PRAISE FOR AND REVIEWS OF *DARK HORSE*

"Ralph Reed, a top-flight political player, has done it again with *Dark Horse*. This political thriller is a spellbinding mix of suspense and intrigue that takes the reader on a behind-the-scenes tour of a bitter and hard-fought presidential campaign. *Dark Horse,* a timely account of the best and worst of American politics, is a must-read."

—Sean Hannity, host, *The Sean Hannity Show*
and co-host, *Hannity and Colmes*

"The crisis-laden plot keeps the pages turning."

—*Publishers Weekly*

"The 2008 presidential election takes center stage in this political thriller by the former director of the Christian Coalition and a veteran of seven presidential campaigns. With both candidates under investigation by the Justice Department, the race is thrown into uncertainty when one of the nominees is assassinated. Terrorism and the ugly side of politics are the themes of this timely tale."

—*Library Journal*

"Ralph Reed takes us behind the headlines to the inside workings of political campaigns, with all of the intense and conflicting pressures that go with that territory. *Dark Horse* will entertain you and also give any reader a better understanding of a world few people have seen as 'up close and personal' as Ralph Reed has over the years. *Dark Horse* is that good."

—Beliefnet

READER REVIEWS

"*Dark Horse* is a fast-paced story that could have been easily lifted from newspapers or right off of the network news programs."

—Bill Wood

"From the opening pages until the final sentence, Ralph Reed captured my attention and held it captive with his political thriller. With his years in politics, Reed has the real-life background to build into the characters and storyline for *Dark Horse*."

—W. Terry Whalin

"With an obvious insider's grasp of political life and surprising skill for a first-time novelist, Ralph Reed, a veteran political consultant and former executive director of the Christian Coalition, manages in *Dark Horse* to present a scenario that is almost as interesting and compelling, if perhaps not quite as dramatic, as the real thing."

—Jeremy Taylor

"Pick it up today. You will not be disappointed."

—Todd Morrissey

"When will the movie come out?"

—Marcia L. Smith

"For a political junkie like me, reading this book was Nirvana. Ralph Reed is a well-experienced political activist and has used his years of behind the scenes political experience to produce a book with intrigue, betrayal, and finally triumph."

—Jean Heritage

DARK HORSE

A POLITICAL THRILLER

RALPH REED

 HOWARD BOOKS
A DIVISION OF SIMON & SCHUSTER, INC.
New York · Nashville · London · Toronto · Sydney

Published by Howard Books, a division of Simon & Schuster, Inc.
1230 Avenue of the Americas, New York, NY 10020
www.howardpublishing.com

Dark Horse © 2008 Ralph Reed

In association with the literary agency of Alive Communications, Inc.,
7680 Goddard Street, Suite 200, Colorado Springs, CO 80920

The Library of Congress cataloged the hardcover as follows:
Reed, Ralph, 1961–
Dark horse: a political thriller / Ralph Reed.
p. cm.
1. Presidents—United States—Election—Fiction. 2. Political
campaigns—Fiction. 3. Political fiction. I. Title.
PS3618.E4357D37 2008
813'.6-dc22   2008005020
ISBN 978-1-4165-7649-5
ISBN 978-1-4391-8241-3 (trade paper)
ISBN 978-1-4165-8434-6 (ebook)

1 3 5 7 9 10 8 6 4 2

Manufactured in the United States

For information regarding special discounts for bulk purchases,
please contact: Simon & Schuster Special Sales at
1-866-506-1949 or business@simonandschuster.com.

The Simon & Schuster Speakers Bureau can bring authors
to your live event. For more information or to book an event
contact the Simon & Schuster Speakers Bureau at
1-866-248-3049 or visit our website at www.simonspeakers.com.

To Brittany

ACKNOWLEDGMENTS

This book began as an outline in 1976, when Gene McCarthy ran as an Independent presidential candidate against Jimmy Carter and Gerald Ford. I wrote the first chapter but then set it aside, recognizing that at age fifteen I didn't know enough to tell the story. I never thought it would take thirty-two years to finish.

Rick Christian, my literary agent, encouraged me to bring *Dark Horse* back to life as we rumbled along in a truck on our way to hunt pheasant in South Dakota. This book would not have happened without him. David Lambert, my superb editor with Howard Books/Simon & Schuster, took me under his wing and tutored me in the art of fiction.

R. T. Kendall's *God Meant It for Good* relates an important truth about God's character that provides a theme of the book.

My colleague Gary Marx read the manuscript and provided great suggestions. My four children endured yet another book in their lives with their usual support and loyalty.

My wife, Jo Anne, read every chapter and was a great encouragement. Since we first met at a campaign rally twenty-four years ago, she has lived a life not unlike that of the women celebrated in this story for their moxie, toughness, and tenderness.

I owe a special debt of gratitude to all those in the political world with whom I have worked. While the characters in this book are not based on real people, their talent and skill, hopes, ambitions, and aspirations inspired me. In particular, I want to thank my colleagues at the College Republicans, the Christian Coalition, the George W. Bush presidential campaigns, the Georgia Republican Party, and Century Strategies for the privilege and honor of working on some unforgettable campaigns, most of them victorious.

There is much in this book that inspires, and perhaps some things readers may find troubling. I wrote it as I saw and experienced it, confident that America's democratic system, for all its flaws, still provides a uniquely redemptive and hopeful way for a free people to choose their leaders.

PART I
THE
CONVENTIONS

1

A SLUMPED FIGURE SAT IN a wingback chair in the middle of the room, oblivious to the crush of sweating bodies that filled the presidential suite of the Chicago Hilton to capacity. Crackling walkie-talkies and shrilling cell phones rang out above the deafening volume of television sets. The Chicago skyline twinkled against the black abyss of Lake Michigan.

The man lazily draped a leg over the arm of the chair, revealing a polished black ostrich cowboy boot. His chin rested on the palm of his hand. "Jay?" he called, his gaze never leaving the television set in front of him.

Another man approached.

"Jay, how did you manage to *lose* a governor?" the man in the wingback chair asked, incredulous.

Governor Robert W. Long of California sat like a dinghy bobbing in the eye of a hurricane. Not a hair out of place, he was a study of calm. His athletic frame was folded into pressed charcoal-gray slacks and a crisp, white shirt, and his well-coiffed, wavy brown hair was streaked with gray. His steely blue eyes surveyed the scene. Senior campaign staff shouted orders to harried subordinates. Clutches of aides huddled in corners, trading the latest rumors in power whispers. After a twenty-month, $400 million, 300,000-air-mile, forty-four-state marathon, the campaign for the Democratic presidential nomination hurtled toward its finish. It had been a clash of titans, an epic battle unlike any witnessed by a major political party in two generations. Everyone in the room had earned their way here, fighting and clawing their way up the sheer, craggy rock of American politics, but all their years of plotting had not prepared them for this hysteria. Senior staff fought off the combined effects of caffeine, alcohol, and exhaustion. They screamed into walkie-talkies while $500-an-hour lawyers gathered at a conference table, poring over delegate lists and plotting strategy for the impending fight over the credentials committee report. Room-service waiters in faux tuxedo uniforms rushed to and fro, dispensing drinks and carrying off discarded glasses and bottles on the trays they held aloft. Governor Long's family tensely gathered on a sectional couch behind him, unsure if they were witnessing a wake or a wedding.

The problem: no one could find Governor Terry Tinford of Tennessee.

"He disappeared like Tinker Bell in a demilitarized zone," said Jay Noble, Long's senior campaign strategist, a grizzled veteran of two decades of Democratic Party politics. His body a compact bundle of energy with a thatch of thick brown hair combed across a high forehead, his shirt soaked with sweat, Noble gave off a faint body odor. "He told someone he was going to the bathroom. That was twenty minutes ago."

"Try his cell." Long's eyes smoldered with frustration.

"It's going straight to voice mail. We have people posted at every entrance in the hall. We sent someone to the DGA suite to see if he went there," Noble said, using the acronym for the Democratic Governors Association.

"You better find him—and I mean right now," ordered Long. They were counting on Tinford to deliver critical votes in the South. "He knew the credentials committee report was coming to the floor, right?"

"Absolutely. I spoke to him two hours ago and he was ready to go."

"He'll show," predicted Long, sounding as if he were trying to convince himself. "I've known Terry for thirty years—since we worked together on our first campaign. He wouldn't stab me in the back."

"We're on it, sir," Noble assured him.

Long rubbed his chin, deep in thought. He had no illusions about Tinford, an ambitious, two-faced climber. Tinford no doubt believed it should be him, not Long, now standing thirty-nine delegate votes from the Democratic presidential nomination. But if Tinford started playing games now—at the eleventh hour—he would commit political suicide. He had endorsed Long and helped him win the Tennessee primary. Was he trying to miss the credentials vote, hedging his bets? It was a distinct possibility. That would be classic Tinford.

Betrayal was part of the game. But Long reassured himself with the thought that Tinford wasn't smart enough to pull it off. He was a lieutenant, not a general.

Noble rushed off sick to his stomach, his heart racing, his mouth dry as cotton. He smelled a rat.

FIVE BLOCKS AWAY, SECRET Service agents in dark suits guarded the door to the presidential suite at the Drake Hotel. Inside sat the senior senator from New Jersey and Senate majority leader, Salmon P. Stanley. His wife and two teenage daughters watched the convention in an adjoining room, respecting his need to be alone at this time of high anxiety. The only sound in the room was the muffled hush of air-conditioning and the barely audible television. Stanley had the thermostat set to the approximate temperature of a meat freezer.

Two raps sounded at the door. Michael Kaplan, Stanley's campaign chairman, glided into the room with breezy confidence. Tall and lanky, he had the build of a long-distance runner. But age had taken its toll, the soft flesh around his jowls beginning to sag. Wrinkles creased his leathery face. His jet-black hair had turned gray at the temples, highlighting piercing black eyes that seemed to bore through people.

"Senator, we have a breakthrough on the credentials report." He paused. "It's a little dicey."

"What is it?" asked Stanley.

"We've been talking to Terry Tinford through an intermediary," related Kaplan.

"But he's a Long man. He drank the Kool-Aid, didn't he?" objected Stanley.

"He did." Kaplan paused. "But it seems he would like to be vice president."

"I can't commit to that," Stanley shot back, eyes unblinking.

"Of course not." Kaplan looked at the ceiling and exhaled, his mind maneuvering in tricky waters. "But the credentials report vote is too close to call. We're up eight votes with 113 undecided. We're twisting so many arms you can hear bones snap, but we've hit a wall. Tinford might break it loose."

"What do you think?" asked Stanley.

Kaplan knew the drill; the boss wanted his unvarnished opinion. "Senator, this is an opportunity to take a key state right out of Long's hide. It would be a devastating psychological blow—a border-state centrist and a governor bailing out on him the night before the nomination." He paused to let the full weight of the opportunity sink in. "The credentials vote will decide the nominee. This is for all the marbles."

Stanley sat silently, eyes narrowed. The crow's feet around his eyes crinkled and the worry lines on his forehead deepened. He wore a blue coat and red striped tie as though at any moment he might be asked to appear in public, the slight paunch of his stomach peeking through his suit, his reddish hair and ruddy complexion highlighted by a receding hairline. He stared unseeing at the cable news talking heads (*Wayne's World* for political junkies, he called these shows) babbling away on the television. He stood on the threshold of the presidency, a goal he had worked for since he was a young man. But he could not have his hands tied in selecting his vice president.

"Promising Tinford the veep is a nonstarter. If we do it, people will say we bought his support." He leaned forward, eyes narrowed to slits, and jabbed the air with his index finger. "Tell Tinford—no witnesses—that we have to be able to say we did not discuss the vice presidency. He will be *seriously* considered—but only if we can deny he is *being* considered—even to him. I must be able to say to anyone who asks, with a straight face, he was never promised anything."

"I'll give it a go," Kaplan responded. He strode from the room. As he twisted the doorknob, he suddenly turned back toward Stanley as if he had forgotten something. "What if he says he can't do it without an ironclad commitment?"

"He won't," replied the senator. "Trust me. And if he does, we can't do business with him anyway."

Kaplan nodded. He was halfway out the door when Stanley stopped him. "Michael, how are you going to have a private conversation with Tinford in this pandemonium?" He pointed at the chaos unfolding on the television screen.

The right corner of Kaplan's mouth rose mischievously in a half smile. "He's waiting for me in a holding room at the convention center."

"Clear that room of staff," ordered Stanley. "No witnesses."

Kaplan nodded and closed the door behind him.

2

MICHAEL KAPLAN SLID INTO the back of a Lincoln Town Car with tinted windows, parked in front of the Drake. "United Center," he said to the driver. "Stat!"

The driver steered the car around the black Caddies and Lincolns triple-parked in front of the hotel and gunned the accelerator. He immediately found himself in a traffic jam. Michigan Avenue glowed with brake lights as far as the eye could see. The driver shot to his right, screaming down Oak Street, looking for an alternate route.

As a political consigliere, Kaplan had no peer. He probably could have been the candidate himself, but the ball had not bounced that way. Sal Stanley had become the vehicle for Kaplan's ambitions, and though Michael remained behind the scenes, the relationship was mutually rewarding. Kaplan had become famous, powerful, rich, and feared. If the meeting with Tinford went well, he was on his way to either the White House or the Cabinet.

The driver zipped in and out of traffic, cutting off cars, weaving through police barricades, running red lights. They screamed up to the rear entrance of the United Center, where an aide waited for Kaplan. The two of them jogged through the bowels of the convention center, their heavy breathing and the fall of their footsteps on the concrete floor mixing with the muffled cheers of delegates. They made a final turn toward an entrance to the convention floor, where another staff member guarded a door to a holding room.

"Is Governor Tinford inside?" asked Kaplan, his voice lowered.

"Yes, sir," said the aide. "He's waiting."

"Stay at this door," Kaplan said, his eyes steady. "No one is to enter or leave this room."

Kaplan entered, closing the door behind him. Governor Tinford sat at a utility table, nursing Diet Coke from a plastic cup. Tinford resembled a human bowling ball, roundish and fleshy, a light brown suit hanging on his rotund frame, his belly hanging over his belt. Beads of sweat glistened on his forehead. His doughy face exuded southern charm; his brown hair swept

into a pompadour; beady eyes twinkling. Kaplan sized him up: he was calcu-
lating, good-natured, and ready to deal.

Tinford's chief of staff stood to one side, body language projecting wari-
ness, talking softly on his cell phone. He ended the call.

"Governor, I need to speak with you alone," said Kaplan.

"If it concerns the governor, I stay," replied the chief of staff.

"My instructions are to have this conversation in private," replied Kaplan. "I just left Senator Stanley." He fixed his gaze on Tinford.

Awkward silence followed. Finally: "All right," said Tinford, relenting.
He turned to his chief of staff. "Give me and Michael a moment."

The chief of staff cast a sideward glance of disapproval and left the
room.

"Governor, forgive me," Kaplan said when the door had closed, "but I
hope you understand the sensitivity. This is an issue of utmost confiden-
tiality."

Tinford nodded.

"Senator Stanley thinks very highly of you, Governor. He thinks you
have done an outstanding job in your state and believes you are one of the
most gifted leaders in our party. Not just in the South, but the entire country." Tinford had won four statewide elections, resolved the state's chronic
fiscal crisis, and raised academic performance at Tennessee schools—but he
never got invited to the Council on Foreign Relations or Davos, the annual
confab for the rich and well connected held in the Swiss Alps. He belonged
to the great unscrubbed masses that the opinion elites looked down upon.
Kaplan chose to play to Tinford's sense of inferiority. "The Leader respects
your previous support for Long. He values loyalty, and he understands that
sometimes people have prior commitments they need to honor."

"I appreciate that," said Tinford deferentially. "That is my situation."

"The senator would have thought less of you if you had not honored that
friendship. But the credentials committee report is a different matter. You
never committed to seat a delegation from Virginia that does not have the
support of its own state party. If the rump Virginia delegation were seated
and Long won the nomination as a result, it would taint him. It would be a
Pyrrhic victory."

"I have problems with the way the process played out in Virginia. I think
a lot of people do," replied Tinford, measuring his words. "Bob is boxed

in—he needs Virginia to win." A wan smile spread across his face. "Of course, so do you. You lost the popular vote and the delegates awarded in the primaries. Only the superdelegates are keeping you alive now. Are you sure you want to win that way?"

"The Virginia state party is on our side," Kaplan said. "Our attorneys have affidavits from Virginia delegates and state executive committee members saying there was no quorum when the Long delegation was selected."

The Virginia credentials battle wasn't pretty. Long had won the nonbinding primary, the so-called beauty contest, but the delegates had been elected at a May convention that featured infighting, fistfights, and chaos. Two delegations had been elected—one committed to Long, the other to Stanley. The dispute had landed at the credentials committee in Chicago, and after reviewing the evidence, the committee had voted to seat the Stanley delegation. Meanwhile, the Long campaign had filed a lawsuit against the Virginia Democratic Party, alleging that it had wrongfully certified the Stanley delegation.

Tinford exhaled slowly. "I hope this can be done without going to court."

"Governor, the best way to ensure that happens is for you to vote for the credentials committee's report," said Kaplan. "You're respected as a voice of moderation and reason. Your endorsement would make the committee's findings unassailable."

Tinford nodded. "It's going to be costly. If I step off that cliff, I want to know there's a net to catch me."

"There will not only be a net, there will be an inflatable cushion the size of two football fields," Kaplan assured him.

Tinford smiled. "Can you be more specific?"

"I don't think I can, Governor," replied Kaplan.

"I would be an asset to the ticket," said Tinford, delicately raising the subject of the vice presidency. "I have three things you need: southerner, DLC member, and Long supporter." He raised the three middle fingers of his hand as he ticked them off. "And I would add a fourth: I've been a national leader on education." He raised his pinkie.

Tinford's willingness to stab Long in the back repulsed Kaplan, and he found himself filled with disdain for the man even as he played him. *Better to go down with the ship*, he thought, *than win as a turncoat*.

Kaplan was skating on thin ice even having this conversation. If he promised Tinford the vice presidential nomination, he would foreclose Stanley's options. But if he mishandled Tinford and the Tennessean got away, they could lose the credentials vote—and with it the presidency.

"Governor, Senator Stanley believes you would make an outstanding vice president. But he is not going to make a decision until he is the nominee. And he will not offer the vice presidency or any other position in exchange for support on the credentials vote. I hope you agree."

"That's not what I'm suggesting," Tinford backpedaled.

Kaplan moved in for the kill. "The senator respects integrity. And for you as a strong Long supporter to vote for the credentials committee report would be a profile in courage. I assure you, the senator will not forget such a selfless act."

"That's good to know."

"Governor, two final points." Kaplan pulled his chair toward Tinford until their faces were six inches apart. "First, this conversation should stay between us."

"What conversation?" Tinford deadpanned.

"Second, you should vote for Long for the presidential nomination. To do otherwise would be bad optics and could complicate the majority leader's ability to call upon you to serve in some capacity later." What Kaplan did not add was that once Stanley had the Virginia delegation, he didn't need Tinford's vote.

"I agree," Tinford said. "If I do a one-eighty on the nomination, it will be a shock to the system. I can vote for the credentials report and still vote for Long for president. That will make me more valuable to you."

Kaplan stood and extended his hand, and Tinford shook it vigorously, his eyes searching. "Governor, it's a pleasure doing business with you." Their eyes locked. "We don't forget our friends."

"I know," Tinford said. A confident smile spread across his face. "By the way—you tell Sal Stanley I can help him get the bubba vote." Kaplan gave him a surprised look. "I'm not like those rich Republicans—pumping iron, jogging, and dirt biking." He grabbed his belly, shaking it. "A potbelly beats a flat belly every time."

"I'll be sure to pass that on," Kaplan said, the corner of his mouth turning up.

As Kaplan left the room, Tinford's chief of staff was standing in the hall-way, arms crossed, eyes narrowed, simmering in a slow burn. "Thanks for understanding," Kaplan said generously, his hand outstretched. "You're working for a good man."

The chief of staff shook his hand warily.

———

THE CHAIRWOMAN OF THE credentials committee, a short, white-haired hotel employee union leader with skin toasted to a desert tan, stepped to the podium. She fumbled with her reading glasses and shuffled her papers, her head barely visible over the massive podium. From Nevada, she was a member of the Democratic National Committee, and in a droning monotone she dutifully read the committee report recommending the seating of the Stanley delegation from Virginia.

To win the nomination, the Long campaign had to defeat the credentials report. The odds were against them, and Long partisans made up for it with feverish intensity. Long whips wearing orange hats moved into position. A low murmur from the delegates belied jagged nerves throughout the hall. The bouncing beach balls fell still.

The chair called for ayes and nays and was about to order the parliamentarian to begin the roll when she was interrupted by the distinct southern accent of Governor Terry Tinford of Tennessee, seeking recognition.

"The chair recognizes the governor of Tennessee."

At the Hilton, Jay Noble glanced up to see Terry Tinford's sweat-streaked face on television. "About time he showed up," he said to David Thomas, the campaign manager.

"Madam Chair," said Tinford in a slow, syrupy drawl, "I rise to appeal for party unity. We have two delegations from the commonwealth of Virginia, one pledged to Senator Stanley, the other to Governor Long. The credentials committee has considered this matter at great length and reviewed all the evidence. It has arrived at a difficult decision. Although I support Bob Long, in the interest of party unity I will vote for the adoption of the committee report, and I urge my fellow delegates to do the same."

Jay Noble's face froze. The snake had cut a deal! He and Thomas moved quickly to Long's side.

"What a backstabbing, lowdown thing to do!" Noble said.

"I can't believe it," said Long. "Has he lost his mind?"

"He's thinking he'll look like a statesman by calling for party unity," said Thomas. "Now he's a man without a country. He just signed his death warrant."

"Get our whips to Tennessee ASAP," snapped Long. "Try to stop Terry from taking the whole delegation with him. We need to stop the bleeding."

"Yes, sir." Noble turned up the volume on his walkie-talkie and began to shout into the mouthpiece for the chief floor whip.

Long interrupted him. "Jay, what happens if we lose Tennessee?"

"It's not good," replied Noble. He turned to Thomas.

"Losing Tennessee would leave us a little over a hundred delegate votes short," Thomas said, his eyes scanning scribbled numbers on a notepad. "Tennessee has eighty-five delegates—we lose 'em, Stanley gains 'em."

"Can we make up the difference with some superdelegates?" asked Long.

"We might get a few, but not one hundred," Thomas replied. "They're still in the tank with Stanley."

"Fight for every delegate you can in Tennessee. We have a while before they get there on the roll call," said Long.

Noble and Thomas bolted for the count room and screamed into their walkie-talkies. No one was answering. If they didn't move fast, the credentials report would pass before they could bolster their forces and fight back.

———

TINFORD'S SWITCH TO SUPPORT the Stanley delegation from Virginia struck like a thunderbolt. Four thousand sleep-deprived, alcohol-addled, sex-distracted, exhausted delegates stampeded with him. The credentials committee had heard three days of testimony from witnesses, pored over depositions, reviewed videotapes of the Virginia state convention, and endured the heated arguments of lawyers on both sides. Who were they to overturn the committee's verdict? It was time to end the fight that was tearing the party apart.

As the roll call droned on, tempers flared. Long whips tried to maintain order, but they could no longer control their delegates. One red-faced Long delegate marched up to a Stanley whip and began jabbing his finger in his chest, screaming until he turned purple and the veins in his neck bulged. Shoving matches broke out. Angry delegates hurled heated words. Fisticuffs broke out in the Michigan delegation. Convention marshals and Chicago police fanned out across the hall and lined the aisles, determined to restore order.

In the pandemonium, someone threw a chair, which hit a Long delegate, opening a gash above his nose. As the TV lights illuminated the blood running down his face and the red blotches on his white shirt, the delegate held an impromptu news conference. "I bleed for my candidate, but I weep for the Democratic Party," he sobbed.

The press corps was euphoric. Blood, tears, drama, man-on-the-street eloquence! It was too good to be true!

Someone grabbed the bleeding delegate, now swaying and woozy from shock, and led him toward a first-aid station. He staggered forward as horrified bystanders stepped back and the paparazzi surged forward, their cameras clicking and flashes exploding. One photographer ran ahead to get a better shot, tripping another delegate and sending him sprawling into the aisle, where someone else tripped over him. Soon a scrum of bodies rolled and clawed at one another in the aisle.

Tears streamed down the faces of Long delegates as they waved wilting hand-scrawled signs. As they saw it, their candidate had been robbed of the nomination by a corrupt credentials report and the eleventh-hour betrayal by Terry Tinford.

Tinford watched all this and decided to leave the floor. The last thing he needed was to be photographed or interviewed in the midst of this rapidly degenerating mob scene.

As the governor rumbled down the aisle, two state troopers in tow, a Long supporter in a rumpled blue suit, coat lapels covered with campaign buttons and face drenched with tears and sweat, caught sight of him. He walked behind Tinford like a crazed, curly-headed asylum patient. "Terry Tinford, you are a pathetic traitor!" he screamed, voice quavering. "You are worse than a traitor, you are a prostitute. You are Judas, a disgrace to this party—and I hope . . . you . . . rot . . . in . . . hell!"

Tinford kept his head down, stone-faced, walking briskly. The delegate continued to hurl verbal abuse. A small crowd gathered, following him down the aisle, venting its anger.

"Traitor! Traitor! Traitor!" the crowd shouted. Cameras gathered to document the faces contorted with anger. This only egged them on, and as the flashbulbs exploded, their voices rose, their faces and gestures becoming more animated. They shook their fists and screamed epithets.

"Benedict Arnold!" shouted one delegate.

"Tinford, you're a quisling!" bellowed another, walking even with Tinford, but held at bay by the state trooper. (The reference to the Norwegian fascist politician Vidkun Quisling, who collaborated with the Nazis during World War II, went over the heads of his fellow delegates, and more than a few reporters.)

Governor Tinford quickened his pace and, head still lowered, avoided eye contact. He entered the tunnel and was gone.

3

THE NEXT NIGHT THE Democrats held their official roll call for the presidential nomination. Long held Tennessee but, with the Stanley delegation from Virginia seated, he lost Virginia, and so also lost the nomination by a razor-thin margin of 2,217 to 2,121 delegates. After twenty-four million votes cast in fifty-four primaries and caucuses, Long won the popular vote but was denied the nomination by a combination of superdelegates and a disputed delegation. With only ninety-six votes separating the candidates, it was the closest contest for a major party's presidential nomination in over a half century.

Cable television talk show hosts had blathered over video footage of screaming, weeping, and bleeding delegates. Stanley decided to give them something else to cover, so he broke with the tradition that the nominee does not appear until the following evening and instead traveled to the United Center. News vans, helicopters, and paparazzi followed Stanley's motorcade as it rolled down Michigan Avenue from the Drake Hotel.

As soon as Stanley walked out onstage, things began to go awry. Angry and thoroughly inebriated Long delegates erupted in a chorus of boos and jeers, and hundreds walked off the floor in protest. Stanley's wife and daughters stood gamely next to him, gritting stage smiles through clenched teeth. One daughter appeared to tear up, her nose reddening and face flushing with embarrassment. Like plastic figures on a wedding cake, the Stanley family waved and pointed to friendly faces in the crowd, looking increasingly awkward and uncomfortable.

Network cameras panned to Long delegates shaking fists at Stanley and shouting insults. Just as the pool camera focused in a tight shot on an elderly woman wearing a blue dress and funny hat, she made an obscene gesture in the direction of Stanley. Twenty million people were watching at home.

"Cut away from grandma!" shouted the director in the control room. "This may be the Democratic convention, but we're still a family-friendly network!"

JAY NOBLE'S BLACKBERRY WENT off at 7:10 A.M. the next morning. To his astonishment, it was Salmon Stanley asking to speak to Long. Noble put his phone on mute, strode across the suite, and rapped on the governor's bedroom door.

The door opened a crack and Long appeared, bleary-eyed, wiping sleep from his eyes. "What is it?" he asked hoarsely.

"Stanley is on the phone."

"I don't think I should take it, do you?" asked Long after a pause.

"No, sir," replied Jay. "If you say anything conciliatory, Stanley will leak that you've kissed and made up. I'm not sure we're quite ready to cross that Rubicon."

"I agree. Take a message." Long closed the door.

Jay returned to the phone. "Senator, I'm sorry, but Governor Long is not available at the moment," he said with barely disguised glee.

Stanley was none too happy. "Let him know I called. I'm at the Drake."

Thirty minutes later, Noble's BlackBerry vibrated on his belt. He pictured Stanley and Kaplan huddled in a strategy session, trying to figure out which card to play next. As he anticipated, it was Mike Kaplan.

"We live in interesting times, Mike," Noble said drily.

"Jay, you ran a first-class campaign—first-rate," Kaplan said with hollow flattery. "You're one of the smartest strategists in this party. You'll be back, and if Stanley has anything to say about it, it will be sooner rather than later."

"Thanks, Mike. But we've got a problem."

"What's that?" Kaplan asked.

"The emotions of our folks are raw," replied Noble. "We've lost control of our delegates."

"I understand," Kaplan said smoothly. "If the shoe were on the other foot, I know how our people would feel. We want to move beyond this, and we believe we have a way to do it."

"What's that?"

"The majority leader wants Governor Long to be his vice presidential running mate."

Noble was taken aback. It was the crowning irony. Four years earlier, Long and Stanley, both rising stars in the party, had been on the short list for veep. Long had been passed over for Stanley. Their battle for the presidency had been a rematch. Now Stanley had prevailed again—and he was offering Long the consolation prize.

"Let me raise it with the governor," he said. "I don't think Senator Stanley should make the offer unless the answer is yes."

"Oh, no—he can't be turned down," agreed Kaplan hurriedly, his voice adamant. "If Long can't accept, the majority leader won't ask. But Jay, this is genuine." He paused. "This is no empty gesture. Stanley wants to unite the party. He wants to win."

Discretion required that Jay not speak for his client. He did not know how Long would react to the offer. But he had a pretty good idea.

———

"IS . . . HE . . . OUT . . . OF . . . his . . . *mind*?" roared Long, his voice rising as he spat out the last word. "He steals the nomination by seating a fraudulent Virginia delegation, and now he wants me to be his running mate? Here's your answer: I'll run with him when hell freezes over!"

Observing this volcanic eruption, slouched in chairs and sprawled out on the couch in the living room, sat Noble, Lisa Robinson, the campaign communications director, and David Thomas, the campaign manager. Joining them was Long's wife, Claire, who always sat in on campaign meetings involving momentous decisions. She sat next to Bob, her pale countenance drained of emotion, bearing the blank stare of a defeated candidate's spouse. It was an impromptu strategy meeting of what had become known in the campaign as "the Brain Trust."

"Governor, that was my initial reaction as well," replied Noble calmly. "But for the purpose of ensuring that you have considered all the options, allow me to make the case for accepting."

"All right," said Long, crossing his arms defensively. It seemed at times to outside observers that Jay was the only person Long listened to, although their relationship was far more complicated and codependent than that.

"If you decline, there's only one way back, and that is a long, bloody fight for the nomination in four or eight years. We just did that, and it ain't a tea party."

Long shook his head and rolled his eyes.

Noble continued. "With the passage of time, new personalities emerge. If Stanley wins, you will have to wait *eight* years—and he will have selected someone else as veep. Incumbent vice presidents don't lose their party's nomination. Look at Nixon, Humphrey, Bush number one, and Gore."

After a short pause, Long said to the entire room, "That makes sense. Anyone care to take issue with it?"

David Thomas waited a bare millisecond before speaking up. The earnest, scrub-faced campaign manager was thirty-six years old but looked as if he had just graduated from college. His baby face peered up from beneath a perfectly combed wave of hair that resembled a helmet; this morning, a day's worth of beard growth incongruously flecked his face, and dark circles framed his tired eyes. Thomas had an IQ high enough to boil water and the discipline of an astronaut going through a NASA prelaunch checklist.

"If you accept the vice presidential nomination and Stanley loses, you're finished," Thomas said. "Today you're a victim, but as Stanley's running mate, you'd lose the moral high ground. A loss would be virtually impossible to come back from. Just ask John Edwards, Joe Lieberman, or Dan Quayle."

"That's not what happened for Sal," Long corrected him.

"He's the Senate majority leader," interjected Lisa Robinson. "It would be much harder for you."

"Forget about the moral high ground, Senator," said Noble. "Were you robbed? Absolutely. Was it criminal? No question. But this is business."

Long shook his head, then mumbled, "Are you talking about the Democratic Party or the Mob?"

Noble smiled. "If the goal is to elect you president, there is only one question: will Stanley win in November? If he is going to win, you *must* be on that ticket."

"So will Stanley win . . . or not?" asked Long.

There was a long pause.

"It's a circular argument," said Noble at last. "I think he loses if you say no. It will be hard to patch up the party. It will be like Carter and Kennedy in 1980. If you reject this offer, I don't think Stanley can put Humpty Dumpty back together again."

"And if I say yes?"

"That's hard to predict," said Thomas, jumping in. "It would be nice if we could test it with a poll, but we don't have time." Thomas was addicted to polls. He pored over the cross-tabs for hours, searching for clues buried in the demographic data. Long once joked that Thomas would probably use a poll to test the names of his children.

"Stanley needs an answer," said Long, suddenly impatient.

"I don't think he wins," said Thomas. "He added nothing to the ticket four years ago. The guy doesn't wear well. He's the candidate of the liberal blogosphere. He's from the Northeast, which is death on the electoral map for us. You would only help him on the margins. People are voting for him, not you."

"I think that's right," said Long, sitting up straighter, animated by a sudden burst of energy. "The last time a vice presidential pick really mattered was when Kennedy picked Johnson. Nobody votes for vice president anymore, if they ever did."

"It's also a poor fit ideologically," said Lisa, jumping into the mix. "You're a centrist, free-trade, third-way, DLC Democrat. Stanley's old-style, northeastern liberal."

Lisa punctuated her point by running her long fingers, fingernails painted bright red, through her mane of jet-black hair, swept back behind her ears. She was smart, with a seasoned toughness that enabled her to fit in with the boys on the bus (critical to her job dealing with the press), but with a caged sexiness just below the surface. Jay knew that only a strong woman like Lisa could avoid being trampled under by the powerful, assertive men in the campaign—not least among them the candidate. Jay considered that attractive. To make matters worse, sometimes Lisa slipped into jeans and a clinging T-shirt when she worked late hours at the campaign headquarters. Jay found it endlessly distracting—and exhilarating.

Long turned to his wife, Claire. She was usually the last to give her opinion. Legs curled beneath her, high heels slipped off, she wore a green St. John top with a matching skirt, its hemline just above the knee. Her strawberry-blond hair framed a face with high cheekbones, a smallish mouth, and steely blue eyes. She was striking in appearance. As she prepared to weigh in, Claire Long sat up regally, her eyes flashing and her jaw muscles tightening with the anger that only a candidate's spouse would understand.

"Sal is *evil*," she said at last, drawing her words out for emphasis. "He stole the nomination. He's Nixonian. You cannot be part of his administration. He's shown what he thinks of you by the way he has treated you. If you tie yourself to him, you'll regret it the rest of your life."

The advisors were stunned. They stared at one another, with cartoon thought bubbles floating over their heads that read: *I thought this was a strategy meeting, not a therapy session!*

"Tell us what you really think, Claire," chuckled Long, trying to break the tension with a little levity. Everyone tittered with nervous laughter.

"What's the verdict, boss?" asked Noble at last.

"The answer is no," said Long firmly. "I can't join the ticket without acting as an apologist for Stanley stealing Virginia. It might be best for the Democratic Party if I said yes. But I fulfilled my obligations to the party a long time ago."

"I'll call Kaplan and give him the bad news," said Noble. The advisors rose to leave.

Long walked them to the door. "Looks like you guys have a new job," he said.

"What's that?" asked Noble, surprised.

"Make sure he loses," Long deadpanned.

Everyone laughed, Long loudest among them. It was the first moment of merriment since Tinford had betrayed them.

Noble thought it was gallows humor. He believed Long had just made a big mistake. Who had ever turned down the vice presidency? Jay could think of no one. In a pique of righteous indignation, Long had punted the chance to be a heartbeat away from the presidency. But as always, Noble would share his counsel only with his client and leave the rest of the world guessing.

The campaign triumvirate walked silently to the elevator, their shoes shuffling on the carpet, the truth that they were out of the game slowly sinking in. Lisa turned to Jay. "What's up with Claire?" she asked. "Why does she hate Stanley so much?"

"When the governor and Stanley were on the short list for veep four years ago," Jay replied, "the Stanley people leaked to the media that Claire had an alcohol problem and had been in rehab. It helped knock Bob out of the running for vice president. Believe me, she hates his guts."

"Wow," Lisa exclaimed. "Was it true?"

Jay looked at her, his face expressionless.

Lisa's eyes widened. She had not known.

"It's always personal, isn't it?" Jay asked no one in particular.

———

IN HIS SUITE AT the Drake, Stanley's own brain trust gathered—but it had only two members: Sal Stanley and Michael Kaplan.

Stanley sat at the end of a long dining room table, lathering a toasted bagel with margarine. The steam from a cup of black coffee rose over his plate. "Bob not taking my call is not a good sign," he said.

"No," said Kaplan. "Maybe he was still in bed."

"Mike, he just lost the presidency," said Stanley, dropping his chin for emphasis, his eyebrows raised sarcastically. "He didn't get much sleep last night. And I bet Claire didn't, either. She's probably hitting the sauce again."

"He knows why we called. Let's give him until noon."

Stanley thought it over. "All right. Noon—but no later."

Kaplan couldn't believe Long would actually turn down the chance to be vice president, regardless of his hatred for Stanley. Anyone angry enough or crazy enough to do that was more than just a fool. They were dangerous.

4

J AY NOBLE TOOK THE elevator down to the Long campaign "war room."
For weeks the room had been jammed with staff hunched over laptops
and huddled around whiteboards, abuzz with energy. Now it resembled a
morgue, with only a few stragglers left. Noble stepped into the bathroom
and closed the door. This was one conversation he would have to conduct in
private. He dialed Michael Kaplan's cell phone.

"Mike, it's a no go," Noble coolly informed him. "I'm sorry."

"Stanley will not be pleased. He's used to getting his way," replied Kaplan. "Would it help if Sal called him personally?"

"No. Long gave it serious consideration, but that's his final answer."

"That's unfortunate. But regardless—we'd still like you on our team, Jay," said Kaplan. "The senator thinks you're the smartest strategist in either party. We need to expand our senior management team for the general election. We want you in the boat."

Noble knew that Stanley thought the best strategist in the party was Michael Kaplan, not him. He was angry at himself for being flattered by the empty praise.

"I appreciate that, Mike," said Noble, "but my guy lost. And if I'm so good, why are you offering my boss the vice presidency and not the other way around?"

"Touché." Kaplan chuckled. "You sure you don't want to come aboard?"

"Not in the cards, Mike. I'm old-school. I live by the rule that you dance with the one who brung you. When your guy goes down, you go down with him."

"That's smart, Jay," Kaplan replied coolly. "Stay in touch."

Jay put his BlackBerry down on the counter and stared into the bathroom mirror. To his surprise, tears filled his eyes. The stress of months of political combat bubbled to the surface. He began to weep quietly, his fingers at his brow, shoulders heaving involuntarily. He caught himself, remembering the staff in the other room. If they heard him crying, they would know their defeat was total. He had to keep his game face on.

Besides, Jay had one last blow to strike. He scrolled through his Black-Berry looking for the contact for Marvin Myers, the most powerful colum-nist in America, whose column had appeared in the *Washington Post* for thirty years and was syndicated to over two hundred newspapers. He also hosted a weekend cable chat show, holding court with the leading politi-cians and journalists in Washington. Myers had written a column about Claire's rehab stint four years earlier; maybe he'd throw a bucket of slime at Stanley.

Jay gave Myers the juiciest nugget in Chicago: Majority Leader Stanley had offered the vice presidential nomination to Bob Long, and Long had declined.

"You don't say," said Myers, his glee apparent in his voice. "That is *very* interesting, indeed. Who can I attribute this to? Can I say a Long campaign official?"

"That's too close for comfort," said Jay.

"How about a high-ranking Democratic Party official?"

"That works."

"When did this happen?"

"We just hung up." Noble could almost feel Myers's panting breath on his cheek.

"Why did he decline?"

"I can't go there," Noble demurred. His objective was to stab Stanley in the back, not give Myers a guided tour of Long's psyche.

"Does anyone else have this?"

"Just you, Marvin."

Noble tried not to enjoy the mating dance, but it was hard. In Washing-ton, one was either a source or a target. By delivering a dog biscuit to one of the nation's top journalistic attack dogs, Noble assured that Myers would spare him any blame for Long's defeat, and instead would laud him for his skill. Noble was sticking a knife in Stanley, but Myers's fingerprints would be on the blade. That was fine with Marvin. Someone was going to get the story; it might as well be him.

"Will Long campaign for Stanley?" probed Myers.

"We have not discussed that," replied Jay. "Until yesterday, we were try-ing to win the nomination. I don't know."

"I see," replied Myers. So Long's senior political advisor could not confirm that his candidate would publicly support the Democratic presidential nominee. The story was getting more interesting by the minute.

"Marvin, protect me," urged Noble. "There are only a handful of people who know about this. If you give me up, I won't be of much use to you in the future."

"I have lots of sources. I could have gotten this from any of them."

Jay hung up the phone with a nasty grin. He had just paid back Kaplan for dropping the dime on Claire four years earlier.

A BLACK LINCOLN PULLED up in front of the Fairmont Hotel and Bob Long burst out of the passenger side, buttoning his jacket, accompanied by senior aides and a security guard. Heads turned as people recognized the man whose dark-horse candidacy had transfixed the nation. Long breezed through the lobby surrounded by his entourage, ignoring hushed whispers and pointed fingers, scribbling an autograph here and there, then disappearing into the elevator.

The Fairmont had hosted the Virginia delegations of both Long and Stanley. The rival delegates had passed in the halls, averting their glances as their attorneys battled to seat them. Now it was over, and Long was paying a courtesy call to his Virginia supporters. It was the final stop of the campaign.

When he entered the large and crowded hotel conference room, the delegates broke into applause. Long flashed a high-watt smile and glided around the conference table, grabbing necks, kissing cheeks, and grasping friends in bear hugs.

"Cleo, my main man!" he called out. Cleo James was a twenty-something African-American activist from Petersburg who had been one of Long's top lieutenants in the Old Dominion. Police had arrested him at the state convention in Richmond when he protested the election of the Stanley delegation, sparking a shoving match with the state party chairman. Later, he testified before the credentials committee and gave a deposition in the still-pending civil suit against the Virginia Democratic Party.

"Governor, we're proud of you. Thank you for fighting for us," Cleo replied. He hugged Long tightly, patting his shoulders affectionately.

"No, thank *you* for fighting for me!" He pulled Cleo close until their eyes were locked. "When you do the right thing for the right reason, you never lose. *You never lose.*" Cleo gulped. Long remembered his name, knew him, and cared about him.

Long walked to the front of the room as all ninety-two delegates and most of the alternates took seats or lined the walls. The room was packed, the quarters cramped and growing hotter, with a number of delegates standing. Long's eyes were puffy from lack of sleep, but his infectious energy filled the room.

"I wanted to drop by on my way out of town," he joked. Relieved laughter rumbled through the room. He turned serious. "I'm here to thank you for all you have done, not only for me, but for the Democratic Party. You came here to take a stand, not for a candidate, but for a principle. We came up short, but not by much. And while my nomination was not to be, the cause for which you stood will prevail."

Several delegates began to cry, wiping tears with their hands or with a tissue.

"Governor Long," said a woman in the front row, "I emptied my savings account to come to this convention. I raised money from friends. I'm not planning to lift a finger for the Democratic ticket in the fall. This is what turns people off from politics, because they don't think they can make a difference."

Taken aback by her raw feelings, Long leaned toward her, eyes narrowed, wagging his finger. "Don't *ever* think you can't make a difference," he shot back forcefully. "That's what they want you to think, and do you know why?" He raised his eyebrows. "So you'll give up. That's not what the people who marched for civil rights believed, it's not what those who protested the Vietnam War believed, and it's not what you should think. You made a difference this week. Stay in the fight and don't give up, and together we can change the direction of our party and the country."

"I'm so sorry," blurted Cleo. His eyes teared up and his lower lip quivered. "I feel like we let you down."

Long was visibly moved. His eyes misted. "You didn't let me down, Cleo. I know this hurts today. But someday, we'll be together again, celebrating victory." He swept an arm to take in the entire gathering. "To me, you will always be the Virginia delegation to the Democratic convention in Chicago. Keep fighting for the right thing. God bless you."

———

MARVIN MYERS FLEW ACROSS town in a hired car, changed into a freshly starched white shirt and fire-engine-red tie, and sat enthroned on the set at the United Center. A makeup artist patted his face with a powder sponge while a technician inserted an earpiece into his right ear. Myers then shared the shocking news: according to "high-ranking Democratic Party officials," Salmon Stanley had spent the morning begging Bob Long to be his running mate and had been rejected. This "stunning development" was "a deep embarrassment for Senator Stanley" and a "major setback in his efforts to unite the party," intoned the anchor, who hung on Myers's every word.

In the control room, joy abounded. This was cable television heaven.

The anchor turned serious, asking Myers to put the news in its proper context.

"This is the tenth Democratic convention I have covered and my seventeenth party convention overall," said Myers, with characteristic self-reference. "The last time I can recall a Democratic presidential nominee in such dire circumstances was George McGovern in 1972. Recall that after Senator Thomas Eagleton stepped down from the ticket after admitting to receiving electroshock treatment for depression, McGovern was turned down by Ted Kennedy, among others, before finally settling on Sargent Shriver. That ticket went down to defeat in a forty-nine-state landslide."

"Marvin, I understand you have learned who may be his second choice," the anchor cued Myers.

"That is correct. Sources in the Stanley campaign tell me that the senator has ruled out Governor Terry Tinford of Tennessee, who was closely tied to the Virginia delegation controversy," Myers said authoritatively. He paused, allowing the drama to build. "Stanley will select Governor Elizabeth Hafer of Pennsylvania, making her the first woman vice presidential candidate since Geraldine Ferraro in 1984."

For the next hour the anchor updated the story with insights gleaned from professors from universities and think tanks. It was unclear whether any of these academics had ever worked on a campaign or even knew what they were talking about. But who cared? Certainly not the cable news executives who watched it all with a mixture of smugness and joy. This was news!

SAL STANLEY SAT ALONE in his suite, following the coverage on television with muted resignation. Only Michael Kaplan was allowed in the bubble at moments like this. Sometimes the silence stretched for long periods. Kaplan could read his friend's moods. He knew it was best to say nothing when watching your life crash on television, like a train wreck in slow motion.

"Long sure paid us back," observed Stanley matter-of-factly.

"Bob took it like the loser he is," Kaplan answered with contempt. "We offered to rescue him from oblivion, and this is how he responds. He's finished."

"Get Betsy Hafer on the phone," said Stanley. "Let's make some history and get this convention back under control."

THE PHONE IN TERRY Tinford's hotel room rang at two minutes after nine.

"Governor, are you watching CNN?" It was the chairman of the Tennessee Democratic Party. "Marvin Myers is reporting that Stanley has picked Betsy Hafer."

It felt like a hard punch to the gut. "That can't be true," Tinford stammered. "That must be a rumor they put out to throw the media off."

"Turn on the television."

Tinford hung up and reached for the remote control. His hands were shaking. Without him, Salmon Stanley would never have prevailed in the credentials fight and would never have won the presidential nomination. He had risked his own future to help Stanley after being assured he would be considered for vice president. Now he had not only been stabbed in the back, he was learning of his betrayal on television.

"Betsy Hafer?" Tinford screamed to his chief of staff, his voice dripping with pain. "She's a total lightweight. She's been in office less than two years!"

"She's a woman," the man replied. "Stanley lied through his teeth—or should I say Michael Kaplan's teeth."

The full weight of the observation took Tinford's breath away. He had been played for a fool. He was about to reply when the jangling phone startled him. His chief of staff reached for it. "Speak of the devil," he said.

Tinford took the phone. "Hello, Mike."

"Governor, the majority leader asked me to call. He is selecting Betsy Hafer. He will call later, but wanted me to tell you that you were seriously considered and that it was a very tough call."

"I appreciate that," replied Tinford. He did not add that he had already learned of the decision on television.

"Terry, you covered yourself with glory, the way you handled this," continued Kaplan. "The senator appreciates it. We'll find something for you down the road. The vice presidency was just more than the system could bear right now."

"I understand, Mike. Tell the senator I think the world of Betsy. I've served with her as a governor. She's great."

"Sal will appreciate that, Terry. Coming from you, that means a lot."

"Count on my help in the fall campaign," he lied again. Tinford lied not to gain any further advantage but to protect his own deeply bruised ego.

"Terry, we don't forget our friends," Kaplan said.

"Right," said Tinford, the edge in his voice betraying his bitterness. He hung up, stunned. As he saw it, Stanley had passed on a border-state centrist, opting instead for a northeastern liberal, a woman governor with less than two years in office, utterly lacking in national or foreign policy experience. Tinford wondered if Stanley had a death wish.

5

BETSY HAFER'S SELECTION ELECTRIFIED the convention. Just as Stanley and Kaplan had hoped, it handed the media a new narrative: the first woman vice presidential nominee in decades. The Stanley campaign banked on bouncing the credentials fight from the front pages so that they could get back on offense. In this single bold stroke, Stanley believed, he could step over the political corpse of Bob Long and replace the story of a split convention with a picture of a united and energized Democratic Party.

But obstacles remained. Long supporters, nearly half the convention delegates, remained bitter and unbowed, and Long had yet to endorse Stanley. The convention was still threatening to spin out of control.

The Stanley campaign decided to highlight the Hafer selection with a rally where the two nominees appeared together in public for the first time. They hastily staged it in Millennium Park the afternoon of the final day of the convention. Police estimated the crowd at eight thousand. Against strenuous objections from the Secret Service, the candidates arrived by hot-air balloon, floating down on the lawn like Julie Andrews and Dick Van Dyke in *Mary Poppins,* warmly embraced by their spouses and the roar of the crowd. Walking across the field hand in hand, they bounded up onto the stage to the beat of U2's hit song "One" and stood before a navy blue backdrop emblazoned with the new campaign logo (it now included Hafer's name below Stanley's) and the slogan "Moving America Forward, Together." Thousands of American flags were waving to the beat of the music while the candidates embraced and waved to the crowd. Dozens of cameras and print reporters and bloggers stood on a riser in the back, stunned by the euphoria and excitement that Stanley and Hafer elicited from the crowd.

Stanley looked like a male Gap model in a pair of olive chinos and a blue, open-collared shirt with sleeves rolled up, sans coat and tie. He appeared at ease and confident, fully in charge. Hafer looked stunning, her body-hugging pink pantsuit accessorized with a string of pearls and three-inch heels that flattered her figure and conveyed feminine sophistication and power. Her brown hair, perfectly coiffed with a touch of blond highlights, wafted in the wind. Giddy with joy, she flashed a triumphant thumbs-up to the crowd, her body swaying to the thumping music. She grinned effervescently and a bit too enthusiastically, occasionally glancing at her bouncing husband, whose wild eyes seemed to say, "Can you believe we got this lucky?" Women in the crowd wore pink buttons with black letters that read "A Woman's Place Is in the House—the White House."

The effect was magical. Stanley, his teeth bared in an irrepressible smile, bobbed on his toes as the full-throated adoration of the audience cascaded over him. Like an aging rocker at a '70s rock band reunion concert, Stanley pumped a clenched fist in the air, revealing a growing circle of perspiration beneath his arm. The temperature on the stage topped out at ninety-two degrees. One could almost imagine the crowd raising cigarette lighters and chanting, " 'Free Bird'!"

"Thank you all for coming. My friends, in choosing our vice presidential nominee, my criteria were simple," Stanley bellowed, his hands gripping the podium. "I wanted someone who shared my vision of moving America forward. Second, I wanted someone who was ready to be president if called upon to serve. And third, I wanted a vice president who would represent every single citizen in the country. I found someone truly special who fulfills every one of those criteria in Governor Elizabeth Hafer." The crowd roared.

"Many of the comments about Governor Hafer have focused on the fact that she is a woman," he continued. Scattered applause.

He paused for effect.

"As you can see, she is, in fact . . . a woman," he deadpanned, to peals of laughter. He turned to her and smiled warmly. "But I did not choose her because she is a woman." (This, of course, was pure fiction. No one believed for a minute that Stanley would have chosen Hafer if she were a man.) "I chose her because she has dedicated herself to children, is committed to public service, and is an outstanding governor and a terrific leader. Ladies and gentlemen, please welcome the next vice president of the United States, Elizabeth Hafer."

"Bet-sy! Bet-sy! Bet-sy!" the crowd chanted.

Hafer hugged Stanley's neck. He pecked her on the cheek. It was a delicate and asexual kiss—his lips had never puckered. The political choreogra-

phy finished, she moved tentatively to the podium, and jerked her head
back, her eyes wide, visibly emotional. Her heart raced. She fought back
tears, wondering if all the hope and history she symbolized was a cause for
celebration—or a burden. As she leaned into the microphone, one thought
kept rattling in her brain like a stainless-steel ball in a pinball machine: *Don't
screw up.*

"First, let me thank Senator Stanley for this high honor," she fairly
shouted. The crowd applauded, allowing her to catch her breath. She felt her
throat constricting. The computer chip that carried a digital version of her
stump speech began to play in her head, and she plowed ahead seamlessly. "I
am the daughter of a steelworker. I was the first woman in my family to
graduate from college. My father worked for forty years in a steel mill to give
me and my three brothers a brighter future. He never imagined that his only
daughter would be standing before you today as the Democratic nominee
for vice president of the United States."

"It's about time!" someone shouted. Everyone laughed.

"My life has been a living embodiment of the American dream. Our
challenge is to fulfill that promise for every . . . single . . . American." Her
voice had a tinny quality to it, like a piano slightly out of tune, as if she was
so focused on her words that she had failed to calibrate their delivery. "I am a
wife and mom. And I think that when it comes to issues like education and
affordable health care, it's about time we had the perspective of a mother in
the White House." (Wild applause and cheering.) "Thank you for the privilege of serving with a man who will make a truly great president. To you, to
Senator Stanley, I make this pledge: I will not let you down."

The U2 song boomed on cue, blaring from gigantic speakers. Confetti
guns fired colored strips of paper across the stage as the two couples linked
arms and raised their hands in a classic campaign pose. Stanley was euphoric.
His hat trick had worked. For the first time since the credentials flap had
threatened to sink his candidacy, he was back in charge. As they walked off
the stage, the music boomed and the cheers of the crowd echoed in their
ears.

In contrast to her running mate, Hafer found herself gripped by a
disconcerting thought. She wondered whether, in their hurry to put the
Long rejection behind him, Stanley's campaign had bothered to thoroughly
check her background. A rush of distant memories filled her head: old

romances, her college years, youthful experimentation with drugs, and more. She had filled out a questionnaire months earlier, but had heard nothing further until that morning's phone call from Michael Kaplan. It had all happened so fast. She wondered if Stanley knew that she was certain to come under withering attack, and whether he would distance himself from her when she did.

————

SIX BLOCKS AWAY, IN a makeshift office on the third floor of a nondescript warehouse building, the Republican rapid-response team swung into action. Like everyone else in Chicago, the GOP had not seen the Hafer pick coming. Now they scrambled to define her before she could define herself.

In a large room known as "the Pit," a dozen opposition researchers chattered away on cell phones and banged away at laptops like stressed-out, sleep-deprived coeds high on diet pills. Fast food wrappers were strewn across their desks. They downed Diet Cokes and inhaled junk food, surfing the Internet like miners looking for gold. They scoured the Pennsylvania state Senate website, flew through a database of executive orders and proclamations Hafer had issued as governor, and searched Lexis-Nexis. Some speed-dialed GOP legislators who had served with her in the state Senate and the consultants who ran campaigns against her, asking probing questions about her record.

Taylor Sullivan paced the floor ferociously. He wore a telephone headset on his shaved head, which shone under the fluorescent lights, carried a piece of paper scribbled with notes, and occasionally hiked up his wool-blend suit pants to cover his bulging belly. He chewed an unlit cigar. He was in full spin mode, shouting talking points in staccato bursts like an army drill sergeant.

"Elizabeth Hafer provides *balance* to the ticket?" he screamed. "What are you smoking?" He cleared his throat before unloading. "As a state senator, Hafer voted against the death penalty for cop killers, against a ban on partial birth abortion, against putting 'In God We Trust' on diplomas for state technical colleges, and she voted forty-two times for higher taxes, including higher property taxes. She's Ted Kennedy in pumps!"

Sullivan ripped his headset from its battery pack and flung it across the room.

"I'm *sick* of these reporters. I have to *spoon-feed* them like babies." He glared at his assistant across the room as though it were his fault. "We need to shift the narrative. Get me a grenade I can roll into their tea party! Now!"

As if on command, one of the researchers bounded in from the Pit and handed him a grainy fax of an old newspaper clipping. The photo was black, the typeface smeared and barely legible. The researcher was grinning foolishly.

"What have you got?" Sullivan asked impatiently.

"It's kind of hard to read," said the researcher. "It's an interview Hafer gave in her first campaign for Congress. She says terrorism is 'primarily an expression of a tragic misunderstanding between Muslims and the Western world.' She compares Christian leaders in the United States who criticize Islam to terrorists on Al-Jazeera. She says they are 'morally equivalent.' Direct quote."

"This is a three-bell ringer," said Sullivan, a nasty grin breaking out on his face, his eyes scanning the text like a supermarket bar code reader. "Will they say we took it out of context?"

"They'll try. But we have the full interview."

"Get this to Merryprankster.com," Sullivan ordered.

Merryprankster.com was to political scandal what British tabloids were to royal family shenanigans. The gossip and news website averaged over four million unique visitors a day and was indispensable show prep for conservative radio talk show hosts. Fashioning itself as a wire service for the new media, it had made a big splash in the previous presidential election when it gained access to the raw data from network exit polls, demonstrated that their demographic turnout models were flawed, and correctly predicted a Republican victory. Merryprankster.com had become a brand name of the new media. In a media universe once dominated by Henry Luce and Bill Paley, the bloggers, Internet smear artists, and Web-based rumormongers now ruled the day.

A satisfied smile slowly crossed Sullivan's beefy face. He knew that within the hour the Hafer story would be splashed across the home page of Merryprankster as a WEB EXCLUSIVE! beneath the screaming headline, "Hafer: Christian Leaders' 'Moral Equivalent' of Terrorists." Like a side of beef dropped in a shark tank, this two-decade-old news clip would send the talk jocks into a feeding frenzy. Stanley and Hafer were about to get hammered.

The researcher bounded toward the door, only to be stopped cold by another shout from Sullivan. "This is great stuff. Get me more!"

Another crazy grin from the researcher. He returned to the Pit to dig some more.

———

SENATOR STANLEY ACCEPTED THE Democratic nomination for president at the United Center to an uproarious and cathartic reception. It was an electric moment. Banners waved, delegates held children aloft, and eyes turned toward the family box, where Stanley's wife and children beamed. The convention floor was a sea of blue signs with white letters proclaiming, TIME FOR CHANGE.

Stanley was introduced by a ten-minute biographical video with the production values of a Hollywood movie. Gigantic screens went black and the hall fell dark and silent. The audience began to clap in time.

"Stan-ley! Stan-ley! Stan-ley!"

They expected Stanley to emerge from behind the curtain and stride onstage. Then, unexpectedly, a single spotlight hit the podium—Stanley was already there, raised by an elevator below the stage. The hall exploded.

The cheering lasted for five solid minutes. Lifting his hands to his sides and raising them up and down like a quarterback trying to silence fans before the ball snap, he implored the delegates to let him speak. But they ignored him.

Finally, the crowd quieted down and Stanley began, slowly and deliberately. An air horn blew in the background. Someone shouted his name from the rafters. As he spoke his opening line, Long delegates from California, the South, and several border states quietly rose from their seats and walked out of the hall. Hundreds of them—heads bowed, eyes staring unseeing, and hands at their sides—moved down the aisles in a staged walkout. Scattered boos rained down on them as they exited. Stanley campaign floor whips moved quickly to place friendly delegates in the empty seats, but the hall was jammed beyond capacity and the fire marshals had blocked the entrances. A few people began to shove one another. Stanley whips and police slid into position to prevent another outbreak of violence. In the corner, out of camera range, a Long delegate gave a policeman a piece of his mind and was wrestled to the floor, handcuffed, and quickly hustled out an underground passageway.

Stanley ignored the commotion and plowed ahead.

"My father was a mailman who taught me the importance of dreaming big and believing in myself. My mother was a devoted wife and homemaker who believed there was no higher calling than caring for her children." The Norman Rockwell picture he painted stood in sharp contrast to the caricature of him drawn by conservative critics as a far-left liberal out of touch with American values.

Next Stanley launched into a scathing indictment of the Republican administration's alleged misdeeds and incompetence. He ticked off the litany of failures by the incumbent party. A botched covert operation in Iran, the inadequate response to an earthquake in California (fifty-eight electoral votes!), a ballooning budget deficit, tax breaks for the wealthy paid for with higher Medicare premiums for seniors—his catalog of horrors consumed two and a half pages of the text.

Then he delivered the kill line. "They promised us compassionate conservatism, but they delivered neither compassion nor conservatism. It is not compassionate to forsake the least and the lost; it is not conservative to double the national debt." A slow roar began to build. "To cut taxes for their wealthy friends, they have saddled our children with a debt they can never repay. My friends, they had their chance, they failed, and now it is time for a change."

The hall rumbled with cheering and foot stomping. The delegates celebrated in full-throated wonder: Here was someone who would fight back! Here stood a candidate who would not outsource the dirty work of tearing down his opponent to the labor unions and Section 527 interest groups. He would do it himself! He understood: when your opponent hits you, you had to deck him.

Stanley warmed to the applause, and then made an announcement that his advisors had debated all day. "Tonight I challenge the vice president to meet me in the city of his choosing one week from tonight for a discussion of the challenges we face as a nation. I propose that we do so every week between now and Election Day. No hiding in the Rose Garden. Let the debates begin!"

The roof nearly came off the hall. Everyone knew the vice president (the

Republican presidential nominee) would decline. But Stanley was on offense.

The Stanley campaign had reluctantly concluded, while planning his acceptance speech, that the Virginia delegation fight could not be ignored.
Stanley was three-quarters of the way through his speech, heading into his
peroration, when he reached the words that had been added to the text only
an hour before the speech. Looking directly into the bank of cameras, he
spoke softly and with uncharacteristic empathy.

"To supporters of Governor Long, let me commend you for reinvigorat-
ing the Democratic Party. Your campaign was one of hope and optimism,
and represented the best of our great party. Tonight I ask for your support.
Your job is not done yet. There is far more that unites us than divides us. Let
us link arms and restore our government to the people to whom it belongs."

The applause that greeted this line was muted. Television cameras panned
to the empty seats that had once held Long delegates. As Stanley beamed
before the adoring delegates, Bob Long sat in a hotel suite four blocks away,
pointedly refusing to issue an endorsement or show up for the speech. The
Democratic Party had come to Chicago to exorcise the demons of two generations earlier. In the same city that had witnessed Richard Daley's blue-
helmeted police cracking the heads of youthful Vietnam War protesters, the
Democrats had staged a divided convention. Back then, the Democrats had
never recovered, and Hubert Humphrey had narrowly lost to Richard
Nixon.

Like a recurring nightmare, history was repeating itself.

HUNKERED DOWN IN ITS warehouse bunker, the Republican war room
swung into action. Salmon Stanley had declared war on the GOP, denouncing eight years of the administration's record, and they were not about to let
him get away with it.

"Look, they promised a convention that would focus on their candidate,
and they promised a positive campaign," bellowed Taylor Sullivan into the
telephone to yet another reporter, his thirtieth press interview of the day. He
pulled the unlit cigar from his clenched teeth and spat into a wastepaper
basket. "After the four nights, and this includes Stanley's acceptance speech,

a word-by-word analysis of the prime-time speeches is as follows: forty-eight percent of the content of the speeches consisted of attacks on the vice president or the president, twenty-one percent praised the Democratic nominee, and the remaining thirty-one percent represented what might be called filler. So in terms of whether they are running a positive or a negative convention, I'd say case closed."

Before him lay a single sheet of paper with facts and figures. His eyes darted across the page, absorbing the data, then spewing it out like a Gatling gun.

"I'm not overstating it," he barked. "If anything, we're underestimating the extent to which their convention is a venom-soaked hatefest consisting of personal attacks and insults. Tonight Reverend Joe Johnson even accused the vice president of being a *racist*. But we're not even counting those caustic comments in the total because they were not made during prime time. If anything, we're understating the negativity. The Democrats have staged a pageant of personal attacks, pessimism, and the politics of personal destruction."

He hung up the phone. Maybe the press would actually report the facts for once. If the campaign could hold the Democrats to a postconvention "bounce" of less than ten points, winning the fall campaign would be easier.

———

BOB LONG WATCHED THE speech in his hotel suite with Claire and a clutch of aides. The room was tense and quiet. Two empty bottles of red wine sat on the counter of the wet bar. People were blowing off steam.

As Stanley finished and the traditional balloon drop began, Long rose from his chair and broke the silence. "It's the same old tired line. I don't see him moving voters in southern Ohio or eastern Kentucky with a speech this liberal and populist."

"Unbelievable," agreed Jay Noble. "He's channeling William Jennings Bryan. Instead of reaching to the middle he lurches to the left on both the veep pick and the acceptance speech. He's not going to add any new voters."

"How much of a bounce will he get from the Hafer pick?" asked Long.

"Three points, maybe four. It will be gone in two weeks," predicted Jay. The prospect of Stanley falling flat on his face infused the room with morbid cheeriness.

"She's an attractive candidate," Long offered, trying not to appear too interested in the running mate slot he had rejected. "She's good-looking. And she has charisma."

"Honey, honestly, Betsy Hafer is an empty suit," Claire corrected him. She was in a fighting mood, having just polished off her third glass of wine in an hour. "Her coal miner's daughter shtick is such revolting *pap*."

Long flinched. "Her father was a steelworker, not a coal miner."

"Whatever," said Claire, rolling her eyes.

Noble found it amazing that Stanley had gone over Long's head and spoken directly to his supporters. It was a deliberate and stunning slight. Such a move could only be the product of astonishing hubris. Stanley believed Long would sit out the election and was therefore irrelevant. Either way, Stanley was clearly done negotiating with the Long camp. He had moved on.

Now the ball was in Long's court. No one knew what he would do.

IN A SKYBOX HIGH above the stage at the United Center, Michael Kaplan was the man of the hour. He circulated amidst a crush of sycophants and straphangers, watching his best friend deliver the most important speech of his career. To his satisfaction, Stanley had performed ably. Donors and fundraisers flitted about him like moths around a flame. They lathered him with flattery, heaped praise on his every word, and shoved business cards into his hand with sweaty palms. They knew if Stanley went to the White House, Kaplan would be the gatekeeper, and could fulfill their dreams: ambassador to an exotic foreign posting or an appointment to a prestigious government board. Kaplan could make it all happen with a single word. He was the candy man.

"Mike, the senator was brilliant tonight," one check bundler blubbered, the stench of red wine on his breath mixed with halitosis. "I think it was the best speech he has ever given. What can the Republicans do? He killed them!"

"The majority leader always rises to the occasion, and tonight was no different," said Kaplan, always on message.

Kaplan's cell phone rang and he excused himself. He stepped to the back corner of the suite to take the call. He recognized the area code and prefix of the number displayed on the screen matched the offices of the *Washington Post*.

"Mike, Dan Dorman with the *Post*."

"Hello, Dan. If you're looking for a quote on the majority leader's speech, I think I'll let what he said from the podium speak for itself."

Dorman ignored him. "Actually, I have a different issue, and I'd like a comment from you or someone from the campaign," he said in a dull monotone.

"Sure, what is it?"

"We're reporting in tomorrow's paper that the affidavits submitted to the credentials committee by your Virginia delegates, which were prepared by the law firm of G.G. Hoterman, were false. We also will report that some witnesses were paid by the campaign to give misleading testimony. According to several sources, some of them perjured themselves."

Kaplan almost dropped his phone. "That's a serious charge, Dan. We stand by the testimony of our witnesses. So I think your question is better directed at the credentials committee," he shot back.

"It *is* serious," replied Dorman. "That's why I want to get your side. I'd like to have you in this story. But if you refuse to comment, this is going on the front page. Is that what you want the morning after Stanley accepts the nomination?"

"Are you threatening me, Dan?"

"Not at all," Dorman said. "I'm just saying there are two sides to the story. If we have a comment from you, we can run them both. If you refuse to comment, it seems to me that makes it an even bigger story. That's all."

"Give me a break," sneered Kaplan. "That's blackmail."

"Those are your words, not mine," Dorman shot back. "My deadline is in forty-five minutes, so have someone call me soon."

The room seemed to be spinning. Kaplan blinked. Through the fog he could see the puffy faces of members of the campaign finance team. In the background he could make out Sal Stanley onstage, accompanied by his wife and daughters and Elizabeth Hafer and her family, bathed in klieg lights. But the images were out of focus. He had hoped that the worst of the convention was behind them, and that the Hafer pick had turned the corner. But the *Post* was going to hammer them across the kneecaps tomorrow. On the front page.

Kaplan fumbled with his cell phone. He needed to find G.G. Hoterman—and fast.

6

G.G. HOTERMAN WAS A big, brazen bulldozer of a man, with the girth of an aging football player and the grace of a confidence man. The most prominent and well-connected Democratic lobbyist in Washington, his client list read like the stock portfolio of a blue-chip investor: AT&T, Apple, General Electric, Philip Morris, and Coca-Cola. His ties to the Democratic Party were evident in his representation of the AFL-CIO, the American Trial Lawyers Association, and the Motion Picture Association of America. His firm also represented numerous foreign governments, among them Saudi Arabia, Nigeria, and Mexico. His biggest clients paid him up to $1 million a year to open doors in Washington. Others paid him $10,000 a month not to hurt them.

At 6 A.M. the morning after the Democratic convention, the barrel-chested Hoterman emerged from the Four Seasons Hotel and squinted through the fog drifting in from Lake Michigan. The sky was still black. A woman emerged behind him, and together they stepped into a chauffeur-driven black Town Car that whisked them to O'Hare Airport, where they would shortly board a chartered aircraft.

The upheaval at the Democratic convention in Chicago had reverberated all the way to the nation's capital, raising questions about how the credentials committee had arrived at the decision to seat the Stanley delegation from Virginia. The *Washington Post* reported that the Virginia State Police were investigating whether witnesses committed perjury in exchange for cash payments. The police were mulling a criminal referral to the Justice Department, which would land like a hand grenade at the feet of a Republican attorney general, putting him in the awkward position of deciding whether to prosecute Sal Stanley's campaign operatives.

Worse, the affidavits of tainted witnesses had been prepared by Hoterman & Schiff, the most prominent Democratic law firm in Washington.

For Hoterman, it was just another day at the office. Nestled in the leather of the car's backseat, he was a study of control. Emblazoned across the front page of the *Post*, above the fold, was an unflattering photo of him (he wondered where they'd found such an ugly picture), but he studied it and the accompanying story with practiced detachment. It was not his first brush with controversy. His first dustup had come decades earlier when his former boss, a member of the House Appropriations Committee, inserted an earmark benefiting a Hoterman client—a client that had subsequently paid Hoterman a $500,000 bonus. Hoterman had been dragged through the mud but emerged largely unscathed. Every time his name surfaced in another imbroglio, it only added to his mystique. The press had used his name to sell magazines and newspapers for years; it was one of the many occupational hazards of being G.G. Hoterman. He picked up the car's cell phone and dialed the home of his firm's managing partner, Anthony Piccillo, who panted as he talked because he was jogging on his treadmill at home.

"Tony, have you seen the *Post*?"

"I'm reading about you, G.G.," Piccillo huffed.

"How bad do you think it is?"

"It's rough. The sister of one Stanley delegate claims he lied to the credentials committee because he was promised an ambassadorship. If that's true, it's a felony. There were payments to a number of delegates and Virginia executive committee members from a pro-Stanley 527. Other delegates may have perjured themselves, including the brother of our associate Deirdre."

"Perjury is hard to prove, in this case," observed Hoterman. "It's he said, she said. Unless someone has notes or a tape recording."

"Or emails. Who knows what's out there?"

"Sure. But this is a party matter. Can you charge someone with a crime for saying something false in a political proceeding?"

"It's not that simple, G.G.," answered Tony. "The witnesses submitted affidavits to the credentials committee. In addition, some people were deposed by Long's lawyers in his lawsuit against the Virginia Democratic Party. Those are sworn statements. If they were deliberately false, that's a felony perjury rap."

"Good grief," Hoterman replied. "It's like Clinton without the sex." He collected his thoughts for a moment. "Tony, given the connection to Deirdre's brother, we need to retain outside counsel."

"Already on it," Tony reported with characteristic efficiency. "Everyone's lawyering up. I spoke with Walter Shapiro at Webster & Underwood. He's the best—and a Republican, which I like, given the dynamics of a Republican Justice Department."

"He's extremely capable. Will he do it?"

"He was favorably inclined, and asked all the right questions. He doesn't have a conflict. He just said he needed to check with his partners."

"Well, move quickly. The sharks are circling, and there's blood in the water. But it isn't mine. I think it's Mike Kaplan's."

"What a nightmare," agreed Piccillo.

"Listen, I'm getting ready to get on an airplane, but I'll be reachable in about two hours. Call me as soon as you hear from Shapiro."

Hoterman hung up the phone and turned to Deirdre Rahall, the strikingly attractive thirty-one-year-old blond associate who was now in the eye of a storm. She wore size four designer jeans, a silk pullover, and black Ferragamo boots that matched her gold-buckled Prada purse. Her thick blond hair flowed down her long neck and fell across her shoulders. Two newspapers rested on her lap, and the passing streetlights lit up her face with strobelike bursts. Her translucent blue eyes were filled with worry.

"I'm sorry we've been sucked into this mess. Brace yourself," warned G.G.

"I talked to my brother," Deirdre said.

"I hope he's not talking."

"No, he knows better. He's dodging press calls. They're asking about you."

"They're a pack of jackals," Hoterman sighed. "Tell him not to worry. The firm will get him a lawyer. And I mean a bulldog. Tell him to stay off email. Anything he has said or written down or says or writes down from now on is discoverable."

Hoterman's razor-sharp counsel was borne of experience. He was the most dominant player in Washington not in public office, combining entrepreneurial acumen with the skill of a fixer. Hoterman & Schiff had reported $55 million in lobbying fees the previous year, billings that did not include what he jokingly called the "reading and writing" lawyers, those who represented hedge funds, venture capital firms, and other Wall Street entities. Copyright infringement cases and class-action lawsuits were the firm's specialty. In a single class-action suit, Hoterman's firm had won a $455 million judgment. The firm had celebrated by flying all its partners and their spouses to Hawaii that year for a week at an exclusive resort on Maui.

Hoterman's rapid-fire instructions and overwhelming confidence made Deirdre feel safe. That was how she'd felt the moment she first laid eyes on him three years earlier, when she was fresh out of the government affairs division of an Internet company and working for another attorney in the firm. Deirdre was a woman in a hurry. She had bumped into him at a fund-raiser at the firm and flirted with him shamelessly. The attraction had been powerful—and mutual. Deirdre placed her hand in his, and he squeezed it. He pulled her closer until her body pressed against his and she nestled her head against his shoulder. He looked down and smiled his winning smile.

THE SUN WAS JUST peeking over the horizon at O'Hare as Jay Noble stepped out of a cab. He wasn't sure where he was going other than as far from the Windy City and his shattered dreams as an airplane could take him.

"Do you have a reservation?" asked the woman at the United Airlines counter.

"No. I want to buy a first-class, one-way ticket."

"To what destination?"

"Mexico," he said. Jay had a cheery thought of sunny beaches and margaritas.

"And what city in Mexico?"

Jay recalled that in a previous life, when he was a partner in a political consulting firm, he had pitched a gubernatorial candidate in Mexico's Camilla district. They had met at an ecofriendly resort that placed a premium on preserving natural habitat. Teeming with wildlife and hiking trails, it was a model of ecotourism. They had lunch overlooking the Pacific, watching a school of dolphins beyond the rocky cliffs. Noble had not gotten the business, but he'd never forgotten the place. He wasn't sure of the resort's name, but he remembered that he had flown into Manzanillo.

The ticketing agent's fingers flew across her computer keyboard as she wrinkled her nose. "The direct flight is oversold . . . mmmm . . . I can get you there with a connection through Mexico City. That flight departs in one hour."

"That will work," Noble replied. He handed her a credit card, fumbled through his briefcase for his passport, and headed for the departure gate. He wanted to lick his wounds in private, to lie on the beach and figure out what to do with the rest of his life.

The round-trip ticket cost him a walk-up fare of $975, but he didn't care. His commission on Long's media buy in the primaries had been 3 percent of a $90 million television and radio buy—15 percent commission to the media placement firm, of which Jay had received one-fifth as the senior campaign strategist—so he had cleared $2.7 million just on paid media. He would make another $2.5 million or so on direct mail through a company in which he was a partner. Ironically, Jay had gotten rich losing the biggest campaign of his life.

Noble boarded the airplane, reclining in his seat in the first-class cabin, and scanned the three newspapers and two magazines he'd bought at a newsstand. On the cover of all three newspapers was a color photo of Salmon Stanley and Betsy Hafer, arms raised in victory, surrounded by their smiling families, with red, white, and blue balloons falling in the foreground. The twenty-point headline in the *New York Times* blared: "Stanley Accepts Democratic Nomination, Vows in Fiery Speech to Wage Aggressive Campaign."

Noble flipped to the jump page, scanning the copy until his eye saw a boxed story on Long in the lower right-hand corner. A paragraph caught his attention:

> For the Democrats, Long's snub marred an otherwise celebratory evening, recalling haunting memories of previous party fissures. It marked the first time a leading candidate refused to publicly endorse the Democratic presidential nominee since segregationist Strom Thurmond staged a walkout at the 1948 convention, bolting the party to run as a Dixiecrat. Stanley strategists worked feverishly to persuade Long to join Stanley on stage for the traditional show of support. But Long rejected their entreaties and remained cloistered in his hotel suite, defiant to the end, remaining tight-lipped on his future plans.

Terrific, thought Noble. The *New York Times* was now comparing Bob Long to Strom Thurmond. He had begged Long to take the vice presidential nomination. But Long, egged on by Claire (influenced either by her own bitterness, or a Bloody Mary or two, or both), had turned it down. Jay had also advised Long to go to the convention hall and endorse Stanley—advice Long had ignored. Why did Long want Jay around if he wasn't going to listen to him? Now Long was probably finished politically.

THE BLACK SEDAN PULLED up on the tarmac and came to a stop next to a Gulfstream 5 jet. Not many lobbyists owned their own jets. But G.G. was no ordinary lobbyist. Besides his law firm, he presided over a business empire known as "Hoterman, Inc." He was a partner in gourmet restaurants in Washington, New York, and South Beach, a ski lodge in Jackson Hole, a film production studio in Los Angeles, a quail hunting lodge in south Georgia, and a golf course in Las Vegas. A decade earlier he had joined the board of a software company, and he sold his stock options for millions. He cofounded a boutique investment bank with offices in New York, Tokyo, London, and Hong Kong. He owned a ski chalet in Vail, a house in the Hamptons, a lake house in the Adirondacks, and a mansion in McLean, Virginia. He kept corporate apartments in Manhattan and London. No one knew the exact size of Hoterman's fortune, but in a cover story several years earlier, *Forbes* magazine had estimated that he was worth $55 million.

The driver opened the doors for G.G. and Deirdre, grabbed their bags, and loaded them into the luggage compartment. Hoterman's cell phone rang.

"G.G., Mike Kaplan."

"Hello, Mike, I'm glad you caught me. We're just about to take off." He waved Deirdre to the plane and stepped back into the car, closing the door. He didn't feel like having this conversation with the smell of jet fuel and the roar of the plane's engines in the background.

"I assume you've seen the *Post*?" asked Kaplan.

"Yes."

"May I gingerly suggest that you have your attorney talk to our campaign's general counsel, Duke Barrett, as soon as possible. This is going to get hairy."

"You bet. We're retaining outside counsel," Hoterman said. "I can't tell you who it is yet, but it will be a Republican, since we may have to deal with a Republican DOJ."

"That's what I'm worried about," replied Kaplan. "The Republicans would love nothing more than to slow-roast us with leaks from DOJ. That's why we need to make sure these witnesses are taken care of. I assume you've taken steps to assure that Deirdre Rahall's brother is buttoned up."

"I don't feel comfortable talking about him," said Hoterman, his voice suddenly icy and distant. "He will have his own attorney—you should contact him. I won't be talking to him, not now."

"G.G., he's your associate's brother. The fate of the Democratic Party hangs in the balance," Kaplan said, projecting gravitas. "I hope you grasp the seriousness of the situation."

"Sure I do," shot back G.G. "This is not my first rodeo, pal."

"I know."

"Mike, I hope no one promised anything in exchange for their testimony to the credentials committee. If what the *Post* is reporting happened, this is going to be hard to get back in the bottle."

"The *Post* is selling newspapers," replied Kaplan. "You know how it goes. Someone works hard on a campaign, someone says something about remembering their loyalty. They hear what they want to hear. There was no quid pro quo, and no violation of law, I assure you."

"Politics has a way of criminalizing the normative," warned Hoterman. "Look, I'm your friend, and I'm telling you that if someone's head has to roll, do it now."

"I'll handle the campaign. You take care of Deirdre's brother," Kaplan volleyed, clearly not pleased with Hoterman giving him unsolicited advice.

"When you say 'take care of Deirdre's brother,' I assume you mean ensuring that he has competent legal counsel and tells the truth if asked to testify."

"Yes, that's what I meant," replied Kaplan sarcastically. "Have a good flight." He hung up.

Hoterman couldn't believe Kaplan was inquiring into the state of mind of a witness in a criminal investigation—and on a cell phone! Witness tampering was a federal felony. G.G. had seen smart people do stupid things once a criminal inquiry got rolling. But he was not just angry about the call;

he was insulted. He was G.G. Hoterman—he didn't need someone telling him how to handle this. He did not *need* to speak to Deirdre's brother because he could guarantee that he would not remember a thing—not a single thing—that was not either exculpatory or innocuous.

G.G. boarded the aircraft, the cabin climate control set to his desired temperature (a cool sixty-seven degrees), its engines warming, a heated granola bar resting on a white Waterford china plate by his seat. Without saying a word, he tore into the granola bar and took a swig of black coffee out of a china cup. He slipped on his blue flight jacket with the initials "GGH" stitched in gold letters over the pocket. Pulling a gold-embossed Mont Blanc pen from his coat pocket, he began to take notes on a legal pad, his eyes darting beneath his furrowed brow. After a few minutes, he handed the legal pad to Deirdre, who sat in the seat across from him reading the newspaper.

"What is it?" she asked, studying his large, looping scribbles.

"Contemporaneous notes of the conversation I just had with Michael Kaplan."

Deirdre shot him a pensive glance. Hoterman read her thoughts.

"Deirdre, when stuff like this hits the fan, people do funny things. Some people turn on their friends, some get indicted, and some go to prison. Well, let me tell you, it ain't gonna be me," he declared, tapping his chest with his index finger for emphasis.

The flight attendant announced that the plane was ready for takeoff. They buckled their seat belts as the plane taxied down the runway and accelerated. G.G. watched the Chicago skyline disappear from view as the sun rose like an orange ball, floating in the soupy fog over Lake Michigan.

THE FIRST THING ONE noticed about Dr. Andrew H. Stanton was the sheer size of the man. At six feet, four inches and 224 pounds, the fifty-six-year-old former college wrestler had a head the size of a ripe pumpkin, large hands that looked like they could crush a soup can, and size fourteen shoes. But it wasn't just his physique that made Andy Stanton a force. Like any performer, he knew how to carry himself, and his persona projected charisma and power, and deliberately so.

This morning, he stepped out of his dressing room and turned down the hall, accompanied by a short, squat security guard with a walkie-talkie on his belt and a .38-caliber revolver bulging under his suit. Death threats against Stanton were a regular occurrence, so security was tight. He stepped onto the elevator and rode in silence.

He had just wrapped up his daily television program, scanned the *Wall Street Journal*, and read through his communications department's daily news clips (the ones mentioning him were always first in the stack), fired through a series of calls, and was on his way to his office for a board meeting. He was always on the move, and today was no exception. He had to be back in the studio for his radio program that afternoon.

To the cultural elite that stretched from New York to Washington, personified by the *New York Times* editorial page, Andy Stanton was a demagogue, a bigoted right-wing crank who channeled Elmer Gantry and Father Charles Coughlin. To tens of millions of others, he was a modern-day Jeremiah who stood for moral values and faith in God. To those who knew him well, Andy was a far more complicated personality than either his critics or admirers cared to admit. As he rode the elevator to the executive suite on the twelfth floor of the gleaming office tower in Alpharetta, Georgia, a bulging suburb twenty-two miles outside Atlanta that was home to his broadcasting, charitable, political, and business empire, he reflected on the fact that he had been attacked *five times* by name from the podium at the Democratic convention in Chicago. He shook his head in disgust. The party of Jefferson,

Jackson, and FDR had been hijacked by the far left. It was yet another sign of the drift of the culture.

"Hello, M.J.!" he shouted to his longtime assistant as the elevator door opened. Andy bubbled with effervescence, his chest jutting with positive energy, his voice sonorous with joy. He had never known a problem too big for his God. His motto: Try something so big that unless God intervenes, you are sure to fail.

"Andy, the board is waiting for you in the boardroom," she said.

"Wonderful!" he bellowed. "I *love* board meetings." He rolled his eyes at her and cackled with laughter.

Andy walked into the boardroom and worked his way around the table, hugging, grabbing arms, slapping backs, making connections, and punctuating his conversation with phrases like "Lord bless you, friend" and "It's so good to see you, my dear brother!"

The board had been handpicked by Stanton, and they knew their place. They were stars in Stanton's universe, but he was the sun. Andy opened the board meeting with a prayer, eyes closed tightly, his hands clasping those of the board members to his left and right until they felt a twinge of pain. He finished with his characteristic drawn-out "Amen," the second syllable stretched twice as long as anyone else would have, and turned to the executive vice president and asked what was on the agenda.

"Andy, first we want to review the latest numbers," replied Bryan Briggs, the executive vice president.

"Great," Stanton nodded. He loved numbers. He studied data the way seminary graduates studied eschatology. A steward brought him a cup of hot tea. He bobbed the teabag and stirred as he listened.

"For the most recent sweeps, *Your World Now* had a weekly cum audience of 15.4 million viewers. That's up about eight percent from a year ago."

Andy nodded and smiled. The faces of the board members lit up like headlights on high beam.

"As usual, it was the highest-rated program on the Spirit Channel."

"It better be," bellowed Andy. "I better be number one on my own network!" Stanton had founded the Spirit Channel in 1979 and it had grown to become the eighth-largest cable network in America, reaching ninety-two million households. The Spirit Channel's revenues were $275 million a year and Wall Street valued it at $4.2 billion, but it wasn't for sale. *The Andy Stan-*

ton Show was carried on 450 radio stations and boasted a daily audience of 13.5 million listeners. Less preachy than its television cousin, the hour-long program featured folksy commentary, celebrity guests, and calls from listeners.

"Next, the financial numbers," Briggs continued. "The conversion rate on prospects generated through radio and television so far this year is twenty-seven percent. The average contribution from donors who have given in the past year is $27.39 one-time, $52.62 cumulative. Based on the telethon results, we're on track for $187 million in contributions this year, and the donor base will be at over 2.9 million."

Another long whistle from Stanton.

Stanton's day job was senior teaching elder at the 26,000-member New Life Church, a nondenominational evangelical congregation. The church had sixty-three ministries, a $35 million annual budget, missionaries in forty-four foreign countries, and five services on Sunday. Satellite congregations in Buckhead and in Fayette County south of Atlanta had another two thousand attendees every Saturday night. Its eighty-six-acre campus boasted a state-of-the-art fitness center (Andy was an exercise nut), a youth facility with games and a bowling alley, a home for unwed mothers, a K–12 private academy, a fully accredited graduate school with a seminary and law school, and modern television and radio studios. The campus also had its own Star-bucks. (Among the hundreds of data points Stanton tracked was the weekly average of cups of coffee consumed at the store, which was the second-highest grossing Starbucks in metro Atlanta.)

Stanton took notes and sucked on the hot tea, which he had sweetened with two packages of artificial sweetener. He asked an occasional question as he flipped through his briefing book.

"How are we coming on the book rollout?" he asked.

"We've put together concepts for the promotional material," replied the publications division head. He passed out advertising mock-ups, cover art, and direct mail inserts.

The book was a follow-up to *Lighting a Candle in a Culture of Darkness,* which had sold twelve million copies, been translated into twenty-seven languages, and was the basis for Bible studies and Sunday school lessons in thousands of churches. The thesis had been that those to blame for the cultural decay plaguing America were not the gay rights lobby and the ACLU, but slumbering Christians. *We have seen the enemy*, Stanton seemed to be saying to conservative Christians, *and it is us*. He had written five other books, all of which had rocketed to the top of the bestseller lists. His latest book advance had been $15 million.

Stanton's bestselling book on relationships and marriage, *Finding Your Soul Mate,* had sold 4.5 million copies. After the book reached number one on the *New York Times* bestseller list, he started an online dating service that matched Christian singles looking for love, friendship, and marriage, which had exploded to one million members worldwide and annual revenues of $135 million. Yahoo! and Google had both come courting, but like the Spirit Channel, it was not for sale.

Stanton had also founded the Faith and Family Federation, which had grown in a decade to three million members in two thousand local chapters, with full-time lobbyists in Washington and all fifty state capitals, and an annual budget of $50 million. The Capitol Hill newspaper *Roll Call* had published an annual survey of Hill staffers that ranked the federation as the fourth-most powerful lobbying group in the nation, behind only AARP, the AFL-CIO, and the National Rifle Association.

As the conversation drifted, it turned to the presidential election. The steward served a lunch of chicken and fruit salad. The banter became relaxed and informal.

"You sure were right about who would win the Democratic nomination, Andy," Briggs said. "Stanley took care of Bob Long."

"Stanley's a junkyard dog," Andy said, shaking his head. "Long was too moderate-to-conservative for the liberal blogosphere crowd. You know, he's actually pretty good on the war with radical Islam."

"He may be in the wrong political party," joked Briggs. Everyone chuckled.

Stanton had caught the political bug from his father, a country doctor from Bogart, Georgia, who served in Congress for eight years before losing a bitter campaign for U.S. Senate. His father's loss scarred Andy deeply. In his second year at law school, Andy was led to Christ by his roommate, then dropped out and enrolled at Fuller Theological Seminary. His later flirtations with politics bore the resentments of the adult child of a defeated father. In the previous election, the Faith and Family Fund, the group's PAC, contributed to eighty-eight candidates for U.S. Senate and Congress, 70 percent of whom won. Andy liked to joke that his father's defeat had contained the seeds of a thousand victories.

Andy's eyes lit up when someone asked what he thought of Betsy Hafer's comment comparing Christian leaders to Al-Jazeera.

"The woman is sinking the Democratic ticket!" exclaimed Andy, leaning forward in his seat. "The worst part is she really *believes* that. The Democrats attack evangelical leaders who stand up to the radicals and accuse them of being mentally impaired."

"It's anti-Christian bigotry," agreed Briggs, who knew how to get Andy's engines running.

"It is the last acceptable form of bigotry in America," said Andy, his eyes lit up, pointing with his index finger. "You can't make fun of minorities, women, or gays—nor should you, by the way. But if you're an evangelical Christian, you're fair game."

The door opened a crack. M.J. stuck her head into the room. "Dr. Stanton, phone call. It's the vice president."

"Vice president of what?" he asked with deliberate comic effect. "I have more vice presidents than Elizabeth Taylor had husbands!" Nervous laughter rumbled around the table. The mercurial Stanton burned through senior executives like a blowtorch, and it was not uncommon for one of them to suddenly disappear without so much as a word.

"The vice president *of the United States,* sir."

"Oh, *that* vice president!" Stanton exclaimed, winking around the table. "Why didn't you say so!" He stood up and stepped into a study off the boardroom.

"Mr. Vice President, so good to hear from you!" he boomed.

"Andy, how are you?"

"Blessed," he answered in a syrupy voice. "I'm sure you must be doing well, given the way the Democrats are shooting themselves in the foot."

"Well, you know the old saying," replied the vice president. "Sometimes it's better to be lucky than good." They enjoyed the joke together, two old warhorses sharing the intimacy of laughter. "Andy, our convention is coming up," he said, suddenly turning serious, "and I'd like to ask a personal favor."

"Sure," responded Stanton. "I'll do it if I can."

"I'd like for you to speak at the convention. We have a prime-time spot reserved on opening night. You could talk about young people, or men being better husbands and fathers. It does not have to be a political message."

What the vice president wanted, Andy knew, was the symbolism of Andy Stanton at the podium and the implicit endorsement it represented. "I'd love to, but I can't," Andy said. "I'm scheduled to be in India that week for a major evangelism blitz. It's all arranged with the government there and I can't back out." In truth, the India trip had been purposely scheduled so Stanton would be unavailable for the convention. Andy had mastered the art of avoiding the limelight when it didn't serve his purposes—he knew the dangers of overexposure.

"As much as I'd love to have you at the convention, your trip to India is more important," answered the vice president diplomatically. "But I'd like for you to do me another favor. I'd like you to visit with David Petty."

Stanton felt a palpitation in his chest. Secretary of State David Petty was the administration's face in the war on terrorism, and more remarkably, a rare face of color in a party that had not won the minority vote in decades. A retired army general who was as articulate as he was charming, he was the toast of the Georgetown set, beloved by the mainstream media (two *Time* magazine covers, one *New Yorker* profile, and a *Vanity Fair* spread) and a suave defender of the administration's often unpopular policies.

But there was a problem. He was a pro-choice moderate who had recently stirred a tempest by testifying before Congress that the ban on gays in the military was no longer necessary to discipline and good order. Stanton realized too late that the veep's convention invitation had been a head fake; his real purpose was to butter up Andy so he would accept David Petty as the running mate. It was a borderline betrayal of trust!

"Are you considering him for vice president?" Andy blurted, a tinge of desperation in his voice.

"I honestly have not decided," replied the vice president, his cards close to his vest. "But whatever I do, I want you and David to have a relationship."

"We have a relationship," replied Stanton.

"I want you to have a close relationship."

"Well, while you're looking for a running mate, I hope you'll consider Tom Reynolds. He's a hero to our people," Stanton suggested plaintively. It was a long shot, Andy knew. The White House disdained Senator Tom

Reynolds of Oklahoma. They viewed him as a preening blowhard who played to the religious right while promoting himself on an endless string of cable television appearances. His favored tactic was to offer amendments to bills dealing with hot-button issues like abortion or gay rights. The joke in the Senate was that the most dangerous place on the planet was between Tom Reynolds and a camera.

"Tom is terrific," the vice president lied. "But he's doing such a great job in the Senate, I'd hate to lose him. I've seen leaders in the Senate get elevated to the Cabinet and the place just doesn't recover."

"I see your point," said Stanton, trying not to sound deflated.

He agreed to fly to Washington and visit with Secretary Petty.

He took a deep breath and plastered a confident grin on his face before returning to the boardroom. The last thing he wanted was a room of syco-phants—who thought *he* was the most powerful figure in the Republican Party—to know that he had just been rolled by the future president of the United States.

————

WHILE ANDY STANTON AND his evangelical executives held hands and prayed, in the deserted back office of a Santa Monica warehouse Rassem el Zafarshan prayed a very different prayer. He prayed for more money. The time for the operation was fast approaching—and he needed cash.

He set a worn leather satchel down on the table and opened it. He counted out the money: $500,000 U.S. It was not enough. He needed more. His men were neither fully ready nor adequately equipped. They needed guns, ammunition, rocket-propelled grenades, and most importantly, SA-88 rockets. They needed a boat that could blend into the scenery.

"How much?" asked one of his lieutenants.

"Five hundred thousand," answered Zafarshan. "Everything will be paid for in cash—guns, ammunition, rental cars, the boat. *Everything in cash.* We cannot use credit cards. The Americans are tracking financial transactions and freezing bank accounts. The banks have been their most effective weapon."

"How much more do we need?"

"One million dollars." Zafarshan had become increasingly frustrated with his Iranian sponsors. They wanted him to do the impossible, and they wanted it done on the cheap. It was delusional. The days of hijacking commercial airliners with box-cutters were over. These operations took money—serious money. Either they would come up with the money or he would walk away.

"They're already in pretty deep," replied the lieutenant. "I can't imagine that another million dollars is a problem. I think I know where we can get it. I have a contact helping to route funds through Caracas."

"Call him. Tonight," ordered Zafarshan. "Make sure you use a hard line and speak in code. We have to assume our conversations are recorded."

The man nodded and departed.

Zafarshan prayed a silent prayer. With adequate finances, his team would strike a blow that would shock the world and bring America to its knees. Their attack would be so devastating it would make Americans forget September 11. Their operation would inspire more freedom fighters around the world to join the jihad.

War between the United States and Iran was inevitable. The only question now was who would fire the first shot. Zafarshan was determined that it would be him.

8

A S SOON AS JAY took his seat on United Airlines flight 110, a flight attendant walked through the first-class cabin carrying a silver tray covered with champagne glasses; some contained orange juice, some champagne, some mimosas. It may have only been 7:45 A.M., but Jay needed a drink. He grabbed a mimosa and drained it. The champagne left a tart aftertaste, but it hit his bloodstream in short order, temporarily lifting his foul mood.

He was snapped back to reality when his BlackBerry vibrated. Surprised that anyone would be calling so early, he glanced at the screen. It was Lisa Robinson.

"Jay, have you seen the newspapers?" asked Lisa.

"Yes. Not a pretty picture."

"Including the *Post*?"

"No, I saw the *WSJ*, the *Times*, and the *Trib*." Typically, Jay had already read three newspapers before most people had gotten to their desks in the morning.

"Check out the *Post* online," Lisa urged.

"Why?"

"Dan Dorman has a front-pager saying Stanley witnesses in the Virginia delegation lied to the credentials committee. Some were paid to give false testimony. G.G. Hoterman's firm did the depositions. The Virginia State Police are investigating, and they may make a criminal referral to the Justice Department."

Noble's heart skipped a beat. "Unbelievable! Is it true?"

"I don't know," Lisa replied. "I got a call this morning from an editor at the *Wall Street Journal* and they have two reporters on it. They're trying to catch up with the *Post*. They want to talk to our attorneys and our Virginia delegates."

"I'm on an airplane, so I have to speak obliquely," said Jay, lowering his voice. "Get them on the phone with the outside people—not internal people—and only on deep background. Nothing on the record, but tell our people to give them what they need, including docs. Got it?"

Lisa knew he was referring to the law firm the campaign had retained to handle the lawsuit against the Virginia Democratic Party. They would be all too happy to do a document dump to the media ripping Stanley for stealing Virginia.

"I'll call the *Journal* editor and get the ball moving."

"Good. Email the *Washington Post* story to my BlackBerry."

"Where will you be later? Reporters may want to talk to you."

"I'll be hard to reach. But leave me a voice mail and I'll get to a hard line and call you back."

"Get some rest," said Lisa, affectionate concern in her voice. Jay had brought her into the Long campaign, given her the shot of her career, and mentored her through the peaks and valleys of the ordeal. He hoped that they could have a closer relationship now, friendship or romance, whatever the system would bear. Was this call a signal that she felt the same? "Jay, I hope we can salvage something from all this."

"Too late to help us. This can only hurt them." Jay hung up. As the mimosa began to take effect, he let himself enjoy the thought of Stanley and Kaplan finally getting theirs. It would be fun watching them deal with an FBI investigation in a general election.

JAY AWOKE AS THE plane began its descent. From the twin effects of exhaustion and alcohol, he had fallen asleep halfway through a screwdriver, rationalizing that it was noon somewhere. Bleary, he gazed out the window at the seemingly endless expanse of Mexico City. From the air the city seemed to spread like ivy, surrounding nearby mountains and climbing up hills. He stared down at the city center, where a massive crowd spilled down the main thoroughfare and into side streets. Clouds of smoke drifted over the mob, all presided over by a gorgeous Latin model reclining in a gigantic tequila billboard. Jay wondered what was going on. A soccer match?

Jay missed his connecting flight to Manzanillo, and the next flight did not leave for four hours. Frustrated at having nothing to do but watch Spanish television in the airline's VIP lounge, he decided to grab a taxi. It was his first visit to the Mexican capital, and he would rather get a nickel tour than sit around and do nothing. His political instincts always led him to circulate with the locals, blend into his surroundings, and find out what was really going on.

The cabdriver informed him that the crowd in the streets was definitely not from a soccer match. The new president of Mexico had been sworn in an hour earlier in a hurried inaugural ceremony disrupted by protests. After a razor-thin victory amid charges of election fraud, his opponent had declared himself the winner and held a counter-inaugural rally, attended by a hundred thousand supporters. The protesters overturned cars and set a bus aflame, its billowing smoke creating a massive traffic jam. In the resulting chaos, with rocks and bottles flying through the air, the new president had called out the police, who were firing on the crowd with water cannons and tear gas.

Incredible, Jay thought. He had left the United States to escape a stolen presidential election and had stumbled upon another.

"Am I safe?" asked Jay.

"Sí, señor. You are in good hands," the taxi driver assured him, the gold caps on his teeth gleaming. The acrid smell of tear gas filled Jay's nostrils. His eyes burned. He felt sick to his stomach, having not eaten since the previous day. He asked the driver to find a restaurant with good Mexican food. When the taxi pulled up, Jay tipped the driver and asked him to wait. As he entered the restaurant, his BlackBerry vibrated.

"Jay, it's Hal Goodman. I hope it's not too soon to call." Goodman was a genuine Bigfoot: the senior Washington correspondent for *Newsweek*. It was Friday, which meant he was under deadline. Jay snapped to attention.

"Not at all, good to hear from you."

"I know it was rough. We sometimes forget that in addition to covering the story, we're dealing with human beings. I hope you're recovering okay."

Noble glanced back at the cabbie with the gold teeth and at the bluish tear gas hanging in the air outside. "Not yet, but I'm on my way. What can I do for you?"

He stepped back so Goodman could not hear the sizzle of the fajitas and the buzz of the lunch crowd in the background. He preferred that Hal not know that he was in the middle of a riot in Mexico City ordering tortillas.

"I'm working on a cover story on how Stanley won. A big part of that story is the fight over the Virginia delegation. Strictly on background, what do you know about whether the Stanley campaign paid delegates to commit perjury?"

Noble went into full-bore message mode. "Our lawsuit against the Virginia Democratic Party laid out the case for why Stanley's delegation was illegitimate," he said, choosing his words carefully. "The lawsuit and the briefs are a matter of public record. I can't comment beyond the public filings because it's a pending legal matter."

"Jay, I've read the lawsuit," Goodman said dismissively. "But you never claimed that Stanley delegates perjured themselves, or that they were bribed. Why not? If you had evidence that it was going on, you would have used it, right?"

Warning lights went off in Jay's head. Goodman was not only writing for *Newsweek,* he was gathering material for his next book. He had made a fortune writing bestselling books about how the winning presidential candidate had prevailed and the loser blew it, sort of Theodore White meets Hunter S. Thompson. He also wrote a daily blog that had become must-reading for the political class. Noble had to tread carefully.

"I'll defer to our outside counsel on that, Hal. If anyone committed perjury, we could not have known about it until after the fact."

The aroma of fresh tortillas filled Jay's senses. A cute waitress in a short blue skirt and white blouse rushed by, carrying a tray of Coronas. Jay wanted to run away and get on with his vacation—and the rest of his life. Goodman was pulling him back to the war, a war he had already lost.

"One last question," said Goodman. "If a police or FBI investigation finds that Stanley suborned perjury and paid bribes in Virginia, would you demand a revote? Wouldn't Long be the rightful Democratic nominee for president?"

"Hal, that's a hypothetical," Jay replied, swatting the question aside. "We made our case before the credentials committee. The convention seated the Stanley delegates. If new information comes out, we'll deal with it at the time."

"It's not a hypothetical. The Virginia State Police are investigating allegations of perjury and bribery."

"Nice try, Hal."

"Better think about it," said Goodman. "My sources tell me the evidence is pretty damning. If Stanley's nomination is invalid, then what? Does the Democratic Party keep him on the ballot with an asterisk?"

"Talk to the lawyers, Hal." Jay hung up.

A waitress escorted him to a table. He ordered coconut strips and a lobster taco as appetizers, downing them with a Corona and bottled water. The restaurant was in the center of Condesa, hardly the glamorous part of Mexico City, but it had great atmosphere and was full of energy. The cuisine was from the Yucatán peninsula, and the waiter recommended tacos with *cochinita de pibil,* a slow-roasted pork.

As he inhaled his food, Jay's brain went into overdrive. Goodman was one of the best reporters in the business. If he thought Stanley's candidacy was in jeopardy, maybe the Virginia delegation scandal had legs. He shuddered at the irony: if Dan Dorman's *Post* story had broken a week earlier, Long would have won.

Jay went back to the airport and boarded the evening flight to Manzanillo. After a bumpy ride in which he settled his stomach with chili peanuts and a Diet Coke, the plane landed. Several taxi drivers stood around in the baggage claim area. One sported a straw cowboy hat, giant silver belt buckle, blue jeans and denim shirt, and brown alligator cowboy boots. He held a sign that read "El Tamarindo." That was it—the resort where Jay had pitched the Mexican gubernatorial candidate.

"Does El Tamarindo have rooms available?" Noble asked in his high school Spanish.

"Sí, señor," the driver replied. "Cabana de muy grande vista de Pacifico."

An hour later, after twisting and turning over winding mountain roads in the darkness, the taxi pulled up to the resort. A bellman took Jay's bags and escorted him up the steps to an open-air lobby beneath a thatched roof. Thick woods buzzed with the sound of crickets, ocean waves crashed on the beach below. A smiling staff member handed Jay a glass of fruit punch with a piece of mango floating in it. He drank deeply.

"You are very fortunate, Mr. Noble," said the man at the small front desk. "We are in the low season. We have an oceanside cabana."

"Fine," Jay heard himself saying. When the man passed him the reservation form to sign, he had him initial the rate: eight hundred bucks a night!

He'd had no idea how expensive the place was; he had only eaten lunch there. But he couldn't leave now; he was in the middle of nowhere.

It was nearly ten o'clock by the time the bellman escorted him to his villa. He couldn't believe it—it was like having his own house on the beach. A spacious patio with comfortable seating, a dining area, dipping pool, and a bar were separated from the large bedroom only by rollaway doors. The living area was decorated with white linen cushions on cane furniture, hardwood floors, and inset mahogany panels. Even at night the view of the ocean was spectacular. He would sleep to the sound of the waves tonight. Peeking into the bathroom, he saw that the shower was a fancy open-air version and the bathroom faucet poured into a granite sink suspended on an oak table.

"Keep the doors closed at night," said the bellman. "To keep out the animals."

"What?" asked Jay.

"Sí," the bellman nodded, smiling. "Monkeys and raccoons."

Jay made a mental note to lock his door at night. After splashing his face and wiping it with a hot washcloth, he changed out of his consultant's uniform of polo shirt, khakis, and a blue blazer, and slipped into a resort outfit: linen shirt, Tommy Bahama shorts, and sandals. He strolled down a rocky walkway lit by tiki torches to the restaurant.

The restaurant included an infinity pool that looked like it flowed directly into the sea. As he walked across a pontoon bridge into the bar, Jay felt all the stress of a losing presidential campaign drain out of him. He sat down at a table and ordered a margarita on the rocks.

"With Don Julio," he said. "A strong one."

"A good one," smiled the waiter.

When his drink arrived, he took a sip, the taste of rock salt on his lips, the blast of tequila hot on his tongue. He glanced across the room and saw two attractive women on the other side of the lounge. One was a brunette, the other a blonde, and they were having a drink with some guy. After a while, the guy got up, shook their hands, and left.

As Jay nursed his drink, he made eye contact with the brunette. She wore white Capri pants, white heels, and a black off-the-shoulder blouse. Their eyes locked for what seemed an uncomfortably long time. He thought of looking away, but why should he? He was in Mexico, he was on vacation, and she was attractive.

His cell phone went off. He answered it.

"Jay, Dan Dorman with the *Washington Post*." Jay couldn't believe it— Dorman must be stressing under deadline. "What can you tell me—on background—about Stanley delegates perjuring themselves? Did you hear rumors about it?"

The brunette eyed him across the room. Jay was piqued at Dorman's timing. Apparently Dorman and Goodman were fighting for the same story. "Dan, once we filed the lawsuit, I turned that over to the lawyers. Call Lisa Robinson at the campaign."

"There *is* no campaign," Dorman protested. "I'm getting a tape machine at your headquarters in Los Angeles. I need you to help me understand how Stanley did it."

"Call Lisa on her cell. She'll get you in touch with the lawyers. They have some documents that you will find most interesting."

Dorman began to hyperventilate. "Documents? Does anyone else have them?"

Jay wasn't about to tell him the *Wall Street Journal* already had them. He wanted a feeding frenzy. "I'm not sure. Call Lisa, she's got a care package for you." He gave him Lisa's cell phone number and hung up.

The cute brunette slinked across the lounge toward him. She stopped, appeared to vaguely recognize him, and then plopped down in the chair opposite him.

"Was that a business call?" she asked. "On a Friday night in Mexico?"

"Yes. And it was a most interesting one."

She cocked her head and raised her eyebrows. "Really? Tell me more." Jay began to speak, but she interrupted him. "I hope you don't think I'm too forward. Is this okay?"

"Of course. Why in the world would I object to a pretty girl coming over to introduce herself?"

"I'm Nicole Dearborn," she said, extending her hand. "So . . . what do you do that requires you to take business calls at all hours of the day and night?"

"I'm a consultant," Jay replied. He kept it ambiguous. The last thing he wanted to do was discuss politics.

"What kind of consultant?"

"I solve people's problems."

"I see," she said, her voice low and seductive. "What services do you offer? If I were looking for a consultant, can I hire your services, or can I just hire you?"

Jay wondered if this was really happening. "You could hire me, or you could make use of my firm's services."

"I see." She threw her head back and laughed. "How much will it cost me?"

"That depends. What do you want me to do?"

"That's a loaded question." She leaned forward, her hair falling off her shoulder. "I've been a bad girl. I have to be honest and tell you something." She paused, leaning forward farther, and lowered her voice to a whisper. "I know who you are."

Drat! His cover was blown.

"You're Jay Noble, aren't you?"

Noble didn't know whether to be thrilled that a hot woman had recognized him or upset that he had been spotted when he was trying to hide from the entire world.

"That's what they tell me," he said.

"So, are you campaigning in Mexico now?" she asked, flashing a smile.

"Not hardly."

"I need to introduce you to my friend or she's going to kill me," Nicole said. "Let's pretend that I just met you. Come up with a name so you don't have to talk politics." She turned serious. "What's your middle name?"

"Ryan."

Nicole took Jay's arm and walked them over to her friend. "Gabriella, I've been talking to this nice man. I brought him to meet you."

"I like nice men," said Gabriella, leaning forward in her chair to shake his hand. She looked like she had been poured into her leopard-skin skirt and black blouse with a plunging neckline. Jay tried not to stare. "What brings you to Mexico?"

"Business and pleasure."

"What's your name?"

"He's the great Jay Noble," interjected Nicole. "He's a famous political strategist."

Jay shot her a confused look—he'd understood that the plan was to use his middle name. She winked. Gabriella's facial expression was blank. She had no clue who he was. Thank goodness for reality television and *People* magazine, thought Jay.

"Gabby and I are here for pleasure only," Nicole said. "I worked on the Scott Ballard presidential campaign. I was in the communications shop."

"Sure, I remember you," Jay lied. Ballard had run for the nomination but never had much of a chance. He had lacked money and name ID and washed out in the Iowa caucuses. He later dropped out and endorsed Long, so at least Nicole was a roundabout friend rather than a sworn enemy. "What brings you two here?" he asked.

"After the campaign, I worked at the DNC in the press shop. Stanley wanted to bring in his own crew, so my last day was yesterday. Gabby and I flew down this morning. To be honest, I can't get excited about Stanley."

"I came along to keep her company and meet men," joked Gabriella. "It was a terrible sacrifice."

"I'm sorry," Nicole said. "Here you are trying to get away, and I'm running my mouth about politics."

"No apology needed," said Noble. "I *am* getting away. This is a great place. I was here many years ago and never got back."

"Well, you're here now." She flipped her hair back and smiled. "Can we buy you a drink?"

"Sure," Jay heard himself say, enjoying the flirting.

The waitress brought Nicole and Gabby red wine. Jay ordered another margarita. Nicole stirred the wine in the glass, letting it breathe, and fingered the edge of the glass.

"So, how was your flight?" she asked, making small talk.

"You don't want to know."

"We changed planes in Los Angeles."

"I went through Mexico City. I missed my connection. But I did get to see a genuine Mexican political rally. Actually, it was a riot."

"A riot?" exclaimed Gabby, sitting up. "You're kidding."

"No," said Jay, warming to his story. "It seems that we in the U.S. are not alone in stealing elections. The new president of Mexico was inaugurated today. Apparently he won in a fraudulent election and there was a massive protest. One hundred thousand people were in the streets."

"That sounds frightening," said Gabriella.

"Tear gas grenades exploding. Water cannons. Buses and cars on fire." Jay embellished the story as he went on. "Mexican soldiers and police on the street with Plexiglas shields and AK-47 machine guns. I felt like I was in a Martin Sheen movie."

Nicole's eyes widened. "Were you scared?"

"Not really." He shrugged, trying to sound macho. "Maybe if *we* had thought to stage a riot, we could have won in Chicago."

Nicole laughed and took another sip from her drink. The wind blowing off the ocean caught her hair, revealing diamond stud earrings that glittered against her skin. She turned toward the waves in thoughtful repose.

They talked for an hour about nothing in particular: vacation spots, what they each might do after politics, the opposite sex. Gabby began to fade, closing her eyes and falling silent. It was getting late. She excused herself and headed off to bed, leaving Nicole and Jay alone. They sat quietly for a minute.

"I thought we were going to use my middle name so I could travel incognito," said Jay.

"Sorry, my fault. I decided to tell Gabby the truth." Her eyes locked on his. "I don't like to live a lie."

"Neither do I."

"So what are you going to do next?" Nicole asked.

"I don't know, but I just ran my last campaign."

"Jay, don't say that. You're one of the best in the business—of all time. You'll be in huge demand. Long can come back and he's going to need you."

"I don't know if Long can come back. Even if he does, I can be a wise man, stepping in when needed. But I can't do another marathon. It's a meat grinder."

The waitress came over, and Jay ordered some appetizers and another round of drinks. It was late, but the conversation flowed easily. After dinner, Jay decided to loosen up. "Cubanos?" he asked the waitress.

"Sí, señor," she replied.

"Do you mind if I smoke a cigar?" he asked Nicole.

She looked at the waitress. "Make it two," she said.

"You smoke cigars?"

"I smoked some in Cuba," she said. When Jay seemed surprised, she added, "It was totally legal. I was there on a humanitarian project."

Jay nodded at the waitress. "Dos Cubanos, por favor."

How had he gotten this lucky? In the middle of the jungle in an ecoresort in Mexico, he had met a beautiful, unattached female—good-looking, smart, funny, and political. And she smoked cigars! Maybe recovering from the worst defeat of his life wasn't going to be so hard after all.

9

B OB LONG SAT AT the dining room table in his hotel suite and scanned the papers, reading his political obituary. The morning light broke through the curtains, splashing the room with a brightness that contrasted with his depressed mood.

The celebration of Hafer was understandable. The media wanted to see the glass ceiling shattered. What really hurt was to have the *New York Times* compare his refusal to endorse Stanley to the 1948 walkout of Strom Thurmond and the Dixiecrats. That was a low blow. Nevertheless, Long got the joke. The press loved winners and hated losers. He had lost, and they were going to kick him on the way down.

The phone rang and Long answered it. The voice of his minister, Jeff Links, crackled through the static. Bob and Claire had been members of his Methodist Church in Glendale for fifteen years. His voice sounded like it was coming from a tin can on the other side of the earth.

"I'm in Malaysia on a mission trip, Bob. I just wanted to call you to tell you that I followed what happened at the convention and you're in my prayers."

"Thanks, Jeff. Claire and I appreciate your friendship."

"Bob, you were *supposed* to run," said Jeff in a firm and confident voice. "God has a plan. I can't wait to see what he has next for you."

Long played along, but he did not share Links's optimism. If God had a plan, it certainly was a bizarre one. Nevertheless, he was grateful for the call. His political handlers, major donors, bundlers, the press, and the friends who were not really his friends had all fallen away. At least Links was still a friend.

"Bob, I'm sending you a book. I assume you're going to get away and get some rest. As you do that, I want you to read it. It's a collection of sermons on the life of Joseph. It focuses on how God uses defeat and injustice to accomplish his purposes."

"You bet." Long gave Links the address of his mountain cabin.

"Bob, do you mind if I pray for you?"

Long was caught a little off stride, but he saw no point in offending Links. "Sure. Go right ahead."

Jeff prayed a short, simple prayer. He thanked God for Long's courage in running, what he had stood for, and the people he had touched. He asked God to comfort and encourage Bob and Claire. Then he closed with what Long vaguely recognized as a phrase from the Bible: "Father, you have delivered Bob from the darkness into your marvelous light, redeemed him, forgiven his sins, and placed him in a strategic place to reach many people. Cover him with your grace. Amen."

Long felt a flood of emotion. "Thank you," he said in a scratchy voice.

"Call me after you read the book, Bob. Remember: you'll find Jesus in a place of suffering."

Hanging up, Bob was not sure his faith was that strong. He believed in God, but he wondered why God seemed at times to be such a disinterested observer of His creation. If death, defeat, injustice, and evil were evidence of God's plan, then what was the evidence of the devil? It seemed illogical to him.

Claire walked into the room, dressed to travel in a white Chanel suit. Bob had heard her talking on the bedroom extension of their dual-line phone.

"That was Kate," she said. "She's having contractions. It could be false labor. But just in case, we need to get to L.A." Their youngest daughter, Kate, was pregnant with their third grandchild. She was due in two weeks.

"I'll call the pilots and tell them to move up the departure time."

"Who were you talking to?" she asked.

"Jeff Links calling from Malaysia. He's sending me one of his books." He grinned awkwardly, still fighting his emotions. "It will be a nice diversion from the newspapers."

Claire looked at him for a moment, then walked over and took him in her arms. They stood in an extended embrace, with Bob clutching her tightly against his chest. Her hair tickled his nose. He felt her forehead grow hot. She began to weep quietly.

"It's going to be okay," he said softly.

"I know, I know," she said through her sniffles. "It's just so hard. I'm so proud of you. What makes me so angry"—she wiped her eyes, trying to keep the mascara from getting on her white suit—"is that what Stanley did was wrong, and he got away with it."

"He may pay for it yet," Long replied.

"What do you mean?"

"Check this out." Long handed her the newspaper. She audibly gasped at the headline: "Stanley Virginia Delegation Subject of Police Investigation." She scanned the story, her eyes widening.

"Well, this story broke too late to do us any good," Claire said. "Do you think they broke the law?"

"I don't know." Long shrugged. "But I know Michael Kaplan, and he'll do anything to win. That goes double for G.G. Hoterman. He'd throw his own mother off a cliff."

"They can't get away with this," Claire protested.

"They just did."

G.G. HOTERMAN AMBLED UP to the cockpit. "Change of plans," he said.

This was no time to be in Southampton, not with his photo on the front page of the *Washington Post* and the paparazzi crawling all over the Hamptons. Gossip columnists would be swarming like locusts. And there was the inconvenient fact that he was accompanied by a drop-dead gorgeous young woman who was not his wife.

He told the pilots to head to Higher Ground, his farm in upstate New York in the Adirondacks. It was beautiful up there this time of year—warm during the day, crisp and cool at night, with blue skies and no reporters. The pilots called ahead so the staff at the farm would be prepared.

An hour later, as they taxied to a stop, a silver Range Rover pulled up to the plane. Out jumped Otis Fernbank, the manager of the farm, in jeans, a flannel shirt, hiking boots, and a green hat sporting a Ducks Unlimited logo.

"What a pleasant surprise, Mr. Hoterman," he shouted over the plane's engines.

"For me, too, Otie. We were supposed to go to the Hamptons, but it's just too hot there right now." G.G. blamed the weather rather than an untimely scandal. "Sorry for the short notice."

"No problem. We're always ready for you, sir."

Otis tipped his hat as Deirdre climbed down the plane's stairs, her long legs seeming to take forever to hit the ground. She gave him a warm smile, and G.G. guided her into the car's backseat. Otis loaded the bags into the Range Rover, climbed into the driver's seat, and pulled away. G.G. caught Otis's eyes in the rearview mirror. He had never brought Deirdre to Higher Ground. He was glad he could count on Otis's discretion. G.G. reached for his cell phone and dialed Tony Piccillo.

"Tony, G.G. here. We just landed. Give me the lowdown."

"Good news and bad news, G.G.," Tony said with a sigh. "The good news is Shapiro's on board. Talked to him an hour ago. He's contacting the Virginia State Police to introduce himself and let them know he is our attorney."

"That'll be quite a shot across the bow. He's first-rate," said G.G. "How can there be bad news when we've got Walt Shapiro?"

"The not so good news," Tony replied, "is that one of Walt's partners heard from another lawyer that the Virginia State Police are asking the FBI to come in."

"That's bad," said G.G. in a somber tone of voice. "This should be handled by a local prosecutor. Bringing in the FBI leads to a lot of places, and none of them are good."

"It's a total cluster, G.G. If the FBI starts poking around, the charges become federal rather than state. Any criminal charges are litigated in the federal courts, with one-year mandatory minimum sentences."

"We've got to try to stop that if we can. When can we talk to Shapiro?"

"I've got him scheduled for a two P.M. call."

"Okay. Talk to you then."

Hoterman put his cell phone in his pocket and stared straight ahead. Deirdre must have heard his comment about the FBI, but she said nothing. Otis bantered away about the weather, the quality of the fishing, the local rainfall, and water levels on area lakes. To G.G.'s delight, he passed on gossip about a neighbor G.G. despised who was going through an ugly divorce and had put his farm on the market.

"That guy complained to the warden about my dock a few years ago and I had to dismantle it," G.G. said. "Wouldn't it be sweet to buy his farm with a straw buyer and then let him know that I got it?" He laughed.

Otis guided the Range Rover over a dirt road beneath a canopy of pine trees, pulling up to Higher Ground. The tires crunched over the gravel on the driveway. Hoterman stepped out of the car and walked into the main house. It was in great shape, its hardwood floors polished, stuffed game he had shot mounted on the wall, a bear rug on the floor, with a huge bay window overlooking the pond in the back. The musty smell of summer blankets, pollen, tree sap, and Pine-Sol filled the room. He unlocked the latch on the screen door and walked out on the back deck, drinking in the scenery, and taking a deep breath.

Deirdre came up behind him and put her arms around his waist, pulling her chest up against his back. The muscles in his lower back relaxed reflexively. He closed his eyes and exhaled. This was better than yoga.

"Would you like to take a nap?" she whispered in his ear.

"I'd like to go lie down." He turned and looked into her eyes. "But I'm not in the mood for sleep."

"That makes two of us."

They walked hand in hand to the master bedroom.

———————

SAL STANLEY AND BETSY Hafer sat across from one another on couches on the bus that carried them from the Philadelphia airport to a downtown noon rally. It was 11:45 A.M., and they were making their third stop of the day. The "Honest Change Tour" had begun shortly after dawn in West Virginia, and after another afternoon rally in Pittsburgh, they were headed for Cleveland and Columbus, Ohio. Five stops in three battleground states—and it was only day one of the general election campaign. By the time the tour ended four days later, the Stanley-Hafer ticket would make twenty-three stops in eleven states.

Sue Bennett, the tough-as-nails deputy press secretary, crouched on the floor, bouncing on her toes, her high heels kicked off, a legal pad in front of her. She gave the candidates a quick briefing. She rocked back on her heels as the bus made a sharp turn.

"The rally is at the Philadelphia Museum of Art, where Sylvester Stallone ran up the flight of steps in *Rocky*. You will go on the stage to the theme song from the movie. You may or may not want to work a *Rocky* line into your remarks."

"Save that one for me, Betsy," Stanley joked with a wink.

"Governor," said Bennett, addressing Hafer, "you'll be introducing the majority leader, as you did in West Virginia. Go straight to the podium when you get onstage. Take as much time as you like—but no more than seven minutes."

Hafer nodded. She already had dark circles under her eyes.

"When you're done, leave the stage," Bennett directed. "Work the rope line. There'll be a press stakeout at the end. Take a few questions and get back on the bus."

Hafer and Stanley looked bored. They knew the drill.

"Three minutes!" shouted an advance man as the bus slowed.

"This is the first press avail since Chicago, so they'll be aggressive. They're going to try to make their bones," Bennett warned. "Governor, you'll get a question about the Muslim statement. Senator, you'll get questions about the Virginia State Police investigation. You know the talking points." She leveled her eyes at them. "Stick to the script and don't mix it up with them. You'll do great."

The bus pulled up to the back of the museum—and there were dozens of reporters leaning over a rope line near the bus, photographers jostling frantically, boom mikes swaying overhead. Sue Bennett's shocked expression seemed to ask, Who let the media gather where the bus pulled up?

"I thought the press avail was *after* the rally!" Stanley yelled. He turned to Bennett, his eyes demanding an explanation. Bennett just shrugged.

"Who let the press here? Who screwed up?" shouted the head of advance. His eyes drilled holes in the forehead of a perspiring advance man next to him.

"Forget it," said Stanley after several seconds of awkward silence. "Let's get it over with."

They stepped off the bus, Hafer and Stanley standing shoulder to shoulder, their spouses standing directly behind them. No sooner had their feet hit the pavement than the shouting and elbow throwing began.

"Senator, are you concerned about the Virginia police investigation into possible perjury and bribery by your campaign?" asked Fox News.

"No," Stanley replied. "The investigation is ongoing and my campaign will cooperate fully. It would not be appropriate for me to comment on a pending investigation. But after reviewing the evidence, the Virginia Democratic Party, the credentials committee, and the Democratic National Committee all determined that I won the Virginia delegation fair and square."

"Will you pledge to fire anyone in your campaign found to have suborned perjury or bribed delegates?" asked the Associated Press.

"I maintain a high standard for my staff, and based on the knowledge I have now, they have held to that standard. They have my full confidence."

"What about Michael Kaplan? Will you dismiss him if it turns out that he was involved in suborning perjury?" asked ABC News.

"As I said, we hold to a high standard. Clearly, that includes Mike. He has my full confidence."

"Governor Hafer, what do you say to Christian voters who find your statement about moral equivalence between Christians who criticize Islam and terrorists to be reprehensible? And will you apologize?"

"That comment was taken out of context. It has been distorted in a manner that in no way represents my views," Hafer replied, blue eyes aflame, her jaw muscles tensing. "This is the Republican attack machine trying to tear me down because they are worried." The press looked up from their steno pads; she was hanging in there. "We all oppose terrorism, but our enemy is the extremists, not Islam, and certainly not peace-loving Muslims."

"Senator, are you concerned that Governor Hafer's comment has become a distraction?" shouted NBC News.

"It's only a distraction to you," Stanley fired back, biting off his words. "It's not a distraction to us. Why don't you report on the record crowds we're attracting today? Reporting the facts—I guess that would be a novel experience for you."

"Thank you. That's all, everybody," shouted Bennett as she waved the candidates along the rope line.

Stanley and Hafer wheeled in the direction of the stage, ignoring more shouted questions. Camera flashes exploded. They bounded up the steps to the stage to the theme from *Rocky*, smiling and waving as the crowd roared its approval. Their spouses stumbled after them as if they had seen a ghost, stricken looks on their faces.

SAMUEL SYMS, WHITE HOUSE chief of staff, walked down the beige-carpeted hallway leading to the Oval Office. He asked the president's personal secretary if he was in, rapped on the door three times, and walked in.

The president was at his desk studying some papers, his brow furrowed, his thinning hair now more salt than pepper. Syms had watched the president age like a time-lapse photograph, the recesses lining his face growing more pronounced, his posture growing more stooped. Reading glasses rested on the end of his nose.

"Mr. President, I just got off the phone with the attorney general. The FBI director has been contacted by the commander of the Virginia State Police, who asked for the bureau's assistance in the investigation into allegations of perjury and bribery in the selection of Sal Stanley's Virginia delegation." Syms read from notes on a legal pad. "He views this request as preliminary to a criminal referral."

The president's eyes widened. "What does the AG say?"

"He thinks the public integrity division should handle it."

"Not a special counsel?" asked the president.

"He doesn't recommend it. He doesn't think the special counsel statute will allow it. That's why you have career prosecutors."

"The Democrats are going to scream bloody murder." The president rose from his desk and walked over to the bank of windows overlooking the Rose Garden. "They'll say it's a political witch hunt by a Republican Justice Department."

"We can write the talking points ourselves." Syms approached the president, who kept his back to him, gazing out the window. "But, Mr. President, if the AG appoints a special counsel, it could get squirrelly. They have a way of chasing down rabbit trails."

"Do they ever," agreed the president. He stretched, looking up at the ceiling. "Look at Walsh during Iran-Contra, the Whitewater investigation leading to Monica Lewinsky, and Fitzgerald going after Scooter Libby. They're accountable to no one. There are no limits on their budget, staff, or tenure. It's Kafkaesque."

"What do we say when the *New York Times* runs the inevitable editorial claiming we're using the Justice Department to target Democrats and cripple Stanley's campaign?"

"I don't care about the *Times*," the president scoffed. He leaned forward in his chair, his eyes steady. "We'll say the investigation is being conducted by career prosecutors who are civil servants, free from any political interference, and if anyone violated the law, they'll be prosecuted to the fullest extent of the law."

"G.G. Hoterman will take no delight in that statement." Syms smiled.

"I'm sure he won't," said the president. "I'm not thrilled we have to investigate the Democratic presidential nominee and the biggest Democratic lobbyist in town. But if Hoterman is smart, and he is, he'd rather have our DOJ than an independent counsel any day of the week."

As he turned and left the Oval Office, Syms imagined where the scandal might lead. If Michael Kaplan or G.G. Hoterman were indicted, Stanley would probably be finished, his candidacy consumed by the scandal. The election would be over before the balloons dropped at the GOP convention, and Republicans would be assured of holding the White House for another four years.

10

V ICE PRESIDENT HARRISON FLAHERTY stood in the ceremonial office he used only for formal meetings in the Eisenhower Executive Office Building, across the alleyway from the White House. The ceiling contained an Italianate fresco painting and extensive handcrafted woodwork, while two Belgian black marble fireplaces dominated the room. Crystal chandeliers hung from nineteenth-century beams. The walls were covered with Venetian plaster and the floor featured intersected planks of mahogany, cherry, and white maple. Flaherty had just finished a photo opportunity with a group of business leaders from Japan and was on his way to the regular weekly lunch of the Senate Republican caucus. He circled behind the ceremonial desk, first used by Theodore Roosevelt, its inlaid calfskin leather embroidered with fourteen-carat gold paint, its top desk drawer engraved with the initials of every vice president since the 1940s, including Truman, Nixon, and Bush. There wasn't a single piece of paper on the desk (his working office was on the second floor of the White House's West Wing). He sat in the burgundy leather chair and picked up the phone.

"Mr. Vice President, I have Sam Syms on the line," said his secretary.

"Put him through." He heard the click of the secretary hanging up. "Flaherty here," he announced.

"Mr. Vice President, I just saw the president and wanted to make you aware of the substance of that conversation. It involves something on the Q.T."

"Fire away."

"The FBI is going to investigate the charges of bribery and perjury by the Stanley campaign in the selection of the delegation from Virginia," Syms reported.

"That's a live grenade that just landed in our lap, isn't it?"

"One hundred percent," agreed Syms in his best official baritone. "I wanted to make sure you knew about it before you read about it in the newspaper."

"Too late." Flaherty chuckled. "It's on the front page of the *Post*."

"That's part of the problem—the state police are leaking like a sieve. Apparently there's an ugly piece in *Newsweek* coming based on police sources."

"It couldn't happen to a nicer group of people," chuckled the vice president.

"The AG is not inclined to appoint a special counsel," said Syms.

"I'm not touching that," replied Flaherty. "We're in an awkward enough position as it is. I recommend we stay far away. And I mean *nothing:* no emails, no talking to the press on background. Loose talk on this by anybody will bite us."

"The president agrees. Just giving you a heads-up," said Syms.

Flaherty placed the phone down. His chief of staff, Bill Diamond, walked in. He had been waiting just outside for the call to end.

"What did Sam want?" he asked anxiously.

"Keep this between us," Flaherty responded, his voice lowered. "The FBI is going to investigate whether any crimes were committed in the selection of Sal Stanley's delegation from Virginia. The whole can of worms is landing at DOJ."

"Incredible," Diamond exclaimed. "Is that good or bad?"

"Both," said the vice president. "A federal criminal investigation of Stanley's campaign is too good to be true. But they'll accuse DOJ of pursuing it for political reasons. Defending an AG that I didn't appoint and don't control won't be a lot of fun, but I'm between a rock and a hard place."

"Why can't the AG just name an outside counsel? Appoint some career prosecutor, an Eliot Ness type, or a retired federal judge—wash our hands of it."

"Not in the cards," Flaherty said. "Special counsels require a conflict of interest—that is, you are investigating yourself. That's not the case here, so the AG is stuck with it." He shook his head. "What a mess."

"The word on the Hill is that the two people with major problems are Kaplan and Hoterman," said Diamond.

"Kaplan's wrapped around the axle," the vice president said. "Hoterman will probably go down with him. It looks like he suborned perjury by paying delegates and party officials to swear to false affidavits. That's a felony, and it means disbarment."

"Stanley needed Virginia. He did what he had to do."

"Guess who I talked to this morning?" Flaherty asked, changing the subject. "Andy Stanton. I asked him to come up here and break bread with David Petty."

"Will he do it?"

"He said he would." He shot Diamond a knowing glance. "And *please* call David and tell him to be on his best behavior. I need him to kiss Andy's ring." He jiggled his ring finger and rolled his eyes. "He requires the full royal treatment."

"Does the secretary have a suck-up bone in his body?" asked Diamond sarcastically.

"He'd better for Stanton." The vice president looked at his watch. "I have to run to the Senate caucus lunch. Keep this FBI matter under your hat." He pointed his finger at Diamond, jabbing the air for emphasis. "No leaks."

Diamond nodded. "This won't go outside this room."

The vice president left his office with a travel aide and two Secret Service agents in tow. The Senate caucus luncheon would be buzzing about the scandal plaguing the Stanley campaign, but Flaherty would have nothing to say about it. He lived by the rule that when your opponent is busy committing suicide, get out of the way.

BOB AND CLAIRE LONG boarded the private jet to fly home to California, their marathon run for the presidency over. Joined by friends and aides, the atmosphere on the plane had a funereal and frat party quality all rolled into one. The Longs killed time playing cards and reading newspapers. A flight attendant poured martinis from a pitcher, while some of the passengers raided the icebox and clawed at a cheese tray. Claire curled up in the seat across from Bob, nursing a Bloody Mary, which she occasionally freshened with more vodka. Bob cast a disapproving glance in her direction, and she stared right back at him as if to say, "I've earned it, so back off."

Lisa Robinson had come along to bid farewell and to begin the decompression process. Most of the staff had scattered. The aftermath of losing campaigns resembled a battlefield amputation more than putting the family dog to sleep. The end was quick and bloody. For Long, a support system of consultants, lawyers, staff, and straphangers disappeared overnight, including Jay Noble, his senior strategist, who had reportedly disappeared for some foreign climate.

As the jet soared over the Rockies, Lisa chose a lull in the rolling card game of spades to plop down in one of the leather chairs opposite Long. "So I understand you're going to be a grandfather. Congratulations."

"My third grandchild." Long beamed. "Kate is having contractions, but it looks like false labor. We're getting home a little early just to be safe."

"Governor, forgive me for talking shop, but I got a call from the *Wall Street Journal* this morning," she reported. "They're looking into the investigation of Stanley's Virginia delegation."

"They're a day late and a dollar short. Where were they when we needed them?"

"They smell blood now. He asked me a question that I . . . well . . ."

"What?"

"He asked what we would do if it were proven that Stanley stole the Virginia delegation illegally," Lisa continued. "Would we demand a revote? And if the DNC refused, would you consider running as a third-party candidate?"

Long broke out laughing. "First they kill me, and now they want to resurrect me and run me in the general election! They will do anything to sell newspapers!"

"Well, would you?" asked Lisa.

"You can't revote on the presidential nomination. If they prove Stanley is a crook, all I can say is, 'You had your chance.' " Long pondered the second question. "As for the independent route, it's hard to get on the ballot, and even if I did, all I would do is split the Democratic vote. I'd be Ralph Nader."

"Governor, you'll never be Ralph Nader," Lisa replied.

"You're right. I'm better-looking and I'm sane." They both laughed.

Claire put down her magazine. She looked elegant in her Chanel suit, her matching high heels slipped off, her feet stockinged. She twirled the lime in her Bloody Mary and took another sip, unwinding. She happily joined the conversation. "It might be worth going down in history as a spoiler, a Dixiecrat or another Ralph Nader to stop Sal Stanley," she said. "He's worse than a Republican."

"Oh, I don't know," replied Long. "There are some distasteful Republicans."

"Sal is crooked, dear," said Claire firmly, a touch of gallows humor in her voice.

Claire can't let it go, Lisa thought. Candidates generally moved on after a defeat, if only for their own psychological survival, while their spouses dreamed of revenge. Jay even had a phrase for it. He called it "Stepford wives sticking pins in voodoo dolls."

———

WHEN THE PLANE LANDED in L.A., Bob and Claire hugged their friends and said their final good-byes. Claire's cell phone rang.

"Hello?"

"Claire, it's Barry." Barry was Kate's husband.

"Hi, Barry, we just landed. How is Kate?"

"Great. But her contractions are getting closer. The doctor wants her to come on in, so we're on our way to the hospital."

"So it's really happening!" exclaimed Claire excitedly. "We're on our way." She hung up the phone and turned to Bob. He was still saying his final farewells. "Bob, we have to go! We have to get to the hospital. Kate is having her baby!"

Everyone cheered and applauded. Claire and Bob loaded their suitcases into the SUV in the parking lot and headed for Good Samaritan Hospital. "She's not due for two weeks, right?" asked Bob. "Is everything all right?"

"Barry didn't mention any problem. Usually the first child is late, not early. But everything sounded fine."

When they arrived at the hospital, they pulled up to the lobby of the women's health wing and a valet parked their car. Barry greeted them with the harried look of an expectant father. "Kate is doing fine," he said. "But before you go upstairs, there's something you should know." He paused. "The baby is breech."

Claire felt a rush of panic.

"We found out about a week ago when she went in for her regular appointment. But Kate didn't want you to be worried about it going into the convention, so we decided not to tell you then."

"What do the doctors say?" asked Claire.

"She's in early labor, but the contractions are still far enough apart, so they are going to try to turn the baby in the womb manually and deliver it vaginally if they can," said Barry. "If that doesn't work, they'll perform a C-section."

"And Kate is all right?" asked Bob.

"She's doing fine but she's a little nervous. She'll be glad you're here."

<hr />

THREE HOURS LATER, KATE's labor had progressed nicely. To everyone's relief, the doctors had succeeded in maneuvering the baby so that his head rather than his feet was facing down in her uterus and would therefore deliver first. Her cervix had dilated to six centimeters. Kate's contractions had increased in frequency and intensity. Everything looked good.

At 8:30 P.M., Bob was in the hospital cafeteria, killing time by drinking a cup of coffee and reading a newspaper. Barry rounded the corner with a look of terror, his face white and bloodless.

Bob stood quickly. "What's going on?"

"They can't find the baby's heartbeat!"

"What happened?" Bob cried.

"I don't know. Something's wrong. They're going in after the baby. They're doing an emergency C-section."

Claire rushed down the hall. Bob could tell by the look on her face that she was already aware of the turn of events. Tears in her eyes, she put her arms around Barry. "It's going to be all right," she said soothingly.

"You don't know that! My son could die!" Barry said, burying his head in his hands.

"Barry, he's not. This hospital has one of the finest OB/GYN centers in the country. Kate is in good hands," Claire said, sounding as if she needed to convince herself as much as Barry.

Bob stood unsure of what to do or say. A doctor wearing green surgical coveralls padded rapidly down the hallway and escorted them into a small cubbyhole, apparently a nurses' station.

"I know you're worried," he said, his voice calm and clinical. "Let me tell you what we're doing. Because the baby was in a complete breech position when Kate arrived, we attempted what is known as an external cephalic version, in which we turn the baby manually so that the head points down and delivers first. That procedure was successful."

"Then what went wrong?" asked Barry.

"In a very small number of cases, the ECV leads to either entanglement of the umbilical cord or prolapsing of the cord. The cord carries the oxygen supply for the baby. That is what happened in this case. As Kate's contractions increased, the cord either wrapped around the baby's neck"—he demonstrated using circular hand gestures—"or became compressed in the birth canal. The baby's heart rate dropped, which is a sign of fetal distress. We need to get the baby out now, so we are performing an emergency C-section."

"Is everything going to be all right?" asked Barry, his voice quavering.

"We don't know yet. We may not know tonight. Kate is a healthy woman and her vital signs are strong. The baby is experiencing oxygen deprivation. There is a danger of complications. If the brain is deprived of oxygen for any length of time, there is the risk of developmental disorders."

"When you say complications, you mean the baby could die," said Barry.

"It's one possibility."

"How long did the baby go without oxygen?" asked Claire.

"We won't know until we run some tests," the doctor replied. "I need to get back upstairs. I'll give you another report as soon as I can."

Barry looked devastated. The euphoria of the birth of his first child had turned into a nightmare. Claire guided him to a bench and sat nearby to comfort him, but she looked like she'd rather collapse on the floor and scream. Bob was numb. He had just lost the presidency; now he was on the verge of losing his grandchild.

Claire rose and came to him, leaving Barry staring at the floor, catatonic. "When it rains it pours, doesn't it?" Bob said.

Claire looked at him, tears in her eyes. "How much can one family take?"

Bob had no answer. His head was spinning, and he was so tired his hands were shaking. Yet even in his confusion, a strange calm came over him. He wasn't sure why at first, and then he realized that parts of his earlier conversation with his pastor were running through his head. He knew where to go and what he had to do. "I'll be back soon," he said to Claire, and headed

down the hall to the reception desk. "Excuse me, where's the hospital's chapel?" he asked.

The receptionist gave him directions. As he turned down the hall, she
called out, "Governor, I voted for you. I hope you run again."

"Thanks," he mumbled in a daze. His stomach grumbled from a combination of alcohol, black coffee, sleep deprivation, and air travel.

The chapel had a plain brown door like any other in the building; the
only difference was that the side panel window held stained glass. He looked
around. No one was watching. At this hour, the hospital was nearly deserted.
He walked into the chapel.

11

B OB LONG CLOSED THE chapel door behind him, his eyes adjusting to the semidarkness. At the front of the room was a makeshift altar covered with a purple felt cloth illuminated by a spotlight. A single panel of stained glass framed in deep mahogany hung from the ceiling, also lit from behind by a spotlight. There was industrial blue-green carpet on the floor and three rows of padded chairs that looked as if they might have been purchased at a bankruptcy sale. The setting was ecumenical and interfaith—no sign of a cross or Star of David to be found. It didn't look like the chapel got much use, yet Bob felt surrounded by echoes: voices of those who had preceded him in their own moment of need, crying out to God. A doctor he had met on a hospital tour had once told him that there were no atheists in ER waiting rooms. He now understood.

Bob was not a praying man. As he got down on his knees awkwardly, it occurred to him that he had no idea what to say. He said what came into his mind: "God, please save my grandson," he began tentatively. "Please don't let him die."

He felt nothing. He heard no harps in the background, no chorus of angels, saw no light from the sky, felt no chill down his spine. Was anybody up there?

"Lord, help Kate and the baby," he pleaded. "Please help me . . . help me."

As he murmured the words, visions of his life began to flash like frames in a motion picture: the day he married Claire, the day Kate was born and he held her in his arms for the first time, the day they bought their first home and celebrated with a steak dinner they could not afford, the night he won his first election. It was odd. Here he was praying for his grandson, but these images had nothing to do with the little one.

And gradually, Bob understood why. It might be the baby whose life hung in the balance, but this conversation between Bob and God was about Bob. He had to end a lifetime of running for office and running from God— and he had to do it right now, before the fate of his grandson was decided.

Religion for Bob had always been a box he checked as he climbed to the top. He had viewed faith as fire insurance, something that kept him out of hell and helped him win elections. Jesus was a great teacher, a prophet, and his savior—but Bob had never made him Lord of his life. That would have meant sacrificing his political ambition, something he was unwilling to do.

Every politician had to learn God-talk, and Long had been no exception. But he was proud of the fact that he didn't need religion as a crutch, like some people he knew did. But that was then. Now he wasn't climbing the mountain of politics, on his way to the top. He was in a free fall, and he needed a branch to grab hold of. A strong one.

"God, I have served myself. My political career was all that mattered," he prayed, despairing that his very words sounded self-important, all about him. "But if you will spare my grandson's life, I will serve you for the rest of my life. I am yours from this moment on. Just please have mercy on this little boy."

He remembered Jeff Links's words: "You'll find Jesus in a place of suffering."

When he'd heard those words, Bob had had no idea that before the day was out, he would be on his knees in a hospital chapel, crying out for his grandson's life—and coming face-to-face with Jesus.

Could this be why he had lost the presidential nomination? So that he could gain something more important—his soul?

How his handlers—and the media—would scoff at that idea. They would think he'd lost his mind.

He rose from his knees and headed back toward the maternity ward, wondering whether his grandson was still alive.

———

JAY AWOKE WITH A start, immediately aware of the sun reflecting off the ocean. After drinks and cigars until nearly 2 A.M. the night before, he had hoped to hit the jackpot. And why not? Nicole had flirted with him outrageously. She had touched his arm and knee suggestively, and their legs had brushed. She had leaned forward and whispered into his ear, her warm breath tickling his neck. When the bar closed, he'd asked her if she wanted to come back to his cabana for a nightcap (absurb, considering the hour, but it was the only line he could think of). She'd declined. She'd kissed him twice on the lips and then disappeared down the path on the way to her own cabana. That was the last thing he remembered.

Yet there she was, curled up asleep on the settee in his cabana. He sat up startled—had something happened the night before and he just didn't remember it? Had he blacked out?

Nicole rolled over and opened her eyes. She stretched and smiled.

"Did you spend the night?" asked Jay.

"You mean you don't remember?"

"Uh . . . well . . ."

Nicole threw back her head and laughed. "I'm pulling your leg. I came by this morning to see if you wanted some breakfast, but you were dead to the world. So I lay down until you woke up. I guess I fell asleep." She gave him a naughty look. "Besides, if I had spent the night, I would think you'd remember that."

"I certainly hope so," Jay replied. "I was running on about four hours of sleep the previous two days and I'd had too much to drink. I was practically in a coma."

"Are you sure it's okay? Do you want me to leave?"

"Are you kidding?" he said. "Of course not."

"Jay, I meant to ask you last night—were you ever married?"

"Twice."

A look of surprise crossed Nicole's face.

"My first marriage was to my college sweetheart. But I spent all my time working on campaigns and building my consulting business. After three years, my wife took me to lunch, told me she didn't love me, said she wasn't sure that she had ever loved me, and asked for a divorce."

"Wow." Nicole averted her eyes, gazing out at the beach. "And the second marriage?"

"I was on the rebound. It was too quick. She was focused on her career and I was focused on mine. She was a management consultant and she would be on a job for six months at a time, commuting home on the weekends. I was running campaigns all over the country. We literally never saw each other. One day I came home from a campaign trip and she was in bed with someone else."

Nicole winced. "That must have hurt. I'm sorry. That's why I'm going to take my time getting married."

"You sure you want to hang out with such a romantic failure?"

"You're not a failure." She sat up, pulling her knees to her chest, showing her long brown legs. "You're nice. I like that. You're like me: you like to live life to the fullest. Passion is very important to me. I have to *feel* it. Do you know what I mean?"

It all sounded like psychobabble to Jay, but he was happy to play along. He had concluded long ago that the psyche of a woman was a mystery. "I think so," he lied. "I'm glad I met you. Thanks for making my escape from a losing campaign something more than just licking my wounds."

They stared into each other's eyes. "What are you thinking?" she asked.

"Do you really want to know?"

"Yes."

"I'm thinking about how beautiful you are and I'm wondering how I got so lucky as to find you, and here of all places. What are the odds? Think about it. I didn't even know you until last night."

Nicole blushed. Jay stared.

"Would you like to get some breakfast?" she said. "Actually, it's probably almost time for an early lunch."

"I would. What's on the menu?"

She jumped up from the settee and leaped onto the bed, landing on top of him, straddling him with her legs. "Me," she said.

G.G. HOTERMAN SHUFFLED INTO the kitchen wearing his fluffy white bathrobe from the Ritz in Paris. He loved to wear the bathrobe on a lazy weekend, the Ritz logo on the pocket bringing back fond memories of the City of Light. He opened the refrigerator and stared into it as if seeking a talisman. After a few moments of staring, he grabbed a Diet Coke and poured it into a glass with ice.

Deirdre came out of the bedroom wearing a baby-blue silk bathrobe. She sat at the kitchen table, gazing out the bay window toward the pond and the woods beyond. She let out a long sigh. "It's so peaceful here."

G.G. nodded, taking a long drink of cola from his glass. He walked over and stood for a moment behind Deirdre's chair.

The escape to the Adirondacks was serving as a steam valve, blowing off the stress they were both feeling. G.G. was on the front page of the *Washing-*

ton Post, all their friends and enemies were talking about them, and there was more artillery coming. There would be questions about the Virginia delegation scandal on the Sunday chat shows. The talking heads would get in their cheap shots. The only way to survive was to hire the best criminal lawyer that money could buy, grab on to each other, and ride down the falls like two fools in a barrel.

"Should I call my brother?" asked Deirdre.

"Not yet. Your brother is a material witness. He'll be interviewed by the FBI, and they'll ask him who he has talked to."

The phone rang, causing different ringtones to echo from phones throughout the house. Hoterman walked back to his study and picked up the extension.

"G.G., it's Tony. I have Walt Shapiro on the line."

"Hello, gentlemen. Walt, we're glad to have you on board," Hoterman replied.

"This one is going to get dicey, G.G. They're really gunning for you, aren't they?" It was a time-honored Washington tradition: expressing false regret at the misfortune of someone caught in a scandal, when the truth was everyone enjoyed it, not only to engage in the schadenfreude of watching the mighty humbled, but also for the sheer entertainment value.

"Comes with the territory," said G.G., keeping his game face on.

"I spoke to the Virginia State Police," reported Shapiro. "I wanted to pre-empt them calling us by offering our cooperation, and to let them know I was representing the firm. They told me they expect the FBI to start doing interviews soon. They will contact me when they want to talk to either you or Deirdre."

"So the FBI is definitely coming in. Did you get a feel for how focused they are on me?" asked Hoterman.

"Not really. It's early. I don't think you'll be the primary focus. That is unless someone impeaches Deirdre's brother's deposition and they can connect you to his testimony."

"Could someone do that, G.G.?" asked Tony.

Hoterman looked at Deirdre, who had walked into his study and curled up in a chair, her silk bathrobe wrapped around her. "It's possible. But most of the depositions were handled by our election law attorneys," he said.

"Did you talk to him at all?" asked Shapiro.

"Not that I can specifically recall. He was a witness and our firm represented him."

"What do you think he will say you said?" asked Shapiro.

"I don't know. But I don't think he'll accuse me of telling him to lie. What about the other attorneys in the firm? Their conversations with him are privileged, correct?"

"Not necessarily," replied Shapiro. "If someone claims your attorneys prepared affidavits they knew to be false, the prosecutors could try to puncture the veil of privilege, and that can get ugly."

"The challenge comes if they have a witness contradicting Deirdre's brother, and they threaten to indict him for perjury," said Tony, jumping in.

"That's why we need to make sure we work with him," agreed Walt. "But I actually think there is a bigger danger."

"What's that?" asked G.G. What could be worse than having Deirdre's brother go funny on him?

"Michael Kaplan. If one of the Virginia delegates says Kaplan offered them something—the press accounts refer to payments and the promise of an ambassadorial appointment—in exchange for false testimony, he could be indicted. We need to make sure that he doesn't turn on you. Do you think he would?"

"I don't know," answered G.G. "I talked to him this morning."

"Good grief. Why did you do that?" asked Shapiro, his voice rising an octave.

"He called me. Believe me, I would never have called him. But I didn't want to make him worried by not taking his call."

"What did he say?"

"In so many words, he said, I'll take care of my people, you make sure you button up Deirdre's brother," Hoterman said.

"You've got to be kidding," Shapiro said in disbelief. "He really said that?"

"Not a good sign, is it?"

"That's a *terrible* sign."

"I was wondering if he was setting me up. I literally thought he might be wearing a wire. I was careful about what I said."

"G.G., that conversation is discoverable and highly problematic. I will call his attorney and tell him I recommend no further conversations between you two," said Shapiro. "We will also need to find a good attorney for Deirdre's brother."

"No kidding," said Hoterman. He looked out the window at the flowers in full bloom. A deer walked across the grass, looking for the deer pops that Otis placed around the main house. Here he was, enjoying such beautiful scenery—while he discussed how to avoid federal indictment.

"G.G., I've been through a few of these. I know you're a smart guy and a lawyer, but I want you to listen carefully and do exactly what I say," said Shapiro.

"Okay."

"There are three rules in a criminal investigation: don't destroy anything, don't alter anything, and don't create anything. You've heard the phrase: It's never the crime, it's always the cover-up? Well, it's true. People get in trouble for trying to cover their tracks. Most don't commit any underlying crime. But they try to alter or dispose of embarrassing evidence, which leads to obstruction of justice."

"I understand," said G.G. "There's one thing you should be aware of. I asked some of my clients to contribute to the group that paid some of the Virginia delegates as consultants. Kaplan asked for my help."

"If all you did was raise the funds I think you should be fine. Even paying someone to do real work is fine. Paying someone to make a false sworn statement is not," Shapiro said. "Unless you had knowledge of funds being paid in exchange for false testimony, you're okay. But Kaplan will have a problem."

"Why?"

"Because I suspect he's going to be hard-pressed to show that these delegates did any real work. If they can't show work product, that's a legal issue."

"One last thing," said G.G. "Can Deirdre talk to her brother?"

"She can talk to him about the weather," replied Shapiro. "But not about the case. The last thing you need is Deirdre accused of witness tampering."

"Walt's right," interjected Tony. "It's amazing how stupid people act at moments like this. They get scared, so they call up a friend and say, 'You remember it this way, right?' " Keep Deirdre as far away from him as possible."

Hoterman hung up the phone "You can't talk to your brother about the case," he informed Deirdre. "Direct order from the attorneys."

Deirdre looked despondent. "I can't talk to my own brother," she said, her voice quivering. "This is so depressing."

"I know, honey," G.G. replied. "But Walt Shapiro knows what he's doing."

"I don't know if I trust anyone anymore, G.G."

"You can trust me." Their eyes locked. His face brightened, as if he had suddenly had an inspiration. "Hey, let's go out to dinner tonight and forget about all this," he suggested. "Why don't we go to the Lake Placid Lodge? You love it there."

"All right," said Deirdre. "I'll have a good time if it kills me." She paused. "I'm scared, G.G."

G.G. got up from behind his desk and walked behind the chair Deirdre sat in. He began to rub her shoulders slowly. She sighed.

"Don't worry," he said softly. "If anyone comes after us, I'll destroy them."

———

THERE WAS NOTHING SPECIAL about the boat. It was your garden-variety, low-slung trawler about thirty-six feet in length, but it was seaworthy. There was a small foredeck and a larger seating area in the back with a mounted chair for deep-sea fishing. Captain Amigo—they didn't know his real name—guided the boat past the rocky cleft that jutted into the Pacific, a cigarette dangling from his mouth. He stared straight ahead as the boat's bow rose and fell in the waves. Jay looked back and saw the white spit of beach of El Tamarindo fading into the distance.

The outing was officially billed as a sunset cruise, but Jay had discovered that like everyone else he had met in Mexico, Captain Amigo was a multitalented entrepreneur. Among the services he offered: scuba outings, parasailing, dirt bike rentals, and maybe an occasional drug run. He also sold real estate. They had spent the morning watching the whales with Captain Amigo, and he had insisted they return for the sunset cruise. Nicole and Jay had just gone to a turtle release on the beach, where newly hatched sea turtles scrambled into the ocean. Whale watching, turtle releases, and touring the surrounding forest—Jay was becoming the ultimate ecotourist.

Nicole wore white cotton chino shorts with a pink and green sash belt, a pink cashmere with cropped sleeves, and matching white shoes with two-inch heels. She looked fabulous. A young, handsome ship's mate with a shock of black hair, wearing black jeans and a tight white T-shirt, smiled a lot and kept offering them beer. Gabriella and her date sat next to the captain. Whenever Jay's Corona reached the bottom third of the bottle, the mate offered him another cold one, his lips parted to reveal gleaming white teeth. Jay had lost count, but he thought he was on his fifth or sixth beer.

"The mate is cute," whispered Nicole in Jay's ear.

"Really?" asked Jay, incredulous. He never could understand what women found attractive. He leaned over to Gabby. "Do you think he's cute?"

"Oh, yeah!" she exclaimed. Her date shrugged.

Jay lifted the Corona to his lips and took another swig. He was feeling good now. He took another long drag off the celebratory Cuban he had purchased on a shopping trip to a nearby village. Nicole reached over and took the cigar from his hand, placing it in her mouth and taking a feminine puff. She handed it back and blew the smoke into the wind, watching it fly past the stern.

Captain Amigo pointed to the bow of the boat. "Look, dolphins!" he cried.

A school of dolphins swam about ten yards in front of the bow, gliding just beneath the surface of the water. Occasionally one would leap playfully above the waves.

"Are they racing us?" asked Jay.

"Yes," replied the captain. "They like to race. They are playing."

The captain had a party CD playing on the sound system. Jimmy Buffett came on, and they all began to half sing, half shout the lyrics to "Margaritaville."

Jay was wasting away in paradise with two beautiful women. He was in such a great mood he didn't even mind sharing with Gabby's date, whose name he could not recall. But somewhere deep inside was a vague uneasiness. The truth was that he'd been drawn to all this fun, sun, and booze for a purpose: to drown his sorrow and his sense of failure. Long had lost, and that made Jay a loser, too. He had gone off the deep end before after other defeats—a four-day drinking and gambling binge in Vegas after one particularly bitter defeat in a top U.S. Senate race came to mind. But this was different. Maybe this time, he was ready to call it quits—just pack it in and move to Mexico for a couple of years. Maybe Captain Amigo could show him some oceanfront property.

The sun began to turn orange as it dipped toward the ocean, shooting shimmering rays across the surface of the water. Jay's skin felt rough and scaly beneath his shirt from the sun, salt, and sand. The dolphins were getting frisky, leaping beside the boat. Jimmy Buffett had given way to the Beach Boys. Now they were all singing "Catch a Wave." How appropriate.

"Guess what?" exclaimed Captain Amigo. "This is my job. I'm working!"

They all laughed uproariously.

"Do you think I could jump in and swim with the dolphins?" asked Nicole.

"Sure!" said Captain Amigo, his face brightening. He killed the engine. The first mate let down the ladder off the back of the boat, gesticulating wildly with his hands and giving instructions in rapid-fire Spanish. Jay had no clue what he was saying.

Nicole gave the ladder short shrift. She slipped off her shoes, stepped over the boat's rail, and tiptoed to the bow. With her back still turned, she pulled the tight cashmere tee over her head, shaking her hair in the wind and adjusting the strap of the white bikini top. She slipped off her shorts, shimmying them down her bronze legs. She was wearing a white thong. Captain Amigo cast a knowing look at Jay and winked, his white teeth gleaming. Nicole dove into the water.

Jay walked to the bow, balancing himself as the boat bobbed. When he got to where Nicole was drifting in the water, he leaned over the rail.

"Is it cold?" he asked.

"A little, but it feels good," said Nicole. "Come on in!" She paddled in the water, her arms and legs turning in circles. The dolphins swam to either side of the boat cautiously. Nicole glided toward them in a sidestroke and they flitted about her.

Gabby jumped in, dressed down to her bikini.

"I don't want to get my shorts wet and I don't have my bathing suit," said Jay, begging off. He could not believe how close the dolphins were getting to Nicole and Gabby. He wondered whether one of the girls might grab a dorsal fin and go for a ride.

"Are you sure you don't want to come in?" asked Nicole playfully. "You're not afraid of the dolphins, are you?"

Captain Amigo giggled uncontrollably, punctuating his laughter with a Spanish word that Jay could not translate: "Muchacha!" The first mate wore a ridiculous grin. What else could he do? Jay slipped off his shoes and dove in, figuring it was worth spending the rest of the night in wet shorts.

———

IN THE RECOVERY ROOM, the only sound was the rhythmic beeping of Kate's heart monitor when Bob entered. Claire sat in a recliner off to one side, looking weary. Kate was pale, her lips puffy and chapped, her face mottled and drained, her brown hair caked with dried sweat. She looked like she had been hit by a train.

Bob walked slowly to the side of her bed, transfixed with fear, his stomach queasy.

Kate opened her eyes. "Daddy, it's a boy," she said, forcing a smile.

Claire looked at Bob and nodded.

"Is he all right?" Bob asked.

"He's fine. We named him Robert Whitney," Kate announced.

"They named him after you, honey," whispered Claire.

"You didn't have to do that, Kate."

"But I wanted to, Daddy." Her eyes conveyed a tangle of powerful and complicated emotions: love for a father she worshipped but who had seemed distant as he chased his political dreams. Bob knew that naming the boy after him was her way of saying what words could not, or would not.

"Can I see him?"

"They have him in an incubator while they monitor his vital signs, but they said they would bring him in for a moment and let us see him," answered Claire. "Bob, it's a miracle."

Bob stood, unable to say a word, tears welling in his eyes. God had heard his prayer. He knew friends who had lost children or grandchildren to stillbirth, severe birth defects, even suicide. Why had his grandson been spared? Bob had little grasp of theology beyond a few Sunday school lessons. All he knew for certain at the moment was that God was real and that he answered the desperate prayers of sinners. His grandson was alive.

And am I now truly alive, too, for the first time in years? he wondered.

A nurse came in carrying little Robert Whitney in her arms, his tiny body wrapped tightly in a cotton hospital blanket. "He's a strong one," she said, her voice dropping to a whisper. "He had a rough time getting here, but he's in good shape now. Someone wanted him to live."

Bob started. Her words seemed almost like a confirmation that the Lord had spared this little boy's life.

"Daddy, why don't you hold him?" asked Kate.

The nurse gently placed the baby in Bob's arms. He was almost afraid to hold him, given what the poor little fellow had been through in the previous several hours. He looked down at his grandson—skin a healthy pinkish glow, eyes closed, a layer of black hair matted on his tiny skull. He was so small! Bob did not remember his own children being so tiny at birth, but they must have been. He felt a revelation: this boy was a sign of the sovereignty of God.

And what would that knowledge now mean for Bob?

He handed the baby to Kate. Her face flushed and tears streaked down her cheeks.

After a few minutes, the nurse took baby Robert Whitney back and explained that they would be able to see him in the infant recovery later.

Claire and Bob gathered up their things to leave, telling Kate to get some sleep.

She nodded. "Dad, we named the baby after you," said Kate. "Now I want you to do something for me."

"What's that?" asked Bob.

"Run."

"What?"

"Run. For president."

He smiled painfully. "I just did, honey."

"I mean in the general election. Run for president. Go for it, Dad."

Bob shook his head. "I don't think that's in the cards, Kate." He didn't want to hurt her feelings, but her request was delusional.

Kate closed her eyes wearily.

Bob put his arm around Claire's waist and they walked out of the room to look for their son-in-law.

It was odd, though—as they headed back to the maternity waiting room,

Kate's words kept echoing in his mind: "Run. Run. Run." Was God speaking to him through Kate? Bob's head swirled. He'd had far too little sleep and too much stress for far too long. He wasn't thinking clearly.

"Why do you think she asked me to run for president?"

"She knows you were robbed," Claire replied. "She thinks Stanley is a crook who stole the nomination. And she thinks you can win."

"But running as an independent candidate is a suicide mission. It's for quacks and self-deluded messiahs."

"Not if *you* run, it isn't."

"Kate must be on something."

"You can say that again," Claire replied. "They gave her enough Percodan to knock out a horse."

12

I T WAS LATE AFTERNOON when Bob and Claire Long arrived at their small cottage in Big Bear, in the San Bernardino mountains, a hundred miles east of Los Angeles. Bob had taken an Ambien with half a glass of red wine the night before as an insurance policy after two sleepless nights. It had done the trick; he felt more rested than he had in weeks.

A large UPS envelope leaned against the cottage's door. Bob opened the door and dropped the suitcases. Claire headed to the kitchen to check the refrigerator and the cupboards for food and provisions.

Bob stepped into the small den overlooking the backyard and the glistening water of Big Bear Lake in the distance. He tore open the overnight package—it was from their pastor, Jeff Links—and pulled out a book. A note was attached with a paper clip: "Bob, enclosed is the book I mentioned. When you run, run for the Lord and you cannot lose. 1 Corinthians 9:24. Best, Jeff." Bob didn't know the Bible verse. Curious, he went to the bedstand in the bedroom and opened the family Bible, flipping the pages. When his eyes found the text, his knees nearly buckled. The verse jumped off the page:

Do you not know that those who run in a race all run, but only one receives the prize? Run in such a way that you may win.

There were those words again: "Run, run, run." On a psychological level Bob felt as though he were driving down a deserted highway, searching for a gas station or a cheap hotel, and every few miles he passed another billboard emblazoned with the same slogan: "Run, Bob, run." He couldn't figure out if it was a sign from God or just a trick his mind was playing on him. Jeff couldn't have known what Kate had said to him in the hospital: "Go for it, Dad. Run." Now his pastor had dictated a similar message eleven time zones away.

Run, indeed. They just didn't understand, Bob thought. He could not run, for the simple reason that *he couldn't win*. And if he could not win, he would not run.

Bob looked at the book's cover: *From Evil to Good: The Story of Joseph and the Victorious Life of the Believer.* He flipped to the introduction and read the opening sentences: "Have you ever experienced defeat, persecution, or false charges at the hands of another? Have you asked yourself why an all-powerful and all-knowing God would allow you to suffer an injustice? The story of Joseph reveals that God always has a higher purpose in allowing defeat and disappointment to befall his children. If you feel cast down and forsaken, like Joseph when his brothers sold him into slavery or later when Pharaoh cast him into prison, perhaps God is preparing you to glorify him and fulfill a larger purpose."

Now Bob understood why Jeff had wanted him to read the book. Did Jeff think that God had allowed the Democratic presidential nomination to be snatched from him so he could achieve something even greater?

Claire called from the kitchen. They munched on cheese and crackers and drank red wine while she finished baking a chicken. They were all alone after nearly two years of planes, trains, automobiles. He had not yet told Claire about his encounter with Jesus in the hospital chapel the night before; he'd been waiting for the right moment.

"I talked to Lisa Robinson," said Claire, taking a bite of cheese and cracker and chewing it methodically, then swallowing. "She said *Newsweek* has a big story coming out tomorrow about Kaplan paying people in Virginia to lie to the credentials committee."

"I heard about it. You're not surprised, are you?" asked Bob.

"Not really," she said, her voice clipped. "But that's against the law."

"So?"

"So, if it turns out to be true, and I think we know it is, are you thinking about running as an independent?" she asked, eyes boring into him. Her erect posture made her seem taller than her five-foot, six-inch frame.

Long was thunderstruck. He knew Claire hated Stanley and would relish the chance to thwart him. Was she conspiring with Lisa and the staff to encourage him to run as an independent?

"Claire—when you run as an independent, you start off with a head of steam and a lot of media coverage. But you drop like a rock as voters turn to more viable candidates at the finish line. That's what happened to Perot. People don't like to waste their vote."

Claire's silence spoke volumes—she had not ruled it out in her own mind.

"What do you think?" he asked.

"If Stanley broke the law, he's finished. The only person who can defeat Flaherty is you. You have to at least think about it."

They deliberately avoided talking politics during dinner. Claire opened another bottle of red wine and drank two more glasses with dinner. Bob hoped she was just unwinding after the stress of the campaign. They talked about their new grandson, life after the campaign, and whether they should take a break in Europe or Asia.

After dinner, Bob returned to the den, put his stocking feet up on the coffee table, and opened the book on Joseph to the first chapter. If Links had gone to the trouble to overnight it to him from Malaysia, the least he could do was read it.

He was on the fourth chapter when Claire turned in for the night. He boiled some water and made a cup of herbal tea. It soothed him. About 1 A.M. he was two-thirds of the way through the book, and finding himself inspired and energized.

The cotton-candy Christianity that Bob had always known—the same kind most other people knew, he suspected—taught that tragedy and God's goodness were contradictions. But the Bible taught otherwise. Like Job, Joseph had suffered apparently senseless tragedy. But what others meant for evil, God turned to good. Joseph became the instrument of salvation for Israel in a way that would have been impossible had he not been sold into slavery.

Bob put the book down and went into the kitchen, freshening his cup of tea, which had gone cool. He walked out onto the small porch off the den, staring into the night. The crickets and bullfrogs played a symphony of croaks and chirps. A half-moon lit up the lake, its waves rippling from a soothing breeze. Bob was deep in thought. He had never felt so alone—or so close to his Creator. He could almost feel God's presence. He took a final sip of hot tea from a large mug.

Reading Joseph's story had been instructive. Though it was a bitter pill, Bob could well believe that God had allowed him to lose the Democratic presidential nomination to do something even bigger. Everyone else seemed sure that they knew just what that was. Bob wished he were as convinced as they were.

———

JAY WOKE WITH A start, the sun shining into his cabana through the white linen curtains. Nicole slept peacefully beside him, her auburn hair draping the side of her face. Her chest rose and fell as she breathed. The crash of ocean in the distance reminded Jay that he was in paradise. He rolled back and closed his eyes, waiting for sleep to catch up with him. Sunlight peeked through the lattices of the shutters separating the bedroom from the patio.

Then, like a lightning bolt in his frontal lobe, he remembered his phone call with Hal Goodman in the restaurant in Mexico City. Goodman had said that the investigation into what the media was now calling the Dele-gate scandal—making it rhyme with Watergate or Iran-gate—might reveal criminal conduct by the Stanley campaign. Now he was wide awake. The Goodman story would be on the *Newsweek* website that morning. He crawled out of bed, slipped on shorts and a T-shirt, and treaded up the cobblestone walkway to the lobby.

In the Internet café below the main lobby, he poured himself a cup of black coffee, sat down in front of the computer, and tapped in the *Newsweek* Web address. When the home page appeared, the teaser for Goodman's story popped up like a missile: "Newsweek Exclusive: Criminal Investigation Haunts Stanley. Will He Survive?" Noble's mouth dropped open. Goodman was twisting the knife. He clicked on the link and read on:

> A criminal investigation by the Virginia State Police into alleged unlawful conduct by Stanley campaign operatives will now be paralleled by a separate FBI inquiry, sources tell *Newsweek*, escalating the investigation into new and dangerous territory for the beleaguered Salmon Stanley. Federal investigators are expected to look into whether the Virginia delegation, which provided the margin of victory for Stanley at the Chicago convention, was awarded as a result of suborning perjury, payments laundered through nonprofit groups, and outright bribery.

Jay speed-read through the copy as his feet danced beneath the table. He could barely believe his eyes:

> Michael Kaplan, one of the most controversial and powerful figures in the Democratic Party, is at the center of the investigation, *Newsweek* has learned. Authorities are investigating whether Kaplan directed payments to family members of elected officials and delegates, along with promises of ambassadorial appointments, administration jobs, and cash in the form of consulting contracts from a pro-Stanley nonprofit group. Documents and financial records obtained by investigators reveal that the tax-exempt group funneled $450,000 to pro-Stanley Democrats who provided invaluable support and favorable testimony before the credentials committee that seated the Virginia delegation.

Clearly, someone in the Stanley campaign had ticked off Hal Goodman! Jay surfed across an array of news sites—*New York Times*, CNN, Fox News, Merryprankster.com, the Drudge Report, and the *Washington Post,* which not surprisingly featured a follow-up to their Friday front-pager about allegations of bribery and perjury engineered by the Stanley campaign. After twenty minutes of adrenaline-addled reading, Noble stopped stone-cold. He lifted his hand off the mouse and gazed out the window at the green foliage outside.

While he was lounging on the white beaches of Mexico, drinking margaritas, whale watching with Captain Amigo, and rubbing suntan lotion on a beautiful girl he had known for only two days, Salmon Stanley's campaign was going up in flames.

———

MARVIN MYERS CLEARED HIS throat and took a swig of java from a blue mug bearing the logo for his television program. A technician asked him through his earpiece to count down for a sound check. "Ten-nine-eight-seven-six-five. It's sunny and ninety degrees here in the nation's capital. Got it?" He shuffled papers on the desk, one last look at his notes and hand-scrawled questions. Like a prizefighter before the bell, he was loose and relaxed. The set director counted down with his fingers. Three fingers, two fingers, one finger, then a balled fist, then a swooping finger pointed toward Myers as his cue. They were live, and Myers felt his energy level pop.

"Good morning, I'm Marvin Myers, and welcome to *Capitol Report*," he began in his best anchorman voice, reading the teleprompter. "We are joined by Michael Kaplan, chairman of Senate Majority Leader Salmon Stanley's presidential campaign. Mr. Kaplan, welcome."

"Marvin, good to be here," said Kaplan. That, Myers knew, was a lie. Kaplan probably felt like he had been strapped to an electric chair. Kaplan had agreed to this interview only because he had no choice. The Stanley campaign had to do something to stanch the bleeding from the Virginia delegation scandal. Besides, Myers had too much clout, too much power, for them to turn him down on the eve of a general election presidential campaign.

"Mr. Kaplan, the Virginia State Police are investigating alleged criminal activity that may have occurred in the selection of your campaign's Virginia delegation to the Chicago convention. There are reliable news reports that the FBI plans to launch its own parallel investigation. Sir, did the Stanley campaign make payments to anyone who provided a deposition or testified before the credentials committee?"

"Marvin, first of all, I think everyone needs to take a deep breath," replied Kaplan, his voice steady. "There is an investigation under way, and our campaign is fully cooperating. Senator Stanley won the Virginia delegation fair and square, and that victory was ratified by the Virginia Democratic Party, the credentials committee, and the convention. This is a political season and while the charges are serious, they are unproven. We should avoid a rush to judgment."

It was a nondenying denial. Myers was not pacified. He knew that Kaplan would have brainstormed, with his campaign leaders, what their talking points would be, and now he was trying not to deviate from them. But it was Myers's job to prod him out from behind that wall. Barely pausing to take a breath, he fired a follow-up. "Were you aware of or did you authorize cash payments to any Virginia delegate, or a family member or relative who gave favorable testimony before the credentials committee?"

"I did not," insisted Kaplan. "There were outside groups, grassroots organizations, and political action committees involved in this process. That is the case in both parties. While it is true that a handful of delegates did some work for outside groups, to my knowledge those payments were at fair market value for actual work done. There were no payments—I repeat, no payments—from our campaign in exchange for the support of any delegate. So the rush to judgment under way in some quarters of the press is simply not justified by the facts."

Myers was displeased. Kaplan had now worked in the phrase "rush to judgment" twice in the first two minutes, undoubtedly part of his game plan. Time to trip him up. "If it comes to light that payments were made or someone was promised a job in a Stanley administration in exchange for support," Myers said, "since it would have occurred under your supervision, will you step down as Senator Stanley's campaign chairman?"

Kaplan blanched. He looked as if someone had stunned him with a right uppercut. This was just the effect Myers had hoped for.

But Kaplan kept his cool. "With all due respect, Marvin, that is a premature and hypothetical question. The investigation is under way, and we are fully cooperating. I'm not going to speculate about anything or anyone until we know the facts."

"So you will or will not resign if there were payments by tax-exempt, nonprofit organizations or promises of jobs?"

"Marvin, I serve at the pleasure of the majority leader. I will chair the campaign as long as he wants me in this position, and not a day longer. The last thing we need is for people to rush to judgment before the facts are known."

A third mention of "rush to judgment." Myers hadn't yet jolted Kaplan off his talking points, but personally he thought the man was starting to sound like a robot.

"Let me shift subjects for a moment if I may, Mr. Kaplan, to Governor Elizabeth Hafer." This would be fun. "Senator Stanley chose Governor Hafer after being rejected by Bob Long," Myers said, slyly working in a reference to the story he had broken. "But since then, Governor Hafer has gotten into hot water for comments about U.S. Christian leaders who have criticized Islam. This week, while defending a remark she made twenty years ago condemning Christian leaders who were critical of Islam, she referred to them as, and let me put it up on the screen so we can all see it, and I quote, 'extra-chromosome so-called Christians.' My question is, do her statements represent the views of Senator Stanley, and if not, will he repudiate them?"

Kaplan delivered his answer rapid-fire, almost as if he had memorized it, which he probably had. "Governor Hafer was frustrated by the distortion of those twenty-year-old remarks and spoke in haste. She regrets those words and has apologized for them. I know Betsy Hafer very well. She respects the faith of others, and I know those comments do not reflect her views. She has apologized, and we are moving on."

"Still, it's an embarrassing gaffe just two days into the general election campaign," said Myers, furry brows cocked in a sarcastic arch. "Does Senator Stanley regret selecting her, and does he wish that Governor Long had not rejected his offer to be the Democratic running mate?"

"Not at all," Kaplan shot back. "Governor Hafer is an outstanding candidate and she brings a lot to the ticket. She is going to help us reach out to women, young people, and voters of all economic backgrounds. She is going to help us carry Pennsylvania and many other states. We're proud to have her as the first woman vice presidential candidate in over two generations."

———

MERCIFULLY, THE INTERVIEW WAS over. Michael Kaplan felt streams of sweat running from his armpits and chest. A band of perspiration gathered at his hairline, hidden by heavy facial powder. He tore the earpiece from his ear, unclipped the microphone from his tie and belt, and stomped from the set, a press aide in tow. The makeup woman politely asked if he wanted her to remove his makeup, but he curtly declined and blew past her toward the door.

Outside was a "stand-up," a clutch of reporters waiting by a stand of microphones for a second ambush. More questions about Dele-gate, the FBI investigation, and Betsy Hafer's foot-in-mouth disease. Kaplan, his face frozen into an expressionless mask, repeated the campaign's talking points in an unconvincing monotone.

In the car, he lit into the press aide with a volcanic and harrowing fury. "Who talked to his producer? I *told* you the entire interview would be about

Virginia and the Muslim comment. The *entire* interview! *Every single question!* This was a setup!"

The press aide sat motionless, eyes staring straight ahead. "You did a great job answering the questions," the aide stammered at last.

"I *know* I can answer the questions!" blasted Kaplan. "That's not the point. We're supposed to be running a presidential campaign, not walking around wearing a KICK ME sign in the bull pen of a rodeo!"

———

THE WAITRESS BROUGHT ANOTHER plate of *polow*—plain rice—to the table at Charlie Kabob's Persian restaurant in Santa Monica, just blocks from the beach. Rassem el Zafarshan had already polished off a bowl of *khoresht,* a thick beef stew, and poured a second helping over the rice. Zafarshan and his friends enjoyed the traditional Persian cuisine from their homeland, which could be found at countless eating establishments in greater Los Angeles. With a population of over three hundred thousand Iranians, L.A. boasted perhaps the largest Persian population of any city in the world outside of Tehran. A teeming polyglot of Shah-supporting dead-enders, democratic reformers, and radical Shiites, the Iranian community was large and diverse.

Zafarshan hardly represented the typical Iranian expatriate. He had slipped into the United States across the porous border with Mexico with forged papers, a so-called OTM in Department of Homeland Security lingo—Other Than Mexican. He was in America not because he loved it, but because he hated it.

The Persian cuisine brought back memories of his childhood in his beloved Iran, when the people, led by the great Ayatollah Khomeini, had built from the ashes of U.S. imperialism an Islamic republic that was a model for the world. They fought off Saddam Hussein's Republican Guard (encouraged by the U.S. military), resisted the meddling of the United Nations, and prospered despite the isolation imposed by the United States. Iran represented the future of a confident, Islamic Middle East.

Then came George W. Bush's invasion of Iraq, followed by civil war between Shiites and Sunnis, economic sanctions against Iran's nuclear power program, and the botched effort by the current Republican administration to overthrow the Iranian government. Things were coming apart in the Middle East—and the United States bore sole responsibility.

Zafarshan had become so convinced that the United States had to be stopped that he had volunteered to serve as an Islamic freedom fighter in Baghdad. Operating in an Iranian-funded, Shiite militia offshoot, he had helped build the bombs and place the IEDs that repelled the American crusaders. After a valiant struggle, they had lost the battle for Baghdad. But the war still raged on.

As he chewed on a piece of meat, Zafarshan wondered how Americans would react when the war came again to their own shores. The first time, on September 11, 2001, they had lost the tallest buildings in New York and thousands of civilians. But no national leader had been successfully targeted. This time, for the glory of Allah, things would be different.

13

C HARLIE! GREAT TO HEAR from you," Bob Long said when he picked up the phone in his study. On the other end of the line was Charles Hector, Democratic congressman from Santa Ana.

"Senator, I hope you are fully recovered," Hector said enthusiastically.

"Getting there. Our daughter Kate had a baby the day after the convention, so we're worn-out. But we're doing great. What's the word?"

"Well, first of all, congratulations on your new grandchild. That's fantastic." Hector paused, then shifted gears. "Bob, have you seen the new Gallup poll?"

"No. What does it say?"

"Stanley trails Flaherty forty-seven to thirty-eight percent," reported Hector. "That's *after* a convention bounce of three points—the smallest convention bounce ever recorded by Gallup." He paused, saving the best for last. "Stanley's unfavorable rating is thirty-nine percent and his favorable rating is only twenty-eight percent. He's upside down."

Long said nothing. He knew Stanley's numbers were in the tank—he didn't need a pollster to tell him.

"They also did a ballot test with you in the race."

"They tested me?" exclaimed Long, surprised.

"Yes, as an independent. You were at twenty-four percent of the vote. Flaherty dropped to thirty-six percent, and Stanley dropped to twenty-five percent, a statistical tie with you, with the rest undecided. That's the highest percentage *ever won* by an independent candidate."

"Still, I'm in third place, and Flaherty wins by a landslide." He was intrigued by Hector's call. Was this another sign from heaven? If so, it was hardly a burning bush—he was in last place.

"But, Bob, you're not even a candidate yet," Hector insisted. "If you announced, you'd be at thirty percent overnight, within range of Flaherty. Stanley would drop like a rock—Dele-gate is crippling him. There'll be indictments, maybe including Mike Kaplan. And Betsy Hafer has been an unmitigated disaster. Sure, the conventional wisdom is that third-party candidacies are hopeless. But no one like you has ever run as an independent. You'd carry California and independent voters all over the country. Please consider it, Bob. We need you. And if you decide to go for it, count me in."

Long could hardly believe his ears. Hector was offering to grab his hand and jump off the cliff like Butch Cassidy to his Sundance Kid. Hector was cochair of the Hispanic Caucus, former chairman of the Democratic Congressional Campaign Committee, and a ranking member on the Appropriations Committee. His would be a major endorsement.

" 'Yet'—what do you mean 'yet'?" Long exclaimed with laughter. "I'm not a candidate!"

"You should be, Bob. I urge you to do this."

Long paused. "Charlie, I don't know what I'm going to do yet. But what Stanley did in Chicago was *wrong* . . . and was probably illegal. If I have it in me, I'm going to make sure they pay."

———

RASSEM EL ZAFARSHAN HAD grown weary of the real estate agent. The presentation had become tedious. Zafarshan tried to signal his boredom by reducing his answers to monosyllabic grunts, but the real estate agent, a Caucasian in a black Armani with a lime-green shirt and Kenneth Cole shoes, too much hair gel, his motormouth enhanced by cosmetically whitened teeth—was not taking the hint. He would not shut up.

"The fitness center downstairs has free weights, Nautilus, elliptical machines, treadmills, and a juice bar," the agent chattered. "You look pretty buff. I'm guessing you work out, right?"

"Yes," replied Zafarshan, unhappy with the intrusion into his personal space.

"Well, your fitness center membership is included in the monthly maintenance fee. There's free parking. And wait until you see the pool." His eyes brightened. "Lots of eye candy—and not just on the weekends. Hot women galore. They have to put a security guard at the pool area to turn the unwanted away." He noticed that Zafarshan's eyes were drilling into him with barely disguised contempt. "It's Miami," shrugged the agent, backpedaling. "But if that's not your scene, no problem."

Zafarshan pulled open one of the large sliding glass doors leading to the balcony and stepped out into the warm ocean breeze. It was amazing how much cooler it was up on the twentieth floor, even on a hot summer day, because of the wind coming in off the Atlantic. He breathed in the salty air. The balcony offered a perfect view of Biscayne Bay, the Port of Miami to his left, Key Biscayne to his right. He could make out the cars as they raced along the Rickenbacker Causeway, and beyond the glistening waters of Biscayne Bay he could see the multimillion-dollar mansions gleaming like jewels, cigarette boats floating nearby, blue rectangular pools reflecting the sun like so many watery mirrors. It was perfect.

"Great view of the bay, as you can see," continued the agent, narrating the setting. "And what's great about the units on this side of the building is that from the far left side of your balcony"—he walked over to the edge to demonstrate, pointing with his right index finger—"you also catch a view of the ocean and the Miami skyline. This kind of panoramic view is usually a lot pricier than this unit."

Zafarshan did not care about the ocean view. He wanted the balcony for other reasons. "How much?" he asked, his eyes never leaving the sight lines that led to the bay, the causeway, and the Intracoastal Waterway. He could almost see the scene he had planned in his head unfolding before him.

"Eight-fifty," the agent answered. "And as you can tell from the other units we've looked at, it's the best value for the price point."

"I'll take it," Zafarshan said. Money was no object. He turned to the agent and smiled, then leaned over the railing of the balcony, taking in the scene below, deep in his own thoughts. "How soon can we close and take possession?"

"It's a motivated seller," the agent replied. "I would say within one or two weeks at the most, assuming no issues with financing."

"I'm paying cash," Zafarshan said. He knew this would raise no red flags. Buyers plunked down cash for high-end condominiums in Miami every day. It was one of the few ways expats fleeing Latin America or the Middle East could move money out of their own country. Wealth poured into the real estate market from Venezuela, Nicaragua, Colombia, Mexico, Qatar, Turkey, and other parts of the world. Some was drug money, some was legitimate, but no one cared and few people asked. The South Florida high-end condo market was the Wild West, with shady expats, cocaine cowboys, art deco architecture, six-hundred-dollar bottles of vodka, and anorexic party girls.

Zafarshan's cell phone rang—one of five he carried. He discarded one and picked up another every few days to make it more difficult to track his movements. He knew from the number displayed on the screen that it was his contact. He spoke in perfect English to avoid making the real estate agent too curious. "My friend," he answered. "Where have you been?"

"Busy," came the answer. His contact was a man of few words.

"How soon will the boat be ready?" Zafarshan asked.

"Soon. Three or four days at most."

"And it has been totally refurbished—the engine is clean and working?"

"Clean and working," the contact answered, code that meant it could not be traced.

"Good. Call me and I'll arrange pickup." He hung up.

"Buying a boat, huh?" asked the agent. "There is a place right around the corner where you can dock it. How many feet?"

Zafarshan had no clue, for the simple reason that there was no boat. The "boat" was an SA-88 missile, the same type that that very moment was being used to down U.S. helicopters along Iran's border with Iraq. "Thirty-seven feet," he said.

"Great!" exclaimed the agent with a chuckle. "I have a friend with a boat. He takes it to the Bahamas on the weekends, hits the casinos, and meets women. He invites them to spend the night on his boat and they lap it up."

The agent would not stop selling. Zafarshan found him insufferable. Like all Americans, the only things he cared about were sex and money. That was why the Americans were going to lose, why their global hegemony was doomed, and why their decadent, sick society had to be brought to its knees. It was why Zafarshan was about to strike a mighty blow at the Great Satan, all for the glory of Allah.

THE GULFSTREAM 5 BANKED gently to the left at an altitude of 4,500 feet, offering a picturesque view of the Mall with the Washington Monument and the Lincoln and Jefferson memorials, its grassy environs ending at the sun-splashed U.S. Capitol. Less visible from the air to the untrained eye was the White House, partially hidden by the Eisenhower Building, which was part of its complex. Turning sharply to the left and heading toward Dulles International Airport, the G-5 shot past the Pentagon and over the seemingly endless rows of white crosses on the grassy hills of Arlington National Cemetery.

It was a view that Andy Stanton never tired of seeing. His father had served in Congress when he was a boy, and he had once roamed the streets and haunted the halls of the nation's capital. He smiled when he thought of some of his rabble-rousing adolescence in his B.C. (before Christ) days. The scene always brought back a flood of memories, most of them pleasant.

When the plane taxied to a stop at Dulles, Stanton made a quick pit stop in the restroom and breezed on to a waiting sedan. Accompanying him was Ross Lombardy, the thirty-nine-year-old executive director of the Faith and Family Federation and former chief of staff to U.S. Senator Tom Reynolds. He functioned as Stanton's senior political advisor and ran the day-to-day operations of his grassroots organization. Lombardy was a strategist-cum-organizer with a killer instinct who could quote two hundred Bible verses from memory and also knew where the bodies were buried in D.C. He had an uncanny ability to cite the precise vote percentages in every key U.S. House and Senate race in the previous three election cycles. A veritable computer hard drive of political trivia, he was sometimes referred to as "Stanton's Dr. Evil," a moniker that caused no small degree of discomfort in their collaborative and competitive relationship.

Ross had tagged along for the trip, but Stanton had made it clear that he would meet with Petty alone. He wanted to go mano a mano with Petty, feet on the coffee table, souls bared, with no staff in the room to leak.

"If Flaherty is going to pick Petty as vice president," Stanton began, "I need to know if I can do business with him."

"Of course it's Petty," Ross said. "Why else would the vice president ask you to meet with him? This isn't about the Middle East peace process—it's an audition. He's trying to give you a comfort level with the inevitable. This is going to cause major indigestion for the base."

"Flaherty wants me to give Petty cover on the right."

"He's setting you up," Ross said coldly.

"How so?"

"He picks a vice president who's bad on abortion and gay rights and then trots you out to defend him. You'll be fragged by your own supporters. They win the White House, you lose your troops."

Stanton gave Ross a troubled look, then gazed out the window as the driver whisked through traffic, past the skyscrapers of Rosslyn and around the traffic circle by the Lincoln Memorial. As they arrived at Foggy Bottom, Stanton, Lombardy, and Stanton's bodyguard entered the building. When they arrived on the seventh floor, the group walked down a long reception hall decorated with nineteenth-century portraits, priceless Oriental rugs, crystal chandeliers, and antique furniture. After they waited for a few minutes in the reception area to the secretary's office, his assistant escorted Stanton in.

Secretary Petty stood in front of his massive desk, surrounded by paintings, with fabric coverings and deep mahogany on the walls. He was a tall man, not as large as Stanton, but as he stood at attention, his chest jutting, his perfectly tailored suit hanging flawlessly on his muscular frame, shoes spit-shined to a mirrorlike polish, he looked as if he had walked out of the pages of a glossy magazine.

Stanton knew he was there to eyeball the secretary up close and personal. Petty's power lay in his biography: eldest son of a civil engineer from Ghana with a Ph.D. from MIT. His mother was a Puerto Rican from the Bronx, the daughter of a janitor, and was the first member of her family to attend college and graduated from Harvard Law School. They taught him by their example that his race was never an excuse for failure or an obstacle to success. He read voraciously from an early age, starred in high school sports, and attended New York University on an ROTC scholarship.

After joining the army, he flew helicopters, training at Fort Rucker and later evacuated Vietnamese refugees during the fall of Saigon. He fought in the first Gulf War, led a battalion during the second war with Iraq, and as the country descended into sectarian violence, he negotiated settlements with Sunni chieftains and Shiite mullahs that led to the pacification of the country. When breakaway Sunni tribal leaders reneged on the deal and launched a second insurgency, he led the forces that defeated them. Petty was a lifelong Republican whose veins coursed with African and Hispanic blood, a military hawk showered with fawning press coverage. He sat in his powerful perch at Foggy Bottom like a running mate straight out of central casting.

"Dr. Stanton, thanks for coming. I guess the vice president is our match-maker," he said with a smile, the joke striking a little too close to home for Stanton, who opted for a "heh-heh-heh" under his breath and shook Petty's hand firmly.

"It's not our first date, but it's the first time we've been alone without a chaperone," Stanton joked back.

"Can I offer you something to drink?"

"I'll have some coffee if you have it, thank you."

Petty nodded to a white-coated steward, who returned moments later with cups of coffee in bone china bearing a gold-embossed great seal of the United States. Petty took his black, Stanton with a touch of cream. As they sipped their coffee, they chatted about the weather and the traffic from Dulles. Each observation was followed by awkward silence. "Dr. Stanton," Petty began in a more serious tone, evidently eager to get the real discussion going.

"Please, call me Andy."

"Andy, there are some things I can't say publicly given the sensitivity of my position as secretary of state. One of them is that I know Sal Stanley well. I worked with him as majority leader, testified before committees on which he sat, dealt with him on budget issues, both at the Pentagon and now State. Andy, he is totally unprepared to lead the global war on terrorism. Totally unprepared." Finished with the soliloquy, which appeared rehearsed, Petty stared at Stanton unblinking.

"He would be a catastrophe," Andy agreed.

"I have fought this war on the front lines—on the streets of Baghdad, on the border with Iran, against global terrorist networks, and as secretary seeking international support for our efforts. This war requires *total* vigilance. There is no margin for error. And our leaders must know the enemy. Stanley can't do that. He has to pacify the MoveOn.org and antiwar crowd in the Democratic Party."

"The Islamofascists want to destroy our way of life," Stanton said, picking up on the theme. "They believe jihad is a holy calling. Their mission is to kill every infidel—which they define as every Christian and Jew in the world. It's more dangerous than communism."

"That's a small minority within Islam," replied Petty dismissively with a wave of his hand. "I know these terrorists. Ultimately they don't believe in anything except murder and terror. They *use* Islam to further their goals because they know they will gain sympathy from the people. But they are not true Muslims."

Andy found Petty's answer shocking. Had he never studied the Koran, or read about the life of Mohammed? Mohammed was the father of terrorism, in Stanton's eyes. Stanton had gotten in trouble a few years earlier for saying Mohammed was the first terrorist. He'd issued a weak apology, saying he had not intended to denigrate anyone else's religion.

"Mr. Secretary, while I agree that national security will dominate the campaign, my audience, which numbers about twenty million between TV and radio, want to know where leaders stand on the issues of faith and family."

"Well," Petty replied, leaning back in his chair, putting his fingers together as he pondered his answer. "My mother was Roman Catholic, my father was a Methodist. So they compromised and we attended the Episcopal Church. Can you imagine me, a black-and-brown boy from the Bronx, as an Anglican?" He laughed. "I believe what the Episcopal Church teaches. If that makes me a Christian, then I guess I'm a Christian."

Stanton felt as though someone had hit him across the jaw. So . . . this was it? Petty believed what his church told him, and that made him whatever he was? Stanton wondered what he thought about the U.S. Episcopal Church ordaining homosexuals as priests, or their support for liberation theology, or their opposition to the U.S. military action in Iraq. He was astonished. He couldn't sell this to his own congregation, much less his radio and TV audience.

"Well, I think with all due respect, Mr. Secretary, social conservatives are going to have to hear more than that," Stanton said cautiously, his head bobbing for emphasis. "They need to hear you address the moral issues burning in their hearts."

Petty stared blankly. It was as if a cartoon bubble had appeared over his head with a caption reading, "He's kidding, right?"

"Look, Andy, I understand the importance of the church people to the Republican Party. We want them on the team. But we have to be able to appeal to independents, the people in the middle. The country is changing. We can't win anymore with just white people who go to Sunday school."

Church people? White people who go to Sunday school? Stanton felt his blood pressure spike. He struggled to suppress his anger.

Petty hiked up his pants, leaning forward in his chair like a defensive lineman in a three-point stance. "You and I need to be clear on something," he said. "If I seek national office, I won't be running for pope or preacher. I'll be running to defeat the terrorists and lead the free world."

Stanton almost fell out of his chair. *This guy just doesn't get it*, he thought. What an incredibly difficult position Vice President Flaherty had put him in! Trying to avert disaster, he threw Petty a lifeline. "Mr. Secretary, this isn't Dwight D. Eisenhower's Republican Party anymore. Evangelicals and pro-family Catholics represent nearly forty percent of the Republican vote. They vote on issues, not personalities. Those issues are faith, family, and marriage. If you won't speak to those issues, they will not be energized. They won't vote for Salmon Stanley. But they may not vote at all."

"Well, they'd better get with the program," snapped Petty in a harsh tone. He had clearly had enough of being lectured by Stanton. "We're at war with an enemy that wants to destroy America and our way of life. They want to set off nuclear weapons in major U.S. cities. Defeating that enemy is the challenge of our time—not talking about abortion or throwing red meat to get votes."

Stanley stumbled through a few weakly offered suggestions and ideas, but he knew it was hopeless. The meeting had confirmed his worst fears about Petty. Stanton was glad there was no staff in the room—but for an entirely different reason than he had planned.

Petty stood up abruptly, his bearing suddenly turning martial and intimidating. "Andy, thanks for coming. I have to give a speech on the other side of town to the Council on Foreign Relations. But let's do it again sometime." An aide stood at the door, his coat buttoned, wearing an expression designed to convey that the secretary was busy and the meeting had ended.

"Looking forward to it," Stanton heard himself say.

CFR? So David Petty didn't have the time to talk to tens of millions of evangelicals, but he had plenty of time for the trilateralists and the one-worlders! Unbelievable.

Stanton left the office in a hurry, rejoined by Ross and his security guard. The uniformed State Department guards at the metal detectors shook his hand and told him they were big fans. This was not uncommon. Everywhere he went the doormen, the front-desk clerks, the valets, and the maids recognized him and told him they watched him on television. The common people loved Andy—it was the powerful and important who treated him like a leper.

Andy said nothing until they got into the sedan and closed their doors, and then he turned to Ross, eyes ablaze and cheeks flushed. "I would not support that man if he were the last person on earth," he said slowly. "Not for vice president, not for president—not for dog catcher."

14

A WAITRESS WEARING WHITE SHORTS, a fitted white T-shirt, and white tennis shoes placed a silver bucket with ice and a bottle of Moët on the table. "Would you like me to open it?" she asked.

"Please," replied Jay Noble. The waitress popped the cork and poured the champagne over ripe strawberries resting at the bottom of fluted crystal champagne glasses. The bubbly fizzed as it hit the fruit. She picked up a small bottle of cognac and put exactly five drops in each glass. It was four o'clock in the afternoon and Jay and Nicole lay back on a daybed on the beach. The champagne had become part of their daily ritual. The ocean lapped peacefully on the beach in front of them, and the sun blazed down like a heat lamp.

"I propose a toast," Jay announced.

"To what?" asked Nicole.

"Life after politics."

"I'll drink to that," she said. He noticed that her red lipstick matched the color of her bathing suit. Nicole reached into her glass and pulled out a strawberry, biting into it with her front teeth. That sight alone—Nicole nibbling on a champagne-drenched strawberry as she lay back in a lounge chair in her bikini—was worth the price of the champagne, Jay thought.

"Mr. Noble, you have a telephone call, sir," came a voice from behind. Jay turned to see an officious-looking man in a white coat and black pants holding a cordless telephone in his outstretched hand.

"A call for me?" Jay looked at Nicole. "Who knows I'm here?"

"It better not be Hal Goodman," said Nicole.

Jay rolled his eyes as he grabbed the phone. "Jay Noble."

"Jay, it's Lisa. I've been trying to run you down for two days."

"How'd you find me?"

"It wasn't easy. Our travel agent told me you took a flight to Manzanillo. We've been calling every resort within fifty miles."

"What's going on?" Jay asked, wondering if there'd been a break in the Virginia delegation scandal.

"Jay, the governor needs to talk to you. There have been some . . . developments," she said. "The Stanley campaign scandal is . . . well, it's mushrooming." She handed the phone to Bob Long. "Here's the governor."

"Jay?" called the booming voice at the other end of the line. "I hope you're tanned, rested, and ready."

"Governor, I'm sorry I've been hard to reach. I needed to get away."

"No problem. You earned it," Long assured him. "Listen, I've got something important to talk with you about that I can't discuss over the phone. I need you to come back to California . . . as soon as you can."

"Sure. What is it?" He took a sip from his champagne and smiled at Nicole. He contemplated the incongruous scene—lounging on a beach with his woman, drinking Moët, and talking shop with the governor of California.

"I haven't made a final decision, but given Stanley's meltdown and this scandal, I'm considering running for president as an independent," he said, then continued after a pause: "I hope you like an adventure."

Jay nearly dropped his champagne glass. He sat bolt upright on the daybed, stunned. Nicole looked up from her magazine. "That's a big mountain to climb, Governor. But if that's what you want to do, of course I'll help you."

"You're not just going to help. You're going to run the campaign!" exclaimed Long. "Get back to L.A. as soon as you can. We need to get the Brain Trust together to kick this around before I make a final decision. Keep this quiet for now, but remember: if I do this, you're in charge."

"I'd be honored, sir," Noble heard himself saying. He had to admire Long—this was clearly a guy with the gonads of an elephant. But an independent candidacy for president? He must be kidding—Jay could only assume that Claire was involved somehow.

"Get back as quick as you can. We can send a plane if you can't get a commercial flight."

"I'll get there right away, Governor."

"See you soon, friend." Long laughed. "All you have to do between now and tomorrow is figure out how to get on fifty state ballots, raise one hundred million dollars, and win a majority of the Electoral College in the next one hundred and ten days. I'll expect a memo from you outlining how to get it done. Welcome aboard!"

Jay hung up the phone and stared unseeing at the beach and ocean, which had suddenly become blurry and indistinct. He wasn't sure he was physically and emotionally up for an independent general election campaign, but the game had grabbed him again, and he knew it would not let him go. Bob Long was about to put a grenade under each armpit and blow up Sal Stanley.

"What was that about?" asked Nicole.

"That was Bob Long. He's going to run as an independent in the fall campaign."

Nicole's jaw dropped. "Is he out of his mind?"

"I think he might be," Jay deadpanned. Nicole looked suddenly hurt, as if she understood that this meant that, among other things, the vacation was over. Jay got up, put on his sandals, and headed to the Internet café. He had to get on the travel websites and find a flight to LAX.

———

BETSY HAFER SAT ALONE in the front cabin of her campaign plane, legs crossed under a foldout table, writing notes to dignitaries and elected officials she had met on that day's campaign stops. Her feminine, cursive writing—interjected with safe and reliable phrases like "You're the best!" and "Great event!"—filled a stack of note cards with "Aboard Victory Two" embossed in blue letters.

In the back of the plane, the press corps seethed. They smelled blood—Hafer was on a deathwatch. The media had panned her selection, her early performance had been universally critiqued as uninspired and stumbling, and she was the butt of jokes by late-night comics. As the press coverage became harsher, her staff had come up with the idea of sending Hafer back to the press cabin with a tray of cupcakes, announcing that she had baked them herself (which, incredibly, was true). The gesture backfired. Women reporters viewed it as patronizing (feminists don't bake cookies, thank you very much), while men saw it as a confirmation of her lack of gravitas. After that disaster, the staff arranged one-on-ones with reporters to try to break the ice. They had initially pitched the sit-downs as off the record, but the press had nearly taken their heads off. Cut the nonsense, they'd protested—she's running for vice president and we're not taking background briefings from her like she is a junior staffer. The campaign caved to their demands and the one-on-ones were now on the record.

It was Dan Dorman's turn, and he ambled up to the front of the airplane, accompanied by Hafer deputy press secretary Sue Bennett, to the whispers of colleagues egging him on. "Don't let her off easy," one of them said in a stage whisper. Dorman was dressed for battle: rumpled jacket, wrinkled khakis, a knotted rep tie that hung at an odd angle, and tousled, matted gray hair. He carried a steno pad and a tape recorder. His reputation preceded him. He had broken the Dele-gate story that now threatened the survival of Sal Stanley.

Hafer wore a red blazer, white blouse, and a wool-blend skirt with a hemline at the knees. She looked prim and proper, but the shattered and confused look in her eyes betrayed her fragile state of mind. Her lips were pressed into a thin line of lipstick. No longer the happy warrior, she braced herself for the interview like a shell-shocked soldier who heard a gun go off every time a car backfired.

"Governor Hafer . . . uh . . . the allegations that have sparked a criminal investigation into whether the Stanley campaign suborned perjury . . . uuh . . . have cast a dark cloud over your campaign. Have you been interviewed yet by the FBI? Would you be willing to be interviewed?" mumbled Dorman, stammering as usual, but his halting speech hadn't slowed him down; he had swung a blade right at her jugular vein.

"Look, it's a serious matter," began Hafer. "The campaign has pledged its full cooperation, and that includes me. I can't comment beyond that. But I have the highest regard for Senator Stanley, for his character and his ethics and his campaign."

"This wasn't what you signed up for, was it? A, uh—a criminal investigation in the midst of your campaign."

"Politics is like a box of chocolates. You never know what you're going to get until you take a bite. It still tastes sweet to me."

Bennett looked as though she might sink through the floor. A box of chocolates! Was this a vice presidential candidate or Forrest Gump?

"Are you concerned," Dorman continued, "that . . . uh . . . your remarks on the criticism . . . er . . . of Islam by Christian leaders, which some have called intemperate, will turn out the evangelical vote for the Republican Party and hurt the ticket? Are . . . uh . . . you a liability to Senator Stanley?"

Her face turned brittle and hard. "I am an *asset* to this ticket," she said. She ran through her talking points about the Muslim comment: it was twenty years old, it was taken out of context, and all she meant was that we should respect other people's faiths. Dorman actually felt a sliver of sympathy for her. He lazily took notes, as bored transcribing the answer as Hafer was delivering it.

Dorman decided to turn to foreign policy, where he was confident she would trip up. He was not a fan of that old standby, the candidate pop quiz—who is the president of Thailand? He knew she had no clue. He decided to go instead with a hypothetical: "If Iran announces it possesses a nuclear weapon, the administration has said that the military option is on the table. Uh . . . would you support the use of force to . . . uh . . . take out Iran's nuclear capability?"

"That depends," she answered, clearly unsure of herself. "Would it change the balance of power in the region and pose a security threat to Israel and other countries? I would have to know more."

"So Iran having a nuclear weapon is not necessarily a danger?"

"Well, as I said . . . I think it . . . depends," she stuttered, her eyes darting. She looked lost. She turned to Bennett. "Sue, help! Where do we stand on Iran again?"

Bennett took a deep breath and tried to parse an answer, but it was too late. Dorman had the gaffe—and his lead paragraph. He shot a wicked look at Bennett over the top of his glasses, the right corner of his mouth turned up mischievously. Gotcha!

————

RON CIDER WAS THE attorney general of Virginia and a rising star in the Democratic Party. The first Democrat to win the chief law enforcement post in twelve years, he had done so in a squeaker, by only 1,251 votes out of over two million cast, and then prevailed in a recount. He planned to run for governor in two years, so he spent every waking hour plotting how to prosecute violent criminals, lock up sexual predators and throw away the key, sue charlatans who preyed on seniors, and get himself in the paper at least once a week. That is, until his cell phone rang while on family vacation at the Homestead in the mountains of western Virginia.

"Ron, Mike Kaplan. How are you?"

"Well, hello, Mike, good to hear from you." Actually it wasn't good to hear from Kaplan at all. Cider had a bad feeling about why he might be calling. Cider was the cochairman of the Stanley campaign in Virginia, had been a delegate to the Chicago convention, and had a painful familiarity with the Dele-gate scandal.

"Ron, I assume you've been following the news regarding the Virginia state convention and our delegation."

"Kind of hard to miss, wouldn't you say, Mike?" he chuckled.

Kaplan ignored the joke. "Rush Limbaugh, Fox News, and the far right are playing this for all it's worth. We did nothing wrong, as you know. But this has the potential to become a major distraction, which is what the Republicans want."

"It's a headache, that's for sure."

"Ron, the Virginia State Police report to you, don't they?" asked Kaplan pointedly.

"Well, that's an overstatement. They're in my department, but they are an independent law enforcement agency," said Cider, his answer lawyerly and evasive.

"I just wonder if it's really necessary to escalate things by calling in the FBI and DOJ," said Kaplan. "If the goal is to get the facts, surely the police can do that without calling in the 82nd Airborne."

Cider said nothing, determined to let Kaplan talk himself out.

"What I mean is," continued Kaplan, "we would appreciate your taking a look at it, if only to protect your own jurisdiction. I am in no way asking you to limit the inquiry. Far from it." Now that he had made the obligatory legal disclaimer, he got down to business. "Could you talk to the commander of the Virginia State Police?"

"Let me check into it," said Cider cautiously. "I'd like to hear from the state police about the requirements of the investigation, their available personnel and resources, and what the FBI might be able to offer."

"I knew you'd know how to handle it. That's why you're the attorney general of the commonwealth and I'm not," said Kaplan. "We just don't want a circus."

"I understand."

"Call me back, if you don't mind, and let me know what you find out."

"You bet. Talk to you soon." Cider hung up the phone. He felt himself a little short of breath, his heart rate accelerated. As he reflected on the call, he wondered if he was being asked to be an accessory to obstruction of justice. He wanted to help Stanley, but not if it sucked him into the scandal. Kaplan's call boded well for his own future ambitions, but he would have to be extremely careful.

15

T AYLOR SULLIVAN WAS AN Irish brawler who fought for the sheer joy of it. He paced as he shouted into the phone, sleeves rolled up to the middle of his sweaty bicep, waving an unlit cigar.

"Did you see our analysis of Hafer's acceptance speech? Out of 3,571 words, she mentioned Sal Stanley's eighteen-year record in the U.S. Senate *twice*. Two times! This guy spends two decades in the Senate, sponsors or cosponsors 2,418 bills or resolutions, and becomes majority leader. But his record is so liberal, so extreme, so out of touch with mainstream America that his own running mate won't mention it more than twice in her acceptance speech! They're running from his record like scalded dogs!"

Sullivan allowed himself a wry smile. Hafer had become a sacrificial lamb—she would either be dropped from the ticket or put into a witness protection program, consigned to flopping around the country in an empty plane to secondary media markets with no press. Sullivan had to retain his artillery on Salmon Stanley.

He paused as the reporter asked a follow-up.

"How much of that is on the record?" he continued. "*Every word of it!* I've given you the story—now you want me to write it for you and email it to you?!" He roared with laughter and hung up.

The glass door to his office opened and a research assistant bounded in. "Dorman's got a mudball on the *Post* website. Hafer asked an aide what her position on Iran was," the assistant announced, bouncing on his toes, fingers twitching excitedly. He let out a giggle.

"She said *what*?" Sullivan's beefy face lit up, his eyes dancing with joy mixed with disbelief. "We need to *prop her up*!" Sullivan bellowed. "She's *imploding* before we can *kill* her!"

"We put together a quick news release. I just sent it to you."

"This is just *too much fun*." Sullivan spun around in his chair, pulling up his email inbox. Moving the cursor to the press release, he opened the document. His eyes scanned the headline and first paragraph. "Oh, this is good." He read some more, going deeper into the body of the copy. "I like this."

Sullivan embodied the old joke about the Irishman who walks up to two other Irishmen pounding each other on the floor of a pub and asks, "Is this fight taken?" That was why he loved the press release: it was a nasty shot, but perfectly within bounds. Hafer had walked right into his punch!

The headline screamed: SO THIS IS SAL STANLEY'S "HIGH STANDARD" FOR VICE PRESIDENT? The press release contrasted Hafer's ignorance with Stanley's statement in Chicago that his main criterion for a running mate was someone ready to become president. Well researched and footnoted, it detailed Stanley's public positions on Iran—diplomatic and economic pressure, worldwide sanctions, but no military intervention—including a line from his acceptance speech in Chicago. "So did Elizabeth Hafer not listen to Sal Stanley's acceptance speech?" it demanded. "Perhaps she was too busy eating a box of chocolates." Then the punch line: "If this is what Sal Stanley believes qualifies someone as 'ready to be President,' it raises serious doubts about his ability to lead at a time when our nation faces a global war on terrorism."

"Blast-email this around midnight," Sullivan ordered. "This should give the sharks something to gnaw on at feeding time!"

The research assistant nodded and giggled, bolting from the room.

NICOLE BOUNDED UP THE stairs to the lobby, her auburn hair lightened by the sun, her legs bronzed to a deep tan. She wore a wraparound skirt and a spandex fitness shirt over her bikini—and the front desk clerk clearly noticed. She asked for a phone and he directed her to a small office in the back. She dialed a number.

"Mike Kaplan's phone," answered a staffer.

Nicole didn't recognize the voice. "Is Mike there?"

"He's in a meeting. Can he call you back?"

"No," she said quickly. "It's an urgent matter and I'm not at a number where I can be reached. I need to speak with him right now."

"Can I tell him who is calling?"

"He'll know." The aide put his hand over the phone and she could hear him saying something in a muffled voice.

"Kaplan here."

"It's Nicole. Listen, I only have a minute. I'm calling from Mexico. Jay got a call from Long today. Long asked him to fly back to California."

"Did he say why?"

"He's planning to run for president as an independent candidate."

Kaplan let out an expletive. "You're sure?" he pressed.

"Positive," Nicole answered. "I was sitting next to Jay when he got the call. I was trying to keep him down here as long as possible. He hasn't even been checking his email. Somehow, Long found him down here."

"This is not what I wanted to hear," Kaplan groaned. "But you've done good work, Nicole. Can you convince Jay to take you with him?"

"I think so."

"Then do it," directed Kaplan. "I hope it wasn't too difficult for you."

Nicole was in no mood to give him the gory details. "I did what I had to do."

"Of course you did. This will be duly noted. We don't forget our friends."

"You better not."

"Call me when you get to L.A.," Kaplan said and hung up the phone.

Nicole stuck her head out of the office, looking both ways before exiting, and padded back down the hall and down the stairs toward the beach.

THE TAXI CARRYING ROSS Lombardy, the executive director of the Faith and Family Federation, pulled up in front of a nondescript Italian restaurant on a cobblestone side street in Old Town Alexandria. It had been a ten-minute ride from Reagan National Airport. The restaurant was off the beaten path and had been chosen for that reason. Waiting for Ross at a back table, scrolling through his BlackBerry, sat Bill Diamond, chief of staff to Vice President Flaherty. As was true with all senior White House staff, his plastic smile masked a besieged soul, his proximity to power tempered by physical exhaustion, professional stress, attacks in the press, and keeping a criminal lawyer on retainer.

Diamond was an aging Hill rat and True Believer. He had come to Washington as a Reagan revolutionary, rising methodically over decades in Congress and multiple Republican administrations to a height from which he now wielded tremendous influence as one of a handful of the most powerful White House aides. His off-the-rack suit, graying, thinning hair, and pale complexion suggested a practiced anonymity that disguised his sway in the West Wing. As Ross rounded the corner, Bill flashed a smile.

"I hope you don't feel like Fredo in *The Godfather*," he joked. "No one gets killed, I promise. But the food is great and it's private."

"It's perfect," replied Ross. "I don't want people starting rumors, which they might do if they saw us having dinner together."

"You mean like claiming that we're plotting the election of Harris Flaherty as president?" joked Diamond.

They ordered dinner and Diamond pulled out a leather-bound legal pad, already filled with notes. He was all business. "I want to cover three things," he began in an official voice. "First, the platform. The vice president will take the same position that we took eight years ago: no change in the pro-life plank."

"Good to hear," replied Ross, squeezing a lemon into his iced tea and stirring it with a spoon. "Can the veep say that publicly?"

"I think so," Diamond said.

"It would be smart. Let the sleeping dog lie. You kick it, and it bites like a Doberman." He let the analogy hang in the air. "Besides, if you mess with the platform, we'd have to take you on and beat you." He did not smile as he said it.

"It's done, let your mind be at ease," said Diamond as the waitress put a plate of penne pasta in front of him. He took his pen and scratched through the item on his checklist. "The second issue is Iran." He took a swig from his ice water. "We're going to the U.N. Security Council to push for tougher sanctions that will bring Iran to its knees. The president is going to take on Iran by name in his address at the opening session of the U.N. General Assembly. There will also be a legislative vehicle in Congress that will land in Sal Stanley's lap. That's where you come in."

"I hope we're not talking about military action," interjected Ross. "We've been there, done that on Iraq. No one's up for invading another Muslim country."

"That's above my pay grade," replied Diamond cautiously. "It is being hashed out at State, the Pentagon, and NSC. Believe me, you don't want to know—it's a bureaucratic cluster. But once the president decides, he will send legislation to the Hill that will frame the election around national security. Stanley will be in a box. If he votes with us to crack down on Iran, his liberal base walks. If he opposes us, he looks weak on one of the rogue regimes in the world having nukes."

"I love it," said Ross. "I'm beginning to think that Senate majority leader is the worst possible place from which to run for president."

"No kidding—especially if you get caught suborning perjury. Anyway, we want Andy's support on this. The veep wants the full monty: radio, TV, direct mail, you name it."

"Andy will like it. He believes the election is going to be about security and terrorism. But what's the angle for the federation?" asked Ross.

"Israel," Diamond suggested. "Iran wants to wipe Israel off the map."

"That's right in our wheelhouse. Can we get the Israeli prime minister to come here in the fall? We can do a big event with Andy and whip up the troops."

"The Israelis are nervous about looking like they are trying to influence the U.S. election. That would make it look like a holy war between Christians and Jews against the Muslim world, which you want to avoid."

"That's the State Department talking," shot back Ross dismissively. "The terrorists are waging a jihad against Christians and Jews. That's what this is all about. They're not killing us because we have Disney World."

"We can't *say* that. And if Andy's smart, he won't say it, either." He scratched the item with his pen. "Third issue: running mate." Here it comes, Ross thought: the big enchilada. "You can't imagine what a pain in the neck this has been." Diamond cleared his throat. "I heard the meeting between Andy and Petty did not go well," he said.

"Two bulls in a china shop," said Ross, shaking his head. "I thought I was going to have to shoot Andy with a tranquilizer gun." They both chuckled.

"If it makes you feel any better, you're not alone."

"Is that so?"

Diamond rolled his eyes. He dug into his pasta, taking a huge bite. The silence hung in the air as he chewed. "Totally between us, you've got nothing to worry about," he said. "The vice president had puppy dog eyes for Petty, but he's over it."

"Well, I mean . . . who wouldn't?"

"Exactly. The guy's a rock star—African-American, Hispanic, war hero, good-looking, articulate, numbers are off the chart. Who can blame him? He wants to win."

"The base would blow up."

Diamond ignored Ross's comment. He reached into his coat pocket and took a note card with the vice presidential seal stamped in gold foil, scribbled, and slid it across the table wordlessly. There were three names written in black ink:

> *Byron Berry*
> *Tad Johnson*
> *Douglas Parks*

Former U.S. senator Byron Berry of Ohio was the former chairman of the Senate Armed Services Committee and a cancer survivor. Terry "Tad" Johnson was the conservative, tax-cutting Republican governor of Texas with movie-star good looks. Doug Parks was a former member of Congress, currently serving as secretary of defense, and was the administration's leading hawk in the war on terror.

Ross picked up the note. The jolt of adrenaline mixed with caffeine almost catapulted him out of his chair. He held in his hands Harris Flaherty's short list for vice president. In Washington, information was power, and Ross had the most sought-after news in the capital. He tried to play it cool.

"They're all friends," answered Ross, choosing his words slowly. "Johnson has the three C's: Catholic, conservative, crime-fighter. He's a former FBI agent, former federal prosecutor, former state AG—all good. As a Catholic, he reaches swing voters."

"What about Berry?"

"Andy likes him. But he's been out of office now for four years. He also has his own C word: cancer."

"And Parks?"

"He's a stud on terrorism and Iran. He's doing a terrific job at the Pentagon. Do you know if he's pro-life?" He smiled. "If he's not, will he say he is?"

"Let's cross that bridge when we come to it. I'd say he's more of a long shot."

"What about my old boss?" Ross felt obligated to at least raise the name of Tom Reynolds.

"No go," said Diamond coldly. "There were issues."

"I understand." Reynolds had invested, Ross knew, in a condominium project that later ran into financial trouble. His partners bought him out for more than his original investment, and his critics had cried foul. Ross leaned back in his chair and pursed his lips, his eyes locking on Diamond's. "I'm glad we don't need to worry about Petty. If that happened, the wheels would come off."

Diamond looked Ross in the eye. "The veep's over it. You've got nothing to worry about."

"When are you going to announce it?" asked Ross.

"I could tell you, but then I'd have to kill you." He smiled. It was a brush-back pitch, a subtle reminder that Ross was a player, but still on the outside looking in. Ross shook it off. He held the short list in his hands, and every name on it was acceptable. That was all that mattered.

"There's one last thing I need you to do for me," said Diamond, his voice grave.

"What's that?"

"Take that piece of paper, put it in your mouth, and eat it."

Ross exploded with laughter.

They got up from the table and slid gracefully out of the restaurant. They shook hands warmly on the curb. Diamond stepped into a government sedan that would whisk him back to the White House, and Ross dove into a cab, barely able to contain his excitement. He whipped out his BlackBerry and called Andy at home.

"Just left dinner with Bill Diamond. Guess what I'm holding in my hand?"

"What?"

"The short list."

"Good for you!" Andy exclaimed. "Who's on it?"

"I'm on a cell phone. I'll drop by your house when I land. I can tell you this much: you will be pleased. The problem we had is now taken care of."

"That's great. God is on the throne, Ross."

"He is indeed," Ross replied.

MICHAEL KAPLAN SAT AT the head of the table in a small, windowless conference room in the Stanley campaign headquarters, his arms folded across his chest, his torso leaning forward from the waist as if he were poised to strangle someone. A copy of Dan Dorman's *Washington Post* story lay on the table like a ticking time bomb. Next to it lay the RNC press release blasting Hafer's latest gaffe. Three senior campaign officials sat around the table, reading their copies in shock. One of them dialed the cell phone for Sue Bennett, the press aide on Betsy Hafer's plane. Sue's voice crackled over the speakerphone.

"Sue, it's Mike Kaplan. I have you on the speakerphone. Could you explain how we ended up with Governor Hafer saying she had no clue about our position on Iran?"

"I don't know, Mike. I briefed her. I went over every possible question. I thought she knew. I tried to cut the interview short, but it was too late."

Kaplan cast a disgusted look around the table. "Why did you let Dorman in the henhouse after what he did to the majority leader on the Virginia delegation story? This guy is an *assassin*! He not only shouldn't have gotten an interview, he should be *booted* off the *plane*!"

"Mike, if we're going to do one-on-ones, we can't do them with *Women's Wear Daily*," Bennett protested. "This is a presidential campaign, for crying out loud. Betsy's going to have to hit major-league pitching."

"The one-on-ones have ended," said Kaplan, his authoritative voice bouncing off the walls. "We have a new policy. No more one-on-ones. Tell Governor Hafer."

"I'm afraid you'll have to tell her yourself."

"Why?"

"We're in the conference room at the FBO in Nashville. She ordered us off the campaign plane after the rally."

"*What*? She kicked you off the plane?" screamed Kaplan, his eyes shooting darts.

"Afraid so," Bennett replied in a dry monotone. "She said she was declaring independence from her handlers."

"That's just great," he said, his voice dripping with sarcasm. "All right, get on the next plane back here," ordered Kaplan. He hung up and immediately dialed the number to Victory Two. An aide answered and he asked to speak to Hafer.

"Governor, this is Mike Kaplan," he began. "Why have you ordered campaign staff off a plane *that we are paying for?*"

"Do you have me on a speakerphone?" she asked.

"Yes."

"Could you please pick up the receiver?" Kaplan put the receiver to his ear. "Mike, I didn't just fall off the turnip truck. Your staff has been dumping on me on background for days. I am not going to be thrown under the bus by your staff," she seethed. "You tell Senator Stanley that I joined this ticket to unify the party and heal the wounds caused by the fight with Long. I've been loyal. But if you guys keep cutting my legs out from under me, then two can play that game. I may have to publicly say what I think about what happened in Virginia. Then you'll really have a firestorm on your hands."

Kaplan was taken aback. Hafer was making a direct threat—against him!

"Betsy," he said, his voice softening, "you're a valued member of the team. But you can't throw staff off the airplane. I can't run a campaign like that."

"I'll throw them out at thirty thousand feet if they continue to trash me behind my back to the press!" Hafer fumed. "I don't want to see them again. Is that clear?"

"Betsy, they're on their way back here. But we need a coordinated media strategy. I need to put someone on the plane with you to handle the press."

"I'm handling the press from now on. I'm done being the punching bag. And you can tell Senator Stanley that at least I'm not being investigated by the FBI."

Kaplan heard a click and the line went dead. He didn't know what to do, but figured it was a bad idea to continue talking into a dead phone. He put the receiver down.

"Assemble a search party," he said drily. "Our vice presidential candidate has snapped her leash and is running loose somewhere in the country."

16

J AY SETTLED INTO HIS seat on the flight from Manzanillo to LAX and braced for his return to civilization. Instead of enjoying a vacation, he was about to run an independent presidential campaign. To calm his nerves, he had downed a pack of peanuts and a bottle of Corona for breakfast in the airport bar.

Nicole sat next to him in stone-washed bell-bottom jeans, Gucci boots, a light brown ribbed T-shirt, black leather jacket with a fur collar, and Chanel sunglasses. Her sun-bleached hair fell across her shoulders. Jay noticed that flights between LAX and Mexico tended to be populated by surgically enhanced California babes and their boy toys or by gray-haired, moneyed men with arm candy. Even in that crowd, Nicole was in a class of her own. In his mind, she was the most gorgeous woman on the airplane—or in all of Mexico. She had a *Los Angeles Times* and a glossy fashion magazine on her lap. Jay glanced at the headline: "Hafer Declares Independence from Campaign Handlers." Good grief, he thought, the woman was bat crazy. If Long had listened to him and accepted the veep slot, everything would have been different.

Jay pulled out his laptop and pulled up the strategy memo he had begun the night before, some of it in barely legible scrawls on the back of a napkin. It was a bold and audacious campaign plan. He spread it out next to the computer and continued writing:

> *The modern Democratic Party is dying. The FDR coalition splintered forty years ago. It has persisted as a patch-quilt of special interests—feminists, minorities, gays, Jews, and the antiwar left. These voting blocs are all declining as a percentage of the electorate.*
>
> *The Democrats' decline is being accelerated by the population shift from the Snow Belt to the Sun Belt. The center of the U.S. population, once near Kansas City, is now near Denver,*

and is moving five feet a day, one mile every year. The states carried by the Democrats in recent presidential elections are hemorrhaging population at a rate of 40,000 per month, or nearly 500,000 annually. States carried by Republicans in four of the last five presidential elections gained 17 electoral votes since the 2000 census. The South, where the Democrats have not won a single electoral vote in the last five elections, will soon have 188 electoral votes. If the Democrats fail to carry a state in the region, their nominee must win 83 percent of all the remaining electoral votes to win—a virtual impossibility. The share of Americans living in the South and West will rise over the next two decades from 58 to 65 percent of the population, while those living in the Northeast and Midwest will fall to only 35 percent. Stanley and Hafer, from New Jersey and Pennsylvania, are on the wrong side of this geographic and demographic divide.

Jay believed demographics drove politics. To him, politics was a numbers game, a problem for both parties. He continued:

The Republicans have bigger problems. A probusiness party with the religious right grafted in like a wild olive plant, it no longer appeals to the center of the country. Libertarians, "leave us alone" voters, secular voters, independents, single women, minorities, and young people now see the GOP as a religious, sectarian party. Its demographic base is white and male, voters who are shrinking as a percentage of the electorate. In the next census, the U.S. population is projected to be 19 percent Hispanic, 13 percent African-American, and 6 percent Asian. Winning with only white voters is impossible, but the GOP is trapped in a failed strategy. An independent candidacy appealing to independents and conservatives (leaving the far left to Stanley) and geographically located in the South and West can win a plurality of the popular vote and a majority in the Electoral College.

Noble ended the memo by listing the failed third-party and independent candidates who litter the pages of history:

James B. Weaver (1892)
Teddy Roosevelt (1912)
Strom Thurmond (1948)
George Wallace (1968)
Eugene McCarthy (1976)
John Anderson (1980)
Ross Perot (1992, 1996)
Ralph Nader (2000, 2004)

This list seemed to catalog the futility of an independent candidacy. But to Jay, it provided a road map to victory.

> *Third-party candidates have failed for three reasons: poor candidate performance, regional candidates (Thurmond, Wallace), or ideological, protest candidates (TR, Anderson, Nader). Long avoids all these pitfalls. If Long assembles a first-rate campaign with a centrist message and runs as a national candidate, he can win.*

To Jay, it was like having Ross Perot's appeal and money without his haircut and theme song: "Crazy" by Patsy Cline. As the plane descended into L.A. Jay turned his computer off and gazed at the city skyline, smoky blue in the smog. Nicole took his hand. He was on his way back to the war, and now he had a woman to share it with.

———

MIKE KAPLAN'S SECRETARY BROUGHT in a fresh mug of coffee and a stack of phone messages. "Ron Cider's on line one. Do you want to take it?"

"Yes," Kaplan answered, his voice rising an octave and betraying his suspense. "Put him through. And close the door, please." He picked up the phone, twisting a paper clip nervously with his right thumb and forefinger. "General, how are you?"

"Very well, Michael."

"What's the word?"

"I talked to the state police commander. I'm afraid I don't have good news," Cider said, getting straight to the point. "I said I had been reading news reports and I thought I ought to check in with him."

"What did he say?"

"He did not appreciate the call. He said his investigators handled election law violations, money laundering, and so forth, but this was beyond their normal purview. He said some of the activities under investigation occurred outside Virginia, so the FBI *had* to come in. He was not budging. He was puffed up like a poison toad."

"I see."

"Sorry, Michael."

"I understand." Kaplan suspected Cider had only gone through the motions. "Did the commander tell you when the FBI was going to begin talking to people?"

"Immediately. If I were you, I'd get in the bunker."

Kaplan hung up and dialed the extension of Duke Barrett, the campaign's general counsel.

"I just spoke with Ron Cider," Kaplan began, "the attorney general of Virginia and our state campaign cochairman there. He talked to the state police commander and has confirmed that the FBI is going full bore. Get your helmet on and get in your hole."

"I need to send a memo to the entire staff on our document retention policy," Barrett replied. "We don't need someone destroying documents or deleting emails and creating an obstruction issue."

"How soon before we get document requests from DOJ?"

"Hard to say. Now that the FBI is involved, a few days to a week at max."

"Can we wait until this afternoon to send out that memo?"

"Sure."

Kaplan hung up the phone and got up from his desk, pacing back and forth, deep in thought. He walked to a file cabinet in his secretary's outer office, opened a drawer, and pulled out a manila folder labeled "Virginia Delegation." Closing the file drawer and returning to his desk, he opened the file folder and began to flip through the contents. It was all there. He pulled over the trash can with the paper shredder on top, pulled out the first document, and fed it into the shredder. He moved quickly and efficiently. He didn't have much time.

"HE'S READY," SAID THE president's secretary to Vice President Flaherty, the gray hair at his temples looking distinguished against his dark blue pinstriped suit and blue Hermès tie. It was noon sharp, time for Flaherty's weekly luncheon with the president. He opened the door and walked into the sun-splashed Oval Office. As he did, he had a happy thought: in 109 days, he would win the office for himself.

"Harris, good to see you, my man," said the president.

"Good afternoon, Mr. President."

Flaherty glanced around while the president finished examining some papers. Blue embroidered curtains draped large windows providing a view of the Rose Garden. The yellow carpet bore a large presidential seal. Paintings on the wall honored the president's personal heroes: Abraham Lincoln, Teddy Roosevelt, and Ronald Reagan.

When the president rose from behind the desk, they walked into a small dining room off the Oval. "Have a seat," the president directed. He sat at the table, picking up a fork and tearing into his shrimp salad. He held the fork aloft and steadied his gaze on Flaherty. "Things look pretty good, don't they?"

"Too good," replied Flaherty. "Between Long refusing to endorse Stanley, DOJ investigating the other team, and Hafer doing a female impersonation of Tom Eagleton, it's about as good a set of circumstances as I can imagine. I always thought it would be Stanley, not Long."

"Me, too," agreed the president. "Stanley's tougher."

"But I thought he would unite the party and move to the middle. Now, I'm not sure Sal ever thought through what came after winning the Democratic nomination."

"The Virginia delegation matter is serious," said the president delicately, not revealing his sources. "Payments to delegates were laundered through tax-exempt groups at Stanley's direction. That brings in DOJ, the FEC, the IRS, and probably Congress."

"It's a full-employment act for lawyers," agreed Flaherty, shaking his head in wonderment.

The president grunted in agreement as he pushed his salad plate to the side. A White House steward picked up the empty plate and ran a blade across the tablecloth to pick up crumbs. The president was a proficient and disciplined conversationalist, and he quickly shifted topics. "Do you think Long will run as an independent?"

"I do," answered Flaherty firmly. The president raised his eyebrows in surprise. "I wish there was something we could do to encourage it, but there isn't. Bob is self-righteous and vain, two character flaws that I think make it likely he'll run. Plus, he hates Stanley. He wants to finish him off."

"If he does, he'll split their vote and take California off the table for Stanley. We might be able to compete in California. Amazing," said the president.

"Don't you wish you could have been this lucky?" joked Harris.

"It would have been nice. But a win is still a win, right?" He glanced down at his grilled salmon, turning suddenly serious. "According to Parks, Iran is about to announce they have weaponized a nuclear device. The CIA is clueless as usual—they don't know if it's true or not. Our human intelligence is nonexistent in Iran. But if *we* don't do something, Israel will, so we need to act."

"We need to cut off oxygen to the current regime," offered the vice president.

"No question. My thought is to proceed on three parallel tracks." He took his hands and laid them out side-by-side on the table to punctuate the point. "First, a regional diplomatic initiative with the Saudis and Egyptians leading the way; second, a diplomatic track at the United Nations; and third, a military option."

Flaherty nodded as he chewed his food.

"The military option will be short of ground troops—supplying Iranian

freedom fighters, air strikes, sealing the border with Iraq," the president continued. "We'll need congressional authorization."

"Closing the border is an act of war. Russia and France will be their usual
profiles in cowardice at the U.N.," said Flaherty.

"Guaranteed," replied the president. "Petty is jawboning them, and they
are just pathetic, believe me. The Russians are making money off the Iranians and the Chinese need their oil." He paused to take a bite of salmon and
chewed vigorously. "On the congressional front, Stanley will have to vote for
the resolution or lead the opposition. Either way, he loses. If Long runs, he's
sort of in the same boat."

"I bet Long supports it."

"He'll probably claim it was his idea," the president joked, arching his
eyebrows humorously. They both laughed.

"Mr. President, there's an issue I'd like to raise with you," said Flaherty,
sensing that his face time was drawing to a close. "I'm announcing my running
mate soon. Can I run some names by you on a strictly confidential basis?"

"Sure. Nothing we say here ever leaves this room."

Flaherty bobbed his head slightly in affirmation. "I've narrowed it down
to a choice between Tad Johnson, Byron Berry, and David Petty. I'd like to
pick David, but I don't know if you can lose him up at State, especially with
Iran coming to a head."

"I can loan him to you for the good of the country. He's the strongest of
those three, but the least political. Can you school him?" asked the president
hopefully.

"I'm trying. He met with Andy Stanton, and apparently it didn't go
well."

"Andy's a challenge," sighed the president. "He once came by and prayed
with me in the Oval. Sweet as he could be. Then he goes to the stakeout and
tells the press every detail of our conversation, including what we prayed
about!" The president chuckled, shaking his head.

"He's a great preacher, but politically naive," agreed Flaherty.

"If you go with David, we could elevate the deputy secretary as a placeholder," suggested the president. "As for the others, I don't have a strong
preference. They would all do well."

"Thank you, Mr. President," said Harris, rising from his chair. "You've
done this before, as I recall."

"Yes, I have," the president said, grabbing Harris by the arm. He pulled himself close. "I hope your decision is as sound as mine was." He winked.

He guided Flaherty to the door. As the vice president headed down the hall, he glanced back to see the president standing in the doorway, smiling and giving him a thumbs-up.

17

R OBERT LONG CAME INTO the room like a force of nature and sat at the head of the table. Two trays of sandwiches, assorted fruit, and chocolate-chip cookies sat in the middle of the table, but no one had touched them. Long eyed the food.

"Why don't we go ahead and eat while we talk, then we can clear away the plates and get down to business." Everyone dove in, filling paper plates and pouring soft drinks. "Thank you all for coming on short notice."

The members of the Brain Trust were intrigued and nervous. Munching on sandwiches around the table, along with Noble and Long, sat Lisa Robinson, David Thomas, pollster Fred Edgewater, campaign finance chairman Perry Aiken, campaign counsel Phil Battaglia, and Scott Morris, the media consultant. The meeting was a kind of suicide pact. They had all made their names as Democrats, and if they helped Long run as an independent, they would be finished in the Democratic Party.

There was a decidedly mercenary quality to their relationship with Long. Behind his back, they called him "the meat," or "the meal ticket." His job was to raise millions of dollars so they could spend it on television, the Internet, and direct mail, making them all rich through their commissions.

"Jay, I read your memo," began Long, his fingers making a box in the shape of a piece of paper. "I have one question: how am I going to run an unconventional campaign with a roomful of aging Democratic political hacks?" They responded with a chorus of laughter. Long's needling broke the ice. Numbered copies of Jay's memo were in front of each person to provide a starting point for the strategy discussion.

"I've thought about this a lot since the convention," began Long. "I think I should run, regardless of the outcome. The political system is broken. It's a game in which Democrats and Republicans vie for power, and the American people are left out. We're not dealing with the real problems facing the country: education, the ticking time bomb of entitlements, health care, the national debt, and the war on terror."

Jay caught Lisa's eye across the table. Long was on his high horse. This was how he talked himself into taking on the bad guys.

"I got into politics to *help* people. But politics is no longer about helping people. It's all about destroying your opponent." The consultants eyed him warily, hoping Long was not opposed to destroying Stanley and Flaherty. He plowed ahead. "I'm as much to blame as anyone. I did the same thing—poll-tested issues, ran my speeches by focus groups." He glanced at Edgewater, who looked at him sheepishly. "No offense, Fred."

"None taken, Governor."

"Now I've been liberated. I can campaign the way *I* want to run. I have nothing left to lose." He paused, glancing around the table. "I'm the dark horse."

"Does that mean we can't run negative ads? Because if that is the case, I quit," blurted Scottie, his mouth twisted into a grin. Everyone exploded with laughter.

Morris, whom Long had nicknamed "Hollywood" because of his background producing films, was a creative genius who wore his hair in a gray-blond ponytail. He had once helped a client win a U.S. Senate race in Arkansas with an ad depicting his opponent as Godzilla, which won him a "Pollie," the Academy Award for media consultants. He had previously won an Emmy for a PBS documentary he produced about the oil industry. Scottie also had a cocaine problem, which everyone, including his business partners, Long campaign colleagues, and live-in girlfriend, pretended not to notice.

Hollywood had another reason for urging more negative ads. Jay's plan called for a $200 million budget in the general election, about $120 million of which would go to paid media. The consultants, including Jay and Hollywood, would split a 15 percent commission, or $18 million. Not bad for a hundred days of work.

"If you do this, you will be the underdog," Noble said. "The whole political system will be arrayed against us. But you're not interested in just making a point about the corruption of the current system. We have to find a way to win."

Long nodded. "Absolutely. I'm in this to win."

"We need to win half the independents, a third of the Democrats, and a quarter of the Republicans. That gives us thirty percent of the total vote and a chance at victory."

"How do we do that?" asked Long.

Noble turned to Edgewater.

"The data indicates you're going to get your fair share of the Dems," Fred began. "Mostly residual support from the primaries. They're mad about how Stanley stole the nomination from you. The message you're talking about—outsider, change agent, problem solver—will resonate with independents. The hard part will be getting Republicans."

"What do you recommend?" asked Noble.

"Stay to the right on terrorism while criticizing the way the administration has conducted the war. Flaherty owns the administration's failures; you don't. You can't get the antiwar crowd anyway."

"They hate me," Long agreed. "I've always been more hawkish on terrorism than the party."

"You also need a values message," Edgewater said. "Evangelicals comprise one-third or more of the GOP vote. The good news is that twenty-five percent of them do not consider themselves to be part of the religious right. That's your target audience. You can get them with a good values pitch."

"I signed the parental notification bill in California. It was a tough call and I caught all kinds of flak, but I did it," said Long.

"It hurt us in the primaries," Noble said. "Maybe it helps us now."

"The way you win is for the Democrats to think you're a Democrat, the Republicans to view you as conservative, and the independents to think you are a reformer," Edgewater said.

"So I have to be all things to all people?" Long said with a frown.

"Exactly," Edgewater replied with calm self-assurance. "Perot did it for a while in 1992. He led the race in the spring. Clinton was in third place."

"Concede the far left to Stanley and the far right to Flaherty," said Jay, jumping in. "You run right up the middle. It's a centrist play."

"And what about the electoral vote?" asked Long.

"We run best in the South and West. The South is 188 electoral votes, plus California's 58 makes 246 electoral votes. We need to get 24 electoral votes somewhere."

"Where?" asked Long. "Arizona? Maybe Nevada."

Noble went to a whiteboard on the opposite wall and began to write with a black Magic Marker:

Illinois	18
Ohio	16
Iowa	6
Arizona	15
Nevada	7
Missouri	10
New Mexico	5
TOTAL:	77

"We need to win two big states or four of the small states to get to 270 electoral votes," Jay said as he finished writing.

"I hate to be the skunk at the garden party," interrupted Phil Battaglia, the outside counsel, whose law firm stood to make upwards of $1 million in fees in the general election. "But unless you get on the ballot, you can't win."

"How much of a problem is it?" asked Long.

"Like climbing Mount Everest in your underwear, Governor," Battaglia said matter-of-factly. "The good news is thirty-eight states have filing deadlines for independent candidates in August or September. The bad news is there are twelve states with filing deadlines between May and July. We've already missed some of those and will probably miss all of them."

"What do we do?" asked Long, worry in his voice.

"We sue the states, choosing carefully to build the strongest case, and we try to win a federal appellate or Supreme Court decision ordering you on the ballot."

"What about the other states?" asked Jay.

Battaglia nodded. "If you run, we'll spend every day between now and Labor Day qualifying you for the ballot. You qualify by petition. In Texas, it's one percent of all the voters who cast ballots in the previous presidential election; in Florida and California, it is one percent of all registered voters. Ohio requires only five thousand signatures. We've divided up the states by region and have lawyers handling each region. We'll have over a thousand lawyers on this before it's over. We'll need a massive grassroots effort, and the Stanley campaign and the DNC will fight us at every turn. There'll be lawsuits galore."

"Don't you hire vendors to do the petition work?" asked Long.

"Yes, but it's expensive—two dollars for each legal signature," replied Battaglia. "The ballot access project will cost about five million dollars. That's why Jay and I are planning to sign up volunteers on the Internet. We'll use vendors to supplement the volunteers."

Long nodded. "I like it." Then his face darkened. "If I don't get on all fifty state ballots, it's not a truly national effort."

"The good news is, the case law helps us," answered Battaglia. "John Anderson won a Supreme Court case out of Ohio after he pulled out of the Republican primary in 1980. Perot and Nader also did a lot to liberalize ballot access. It's easier now than it used to be."

"The Ohio case is a good precedent?"

"Very," Battaglia replied. "Ohio moved their filing deadline from before the primaries to seventy-five days before the election. If the courts stick to that standard, we'll overturn the early deadlines."

"What about sore loser laws?" asked Long. "Can I get on the ballot even though we signed oaths agreeing to support the Democratic nominee?"

"Sounds like you know more about election law than most lawyers, Governor," Battaglia said, flattering his client. "It's generally not a problem—legally, people are not voting for you. They're voting for a slate of presidential electors pledged to you. That's a loophole we can drive a Mack truck through. There are a few states where sore loser laws apply to presidential candidates, including New Jersey, ironically enough. There again, we'll have to go to court."

Long stared blankly at Battaglia.

"It gets worse," said Jay.

"How can it get worse? I just found out I've already missed filing deadlines in some of the largest states in the country!" said Long.

"The filing deadline in California is in twenty days. We will have to file 167,000 valid signatures, so that means we'll need 225,000 signatures."

"Good night," said Long slowly, stunned. "Can we do it?"

"Yes, but we need to flip the switch right now," said Jay, trying to cheer him up and force a decision at the same time. "It's been done in less time, and we have a kick-tail organization in California. We have more than a hundred thousand volunteers in the state in our database. We'll go to them and ask them to sign up friends and family, then back it up with paid petition gatherers."

"Folks, we need to move," Long said, his eyes wide as he sat erect in his chair. "I need to make a final decision and then schedule some kind of announcement. How do you think we should do it?"

"I would do it in two stages," suggested Lisa, who had been doodling on a legal pad. "Announce your independent committee on a television show. The networks will fight for your first postconvention interview—you drop the bomb on live TV, and we get fifty million dollars in earned media. The formal announcement follows a few days later with a rally at the state capitol, which we can use to launch the ballot access petition drive."

"I like it," said Long. "I need to think and pray about it, but let's go ahead and book the interview. If I decide not to go, we can always pull the plug."

Jay made a mental note: Long had said he wanted to *pray* about it. That wasn't how he usually described his decision-making process. Something else: Long *looked* different—more serene, more at peace, more comfortable in his own skin.

"What about the money?" asked Long. With a proposed budget of $200 million, Long would need to raise roughly $2 million a day.

"Jay's budget is optimistic," said Perry Aiken, the campaign finance chairman. He had remained silent up to this point. Political strategy was not his game, and he did not pretend to know how to win elections. His skill was raising the dough, and he relished being Long's bagman. "We're flying in the dark. I need to get on a conference call with our bundlers, but I can't do that until you announce your decision. Otherwise, it will leak."

"What's your best guess today?"

"The calendar is not our friend. My guess is we raise $60 million in California, and about the same amount in the rest of the country. I think we can do another $50 million with direct mail, telemarketing, and the Internet. So a conservative estimate is $100 million, but it could go as high as $170 million."

Mental calculators whirred around the table. Noble tried to mask his disappointment. He was planning on building his dream house in Santa Monica. Rats! The commission pool on paid media to be split among the consultants had just shrunk from $18 million to $13 million in a single meeting. Someone had to lay a cattle prod on the finance people and get them into gear. Thirteen million dollars was still a lot of money, but nothing like what the Stanley and Flaherty consultants would make, and Jay had to assume this would be his final payday in the Democratic Party.

"This has been very helpful," said Long, his face wearing a slightly shell-shocked expression. "I'll sleep on it tonight, and then we make an announce-ment one way or the other." Long got up, shook hands with everyone, and left.

"Please pass back your copies of the strategy memo," said Jay. Everyone slid their copies across the table. Jay flipped through them to make sure he had all nine copies, which were numbered sequentially.

He walked back to his office. Nicole came in and closed the door behind her. "So what's the verdict?" she asked.

"He *wants* to do it," sighed Jay. "But raising $150 million to $200 mil-lion, recruiting a million volunteers, and getting on the ballot in fifty states, all in the next hundred and eight days, is daunting."

She walked behind Jay's chair and began to rub his shoulders. It felt won-derful. He slumped, his muscles relaxing. Out of the corner of his eye, he noticed Nicole peering over his shoulder, reading the first page of his memo-randum with great interest.

18

A CHARTERED PRIVATE PLANE SAT on the runway at the airport in Austin, Texas, its jet engine humming. The pilots had no clue as to their ultimate destination. Camera crews stood on the tarmac, sweltering in heat already pushing ninety degrees at midmorning.

Half a continent away, a second jet sat outside the hangar at Signature Aviation at Cleveland Hopkins International Airport, its crew in the dark as to whether they would be flying to Washington with an empty cabin or the next vice president of the United States aboard.

The Flaherty campaign had spent fifteen thousand dollars on the chartered planes. Normally, this extravagant expense would have been a waste of money, but on this day it was a pittance for the free media they were getting from the lapdogs in the press, who gobbled it up. The cable shows ran pictures of the two jets on a split screen, the anchors speculating about which vice presidential pick might bring the most punch to the Republican ticket.

Except for Vice President Flaherty and Bill Diamond, no one knew which jet was the decoy and which was the real thing. In a town known for leaks, the Flaherty campaign had kept the selection of his running mate a total secret.

At exactly 11 A.M., Vice President Flaherty and the second lady appeared on the back porch of the vice presidential residence at the U.S. Naval Observatory, accompanied by an explosion of noise from still cameras that sounded like electronic crickets coming from the press riser. Flaherty and his wife stood at attention by the threshold, enjoying the moment of almost unbearable suspense. He held the door open as two figures stood in the shadows of the doorway, reporters straining to make them out.

"It's David Petty!" a disembodied voice shouted. Out of the house and into the blazing sunlight emerged the secretary of state holding the hand of his wife, Anne, walking with Flaherty and the second lady down the lawn and toward the assembled media throng. That Flaherty had selected Petty shocked everyone. The press had bought the leaks that Petty was too important in the Iranian crisis and was out of the running, and everyone fell for the head fake of the chartered jets. As the foursome strolled across the grass, they looked as glamorous and confident as Kennedys on their way to play touch football. It was magical—the first African-American/Hispanic candidate for vice president in U.S. history. Audible gasps could be heard from the riser.

Yes, it was David Petty—the toast of Georgetown, darling of the media, soldier-statesman, a man who transcended partisan politics and could heal the nation's racial divide. Unlike some minority candidates, Petty embodied not racial protest, status politics, or ideological fervor, but their very opposite. He symbolized not America's failures but its successes, not its racial sins but its redemption, not its racially divisive past but its multiethnic future. Because he claimed Hispanic and African-American lineage, he was the everyman of postracial politics. Beyond serving as a symbol for the way forward as a nation, he was a Republican—the good kind of Republican, a moderate who loathed the far right. The media was in love!

Vice President Flaherty beamed like a proud father, wearing a blue suit with an open-collared shirt. He stopped at his "mark," a spot designated by a small X of white tape on the grass. Petty glanced down to make sure his wing-tipped toe touched the tape mark, and a crackle of camera clicks captured the moment of earnest spontaneity.

"Thank you all for coming," Flaherty began, his tight smile revealing nervous excitement. "It has been a great privilege for me to work closely with Secretary of State Petty as we rallied freedom-loving nations against terrorism. He has done a truly superb job." He paused, the sound of whirring and clicking cameras in the background. "He did an equally outstanding job as the general who led coalition forces in defeating the enemy in Iraq. He has been tested and proved in times of crisis. This is no time for on-the-job training." Here was Flaherty's thinly veiled jab at Stanley for selecting Betsy Hafer. "So it is a great honor to introduce you to my running mate, the next vice president of the United States, Secretary of State David Petty."

Petty turned toward Flaherty, grinned widely, and gave him a firm handshake with two pumps. He turned back to his wife and pecked her on the cheek, then turned to face the press. "Thank you, Mr. Vice President. When this call to serve came, I gave only one answer—the same answer I have given my entire career. I said yes to serving my country, yes to patriotism in the best sense of that word, not a false and patronizing jingoism but the humble responsibility that comes with America's role in the world, and yes to serving a man that I believe will make an outstanding president and who has the values and leadership ability to serve as commander in chief. Thank you again, Mr. Vice President. I am honored to be on your team again."

Shouted questions exploded from the press corps. Flaherty pointed to the AP reporter.

"Mr. Secretary, you've never run for office before. Will you be able to make the adjustment from being a general or diplomat to being a candidate? And will you be able to take orders from the vice president's campaign handlers?" shouted AP.

Petty smiled confidently, clearly at ease. "I have not spent my life in politics, and I think that is a positive. The American people want their leaders to put the country first and partisan politics second." He paused and flashed another quick smile as if to say, "Look, Mom, no hands." Then turning to the tricky part of the question, he answered, "As for taking direction, I spent twenty-nine years in the army. I've saluted more than a few orders in my career." Knowing chuckles filled the air—he was passing the audition with flying colors, parrying their questions and matching their wits! Flaherty grinned widely.

"Mr. Secretary, you are known as a centrist—some would say more moderate to liberal than the base of the Republican Party. Are you worried that is going to cause difficulties for Vice President Flaherty in the days ahead as you seek the support of conservatives in the party? And I wonder if the vice president could answer the same question," asked the *New York Times*.

"Did you say I was liberal?" Petty shot back, his voice raised and eyebrows arched in comic indignation. More chuckles from the press corps. They glanced at one another as they scribbled on their steno pads, exchanging knowing smiles—what a performer! "I have been a conservative and a Republican my entire life and am proud of it. I support the vice president's stand on the issues. No one will ever agree with me on everything, but I believe in the big tent. I think Ronald Reagan had it right when he said an eighty percent friend is not a twenty percent enemy."

The press corps was abuzz now—he had used the phrase "big tent." Was his use of the euphemism intended to signal backpedaling by the Grand Old Party on abortion and gay rights? The reporter from the *Times* fired a follow-up: "I was specifically referring to your pro-choice position on abortion, for example, and gays in the—"

Flaherty jumped in to cut off the line of questioning. "The secretary supports my positions, and he supports the party platform," he said firmly. "I had no litmus test in the selection of a vice president. I wanted someone who shared my conservative philosophy, and Secretary Petty does."

"Thank you all very much," said the vice president, ending the news conference, stepping between the Pettys and wrapping a paternal arm around their waists, heading back toward the residence. The power foursome walked into the distance, arm in arm, like two couples on a double date, by all indications on their way to the White House. More clicks from still cameras echoed across the lawn.

Dan Dorman of the *Washington Post* ambled over in an awkward gait in the direction of Bill Diamond, eyes peering out over his glasses, a blue roller pen in one hand and steno pad in the other. Diamond watched his approach with the trepidation of a hyena watching an approaching tiger.

"How are you going to handle . . . uh . . . ah . . . the reaction to Petty by the religious right?" Dorman inquired. "It's going to be pretty ugly, isn't it?"

Diamond sucked a gulp of hot, humid Washington air. It didn't seem to reach the bottom of his lungs. So this was how Dorman reacted to one of the most historic veep picks in U.S. history? "This is not for attribution," he replied, trying to keep his temper in check. "Secretary Petty made it abundantly clear today that he supports the vice president's positions on the issues. That's what social conservatives care about. They also want a vice president who understands terrorism and knows how to defend our country at a time of war."

"So Petty is no longer pro-choice? Is that what you're claiming?"

Diamond felt the blade coming in under his third rib. Was Dorman going to call the leading television evangelists and trick them into making critical comments? He mentally worked up a call list. "I'm not going to characterize the secretary's personal views. He has agreed to join the ticket by stating that he supports the policy positions of Vice President Flaherty and the Republican Party platform."

"Was that a condition of his joining the ticket?"

"The vice president answered that, Dan. There was no litmus test."

Dorman shot Diamond a look of frustration. "Bill, no one's going to buy that from one of the leading moderates in the Republican Party."

"I have to get back to the office, Dan. Thanks for coming," shot back Diamond. He buttoned his coat and turned on his heel to head back to the residence. He needed to get Andy Stanton on the phone. Boy, was he ever going to be steamed!

19

Andy Stanton stood in the living room of his suite at the Bombay Intercontinental Hotel, watching the television in a state of shock. A clutch of aides, including his senior vice president for missions and his press secretary, stood beside him, transfixed as they watched the announcement of David Petty as the vice presidential running mate of Harrison Flaherty on CNN. It was eerie, watching it in a hotel room eleven time zones away. No one said a word. The tension in the room was thick.

Stanton almost reached for the couch to stabilize himself. Harris Flaherty—his friend, his trusted ally, his fishing buddy, for goodness sake—had stabbed him in the back! It was unconscionable, inconceivable, and dastardly—yet it was happening.

"Turn it off," Stanton said with a sigh. Stanton's security guard turned off the set.

"We're going to get press calls," warned his press secretary, his voice low. "We better figure out what to say."

"What in the world can I *possibly* say?" thundered Stanton, raising his voice, his eyes desperate. If he said something complimentary of Petty, his supporters would not understand. If he said nothing, the silence would speak volumes about his impotence. "I can't believe Flaherty did this to me."

"What if you just tell the truth," suggested the press secretary. Now there was a novel concept in politics! He had gotten Andy's attention. "Say Petty has done an outstanding job as a general and as secretary of state, but that you're concerned his selection may send the signal, however unintentionally, that the Republican Party is somehow backing away from its support for family values."

"That's mealymouthed," scoffed Stanton, his face twisted in disapproval. "That's spinning. It's not the statement of a Christian leader."

The press secretary was flummoxed. This was an ideal time for one of Andy's "horsehair and locust" moments—as his bone-rattling statements were known around New Life Ministries—when he just let it rip, politics thrown to the wind. One could almost see the headline on the front page of the *New York Times*: "Religious Leader Lashes Out at Petty, Calls Him 'Half-Baked and Unacceptable.' "

"It's late here—can't we just say I've turned in for the night?" asked Stanton plaintively.

"Sure, but only for one night," said the press secretary. "If we don't feed the beast, they'll track you down."

Stanton went to the huge bay window in his suite and looked out over Bombay at night. The spires of Hindu temples stood side by side with towering skyscrapers, citadels of encroaching modernity, glass-and-steel signs of India's exploding economy. "Get Ross on the phone and we'll war-game it in the morning," he said. He wheeled, suddenly back on his game. "Gentlemen, since our story is that I have turned in for the evening, I'm going to bed."

Stanton's posse filed out of the room. After the door had closed behind them, Andy walked back to the bay window and gazed out at the glorious Indian evening, deep in thought, his hands clasped tightly behind his back.

———

IN AN ABANDONED WAREHOUSE in South Miami, a few miles from Coconut Grove, just off Dixie Highway, Rassem el Zafarshan drew a diagram on the chalkboard. There were maps and building schematics laid out on the worktable in the center of the room. His team assembled and their training completed, the final preparations for the operation were under way.

As usual, Zafarshan was all business. On the chalkboard he had drawn a rough outline of Biscayne Bay with numbered squares representing various crucial landmarks: the Ritz-Carlton hotel on Key Biscayne, the Four Seasons, the condominium he had purchased, and a boat anchored in the bay. There were eight people sitting around the table, some with eyes glued to the chalkboard, a few poring over maps.

"Make no mistake, comrades," said Zafarshan, speaking in Farsi. "We will have only a split second to act. The cruising speed of the Sky Knight helicopter is sixty-five kilometers an hour, so everything will happen very fast. That is to our advantage. There is no margin for error for us or the enemy." He pointed to the chalkboard. "The anticipated route of the first secure package will be from a helipad at the Ritz, heading across Biscayne Bay toward Miami International Airport"—he drew a sharp line with a piece of white chalk—"and it should cross over the Rickenbacker Causeway here." He took the piece of chalk and drew a small X on the diagram.

"Ali," he said, pointing to one of the members of the group, "your team will be here in the boat near the causeway. When you visually identify the first shot, that is your signal."

"God is great," Ali replied.

"The second secure package will leave the Hotel Mandarin," Zafarshan continued, pointing to a numbered square. "All I will need is visual confirmation of the motorcade leaving the hotel from the surveillance unit. We will take it from there."

"What if the timing of the motorcade from the Mandarin and Marine Two don't match?" asked one of the team members. "Do we have a backup plan?"

"There is a backup plan. You stay focused on your job," shot back Zafarshan. As usual, he revealed only what was necessary for the men to execute their mission. "Any other questions?"

There were none. By now the team had worked together for nearly two months as a cohesive unit, running through every contingency and planning the smallest detail. Everything was now ready, with one exception. The only missing piece was the purchase of a suitable boat by Zafarshan's contact, with whom he had spoken an hour earlier and who was in the Bahamas at that very moment making the necessary arrangements. He had a lead on three boats. He would purchase one of them with cash and deliver it within forty-eight hours. If Zafarshan was unsatisfied with the contact's progress, he was prepared to charter a plane and fly to the Bahamas himself. Now that Vice President Flaherty had named his running mate, Zafarshan knew the identity of the second target: Secretary of State David Petty, the self-glorifying tinhorn general who had waged war on the mujahideen in Baghdad. He would pay for the death of Zafarshan's brothers in Iraq with his own blood.

———

"ANDY, I'M AFRAID WE don't have a lot of options," said Ross Lombardy. He was surprised how clear the phone line was from Bombay. "If we turn on Flaherty now, there's no upside. He's going to win and it's not even going to be close. But if you say something supportive of Petty, we'll have a rebellion on our hands."

"Ross, you called it when we went to Washington to meet with Petty," said Stanton with a trace of bitterness. "This whole thing was a setup."

"I'm sorry I was right. The worst part is, they lied to us," Ross lamented. "Diamond assured me that Flaherty was over Petty and had moved on. He gave me the short list, for crying out loud! *He lied to my face*."

"Flaherty was more careful. He played me like a fiddle," said Stanton. "I think I've lost my political virginity." They both chuckled at the analogy.

"At least we know where we stand," observed Ross. "Better to know it now before the election than to burn our political capital getting these guys elected and then get stabbed in the back."

"You've got that right."

"By the way, Dan Dorman with the *Washington Post* called," Ross reported. "He's looking for a comment. I could fire a shot across their bow."

"Let's not rush into it. I don't want to look like I'm hiding behind the skirts of my executive director." As usual, Stanton was in charge, and he would call the shots.

Lombardy's assistant opened the door a crack and stuck her head in, signaling that he had a phone call. Ross strained to read her lips. "Speak of the devil," he said. "Guess who's on the phone?"

"Who?"

"Bill Diamond. He must be tapping my phone."

"Remember, I've gone to bed," Stanton said wearily. "Call me tomorrow, preferably early my time."

Lombardy picked up the other line. "Hello, Bill. Congratulations on the Petty announcement," he said in his best deadpan.

"Ross, I wanted to call you last night but we were in lockdown mode. Look, I know Andy's probably unhappy—"

"Try up on the roof with a carbine."

"Everything I told you the other night was true. In hindsight, I should have been more circumspect. When it came time to pull the trigger, the veep was underwhelmed by the options beyond Petty. He wanted someone who could lead the world in the war against terrorism. I'm not going to sugarcoat it. It is what it is."

"Well, I just hung up with Andy, and he's officially off the reservation."

"Does he want to commit political suicide?" asked Diamond, the edge in his voice turning jagged. "David Petty is a war hero. The media's eating out of his hand. His job approval is sixty-eight percent! Does Andy want to jump in front of that train?"

"Andy doesn't care about polls," Ross shot back. "All he cares about is what's right and wrong. This puts a pro-choice moderate in line for the presidency—and who knows how many Supreme Court picks he might have? It's a repudiation of everything the profamily movement stands for, Bill."

"Petty supports the vice president's positions on the issues. What more does Andy want?"

"He wanted a social conservative. Didn't the vice president understand that?"

"Sure he did. But his main consideration was choosing someone qualified for the job. We're at war. It's like FDR picking Truman."

"Even FDR cleared the Truman pick with the labor unions," corrected Ross. It was a warning shot, fired with undisguised pleasure.

"Look, let me try to smooth things over. Can you have your assistant email me a number where Stanton can be reached in India?"

"I'll email you his hotel room number and the number for the satellite phone his security guard carries. Keep in mind they're eleven hours ahead of us."

"Petty will call him today, and this time he'll suck up big-time."

"Dan Dorman is rooting around," revealed Ross. Another warning shot—this one at the head. "If we don't get Andy back in the boat before he gets back from India, Lord only knows what he's going to say on the radio or on his TV show."

"I *said* I'm on it," Diamond replied, and quickly hung up.

JAY NOBLE ANSWERED HIS cell phone as he walked to his car in the parking lot. His cell phone had been ringing constantly since the release of the Gallup poll. All of a sudden, Jay was popular again. "Noble here," he answered.

"Jay, Marvin Myers," said the voice on the other end of the line. "Unless I'm misinformed, it sounds like you are back in business."

"How's that?" asked Jay, taken aback. *This guy is uncanny,* Jay thought. He had sources everywhere. *Is somebody on our team leaking?* "What are you hearing?"

"I'm hearing Long is going to announce his independent candidacy for president as early as Friday. True?"

"Not true," Jay lied. "He's thinking about it, but raising the money, getting on the ballot, and taking on the entire Democratic Party has been a cold shower. As of now, it's Christmas Eve and there's no Santa Claus."

"What have you recommended?"

"Can't go there, Marvin," Jay said. "I only give my advice to the governor."

"What's your best guess?"

"The governor doesn't tilt at windmills," replied Jay. "Look, an independent candidacy faces incredible challenges—money, organization, getting in the fall debates. Because it's so late, there are huge ballot access issues. There's a reason no one has ever pulled it off."

"So he won't run? Even though Stanley stole the Democratic nomination in what increasingly looks like a criminal enterprise?"

"I think he has support for that reason. The Gallup poll shows it. But Long is smart. And the smart move is to let this cup pass, play the victim, buy a front-row seat to Salmon Stanley's political funeral. We'll see you in two years in New Hampshire."

"Did you see the Pew Research poll?"

"No. What did it say?" asked Jay, curious.

"Sixty-five percent of white evangelicals said they would consider supporting a third-party candidate for president in a three-way race with Stanley and Flaherty. It shows real discontent on the right over Flaherty's picking Petty. That's quite an opening for someone like Long if he could move to the middle on social issues."

Jay gave a noncommittal grunt.

"So you're telling me that my sources are wrong?" Myers asked, making no attempt to disguise his skepticism. "You better not be spinning me."

"Your sources are wrong," Jay lied again. "I'm your best source in the Long campaign, and it ain't happening, Marvin."

"Then why are your people trying to book him on my show?"

"Marvin, he's been holed up at his mountain cabin since he left Chicago. We want a venue where he can announce his plans, or lack thereof, with maximum impact."

"The independent trial balloon is him showing leg to get a high-profile show?"

"Bingo," replied Jay. "You've connected the dots. If you're not going to run as an independent, you don't announce it with a whimper by releasing a statement. You want to fly a B-2 bomber over Yankee Stadium. We're going out with a bang."

"My show's already booked this week, so if you don't mind, I'll take a pass."

"No problem." Jay thought, *Marvin was sure going to be ticked when Long announced on a rival program!*

"I'll have him on later, sort of a postmortem interview on the campaign."

"The governor will look forward to that."

Noble hung up the phone and started the engine. He had just lied through his teeth to Marvin Myers, a very dangerous thing to do. He hoped he had succeeded in warning Myers off the story.

He banged his fist on the dash. He didn't know who was leaking, but he was going to find out and break their neck.

————

ANDY STANTON STEPPED OUT of the bathroom wearing a white cotton bathrobe as a room service waiter laid his breakfast on the dining room table: a bowl of steaming oatmeal with plump raisins and brown sugar, a plate of yogurt with fresh mixed berries, a kettle of hot green tea, and assorted breakfast breads. Stanton was about to sit down and pour himself a cup of tea when he noticed the phone's message light blinking red. Someone must have called in the middle of the night. Maybe someone making arrangements for his meeting later that day with the Indian prime minister?

The voice on the recorded message took him by surprise. "Andy, it's your old friend David Petty here," the message began, Petty's voice hushed to a whisper. "I know you're out of the country, but I wanted to call you right away. The vice president and I talked about you earlier today, and your help means so much to us. I know you and I have had some differences in the past, and I want to put that behind us. I want to sit down as soon as possible on the phone or in person—whatever works best for you—and discuss things. Andy, I don't just want to ask for your help. I want to *earn* your support." He dragged the word out so that it had two syllables. The message continued, "I look forward to our future friendship. Call me as soon as you return. You know how to reach me. Thanks, my friend."

Stanton hit the number on the telephone keypad to replay the message. He listened to it a second time, playing it back to make sure he had heard it correctly. The message was flattering, slightly embarrassing, and borderline obsequious. It was an Oscar-winning performance of sucking up, yet it also had the eerie quality of a hostage tape—he pictured Petty at his desk, someone holding a gun to his head as he read the words from a piece of legal-pad paper. Quite a change from the dressing-down Petty had given him at Foggy Bottom a few weeks earlier!

For Andy, it was too little, too late. The Republican convention was only days away and he felt no obligation to save Petty's hide. He knew he would have to return Petty's phone call, but first he had to figure out what he was going to say. He went back to the dining room table, poured a cup of green tea, and bowed his head to bless the food. He prayed a silent prayer asking God for guidance. He asked for wisdom and understanding, struggling with how to balance his friendship with Harris Flaherty with his spiritual calling to speak truth to power. The prayer finished, he felt a strange peace. As he opened up his Bible to have his morning devotion, he picked up his spoon and dug into his oatmeal.

20

J OINING US THIS MORNING, former Democratic presidential candidate and California Governor Robert Long," said the news anchor from a studio in New York, reading the scrolling copy from the teleprompter. As she teased in her best Ron Burgundy voice, viewers saw a tight shot of Bob Long from Los Angeles, his jaw jutting and lips pressed. "Are the rumors that Long may run for president as an independent true? We'll ask him in his first live broadcast interview since losing the Democratic presidential nomination to Senate Majority Leader Salmon Stanley."

The teaser finished, the floor director in the Los Angeles studio drew a line across his neck with his index finger. The clock read 4:01 A.M. Pacific Time. Long's segment, scheduled to last seven minutes—an eternity in morning television—had been negotiated over two stress-filled days with all the gamesmanship of an international summit. The Long campaign had twice threatened to walk, and both times the network had made concessions. The agitated floor director, throwing off flop sweat, made no effort to disguise his disapproval of Long getting up from his chair. But Lisa Robinson had insisted. She was not about to leave her candidate wilting under hot lights for eight minutes while the New York anchors did the morning headlines and the weather. She and Long retreated to a small dressing room.

"So?" Long asked no one in particular as he alternately sucked on coffee and an ice water with a wedge of lemon in a small Styrofoam cup—black coffee to wake him up, water to calm him down. Crammed into the tight quarters were Lisa, Jay Noble, and Hollywood.

"Kim Banning's doing the interview," Lisa said. "She's got ice coursing through her veins. Cute as a button, but with fangs like a cobra—she loves to go for the jugular."

Long looked like he had just been told he had to step into the ring against Mike Tyson.

"It will work in your favor, Governor," Lisa insisted, bucking him up. "Give it right back to her. She will try to provoke you—probably by getting you to rip into Stanley. Stick to your message, and above all, smile and be upbeat."

Long nodded. He was sucking down the water now. His mouth felt like cotton and his tongue stuck to the roof of his mouth. His nerves jumped and his eyes darted from friendly face to face, seeking encouragement. He felt as if he were about to bungee jump off the Golden Gate Bridge.

"Do you know what you're going to say yet?" asked Jay hopefully. "Is it a go or a no-go?"

"Yes, I know what I'm going to say."

"Can you tell us?" A panicky smile filled his face.

"No." Long had insisted that he tell no one his final decision other than Claire and the children. He had called Jay the night before to make sure the campaign website was still up. It was a clue, but that was all.

"All right," Jay said, throwing in the towel. "If you're not running, and she asks about the Virginia delegation scandal, say it's a pending legal matter and no one is above the law. If you announce you're running, hit Stanley hard. Say that anyone responsible should be dismissed from his campaign— and smile while you say it."

A knock came on the door. It was the floor director. His face was red and flushed, his forehead beading with perspiration. "I need the governor in the chair! New York is going ape!"

"Jay, I'd like a moment alone with the governor," said Hollywood. Jay nodded. He and Lisa stepped out of the dressing room, standing guard outside.

"Okay, Hollywood." Long smiled. "Give me your best advice."

Morris leaned into Long, his face no more than six inches away. "Governor, you're ready for this," he said slowly, his voice so low that Long had to strain to catch every word. "You've been preparing for this moment your entire life. In your mind, I want you to shoot all the pollsters and all the consultants, me included. I want you to do just one thing. Look into that camera and talk to the voters . . . from your heart. Let them see into your soul."

"Got it," said Long.

"One last thing," advised Morris. "Forget about Kim Banning. She's a prop. She trips people up because they focus on her instead of the people in

TV land." He paused, his face intense, the veins in his forehead bulging. "This isn't about her. It's about the country. This election is about the people, not some talking head who eats people for breakfast on national television. Talk past Kim, talk over her head directly to the voters, and you say what you came here to say." He paused, staring directly into Long's eyes. "Be yourself. You own this moment."

Long felt a surge of adrenaline. He suddenly felt like a prizefighter bouncing up and down on his toes in the dressing room, his name emblazoned across the back of a black silk robe, punching his boxing gloves together in anticipation of the opening bell, the cheers of the crowd reverberating in his ears. His stomach was queasy, the butterflies in full flutter. The announcer was calling his name. *Let me at her!*

"Break a leg," said Morris, but Long could no longer hear him. He was in the zone, his brain locked on its target, his ears tuning out the background noise. He felt as if he were watching a movie of himself in slow motion. He sensed that a new, higher power infused his being. Was this God's Spirit? If so, it was more powerful than money, politics, or the press. The world did not understand it, but Long was beginning to. A Bible verse he had memorized the day before kept rattling around in his head: *I can do all things through Christ who strengthens me.*

Whatever this was, he was glad he had it.

He saw himself being guided past work cubicles, onto the dark set, where a makeup artist patted a layer of powder on his face and sprayed a last blast of hair spray across his scalp. Someone placed a coffee mug filled with water on the small table next to him. A hand ran a cord up his back and gently maneuvered an IFB into his ear. He heard the director in New York asking him what the weather was like in Los Angeles. The set was dark and eerie. His heart pounded like a jackhammer, his throat felt dry as a bone. He said a quick prayer—*Lord, protect me and put a guard over my mouth*—and the next thing he heard in his ear was:

"And now, in his first interview since the Democratic National Convention, a man much in the news these days, former and perhaps future presidential candidate Governor Robert Long of California. Governor, welcome."

"Thank you, Kim, good to be with you."

"Governor, there are allegations of bribery and perjury swirling around the selection of the Virginia delegation to the Democratic convention, which provided the margin of victory for Senator Stanley. Do you believe that the Majority Leader won the Democratic presidential nomination by committing a crime?"

Wow, Long thought, Banning wasted no time going for the headline.

"Kim, we don't know. My campaign made its case before the credentials committee of the Democratic convention." His face suffused confidence. He spoke firmly. "I still believe that our Virginia delegation was the proper and legal one under the party's rules. Had it been seated, I would have won the Democratic nomination. But there are now investigations under way by the Virginia State Police and the FBI, and like everyone else, I await its conclusions. I do think"—he paused and downshifted—"if it is determined that anyone in the Stanley campaign acted inappropriately, that needs to be dealt with under the rules of the Democratic Party and the law."

"You refused to appear with Senator Stanley onstage in Chicago and have still not endorsed him. Why?"

"Well . . ." It was an uppercut, and Long shook it off. "I've been a Democrat all my life, so that was a hard decision. Given the questions about the outcome at the convention, I needed to take some time before deciding if I should remain in the Democratic Party or chart a new course. I don't rush decisions this large. So I've been thinking about how I can best contribute to making America better."

———

BACK IN THE GREENROOM, standing in front of a television monitor, Jay turned to Lisa and chuckled. "Only Bob could turn his Hamlet-like equivocation into deep thinking about charting a new course for America," he joked.

"What's he waiting for?" asked Lisa in frustration. "When will he say he's going to run? Spit it out already!"

"Don't worry," Jay assured her. "He's about to drop the bombshell."

———

"ARE YOU THINKING OF running for president as an independent?" asked Banning.

"I am," said Long. "Given the positive response I've received, yes, I am planning to seek the presidency as an independent Democrat. I think people are tired of the bickering and fighting from both parties in Washington. They want an alternative to the Democratic and Republican parties. I want them to have a real choice in November. So I will file papers with the Federal Election Commission today for an independent campaign committee. I will see if there is sufficient support for me to qualify for the ballot in enough states to be viable. I think I owe that to myself and my supporters."

"So . . . are you running or not? You sound like you're hedging."

Long understood why Banning made the big bucks. She had the face of a Kewpie doll, the svelte figure of a runway model, and the interviewing style of a serial killer. "Kim, I'll make this promise: I will run if the American people want me to run," Long said, fouling off her fastball. "But if they do, then they need to get some skin in the game. Should I run, this is not going to be your typical, top-down, special interest campaign in which the candidate is sold like a tube of toothpaste. I will be running independent of any party machine. So I will need the grass roots—hundreds of thousands of volunteers. If they want me to run, they need to go to www.voteboblong .com or email me at bob@voteboblong.com. That's my only commercial," Long said, flashing a relaxed smile.

Banning was not smiling. Her facial features had visibly hardened; her eyes glistened like two blue ice picks. Here she was, one of the toughest interviewers on television, and she was being reduced to a potted plant on Long's magical mystery tour! She shifted her notes in her lap and went for the kill shot. "As you know, Governor, Democrats are already attacking you, saying this is just sour grapes. They say you pledged to support the Democratic nominee, but now you've changed your tune. Aren't you just a sore loser?"

"No, not at all—"

"But you promised to support whoever won the Democratic—"

"Hold on, Kim, let me finish. I said what I believed at the time," replied Long, "and it was my intention to support the Democratic nominee. But circumstances have changed; there is a criminal investigation under way and I have to recognize that reality. I was elected to serve one state, one country, and one people—the American people—not one political party. What turns so many people off about politics today is politicians are putting their party first and the country second."

IN THE GREENROOM, THE campaign team waxed euphoric. Hollywood balled his hand into a fist and pumped it in the air, letting out a high-pitched "*Yes!*" Lisa grinned from ear to ear. "He turned it back on her!" exclaimed Scottie. "He took a hardball question and threw it right back in her face. He's on a roll."

"Watch this," predicted Jay. "It'll get even better."

"LET'S TURN TO IRAN," said Banning, reloading. "You supported the administration aiding groups seeking the overthrow of the Iranian government. How do you respond to the United Nations' claim that this violates international law?"

"Kim, Iran armed with a nuclear weapon poses one of the most serious threats to the United States and the world that we have ever confronted," replied Long, his face grave. "As for the U.N. secretary-general's comments, Iran's actions are themselves a violation of U.N. resolutions and international treaty obligations. Iran has threatened Israel, as well as what its foreign minister has called 'agents of U.S. hegemony,' meaning moderate Arab states. So yes, I favor working with groups promoting democracy and human rights in Iran, and we should—"

"So when the U.N. says we violated international law, you are not concerned with what that does to our image in the world?" Banning interjected, cutting him off.

"I care about our image, certainly," answered Long, keeping his cool. "But I don't think the U.N. should determine U.S. foreign policy. I care more that the American people are safe from nuclear blackmail by a terrorist-sponsoring state. I've been very critical of the administration for failing to fully disclose its actions to Congress. Part of the reason for our current quandary with Iran, I say with sorrow, is the utter failure of the administration to be transparent. That will change should I be elected president."

"Governor, you say you plan to run as an independent Democrat. So which is it, Democrat or an independent?" She crinkled her face theatrically. "Aren't you trying to have it both ways?"

"I think people are tired of partisan politics practiced by both parties, and that's why I describe myself as an independent . . . an independent Democrat," replied Long, his jawline sharp and unyielding. "I'm probably more conservative than some Democrats on foreign policy and defense issues, and I'm probably more focused on education and health care than some Republicans. Neither party has a monopoly on the truth. That's why, should I seek the presidency, I will do so as an independent. When you are trying to change, you can't pour old wine into new wineskins. You need to pour new wine into new wineskins."

Banning's face went blank. Long assumed she had no clue that the wineskin allusion was to the New Testament.

"I'm afraid that's all the time we have, so we'll have to leave it there, Governor." She bobbed her head. "I think it's fair to say you made some news this morning. Thank you for coming."

"Thank you, Kim."

As a technician removed the IFB from his ear and unclipped the microphone from his tie, Long felt the full gravity of his announcement. He was running for president again. As he stood from the chair, the technician said in a stage whisper, "You did great. Thanks for giving us a choice."

"Glad to do it," replied Long. He said another quick, silent prayer: *God, I obeyed you, so please bless it*. As he walked through the stage door of the studio, he was greeted by Jay, Scott, and Lisa, all smiling broadly and clapping. Lisa let out a shrill whistle.

"Well, guys, I'm in," said Long, spreading his arms to either side and opening his hands, palms out.

"No backing out now, Governor," said Jay, beaming.

"Did I sound corny when I mentioned the website? I hope I didn't sound like a huckster," he asked.

"You *better* mention the website!" shouted Lisa. "You did it once, which was just right. You didn't overdo it."

"Okay," Bob said, "let's get back to headquarters." They walked through the deserted newsroom, almost floating on air.

"How do you feel?" Jay asked.

"Like I'm involved in something bigger than me," replied Long, his face full and expansive. "Like I'm being carried along by a wave. I know it sounds a little far-fetched, but I think we're on our way. And it's not about me anymore."

Jay shot a surprised glance at Long.

"Okay, but you better get some rest sometime today," instructed Lisa. "We have to tape the video announcement to post on the campaign website. Then we've got CNN at one o'clock this afternoon, you tape the *Tonight Show* at six, and then we have to rush back to headquarters to do a live interview with Sean on Fox News."

They stepped out of the building into the cool, crisp morning air. It was still dark, but there were already three television camera crews and several print reporters waiting, including the Associated Press and the *Los Angeles Times*. Long could see the vans for the local network affiliates and cable news networks parked on the curb. A motley crew of technicians jogged across the street, lugging handheld cameras and trailing cables. Apparently the news was spreading fast.

LONG ANNOUNCES INDEPENDENT PRESIDENTIAL CANDIDACY; CLAIMS TO REPRESENT PEOPLE, NOT SPECIAL INTERESTS, shouted the twenty-point headline on Merryprankster.com. Michael Kaplan shook his head in disgust and clicked on the link with his mouse as he worked the phone. He could not believe Long was getting such a creampuff coming-out party. After what they had been through, it was enough to make him puke.

"Well, he's made it official," he growled into his cell phone. "It's going to be a Bob Long telethon for the rest of the day: Fox, CNN, a live Webcast, and he tops it off tonight with the *Tonight Show*."

"Smart. He lay in the weeds like a snake in the grass, waiting for the right moment to pounce," said Salmon Stanley on the other end of the line. He was in a bus rolling across Florida on I-4, somewhere between Orlando and Tampa. "He'll have his day in the sun. Then the Republicans will have their convention and his fifteen minutes will be up."

"Stay above the fray," advised Kaplan. "Welcome him to the race, stay positive, stick to the 'I look forward to a spirited campaign on the issues' message."

"Right."

"The media will be looking for us to be rattled."

"I'm going to kill him with kindness," offered Stanley, the rumble of the bus engine in the background. "He's a fine man and a good public servant, all that nonsense. Blah, blah, blah. I want no personal attacks today on Long. I mean it."

"Yes, sir. We're doing a conference call for our surrogates to keep everyone on message. The better we handle this now, the harder we can hit him later. Then we'll have the DNC hit him high and hard as a flip-flopper and a sore loser. We'll do that as a research backgrounder, 'Meet the Real Robert Long.' We won't let the DNC chairman go on television to talk about it. That's too hot. We'll blast-email it to the entire press corps and have the DNC press shop background it."

"Now that he's in, someone needs to tee up a 501(c)(4) or a 527 group to really take the bark off him," suggested Stanley. "How does that happen?"

"Very mysteriously," replied Kaplan.

"Who's going to do it?"

"You'll never know."

"Of course," said Stanley. "I temporarily forgot." They chuckled in a low, masculine guffaw. Kaplan could hear the rustle of papers, a swarm of bodies, and the sound of high screeching brakes in the background. The bus was coming to a stop.

"Got to go," announced Stanley. "We're at our stop in Kissimmee."

AT THE CAMPAIGN HEADQUARTERS in downtown L.A., Jay's BlackBerry went off. The number on the display belonged to Marvin Myers. Jay took a deep breath and answered it.

"Jaaayyy," Myers drawled in his deep baritone. "I have a bone to pick with you."

"Marvin, I swear I told you the truth the other day," Jay lied, trying to sound as earnest and chagrined as possible. "I did not think he was going to run."

"Then why did you book him on the *Morning Show* in the seven A.M. half hour?" seethed Myers. "Come on, Jay, don't insult my intelligence. You lied to me."

"Marvin, do you know when I found out he was going to run for president? Do you want to know the exact moment I found out?"

Myers was silent, still in slow-burn mode. He was beyond angry. He did not like to be scooped, especially by a blow-dried TV host like Kim Banning.

"When he said it on national television!" Jay shouted into the phone. He was really exercised—and he hoped it was working. "Marvin, believe me, I found out at the same time you did—watching it in the greenroom. He fooled us!"

"I find that hard to believe, Jay."

"We didn't even have the website ready," Jay lied. "Just look at the announcement video—it looks like a homemade video on YouTube. We shot it this morning with a handheld digital camera. Do you think that I would compromise our production values unless I was forced to scramble? Think about it, Marvin."

"Are you telling me that he didn't tell his own advisors that he was going to announce he was running for president?"

"Only two people knew: Bob and Claire Long. That's it. I asked him thirty seconds before airtime and he wouldn't tell me. I had to give him two briefings—one if he was running, the other if he wasn't."

"Wow," said Myers, sounding slightly sympathetic. "Can I use that?"

"Sure, on deep background. It may be crazy, but it worked. It's the biggest launch of an independent candidacy since Ross Perot in '92." Myers sounded as if he was beginning to calm down. Jay hoped he had convinced him—he didn't want to be in Myers's gunsights for the rest of the campaign.

"I want him this Sunday," said Myers, ratcheting up the pressure.

Jay gulped. "Let me see what I can do. He's tired. He had a two-thirty A.M. wake-up call. He's flying high right now, but he's going to crash."

"He can crash after he does my show."

"I'll talk to him."

"Do that. Call me back. I want him." Myers abruptly hung up.

Jay hung up and stared at the wall. He had no idea how he was going to convince Long to do Myers's show. Long loathed the Sunday chat shows the way most politicians pined for them. But if Jay didn't find a way to deliver him, Myers was going to bury them.

———

VICE PRESIDENT FLAHERTY WAS in the motorcade on his way to the final campaign appearance before the Republican convention when he learned of Long's reentry into the race. Billed as a coming-home event for David Petty, it highlighted his upbringing as the son of an engineer from Ghana and a Puerto Rican mother in Brooklyn. Petty's candidacy brought the Grand Old Party to the belly of the beast, the capital of blue-state America, the Big Apple. It was like JFK going back to Ireland, only better.

The motorcade pulled up in front of the local precinct police station, the hub of neighborhood patrolling that had succeeded in reducing violent crime in the area by 70 percent in two years, with the help of a generous grant from the Department of Justice (the same department that was now investigating Salmon Stanley). Flaherty stepped out onto the sidewalk and did a quick turn to his left and right, lifting his right arm in a stilted wave. Petty stepped out of the car on the other side. A crowd of angry protesters, many of them from ACORN, AFSCME, and an assortment of other left-wing groups, shouted at the end of the street, kept back by a yellow blockade guarded by New York City's finest. They shouted tried and true slogans: "*Stop the war against the poor!*" "*Jobs, peace, and justice!*" "*Money for books, not for bombs!*" It was a rent-a-riot.

The campaign had surrounded the police precinct building with a rope line and organized a small, friendly crowd. They waved signs and applauded as Flaherty and Petty stepped out into the morning sunlight.

"There he is!" shouted one woman, pointing at Petty and jumping up and down.

"I can't believe it. He touched me!" cried another after he had quickly grabbed hands along the rope line.

The vice president and his running mate decamped to a holding room upstairs. They sat at a long table drinking Diet Cokes and talking on their cell phones. The press secretary stuck his head in and suggested they invite a small press pool in to get their comments on Long's announcement—he didn't want the event itself dominated by shouted questions.

"Bring them in," Flaherty said.

A moment later five reporters filed into the holding room, thrilled to be escorted into the inner sanctum.

"Mr. Vice President," asked Fox News, "Governor Robert Long announced this morning that he is forming a presidential campaign committee to run for president as an independent. Your reaction?"

"I know Bob Long well, I have worked with him in his capacity as chairman of the National Governors Association, and I like him personally," said Flaherty methodically. The reporters all glanced at one another. He was kicking Stanley in the teeth by kissing Long. "This is democracy. It's what is great about our country—people choose their own leaders. So I welcome Bob to the race." He stopped talking and flashed a wide smile as if to say: "What, me worry?"

"Would you favor his inclusion in the presidential debates? He's polling over twenty percent. Shouldn't he be included?" asked *USA Today.*

"I'll leave that to the presidential debate commission, which has its own criteria for the inclusion of candidates," responded Flaherty, choosing his words cautiously.

"You don't have an opinion? You're not for excluding him?"

"I wouldn't seek to exclude anyone. But I think the criteria for inclusion is set by the debate commission, so I think that question is better directed to them."

"Don't worry, we'll be asking them," said the *New York Times* to laughter.

"Okay, one more, everybody," said the press secretary.

"A question for Secretary Petty, if I may," said AP. "Won't Long split the Democratic vote? Doesn't this help the Republican Party?"

"I'll leave the speculation about who it helps or hurts to the political people and all of you in the media," responded Petty. "That's your job. My job is to run for vice president. I think if Vice President Flaherty and I make our case to the American people, we will win in November regardless of who else runs."

"You know, my mother used to have a phrase, 'stick to your knitting,' " added Flaherty, jumping in. "We're going to stick to our knitting and run our own campaign. But I welcome Bob Long to the race." He flashed a hundred-watt grin again.

"Thank you all very much!" shouted the press secretary.

Flaherty and Petty, Secret Service agents and staff in tow, clambered down the stairs toward the briefing room, where several dozen police—

human props for the day's photo op—waited in full-dress blue uniforms. The candidates exchanged confident smiles as an aide handed Flaherty the cards that contained his brief remarks. They all knew they were merely going through the motions. The only thing they would say that day that would appear anywhere would be their comments on Robert Long's entry into the presidential race. That was fine by Flaherty. As he headed into the Miami convention, he was on cruise control. If Bob Long wanted to strap plastic explosives to himself and blow up what remained of the Democratic Party, what was that to him?

JAY WAS ON THE phone, his headset strapped to his skull as he fielded his one hundredth call of the day—he had lost track, the call sheet stretched for three pages—when he noticed the campaign webmaster standing outside his door, bouncing like an eight-year-old with a full bladder. *What's going on?* Jay wondered. He had deliberately had a window installed on the wall and door of his office overlooking the cubicles where his field staff toiled away so that he could see who was really doing their job and who was just a blowhard who drank coffee and ran their mouth. He also wanted to know who was waiting to see him—and if it was the campaign webmaster, it usually was not good news. He ended his call.

"What is it?" Jay asked.

"We've got a problem with the website," said the webmaster, sweating bullets.

"How can you have a problem? It's the same system we used for the entire campaign."

"It's the volume," the webmaster replied, fingers fidgeting, perspiration beading on his forehead. "It's overwhelming our server capacity. If I don't get a backup server in the next hour, we'll crash. If that happens, we'll be down for hours . . . maybe a day or two."

"What?" shouted Jay. "This is a disaster! How did this happen?"

"Jay, we've had over 9.5 million hits on the website already."

"You've got to be kidding. He only mentioned the website once."

"It wasn't just his mentioning it on television. About half the traffic is coming from links to our website on Merryprankster.com, Drudge, and the news sites. And the blogosphere is running on crack. It's viral."

"So what are they doing—watching the announcement video?"

"No, they're signing up as donors and volunteers. Of the 9.5 million hits, 7.2 million are unique visitors, and we're still tallying numbers, but it looks like over 475,000 of them have signed up as volunteers. We're setting links so they can download state ballot petitions."

"Holy smoke!" shouted Jay, letting out a long whistle. "In five hours? That's unprecedented. We've signed up half as many volunteers in one day as we did during the primaries!" He took some notes on a memo pad on his desk. He did the math quickly—the conversion rate was way above industry standards. "What about the money?"

"Eleven and a half million so far. Because it's on credit cards, it hits the bank today. The average contribution is forty-two dollars. It's pouring in."

"That's the biggest single-day take of the campaign, even more than the day after we won the Iowa caucuses and landed on the cover of *Newsweek*."

"There's more. Bob has received over nine hundred thousand emails. Guess what the number one subject line is?"

"What?" asked Jay.

"Skin in the game."

"Un-be-lievable," said Jay, a look of awe crossing his face. He quickly regained his composure, pointing at the webmaster with the end of his pen. "Listen, you get on the phone right now and find a backup server. Try some of our friends in Silicon Valley who set up the Internet marketing program for the primaries—they'll have excess capacity and they'll let us tap into their T1 lines. Get state petition links for all fifty states up on the website ASAP. Link to secretary of state websites around the country if you have to, just to get through today. And coordinate everything with David Thomas and the field folks."

The webmaster took notes on a legal pad while he nodded affirmatively to each instruction.

"Go! You've got twenty-six minutes to find a backup server! If our server crashes, I'll have your head!"

Jay gazed out the window, watching the cars inching along bumper-to-bumper on 405. He spun in his chair and pulled up the campaign website, just to see for himself what was happening. Clicking on the announcement video with his mouse, the video popped up and froze on the opening frame. The screen flashed a message: "Adjusting for Excess Volume . . . Please Wait."

The Long campaign was sweeping the nation like wildfire. They were going to have the biggest email list and the most extensive netroots organization in history. They were drinking water from a fire hose.

Jay had an inspiration. He opened a Word document and began to peck away on the computer keyboard, composing an email from Long to his supporters. "Dear NAME," the email began (the campaign Web team would personalize it for each supporter). "Today I announced that I am forming an independent campaign committee that will enable me to run for president in the general election. But I can't do it alone. Without your help today, I won't have the funds to wage an effective campaign or qualify for enough state ballots to be a viable candidate. I need you to make your voice heard right now." The email provided links to download a petition and make a contribution. The subject line read: "Skin in the Game."

After he finished his draft, he shot it over to the webmaster with a sharp instruction: "Get this out to the entire campaign email list by COB today. Use an outside vendor if you have to. Make it happen." Jay figured the email might bring in another $2 million, bringing the total to $14 million raised in a single day—with no fund-raising costs. Jay leaned back in his chair and smiled. It was working beyond his wildest dreams.

21

I T WAS 12:30 A.M. and the party was just getting into full swing on South Beach. Over at the Shore Club, waitresses in short black skirts and white tuxedo shirts at Skybar floated by with trays loaded with rainbow-colored cocktails, while a team of bartenders churned out martinis and mojitos. Couples dressed down in designer jeans and black shirts or cocktail dresses—they had shed their suits from the convention's evening session—swung lazily in hammocks or sat at tables nibbling sushi from Nobu, the restaurant. A giant elephant made from red, white, and blue balloons floated in the pool, illuminated by strobe lights that blinked to the beat of club music, while revelers lounged around in clusters on beds and chairs around the pool. Dancers and models in exotic costumes paraded through the crowd—a female twosome dressed as Peter Pan and Tinker Bell, a threesome wearing black and yellow tights with bumble bee wings, a pair of tall redheads wearing playing cards as sandwich boards and six-inch heels—posing for photographs with delegates. For all the talk about the Republicans being the party of Ozzie and Harriet and the biggest squares and killjoys this side of Mayberry, no one could party like pachyderms under a full moon in Miami.

They had plenty to celebrate. The new Gallup poll showed Flaherty's lead over Stanley yawning to fourteen points. The L-word was on everyone's lips—*landslide*. The press, the pollsters, and the pundits all predicted smooth sailing for the Grand Old Party now that Long had jumped in and the Stanley-Hafer ticket had gone into a death dive. This was not a convention; it was a coronation!

The president had kicked off the convention on opening night in style, delivering the valedictory political address of his career. He brought the delegates to their feet with a speech laced with humor and reminiscing, a moving tribute to the first lady, and a stirring defense of his administration's achievements. Then, pivoting like a quarterback in the pocket, he turned his rhetorical fire on the Democrats, hammering them as tax-and-spenders and weak in prosecuting the war on terrorism, all the while lavishing praise on Vice President Flaherty. The delegates cheered themselves hoarse. By tradition the president then exited stage left, so as not to distract attention from his successor. The baton formally passed, Harris Flaherty had been officially nominated for president in an uneventful roll call vote a few hours earlier. Now the convention hall had emptied, creating a traffic jam of cabs and limousines that had turned Collins Avenue into a parking lot, and delegates poured into the hotels and clubs along South Beach, protected from the unwashed by red velvet ropes and security guards wearing black Prada. Everyone was partying like it was 1999.

The Republicans had last come to Miami in 1972 on their way to an earlier landslide. Like a bad '70s sitcom, that convention had featured Sammy Davis, Jr. (looking embarrassingly like the GOP's token African-American), hugging Richard Nixon, Spiro Agnew staring down the "nattering nabobs of negativism" in the left-wing press, and the clean-cut Youth for Nixon contrasting themselves with the hippies and yippies who had nominated George McGovern in the same city. Nixon went on to destroy McGovern in a forty-nine-state landslide. Then followed Watergate, resignation, shame, a crushing congressional defeat in 1974, and the entire party came crashing down. The Republicans had never returned. Now they were back in sunny, sexy Miami with a swagger. They were burying the ghost of Tricky Dick.

Bill Diamond breezed into the pool area like a rock star. As he walked across the patio to wrap an old friend in a bear hug (who was that—was he important?), the crowd parted. Delegates, lobbyists, bundlers, reporters, and elected officials swarmed like groupies, lathering him with compliments, showering him with accolades, telling him how great everything was going. Bill was . . . a genius! He had engineered the fairy-tale rise of Harrison Flaherty, masterminded the selection of David Petty, and had the Democrats so tied up in knots they didn't know up from down. Rumors flew that Bill had even played a role in Bob Long running as an independent, which further divided the Democratic vote. Was it true? No one knew, and no one cared. Bill was the smartest guy in the room—and he was theirs! They peppered him with obsequious questions: Wasn't the president's speech just terrific? (Answer: I've never seen him stronger.) Don't the polls look good? (Yes, but ignore the polls and work harder.) Did he think Petty could help us with black and Hispanic voters? (You bet.) How did he feel? (Great, ninety-eight days to go, we're going to win, now go raise more money!)

The governor of a large battleground state who lusted after a Cabinet post snuggled up to Diamond like a starry-eyed coed, whispering sweet nothings in his ear, one arm wrapped around him as he clawed a platter of snow crab with his free hand. No one could hear what the governor was whispering to Bill over the loud club music, but Bill kept nodding in agreement. The governor was monopolizing him, refusing to share.

A trade group lobbyist decided it was time to break it up. He had paid big money to get into the party and was determined to get his face time with Diamond, if only to recount it later to his clients. Among Republicans in Washington, it had become a common practice to seize control of a conversation by saying in a self-important voice, "I was talking to Bill Diamond the other day, and he said . . ."

"Bill!" shouted the lobbyist over the thumping music. "What do you think will be the impact of Long getting in?"

Diamond stared at him blankly. The music thumped its rhythmic beat. *Doomp-doomp-doomp.*

What was this, he thought, a skull session at a Prince concert? He yearned to say what he was thinking: raise the money and leave the strategy to me, kid. Instead, he graciously endured yet another imposition on his brain power.

"Hard to say because it's so early," he shouted over the *doomp-doomp-doomp* of the music, the veins in his neck showing. "He's polling high now, but historically third-party candidates fade. George Wallace started at twenty-four and fell to thirteen, Perot began at thirty-three and ended at nineteen percent. My guess is Long does the same, but we'll have to see."

The lobbyist nodded. Brilliant! "Will he win evangelical votes?"

"What?" shouted Diamond, the music booming in his ears. *Doomp-doomp-doomp-doomp.*

"Evangelicals! Does he get any votes from the religious right?" *Doomp-doomp-doomp-doomp.*

"No, I don't think so." He thought about it a second. "I sure hope not!" *Doomp-doomp-doomp-doomp.*

The question caused synapses in his brain to fire like spark plugs. His mind raced back to Andy Stanton, who was holed up at a hotel in Bombay, India, threatening to parachute over the Miami convention center and blow up the entire Republican Party. He wondered how Petty's call to Stanton had gone. He made a mental note to follow up.

DAVID PETTY'S SUITE AT the Four Seasons Hotel, in the heart of downtown Miami, had the quiet hush of a royal palace drawing room. With few staff and hangers-on around, David and Ann Petty had all 2,830 square feet of one of the finest suites in the city—with a spectacular view of the Port of Miami, the city skyline, and Biscayne Bay—to themselves. Petty had already done his walk-through at the convention center, playacting as he checked the podium height and teleprompter, reporters gawking and photographers clicking away. He had gone through his speech twice with the writers assigned to him by the campaign. But the speech was completely his. He knew it by heart—he had been giving the same speech for nearly five years, and he was ready.

"General," came the quiet and unobtrusive voice of an aide. "Dr. Andy Stanton is on the line."

Petty paused to collect his thoughts before picking up the phone. "Andy, thank you for calling me back!" he said a little too enthusiastically. "How is India?"

"It's wonderful, Mr. Secretary—"

"Call me David. I resigned as secretary of state, so I'm just a civilian now."

"David, it's fabulous," replied Stanton, starting over. "We're having a glorious visit here. We're doing leadership training with pastors and businessmen and I am speaking to one hundred thousand people tonight in a soccer stadium. I've had terrific meetings with the prime minister and other leaders, as well as some of the opposition parties."

"The prime minister is a good man," said Petty as he tried to figure out how to shift the topic from Andy's Indian adventure to the matter at hand. "Listen, I called because I want to sit down with you as soon as possible." His voice dropped an octave. "I'm sorry we got off on the wrong foot, and I want to set it right."

"I look forward to sitting down. I'll be back from India in three days."

"Good. Harris and I really want your support, Andy. You are one of the most important leaders in the country."

"I want to visit with you, but I also want to be transparent with you because I respect you so much," said Andy, sending a warning flare with a hollow compliment.

"I appreciate that," Petty lied.

"My ministry has a policy that forbids me from endorsing candidates. My board does not allow me to do it. I do speak to the *issues,* however, and when it comes to where you stand on some of those issues, such as human life and the family, I can't really embrace your positions. Unfortunately, I think that is where we find ourselves."

Petty's eyes narrowed as he gazed over the cruise ships in port, the Atlantic Ocean in the distance. *What a coward,* he thought—*hiding behind his board, pretending he was not the one in charge.* He would not give Stanton a platoon to command. He wanted to scream into the phone: *Tell the truth—you won't endorse me because you're afraid you'll be fragged by your followers.* Petty couldn't believe the Republican Party had let self-appointed king-makers like Andy call the shots for years. He was now paying the price for their self-importance, single-issue litmus tests, and insufferable sense of entitlement.

"Andy, you need to keep your ministry first. That's the most important thing, a lot more important than politics," he said through gritted teeth.

"We've gotten a lot of press calls," Andy continued. "I've avoided them by being out of the country, but I'm going to have to say something, so I'm releasing a statement. It is very complimentary, but acknowledges our differences. I hope it doesn't cause any indigestion."

"Thanks for the heads-up," replied Petty, his voice devoid of feeling. What a low blow—releasing a critical statement on the day of his acceptance speech! Stanton was not only a wingnut, he was impolite as well. "You have a role to play and it is different than mine. You're a religious leader. But, Andy, I'm not a pastor—I'm a public servant. It's a different role. I just want us to have a good relationship."

"I would like that as well," said Stanton.

Petty hung up the phone, staring out at the ocean. If Andy Stanton thought he was the Boss Hogg of the Republican Party, then he was about to get a lesson he would not soon forget.

DAN DORMAN HUNCHED OVER his laptop in the *Washington Post*'s cramped quarters in the bowels of the Miami Beach Convention Center. The hair on his balding head was more matted than usual, his glasses lower on the end of his nose. He was perturbed at being forced to toil away like a church mouse in this concrete bunker, far from the glitz and glamour of the convention stage. The pecking order at the GOP convention was clear from the space assigned to news organizations. Fox News, which Dorman derisively called "GOP TV," had the spot not far from the Starbucks. The right-wing bloggers had glass-encased offices with refrigerators stocked with cold drinks. The *New York Times* languished near the bathroom.

Dorman was in a deep funk. He was a *news* man—emphasis on news, not the tabloid trash and ratings-driven drivel that passed for news these days—and this convention was as exciting as watching paint dry. Dorman wanted something *new,* something interesting, something revelatory—and controversial. Where was it?

As he leaned back in his metal chair and took a swig of bad coffee from a Styrofoam cup, his email inbox let out its characteristic "ping." He opened it. To his pleasant surprise, it contained a heads-up from another reporter. It was pure gold.

The subject line read "Statement by Dr. Andrew H. Stanton." Dorman read it avidly:

STATEMENT OF DR. ANDREW H. STANTON

Since the selection of David Petty as the Republican vice presidential nominee, I have been asked for my views. New Life Ministries does not endorse candidates, so my comments are as a private citizen. The protection of innocent human life, sanctity of marriage, and the family are issues that burn in the hearts and give meaning to the souls of millions of Americans. If the Republicans do not speak to these issues with clarity, they cannot win in the November election. David Petty is a war hero and a patriot. However, he has not been clear where he stands on the moral agenda. The Bible teaches that if the bugle gives an indistinct sound, who will respond? If the Republican ticket does not embrace life, marriage, and family, it will not receive the support of people of faith, nor should it.

Dorman's eyes widened over the top of his glasses, taking it all in, including the editorial comment from the colleague who had passed it on: "Jeremiah has spoken! Have fun!" Dorman licked his lips. What a smackdown! He pulled up the Faith and Family Federation website—and there was Stanton's statement for the whole world to see. He wondered how Petty and the Flaherty campaign could have handled Stanton so badly as to cause him to throw this grenade. Inquiring minds wanted to know, and Dorman would find the answer. The Mad Hatter had crashed the tea party—and he was carrying a King James Bible. Dorman picked up the phone to call his first source in the Flaherty campaign. He was off to the races.

———

FOLLOWING THE CURRENT SECOND Lady and soon-to-be First Lady to the podium had not been easy. But as the speech built momentum and picked up thematic speed, David Petty had the crowd eating out of his hand.

"I am the son of immigrants, one of millions who came to America's shores seeking a better life," he said. (This was his rhetorical shot at the "seal the border" xenophobes in the party whom he so despised.) "My father grew up in Africa. My mother was the youngest daughter of a Puerto Rican janitor from Brooklyn, and she was the first member of her family to attend college. She later graduated from Harvard Law School. Imagine that—a Puerto Rican Republican from Harvard!" The hall erupted in delighted laughter.

"But, my friends, our work is not done until we make that dream a reality for every . . . single . . . child . . . in . . . America." (Applause.) "We cannot deny that we once forced children to attend segregated, substandard schools solely because of the color of their skin." The hall grew strangely quiet. "We cannot deny that even the party of Lincoln has not always lived up to its heritage." (Ouch!) "We *can* bring about a new era of opportunity by saying to every American, regardless of their skin color, ethnicity, gender"— applause began to rumble up from the back of the hall—"national origin, and socioeconomic status, that you are welcome in our party, and our vision for America includes you." He held his arms from side to side, then pulled them in dramatically as if to say, *Welcome, welcome.* The delegates cheered wildly. For them, Petty gave the lie to the charge that the Republicans were the party of intolerance. Here was the first African-American (with a Hispanic mother, no less) ever nominated for vice president—and he was theirs!

Petty's blue suit, blue tie, and perfectly combed hair presented a deeply masculine appearance; his gestures projected strength. "I'm an old soldier responding to another call to serve. Tonight, I speak for those who have gone before," he said, the hall falling deathly quiet. "On a thousand battlefields on every continent, rows of crosses and Stars of David give silent testimony to those who paid the ultimate price." No one moved. A solemn stillness came over the delegates. Even the high-dollar crowd in the skyboxes stopped clinking glasses and rattling their jewelry, hanging on Petty's every word. "These patriots gave their lives to defeat evil, liberate millions, and give birth to freedom. All they ever asked for in return . . . was enough ground to bury their dead." The network pool camera zoomed in on a white-haired, prune-faced veteran wearing an American Legion hat, tears streaming down his face. "Let us ensure that they did not die in vain," Petty urged the delegates. "Let us begin this great work together. Let us elect Harris Flaherty as president and keep the promise of America."

The convention director threw up the house lights and ordered the release of balloons from gigantic nets in the rafters, causing a steady stream of balloons to fall on the stage and in the crowd. Petty waved and pointed to friendly faces in the crowd. His wife, Anne, stunning in a double-breasted pink dress with stylish black buttons and fringe, came out to join him onstage, greeted by a huge roar. It was a moment of magical possibility. The Pettys stood gripping hands as the delegates sent up waves of cheers and applause.

Up in the press box, Dan Dorman ignored the cheering. He was busy putting the final touches on his story, which he was confident would land on the front page. He tapped away on his laptop as though calibrating an engine, turning a phrase here, highlighting a quotation there, getting it just right before he turned it over to the editors in Washington. He smiled as he read the lede:

> *Before former Secretary of State David Petty mounted the po-*
> *dium to accept the Republican nomination for vice president last*

night, the Flaherty campaign absorbed a blistering attack on the Republican ticket that revealed fierce warfare and deep divisions in the party. Even more troubling, according to Republican strategists who spoke on condition of anonymity because they did not wish to offend the Flaherty campaign, the attack came from one of the most popular evangelical leaders in the nation, Dr. Andrew H. Stanton.

Satisfied, Dorman hit the send button.

———

THE CITY THAT THE Republicans had returned to bore no resemblance to the one they'd left behind decades before. The Las Vegas–style shows that had once played at the Fontainebleau had been replaced by the art deco revival symbolized by the Delano, the Shore Club, and the Raleigh. Restaurants that once held tables for Frank Sinatra and the Rat Pack had given way to Opium and the Mansion, clubs that specialized in catering to the decadent desires of rappers, professional athletes, celebrities, and party girls. In these dark fleshpots of South Beach, the music was deafening, everyone was thin and beautiful, and the martinis cost thirty bucks a pop.

When the Republicans rolled into town for their convention, it portended a culture clash not unlike the Southern Baptist Convention showing up in New Orleans for Mardi Gras. Red-state America had invaded one of the bluest enclaves in the country. The locals cringed while the GOP wondered if it could handle the chest hair and gold chains. But the Republicans wanted Florida's electoral votes, and once there, they adapted to their new surroundings—sleeping late, lounging by the pool, and clubbing until dawn. They were winning—and hey, this was real fun!

In the VIP suite at Nikki Beach, at Ocean Drive and First Street, a different kind of party unfolded. For $7,500, a party of men of Arab descent had reserved the most expensive table in the club. The manager noticed happily that they were spending a small fortune on champagne, caviar, sushi, and vodka. The leader of the group was passing around hundred-dollar tips. The VIP suite had plush couches, its own bartender and waitress, a fully stocked refrigerator, and a balcony overlooking the dance floor. One of the men raised his glass and proposed a toast. Two beefy security guards with earpieces and arms the size of tree trunks guarded the suite, shooting dirty looks at anyone who tried to get too close. This was a private party.

"Gentlemen, tonight is a night that we will remember forever," said Rassem el Zafarshan. "And it will also be remembered by hundreds of millions of people around the world, for all of eternity. To bravery, courage, and immortality!"

"Yes! Yes!" they cheered as they banged glasses.

"Soon we will all be in paradise. We are brothers forever!"

"Yes! Yes!"

Four high-priced call girls joined the fun. They moved from couch to couch, dancing with the men, downing shots and showing off their wares. Their low-cut blouses, tight jeans, and stiletto heels left little to the imagination. Zafarshan had paid each of them two thousand dollars, a price that included "anything goes." At 1:30 A.M. one of the girls stood on a table and began to slowly gyrate to the music, unbuttoning her blouse as she swayed. Zafarshan looked at the bartender, who just winked.

When the club began to slow down around 4 A.M., the party loaded into a double stretch Hummer limo. Zafarshan ordered the driver to cruise down Collins Avenue and look for more action. The bar was stocked with booze, a refrigerator filled with champagne and beer, mirrors on the ceiling, a stereo blaring rap music, and mood track lights that changed from maroon to green to yellow. One of the girls brandished a bottle of champagne and stood on her seat, her head sticking out the sunroof, and jokingly propositioned Republican delegates straggling back to their hotels.

Zafarshan had seen enough—it was time to call it a night. The last thing he needed was the cops pulling them over, asking a bunch of questions and requesting IDs. It could blow the operation. He tapped on the smoked window separating the driver's seat from the back of the limousine. The driver lowered the window.

"Yes, sir?"

"Take us home," said Zafarshan. "Now." He would take the girls and his men back to the condominium where they could finish the party without drawing attention.

Through the fog of a night of alcohol, he felt a twinge of adrenaline. They were twenty-eight hours away from participating in one of the most spectacular acts of religious martyrdom in history.

———

"FLAHER-TY! FLAHER-TY! FLAHER-TY!" THE CROWD'S chant echoed off the
rafters, ricocheted off the walls, and threatened to raise the roof of the Miami
Beach Convention Center. It was the final night of the convention, and the
climax had arrived. Vice President Flaherty was formally accepting his party's
presidential nomination, and he was hitting it out of the park.

"My friends," he continued, waiting for the applause to die. "My friends,"
he tried again. He finally gave up and spoke through the applause, hoping
that would shut them up. "My friends, don't let the rhetoric from the other
party fool you. The last time the other party was in charge, we inherited an
economy in the ditch, with high inflation and unemployment—at the same
time. Today inflation is under control, interest rates are low, and we have created over ten million jobs in the last six years." The crowd applauded. Horns
blew. "Don't think it happened automatically. It happened because we cut
taxes, tightened our belt, and kept spending under control. And as president, I'll control spending even better if I have the line-item veto, and I intend to fight for it." More cheers.

"No issue is more important to the American people than protecting the
homeland and securing the peace," he continued, going for the weak underbelly of the Democrats. "You heard the president say the other night that as
long as we're in charge, we will not tolerate a radical regime that sponsors terrorism armed with nuclear weapons." It was a clear reference to Iran, and it
generated loud applause. "History teaches that strength repels aggression
while weakness invites it. As president, I will use military force only as a last
resort. But let me be clear. On my watch, I will not allow state sponsors of
terrorism to intimidate the world with the most dangerous weapons known
to man . . . not now . . . not ever." The hall erupted. "And with David Petty
as vice president, I will have a man at my side who has been on the front lines
of the war on terror as the general commanding coalition forces in Iraq and
as secretary of state." He skipped a beat. "And David Petty *knows* our policy
toward Iran . . . he helped develop it." The delegates laughed uproariously,

turning to one another with wide eyes, enjoying the joke at the expense of the hapless Betsy Hafer.

"For seven and a half years, it has been my privilege to serve at the side of a great president. I know the awesome responsibility, the unspoken burden, the life-and-death decisions, and the quiet compassion that this office requires of its occupants. Tonight, I stand before you ready to hold that office. I ask for your vote, for your support, and for your prayers. Thank you, and God bless you all."

"Flaher-ty! Flaher-ty! Flaher-ty!"

The technicians backstage electronically lowered the podium into the floor so Flaherty could stand in the center, the sight lines of the delegates unbroken. As the balloon drop began and the confetti fell, Flaherty was joined first by the second lady, then by David and Anne Petty, then a parade of children, sons- and daughters-in-law, and grandchildren. On cue, Flaherty picked up one of his adorable granddaughters, a four-year-old blond beauty, and hoisted her into his arms, waving to the crowd with her and pulling her tight to his chest. The convention center rocked. The Republican consultants, pollsters, and strategists stared down from the skyboxes and saw victory in the person of Harrison Flaherty. They could hardly wait until the next Gallup poll. Some wondered: was it too early to book rooms in D.C. for the inaugural?

Flaherty stepped gingerly through the balloons, gently kicking a few aside with a black wingtip, heading for a stairwell behind the stage. A bulletproof limousine waited to drive him across the parking lot to Marine Two, which would fly him back to the Ritz on Key Biscayne for the night. He caught sight of Bill Diamond standing in the semidarkness, arms folded across his chest. He waved him to his side and they clambered down the stairs to the parking lot, followed by Secret Service agents.

"How did I do?" he asked, smiling as if he already knew the answer.

"Home run, sir," Diamond replied.

"It felt good out there."

"You hit all the notes, Mr. Vice President. The networks are saying it's the best speech you've ever given." Flaherty moved down the steps at an aggressive clip. Bill tried to keep up, careful not to trip.

"Now all we have to do is make sure Long stays in," joked Flaherty.

"We'll fund him ourselves if we have to," Diamond replied with a chuckle.

At the bottom of the stairwell, a Secret Service agent held the door open, the vice presidential limousine steps away.

"See you bright and early," said Flaherty.

"Yes, sir, wheels up at eight A.M. See you on the plane. Good night, sir." Flaherty nodded and turned toward the limo. "And sir?" The veep wheeled, his adrenaline still flowing. Their eyes locked. "Congratulations."

"Thanks," Flaherty said. "You've done a very impressive job, Bill. After November, I want you to keep your dance card open."

Flaherty stepped into the limo along with the second lady and other family members, including the blond granddaughter, and headed across the parking lot. A Marine guard in full-dress uniform stood in front of a red carpet leading to Marine Two. Diamond watched as the limo pulled up to the helicopter, as the vice presidential party boarded, and as the helicopter took off and headed into the night, the white taillight blinking in the dark. His thoughts rushed ahead to Labor Day, the debates, the homestretch, and finally, victory. *That man is going to be president of the United States,* he thought, *and I'm going to be his White House chief of staff.*

PART II
THE GENERAL ELECTION

22

Harris Flaherty walked through the bright and cheery presidential suite of the Key Biscayne Ritz-Carlton, its beige carpet and yellow paint reflecting his own upbeat mood. The night before couldn't have gone better, he thought as he checked the knot in his tie in the dining room mirror, and today was the first day of the general election campaign, with ninety-six days to Election Day. He took one last look at the panoramic view of the Atlantic offered by the large windows trimmed with tropical floral curtains. He walked through the door and stepped onto the elevator, accompanied by the secondlady and a travel aide. Racing up to the roof and the helipad—an elevator carrying the vice president never stopped at other floors—to a cordoned-off storage area, they suddenly stopped when an advance man held up his palm.

"What is it?" asked the second lady.

"They think they saw something moving in the woods. We have to hold here while they check it out," replied the travel aide. Flaherty looked at his watch. It was 7:27 A.M. They were scheduled to be wheels up on Air Force Two in thirty-three minutes.

After a minute or two, whatever the Secret Service thought they had seen among the lushly landscaped foliage, trees, and flowers on the forty-four-acre grounds of the resort had been determined to be safe to their satisfaction.

"Eagle is on the move," said the lead agent into his sleeve as the door opened, using Flaherty's Secret Service code name.

In the security office at the Four Seasons, the lead Secret Service agent had made a command decision. There was no reason to drive across the Rickenbacker Causeway to Key Biscayne just to load David and Anne Petty onto Marine Two and fly to Miami International. The airport was five minutes from the hotel. There would be no press, no crowd, and no reason to retrace in the air what they had just covered on the ground. Petty's lead advance man pitched a fit—he wanted Petty on the helicopter because it signified his boss's importance. But the Secret Service pulled rank. Vice presidential advance was notified that Petty would travel to Miami International via motorcade and would meet the vice president there.

Stepping off the elevator, David and Anne Petty greeted the hotel employees that lined the short hallway from the elevator to the garage with enthusiastic hand pumps, high-fives, and witty asides. Even though it was only 7:31 A.M., they both looked like they had just stepped out of a catalog. He wore a custom-tailored brown suit with red patterned tie, she wore a yellow pantsuit. Petty signed autographs for employees who gathered in the parking garage. As they prepared to slide into the backseat of the Lincoln Town Car with smoked windows, Petty turned on his heel, leaned back toward the employees, and pointed at them with his index finger.

"Don't forget to vote!" he joked. They all laughed, assuring him they would.

With a Miami-Dade police escort leading the way, the motorcade pulled out of the garage and onto Brickell Avenue, and picked up speed as it moved North to I-95. A small crowd of supporters, mostly delegates who had not slept the previous night, lined the road, waving and cheering.

"Wasn't that nice of them to get up this early to see us off?" said Anne. "Who says the party doesn't love you? Just look at them!"

———

IN A STARBUCKS JUST off Brickell Avenue, two Arab men sat alone at a table sipping espresso. As the motorcade passed, one glanced at his watch: 7:32 A.M. He flipped open his cell phone and dialed a number. "The package is moving," he said, and hung up. They got up from the table, leaving their espresso, and left.

The woman at the cash register watched them depart, thinking it odd that they had left after barely drinking their coffee. She could not recall having seen them in the store before.

———

FLAHERTY, HIS WIFE, AND the travel aide moved briskly across the roof, flanked by two Secret Service agents wearing sunglasses, their heads on swivels and eyes like lasers. A soft morning wind blew and the sun was already above the horizon, its glow reflecting from the ocean. Four U.S. Army sharpshooters peered down from each corner of the roof, rifles poised. Flaherty walked the short distance to Marine Two, the official designation given to any helicopter carrying the vice president, and snapped a quick salute to the U.S. Marine guard standing at attention in his blue dress uniform. Flaherty strode across the red carpet, pulled his body up the stairs on the handrails, his wife and travel aide trailing behind him, and slid into the cabin. Settling into the spacious leather seat reserved for him, he grabbed copies of the *Miami Herald* and *New York Times* from the stack of newspapers on the jump seat across from him and fastened his seat belt.

The door secure, the red carpet rolled up and taken away, the pilot started Marine Two's engines and the rotor blades of the helicopter began to turn— slowly at first, then accelerating. The helicopter's tires lifted off the roof and drifted slightly to the right in the wind, and then the helicopter shot upward over the swaying palm trees. Two identically marked forest-green and white helicopters serving as decoys flew in from the east and west. The three aircraft moved in formation, weaving in and out to fool any would-be assassins on the ground. Among the pilots in the Marine Corps' elite HMX-1 "Nighthawks" squadron, based in Quantico, Virginia, with eight hundred Marines supervising all presidential and vice presidential helicopter travel, this was referred to as the "shell game" maneuver.

As the pilot surveyed the scene through the windshield, he guided the chopper with his right hand and slowly turned toward Biscayne Bay. He could see the green foliage and bunker-studded golf courses on Key Biscayne, the Rickenbacker Causeway, the bay, and beyond it Miami International Airport, where the secure package would shortly board Air Force Two. Marine Two was moving at 110 knots an hour. They would be at their destination in seven minutes.

Harris Flaherty scanned the front pages of the newspapers. He passed a copy of the *Herald* to the second lady. She read the headline and smiled, and he squeezed her hand. As the helicopter sped along, he glanced out the window. Cars and people moved like Tonka toys and ants from his bird's-eye view. The glistening water of Biscayne Bay raced by, an occasional boat bobbing in the waves. He drank in the view.

Marine Two was not a lone bird over Miami that August morning. Flying above was a squadron of F-22 Raptors, each armed with GPS-guided munitions and air-to-surface missiles. They patrolled a fighter jet cap maintained by the Federal Aviation Administration for a distance of eighteen miles, up to 30,000 feet. No aircraft was allowed to enter this zone. The FAA maintained a second safe zone for an additional ten miles. An AWACS plane flew at an altitude of 42,000 feet, boasting the most sophisticated air-to-air and air-to-ground radar system in the world. With the ability to detect automobiles moving on local roads, its job was to signal the F-22 pilots, the helicopter pilots, the U.S. Army sharpshooters, the Coast Guard cutters and speedboats patrolling the bay, and the Navy SEAL divers in position in the water.

As Marine Two's pilots steered in a westerly direction toward the airport at an altitude of 2,100 feet, an eight-knot wind at their back, they were operating within the strictest set of security protocols in U.S. history. Most had been put in place after the attacks of September 11, 2001, and had successfully protected the president and vice president ever since. Until this morning, they had never failed.

———

RASSEM EL ZAFARSHAN STOOD motionless on the balcony of apartment 2702 of Bristol Tower, waiting for the chopper to get within five hundred yards of the causeway. His heart pounded. In the distance, a white van moved east on the causeway, then slowed and pulled onto the shoulder. It was going to be glorious, Zafarshan thought.

He took a deep breath and exhaled. His right eye closed as he peered through the scope with his left. The helicopter, silhouetted against the sun, seemed to hang in the air. Zafarshan held his breath and pulled his index finger forward on the trigger of the shoulder-fired SA-88 missile launcher.

"All glory to Allah," he whispered.

He felt a strong kick from the launcher as it fired. The missile rocketed across the bay, leaving a trail of white smoke.

A woman taking her morning jog along the sidewalk abutting the water heard a muffled explosion and loud hissing sound. She looked up, instinc tively ducking, as the missile passed directly over her. She would later tell everyone that she knew right away that something was terribly wrong.

———

IN THE VAN, THE driver kept his gaze fixed on Bristol Tower. The crew in the back saw the flash, then the trail of white smoke. This was their signal. They scrambled out of the van.

"Go! Go! Go!" shouted the driver.

The men brandished AK-47 automatic rifles, barrels held up in the air. The strict orders from Zafarshan were to hold their fire until the first missile had reached the target.

———

THE LEAD PILOT IN Marine Two saw the missile immediately. The telltale flame flashed at one o'clock. Simultaneously, the helicopter's early warning system blared deafeningly. The alarm alerted the pilot to fire the flares and release the chaff that would throw off the incoming missile.

"What happened?" asked the second pilot, confused. He had not yet seen the missile.

"Incoming!" the lead pilot shouted.

The vice president heard the early warning alarm and looked up from his newspaper, heart suddenly pounding.

The pilot pushed the button to release the decoy flares. He pulled the helicopter into a sharp evasive maneuver. The missile screamed into one of the flares and exploded, the concussion shaking the cabin, its blinding white flash causing the passengers to jump in their seats. Panic filled the cabin.

"Everyone down!" yelled the Secret Service agent from the jump seat as he came across the aisle, using his body to cover the vice president. "Lean forward and put your hands over your head!"

———

A FIBERGLASS PLEASURE BOAT swayed in the waves beneath the causeway, hidden from view. As the first missile exploded, it accelerated into the morning sunlight. What happened next seemed to occur in slow motion. A member of Zafarshan's team balanced himself against the side of the boat, turning his missile launcher toward the sky. He saw the helicopter bobbing and weaving in front of him and fired at close range, sending a missile toward the fuselage with a low whining sound.

The pilot pulled the stick hard to his left to avoid the second missile. But it was not a heat-seeking missile, so the helicopter's decoy flares provided no protection. The missile screamed through the front rotor blades, clipping off the end of one of them. Amazingly, it did no additional damage.

"We've got major incoming!" shouted the pilot. "I need air support . . . Stat!"

"Roger that!" replied the lead F-22 pilot ten thousand feet above him. He pushed forward on his joystick and went into a straight dive, hurtling toward Marine Two at 400 miles per hour. The rest of the squadron roared in behind him. They would be on top of the causeway in less than a minute.

Small-arms fire unleashed by AK-47-wielding assassins on the causeway peppered the side of the helicopter with a sickening sound. The second pilot slumped forward, bullets lodged in his chest and stomach. He glanced down to see a pool of blood forming on his flight suit and went into shock.

A second missile fired from the deck of the boat scored a direct hit on the helicopter's rear fuselage. The explosion rocked the cabin, eliciting screams from the passengers. The missile blew apart the rear rotor casing. The chopper vibrated uncontrollably, then began to spin slowly.

The second lady screamed. The vice president grabbed her hand tightly, and she looked at him with panic in her eyes. The travel aide went white and looked like he was going to get sick. He doubled over with his head between his legs.

The pilot of Marine Two had veered the craft away from the direction of the first missile, but it put him directly over the causeway, where the second team of assassins awaited. They popped clips into their AK-47s and blazed away at the wounded vice presidential helicopter. The six gunmen had already emptied two clips apiece into the fuselage of the chopper—a total of twelve hundred rounds of ammunition at close range. Their accuracy came from similar missions against U.S. Army helicopters along the Iran-Iraq border. Now the war had come to U.S. soil.

Cars began to slow on the Rickenbacker Causeway. Some passengers got out of their cars to watch in horror. A toll booth operator at the intersection with I-95, hearing the first explosion, whipped around just as the third missile slammed into the helicopter, sending it twisting in the air. She later recalled thinking that the aircraft was going to crash on the causeway. She had no idea it carried the vice president of the United States.

A rocket-propelled grenade smacked into the cockpit and exploded with a loud bang. Bullets bounced off the fuselage with a *ping-ping*. Marine Two was a sitting duck.

THE PILOT IN THE lead F-22 Raptor surveyed the GPS display in his flight helmet to see where the fire was coming from. Seeing flashes on the radar, he locked the target and prepared to launch one of his missiles. He placed his thumb on the red button. Given the plane's stealth construction and his high rate of speed, nothing on the ground would pose a threat.

Just as the F-22 pilot was about to fire, one of the decoy helicopters swung in from the left and fired an air-to-surface missile at the pleasure boat, blowing it to pieces. Its hull exploded in a giant plume of burning gasoline, orange flames, and black smoke. As he flew over the top of the burning wreckage, he could make out several bodies floating in the waves, one of which appeared to be with its arms. He sprayed the water with machine-gun fire, instantly killing them all.

"I got the boat!" he shouted into his radio. "I think I got them all!"

Marine Two trailed black smoke and spun wildly as it fell out of the sky, its nose pointing toward the water.

"Marine Two going down!" shouted the lead pilot. "I repeat, we are going down!"

He pressed the button to deploy the inflatable airbags. He knew the amphibious hull of the EH-101 helicopter could float for up to ten minutes if he could land it on the water properly. But the aircraft was crippled, impossible to control. He fought to keep it from flipping over. As it crashed onto the causeway, a burst of machine-gun fire sprayed its side, and the vice president slumped across the second lady's lap.

The second lady let out a bloodcurdling shriek.

The tail broke off at impact as the helicopter skidded, throwing up sparks and smashing into a sedan. The rotor blades spun into the concrete, snapping off as they turned. Then the hull slid over the rail and plunged nosefirst into Biscayne Bay.

"Eagle down!" shouted one of the decoy pilots as he hovered over the wreckage. "I repeat, Eagle is down!"

DAVID PETTY'S MOTORCADE TURNED slowly onto Eighth Street, accelerating as it headed toward Interstate 95 en route to Miami International Airport. Squad cars from the Florida Highway Patrol and Miami-Dade Police Department blocked traffic coming from each direction. Relying heavily on limited access roads, the Secret Service ensured that the motorcade would have minimal contact with other vehicles. In addition, roadblocks at key intersections prevented rush hour traffic from entering the route of the motorcade, though traffic was allowed to move in the opposite direction.

Two Florida Highway Patrol officers supervising the roadblock on the southbound exit ramp to Dolphin Expressway from I-95 both saw a white van slow to a stop at the top of the cloverleaf. It sat there for a full minute. They glanced at each other. "We have a white van that has come to a stop on 395 East at the cloverleaf. It is in full view of the secure package. I repeat: it is in full view of the secure package," barked one of the state patrol officers. "We need a unit up there pronto to check it out."

"Roger that," said dispatch. A state patrol car carrying two officers shot up the ramp and pulled behind the van, blue lights flashing. The officer riding shotgun tapped the van's license number into an onboard computer and learned only that it was a rental vehicle. The motorcade was minutes away. They had to move fast. They stepped out of the patrol car and walked toward the driver's side of the van.

Two men jumped from the rear of the van firing Glock pistols. One officer was killed instantly. The other pulled his .38 police revolver from his holster and got off four quick shots, killing one of the two assailants before taking a fatal shot to the chest. The shots could be heard over the radio.

"Officers down!"

The Secret Service agent in David Petty's motorcade heard the radio traffic. Someone was shooting at police officers on the causeway. He turned to the driver.

"Turn around and go back to the hotel!" he shouted to the driver.

As the driver whipped the limousine around in the middle of the empty highway, a rocket-propelled grenade exploded just ten feet away. Machine-gun fire bounced off the bulletproof exterior of the car with a terrifying *thud-thud-thud*.

"Floor it!" screamed the Secret Service agent.

David Petty grabbed Anne and shoved her to the floorboard, diving over the top of her. Her muffled sobs could be heard over the squeal of the tires.

"What in God's name is going on?" he shouted.

"We're under fire! Everyone stay down!" ordered the agent.

———

FROM THE ROOFTOP OF University of Miami Hospital, an FBI sniper fired on the white van, aiming for several men in white painter's overalls holding AK-47 machine guns and a rocket-propelled grenade launcher. His first shot entered the side of the van. Holding his scope steady, he pulled the trigger again and saw one of the men hit the deck, the top of his skull blown off. *Got one*, he thought.

He was about to get off a third shot when an F-22 came screaming overhead, rattling windows and causing people in the parking lot below to scramble for cover. An air-to-surface missile spat forth from the fighter jet in a reddish glow. It whistled toward the cloverleaf and slammed into the van, blowing it into the air in a fiery explosion. The sniper, his trained eye peering through the scope, looked to see if anyone was still standing. All he could see was the flame of burning gasoline and black smoke rising from the charred remains of the van.

Two more Florida patrol cars and a SWAT team in a police van came squealing onto the scene, their burning tires leaving a trail of blue smoke. Black-uniformed, blue-helmeted SWAT team members jumped out, shot-guns and high-powered rifles drawn. One of them glanced over the barricade and saw that one of the terrorists had been blown over the side by the blast of the missile. His clothes on fire, his crumpled body lay on the pavement.

———

BACK IN THE CAR carrying the Republican vice presidential nominee and his wife, David Petty could distinctly hear shouted orders crackling over the lead Secret Service agent's walkie-talkie.

"Eagle down!" a disembodied voice shouted over the walkie-talkie.

Anne looked into his eyes. They both knew what it meant.

———

ZAFARSHAN PLACED THE SHOULDER-FIRED missile casing on the floor of the balcony and dashed into the condominium, gathering up his things. From a distance, he had seen the explosion from the second unguided missile. Planned redundancy had been critical, with multiple missiles fired from different lines of fire, supported by small arms. As expected, the helicopter's early warning and defensive systems had stopped the first missile. He hoped that the team on the bridge had finished the job, but he had no time to find out. He exited the apartment, locked the door, and stepped onto the service elevator. He rode down to the pool area on the third level, left the building by a back door, and walked across the patio to a fire escape stairwell, by which he descended to the street below. A blue Ford Taurus, its nervous driver glancing around for any sign of police, waited on the curb.

Zafarshan, wearing jeans, brown Puma shoes, and a black T-shirt, climbed into the car and lay down on the backseat. The driver pulled away, turned right on Brickell Avenue, and headed north toward I-95.

"Turn on the radio," Zafarshan ordered. "I want to hear it."

As they reached the intersection of Biscayne Boulevard and I-95, they saw several police cars coming the other way at top speed, their blue lights flashing and sirens screaming.

———

"MR. PRESIDENT, SOMETHING'S HAPPENED," said the Secret Service agent.

"What is it?"

"I don't know, sir. But Mr. Syms needs to see you right away."

The president jogged up the path from Laurel Cabin to find Sam Syms talking on his cell phone.

"Sam, what's up?" asked the president.

"There's been a terrorist attack on Marine Two, Mr. President. The vice president was on board. There were shoulder-fired missiles, small arms, multiple shooters."

"Good Lord!" the president exclaimed. "Is Harris all right?"

"We don't know, sir. The helicopter went down. David might have been on board as well."

"Dear God." Shock crossed the president's face as he absorbed the news. He stood motionless, collecting his thoughts as to what his next steps should be. "Get the director of national intelligence on the phone. You realize what this means."

"What?"

"We're at war," said the president.

"With whom?" asked Syms.

"I don't know yet," replied the president. "But I will soon enough. If I had to guess, it would be Iran."

———

A MOB OF MEDIA gathered outside the emergency room at Jackson Memorial Hospital, seeking information from anyone who passed by. The hospital spokesperson had proven to be no use at all, overwhelmed at being thrust into the national spotlight in the midst of an assassination attempt on the vice president. An ambulance had transported the vice president and Mrs. Flaherty to the hospital after an amphibious rescue by the Coast Guard. News crews monitoring police radio traffic rushed to the hospital. Pandemonium reigned. Rumors flew—David Petty had been on board the helicopter, several crew members were dead, the vice president had been rescued, al Qaeda had already taken credit for the attack in a statement posted on an Arabic website. No one could separate fact from fiction.

The attack had occurred just as the morning news shows were coming on the air, and the shocking news filled every channel. Nothing was known about the identity of the assassins. Were they terrorists? The picture of Marine Two floating in the shallow water of Biscayne Bay was on every television screen.

At 8:45 A.M., Vice President Flaherty's press secretary stepped to a podium in the jammed auditorium at Jackson Memorial. It had been an hour and fifteen minutes since the attack. Three hundred reporters awaited the statement with a mixture of anticipation and dread. The spokesperson walked to the lectern, unfolded a piece of paper, and began to read.

"At approximately 7:30 A.M., the helicopter carrying Vice President and Mrs. Flaherty to Miami International Airport was deliberately attacked by terrorists. Vice President and Mrs. Flaherty were brought here to Jackson Memorial Hospital, where a team of doctors treated them. Mrs. Flaherty suffered serious injuries and is now in surgery. After valiant efforts to revive him, the vice president"—his voice cracked—"was pronounced dead at 8:23 A.M., Eastern Standard Time." The press secretary paused, his hands gripping the podium, his eyes filling with tears, voice shaking. He stopped to regain his composure, licking and biting his quivering lower lip. "Ladies and gentlemen, Vice President Flaherty is dead." He began to break down. "That is all."

Reporters bolted for the door to file their stories. A sitting vice president was dead, the United States was undoubtedly at war, and the presidential election had been thrown into chaos with only ninety-six days left before Election Day.

23

THE BODY OF VICE President Harrison Flaherty lay in state in the Capitol Rotunda beginning on Saturday evening, his coffin draped with an American flag and resting on the black velvet catafalque that had once borne the body of Abraham Lincoln and on which later rested the remains of John F. Kennedy and Ronald Reagan. A shocked nation absorbed the macabre scenes on television: the battered hull of Marine Two floating in the turquoise water of Biscayne Bay, the black scar left on a causeway by a missile that had destroyed a van loaded with terrorists, the body of their assassinated vice president lying in state. An estimated one hundred thousand spectators waited patiently at the Capitol in a line that stretched for six blocks, some for as long as eight hours, to walk solemnly past the vice president's body and pay their last respects.

The state funeral brought the nation to a halt. Foreign heads of state, presidents, prime ministers, dignitaries, members of Congress, ambassadors, leaders in business, and captains of industry traveled from all over the world to gather at the National Cathedral for a ceremony that featured Bible readings, hymns, poems, and a eulogy by the president. Among those in attendance were the prime ministers of Great Britain and Japan, the presidents of Iraq and Afghanistan, and the king of Spain. The nation combined collective mourning with a grim determination to strike back at those responsible for Flaherty's murder. The vice president's body was carried with full military honors from the Capitol to the cathedral on a caisson drawn by eight gray horses, accompanied by a Marine drums corps and the traditional black riderless horse with the boots turned backward in the stirrups. The police estimated the crowd along the parade route at a half million people. The roll of muffled drums and the clopping of horses' hooves broke the eerie silence.

Tight security befit a nation at war. U.S. Army assault helicopters buzzed overhead and fighter jets streaked across the sky. Snipers stared down from the spires of the cathedral and surrounding buildings. Ten thousand troops descended on Washington, guarding intersections, patrolling Metro stations, strolling through the streets with machine guns, and blocking roads with tanks and machine-gun nests. America resembled a third-world country on war footing.

Four thousand mourners filled the sanctuary, including the president and first lady, four former presidents and their wives, and the Supreme Court. Dr. Andy Stanton sat in a prominent location after flying through the night from India. In an awkward display of nonpartisan seating, Sal Stanley and Bob Long sat with their wives no more than ten feet apart. They avoided eye contact and exchanged no small talk.

The president eulogized his late protégé by recalling his loyalty, decency, and visionary commitment to freedom. "Harris Flaherty was a man who saw public service as a higher calling, not merely holding office," he said. "That is why he sought to bring freedom to those who had only known tyranny, healing to those plagued by sickness and death, prosperity to those who suffered in poverty, and understanding to those who had known only hatred and division." As sobs filled the sanctuary and mourners wiped tears with handkerchiefs, the president nearly lost his composure. But, his voice firm, he vowed: "We commend him to the ages, and we will honor his memory by finishing the fight for freedom for which he gave his life."

AT 7:30 A.M. THE president sat down in the leather chair at the head of the table in the Situation Room. He called the meeting of his war cabinet to order and wasted no time getting down to business. "Okay, what have we got?"

Seated around the oblong table were Secretary of Defense Douglas Parks, the interim secretary of state, the national security advisor, attorney general, director of national intelligence, the directors of the FBI and CIA, the chairman of the Joint Chiefs, and Sam Syms, White House chief of staff. Other staff members sat against the wall, legal pads ready, preparing to take notes and record directives.

Hal Sikorski, director of the FBI, spoke first. A former cop who grew up on the hardscrabble streets of the south side of Chicago, he earned his law degree at night and later became a prosecutor and a federal judge. Sikorski's background caused him to view the world in Manichaean terms: black and white, good and evil.

"We believe the leader of the terrorist cell is an Iranian by the name of

Rassem el Zafarshan," Sikorski said as an overhead projector flashed a photograph of Zafarshan on a screen. "During the height of sectarian violence in Iraq, Zafarshan was a major arms supplier of a breakaway Iranian-supported Shiite militia called Abu Walid. The militia operated in Baqouba, the provincial capital of Diyala province, northeast of Baghdad. Like a lot of foreign fighters, once the surge turned the tide in our favor in the capital, he disappeared into thin air. We believe he returned to Tehran."

"How did he get into the U.S.?"

"We don't know. Based on our review of immigration and customs databases, it wasn't legally. He probably came in surreptitiously, perhaps across the Mexican border, but we don't know for certain." Sikorski frowned. "We're flying blind."

"What about his crew?"

"So far, we know of eighteen terrorists. Four were on the Rickenbacker Causeway," said Sikorski, as a diagram of the scene of the terrorist attack appeared on the overhead projector. "Six more on the boat—this is the crew that fired the fatal missile." He took a red laser and pointed at the spot on the diagram. "Four more in the crew that fired on David Petty's motorcade. These crews were all eliminated." He looked around the room. "We have one of the terrorists in custody. He is being interrogated now."

"I trust you are utilizing enhanced interrogation techniques."

"Yes, Mr. President. We'll break him." The FBI director continued with the briefing. "Two spotters were seen at a Starbucks here"—he pointed again to a location on the diagram near the Four Seasons—"and they reported the departing of the Petty motorcade. An employee at Starbucks saw them. We have traced their cell phones, and their call corresponds to the attack. We'll get them soon. Those two, plus Zafarshan and we believe an associate, are still on the loose."

"Find Zafarshan. He's the key to finding out who was behind this," ordered the president, tapping the table.

"We will, Mr. President," replied Sikorski.

The president turned to the director of national intelligence, Admiral David Dickerson. "David, what do we know about who might have hired and funded Zafarshan and his team?"

Dickerson was a ring-knocker who graduated in 1987 at the top of his class at Annapolis, a former navy fighter pilot who later became a naval intelligence officer and then chief of naval operations. He was a no-nonsense manager with little use for the bureaucratic niceties and watered-down consensus of the intelligence community—which was why the president liked him.

"Mr. President, this was a cash operation, and a large one," Dickerson reported. "Zafarshan bought the condominium he used as the base of the operation for $850,000. The boat was purchased in the Bahamas. The SA-88 missiles were Russian made. They probably came from Iran but could have been purchased on the black market. The going price for their supply is $120,000 per missile. So we're looking at a total of $2 million or more. By comparison, the entire amount expended by the terrorists in the planning and execution of the attacks of September 11 was $250,000. Sir, this operation had a major financial sponsor."

"Who? Iran? Syria? Al Qaeda?"

"Some of the bills have been traced to a bank in Caracas," Dickerson replied.

"So you're telling me that we do not know who was behind it?"

"That's correct, sir. If it was Iran, they don't want to be the next Afghanistan. They covered their tracks."

"Why didn't they target me?" asked the president.

"You're gone in five months," answered Sikorski. "Their target was the next administration. They thought Petty would be in Marine Two with the vice president—and he was supposed to be." He made a chopping motion with his hand, as if waving an imaginary machete. "Had Petty been on that chopper, he'd be dead. They would have crippled the government and thrown the election into chaos."

The full weight of Dickerson's observation sunk in around the table. It was hard to believe that a last-minute change by an unknowing Secret Service agent had spared Petty's life.

"Doug, what do you think?" asked the president.

"Mr. President, given Iran's nuclear ambitions and their support to terrorist organizations like Hamas and Hezbollah, I have my suspicions," said Secretary of Defense Parks, his face hardened like flint, his eyes a steely blue. "The militia that Zafarshan supplied in Iraq was the armed wing of an Iranian-backed Shiite radical organization. That is a direct tie to Tehran."

The president nodded.

"We cannot take military action against Iran without proof. We do have contingency plans, obviously. Mr. President, the options give you a great deal of latitude: air strikes on purely military targets, moving carrier groups, positioning more ground forces near the Iran-Iraq border. And we also have the option of providing logistical support to an indigenous fighting force within Iran."

"As we did in Somalia with the Ethiopians?"

"That's correct, Mr. President. We would have deniability."

"All right," said the president. "David, you are authorized to get the information about Zafarshan's Iranian militia connection out to the media. Brief both intelligence committees. I think we can count on a leak from them. That will set up the case for military action against whoever did this, whether it's Venezuela, Syria, or Iran. Doug, I want you and the Joint Chiefs to review your plans and present actionable options."

"Yes, sir, Mr. President," answered Parks. He had been lobbying for forceful action against Iran for months. Passed over for the vice presidency in favor of Petty, whom Parks viewed as timid and overly enamored with his image in the media, he'd been craving a chance to move against Iran. With Petty out of the picture, he now had his opportunity.

Sam Syms had sat silently throughout the meeting. He rarely spoke in a group setting. He was the implementer, the one the president tasked to herd the cats in the bureaucracy and bend it to his will. But as Syms listened to the conversation, he became deeply concerned. Groupthink was setting in. No one was raising the possibility that Zafarshan's operation was purposely designed to look like an Iranian one. It could have been al Qaeda, which had reconstituted itself in the tribal regions of Pakistan, or the Taliban, newly resurgent and awash in cash from the opium trade. He felt a word of caution was in order.

"Mr. President, if we're going to blame someone for the assassination of the vice president as the pretext for military action, we have to be prepared for a lot of skepticism," he warned. "Look at the September 11 commission. The case has to be airtight. We don't want another situation like not finding the WMD in Iraq."

The president stared back at Syms, unblinking. He seemed startled, as if he could not believe that someone was questioning his decision-making capacity. "Second-guessing is for armchair generals," he snapped. "I can't defend the American people if I'm worried about covering my backside." He glared around the table. "As long as I'm president, we're going to find out who did this—and we're going to hit them with everything we've got."

After the president's furnace blast, the room fell quiet. People studied the wood texture of the table or looked down at the joltings on their legal pads. Everyone avoided eye contact with Syms. The only noise in the room was the low hum of the overhead projector. The president stood up from his chair and walked out.

———

"WELL, THIS CHANGES EVERYTHING," Long began. "After JFK's assassination, Nixon and Rockefeller took a pass and Goldwater went down in flames. Dallas made LBJ's election inevitable. Does this do the same?"

Everyone waited for Jay Noble to speak. No matter what they said, Long would listen to him, so why burn the calories?

"There's no way to know," answered Noble matter-of-factly. "Everything in a campaign falls into two boxes. In one box are all the things you can control: message, budget, paid media, and schedule. In the other box are the things you can't control: war, the economy, natural disasters, and in this case a terrorist attack and an assassination. We can't control what we can't control. We just have to keep doing our jobs."

Long stared unblinking, his body language saying nothing. In truth, he was still shell-shocked. He had been in a hotel room in Lansing, Michigan, getting dressed for a rally with petition gatherers when he'd received the call from Jay telling him Flaherty's helicopter had been shot down. An hour later came the news that Flaherty was dead. Long suspended the campaign and attended Flaherty's funeral. Suffering from the twin effects of jet lag and emotional stress, he poured himself a cup of black coffee and sought the counsel of his Brain Trust. He had contemplated dropping out, but he did not share that with his campaign team.

"Let's face it," said Fred Edgewater. "We're here because of two events we did not control: Dele-gate and Flaherty picking Petty. We're not in the game without them."

"True," Long said. "We've never controlled our own destiny."

"I think the Republicans are in a whole heap of hurt," insisted David Thomas.

"How's that?" asked Long.

"If they elevate Petty to the presidential nomination, it's a bullet fired right into the temple of the social conservative base," argued Thomas. "The religious right will either bolt the party or stay home in droves. Then Petty picks a running mate. If he picks a right-winger, he looks like he's pandering to his base, which will turn off independents. If he picks a moderate, he disses his base more."

Long nodded. It sounded well reasoned, even brilliant. Even Thomas's zany ideas sounded rational. Flaherty's assassination was a tragedy of such magnitude that it was bad form to discuss who benefited politically. But Long's campaign team had no choice. On paper, in spite of Thomas's assessment, the Republicans looked like winners. The attack made the election about national security and terrorism. Stanley, a dove on Iran, looked weak. Long was hurt because he had to suspend his campaign while ballot access deadlines loomed. There was one wild card: whom would the Republicans choose to take Flaherty's place as their standard-bearer? David Petty was the logical choice, but his elevation would inflame the right. And it was not entirely clear who would make the decision—the president, the Republican Party, or Petty himself.

"If they go with Petty, it plays right into our hands," argued Jay. "Our strategy is simple: run everywhere and win somewhere. You are a national candidate. If Petty drives social conservatives into our arms, we can win most of the South and we'll be over two hundred electoral votes"—he snapped his fingers—"just like that."

"The Republicans will have a ticket with two candidates, neither of whom has won a single vote in a single primary," added Lisa. "They go into the general election cold, and totally untested."

Long leaned forward, his blue eyes dancing. "That's right, Lisa. Petty's never been on a ballot. He's never taken a real shot, not like I did in the primaries."

"Let's not get carried away. Bill Diamond will stay on. He's first-rate. We have to assume the Republicans will run a good campaign," said Jay. "We just don't know who the candidates are yet."

"But candidates matter," argued Lisa. "Bill Diamond's not on the ballot. And if Petty screws up the veep pick, he'll have a rebellion on his hands."

Jay glared at Lisa, not used to being corrected. She stared back.

"When will they decide?" asked Long.

"The rumor is Friday at an emergency meeting of the Republican National Committee," answered Jay.

"When can I get back out there?"

"Right away," interjected Lisa. "We don't have a choice. There are only ninety-two days left and we have to keep the ballot access petition process going."

"The California filing deadline is in three days," Jay pointed out. "We have to turn in those petitions, and we have a big rally scheduled. We file in Iowa four days later, and we want you to travel there because it's a battleground state."

"All right," sighed Long. "But I hate to look like I'm stepping over Flaherty's corpse."

"Petty has to do the same thing," pointed out Lisa.

"Just make sure you come out with a light touch, Governor," urged Hollywood. "It's a delicate time. You need to show the love."

"I *love* . . . everybody!" exclaimed Long. His ironic outburst elicited gales of laughter from the Brain Trust.

They got up from the table, the meeting adjourned. Long waved Jay to follow him to his office. He closed the door.

"I don't want an answer now. I want you to think about it first," said Long. "But I'd like your thoughts on who I should choose as my running mate."

Jay sucked in a gulp of air and slowly exhaled. "Yes, sir," he replied, clearly relishing the chance to provide input. "Thematically, there are two ways to go. One is the complementary choice: you make up for your perceived shortcomings by choosing a running mate who complements you. Cheney was a complementary pick—he knew Washington and the world. Bush had never served in D.C. and had no foreign policy experience. The second strategy is the reinforcing pick—you put an exclamation point on your strength. Like Clinton picking Gore—fellow baby boomer, southerner, and DLC centrist. It was brilliant."

"What's my shortcoming and strength?" asked Long, probing.

"Easy," Jay answered in a millisecond. "Shortcoming: no military or foreign policy experience. Your strength is you're a reformer and an outsider."

"I'd like to get both in one person if I could," said Long, his face serious. "A reinforcing complement. And there's one other thing I'm really looking for."

"What?"

"Somebody crazy enough to end their political career by signing on with us," Long deadpanned.

"That'll be the hard part!" laughed Jay.

"Sleep on it. Give me your thoughts in a memo."

"You bet," said Jay. "Now there's something I need you to do, Governor."

"What's that?"

"You need to call the good doctor, Andrew H. Stanton."

"Really?" asked Long, his brow furrowed, a slightly bewildered expression crossing his face. "He's a porcupine—if you get too close, he sticks you." He fidgeted as he leaned against the desk. "What do I say?"

"Tell him you want to work with him. Stanton hates Petty. With Flaherty now gone, Andy is feeling lonely. I want you to hold his hand."

Long arched his eyebrows at the choice of metaphor. Noble pulled a note card from his coat pocket and wrote down a number with a blue felt pen, handing the card to Long. It was Andy Stanton's home phone number. Long stared at it. If he got lucky and the Republicans elevated Petty, he just might have a new card to play. And it might turn out to be an ace.

24

RICHARD PEPPER, CHAIRMAN OF the Republican National Committee, was on his way to his office after a breakfast meeting at the Mayflower Hotel when his car phone rang. A White House operator was on the line. Pepper was a prominent Republican lobbyist, former chairman of the Ohio Republican Party, and big-time fund-raiser for the president. He maintained homes in Columbus and Washington and commuted to Ohio on the weekends. He had been asked by the president to serve as chairman of the RNC the previous year and had not figured out a good excuse to decline. He suffered from no health problems, was not going through a divorce, and had not recently been the subject of ugly press coverage over one of his clients. Just like that, tag—he was it.

"Dick, Sam Syms here. The president asked me to check in with you regarding the presidential nomination."

As usual, Sam had gotten right to the point. "Sure. How do you want to proceed?" Pepper asked.

"Can we get the RNC members in town quickly?"

"I don't see why not. But who's our candidate?"

"Keep this under your hat," Syms cautioned. "The president feels strongly that David Petty should be the nominee."

Even though Pepper had expected that, it still hit him like a load of bricks. His body sank deeper into the car's leather seat. This was going to be a problem on the right. "I see," he said.

"What do you think, off the record."

"It's going to raise hackles with conservatives," he said, his words measured. "But I think that is probably manageable, assuming the president has the political will to make his preference clear."

"I don't think you have to worry about that," Syms replied vaguely.

"I'm relieved to hear that," said Pepper, always the loyal supplicant. "What about Andy Stanton and the socos?"

"They are not going to matter as much as in the past," replied Syms, his voice steady. "This election is about terrorism, not social issues. That's doubly true after the assassination of the vice president."

Pepper could hardly believe what he was hearing. He wondered if everyone in the White House was drinking the same Kool-Aid. But Pepper knew that the only thing the West Wing expected him to do was to salute and obey orders.

"The moment I issue the call for an emergency meeting, the press will start calling members, asking who they support for the nomination," said Pepper. "I'll need some talking points."

"You're going to have more than talking points, Dick." As usual, Syms held his cards close, revealing nothing. "Come over here in the morning around eight o'clock and we'll hammer it out."

"See you then," replied Pepper. He hung up, gazing out the window as the cars on Constitution Avenue whizzed by. Pepper had not seen the inside of the West Wing in three months. Clearly, something big was about to happen.

RANDOLPH SNOW DIALED THE conference call access number and heard a series of gongs as others joined the call. Snow was the grizzled grassroots organizer and the longtime RNC committeeman from Michigan. He chaired the John Winthrop Institute, a free-market think tank based in Grand Rapids, and sat on the boards of the NRA and the American Conservative Union. A movement conservative with the jagged scars to prove it, he had no intention of letting the party establishment foist David Petty on the Republican Party. He was the commanding general of the conservatives on the RNC.

"Who's joining? Please identify yourselves," he instructed. (Randolph was paranoid about spies joining the call.)

After the roll call, Snow called the meeting to order. "I know I speak for all of us when I say that I am shocked and saddened by the tragic death of Vice President Flaherty," Snow began in an officious baritone. "He was a great American."

"Amen," someone chimed in.

The purpose of the call was to discuss Rule 27, which stated that if a presidential or vice presidential nominee died, his replacement would be chosen by the RNC, with each state casting votes equal to the number of delegates from their state to the national convention. The rule had last been invoked in 1912 when William Howard Taft's running mate died, but a presidential nominee had never died prior to an election in U.S. history. Technically, the RNC members chose Flaherty's replacement. The unanswered question was, Would the White House let them do it?

"We are all friends, so let me speak freely," Snow said. "David Petty, who is anathema to all of us on this call, is our vice presidential nominee. We agreed not to oppose him based on his support for Vice President Flaherty's positions on the issues. But Harris Flaherty is gone. Although we do not know what Petty's plans are, I am hearing rumors the White House will try to elevate him to the presidential nomination. Such an occurrence, in my opinion, would be a disaster for the party."

"Total disaster!" shouted someone.

"Precisely," seconded Snow. "David Petty is pro-choice, pro–gay rights, pro–affirmative action, and he supports illegal immigration. Need I go on?"

"What else is there?" cried an RNC member with theatrical flair.

"All right, then, what do we do about it?" asked Snow in his best professorial voice. "I suggest we make clear our opposition to Petty in a way that is respectful but firm. Second, we should unite behind a single conservative candidate."

"Randolph? May I ask a question?" The voice belonged to Beverly Hunt, Republican national committeewoman from Alabama.

"Of course, Beverly."

"I don't care for Petty," she continued. "But you can't beat somebody with nobody. Have you approached someone about placing their name in nomination? Will they run against Petty? They need to have the stomach for a fight."

"Indeed, I have," replied Randolph with dramatic effect. "I spoke with Senator Tom Reynolds just this afternoon. We had a good conversation, and I believe if he felt there was support on the committee, he would give it serious consideration."

Someone let out a long whistle. "He would be terrific!" exclaimed Hunt.

"Randolph, this is Russell May from Texas. We have a bit of a chicken-

and-egg problem. We need a candidate, but we'll have a hard time getting a candidate without a large number of solid votes on the committee."

"Correct," said Randolph, setting the trap. "Let's get on the phone with friends and allies and see if we can expand our caucus. Let us meet again tomorrow evening at this same time. We'll seek to ascertain how many votes we have."

"And what about the candidate?" asked someone.

"If there is no objection, I can act as the emissary from this group to Reynolds. Assuming he agrees, I will ask him to join us on tomorrow evening's call."

"I second that motion," said a voice.

"All in favor, say aye," moved Randolph. A chorus of ayes filled the air. "All opposed." Silence. "My friends, the future of the Republican Party hangs in the balance. This is a fight we did not seek, but it is a fight we cannot avoid. Let's get to work."

"Hear, hear!" someone said, and the call came to an end.

After four decades of toiling in the vineyards of the Grand Old Party, watching others from his generation pass him by on their way to Cabinet posts and elected office, Randolph Snow was on the verge of realizing his dream. Like other movement conservatives, he had learned that it was more important to control a political party than it was to govern the country. David Petty's nomination posed a threat to the conservative movement's role in the Republican Party. Randolph was determined to put a Reagan conservative in the White House—even if it meant an open break with the president.

———

THE MOTORCADE PULLED UP to a raucous and massive crowd at the California state capitol in Sacramento, giant loudspeakers blaring Bruce Springsteen. It was more like a rock concert than a political rally. Twenty thousand people spilled over the grounds and into the street. Three hundred credentialed media—including camera crews from Japan, South Korea, and the Czech Republic—crowded onto a massive riser. Bob Long, his shirt sleeves rolled up, his shirt matted with perspiration, led the way, standing atop a stack of petitions in the bed of a covered wagon that had carried some of the original settlers to the California territory during the 1849 gold rush. (Having Long ride to the rally in the front of a covered wagon used by the forty-niners had been Lisa's idea, and it had turned out to be a stroke of genius.)

The Long campaign had gathered the requisite 167,000 valid signatures needed in only twelve days, a modern record that shocked the political establishment. Using a hundred thousand "e-activists" recruited on the Internet and supporting them with a paid force of a thousand petition gatherers, Long was achieving the impossible. Pundits had questioned whether he would qualify for the ballot in his own home state.

Long bounded down from the wagon and jogged up onto a stage that featured volunteers dressed as forty-niners, the women in plumed dresses and bonnets twirling parasols, the men wearing overalls and floppy hats. Aides ran to and fro, stacking the petitions four feet high around him to provide a visual for the cameras. One of them handed him a microphone.

"Ladies and gentlemen, today we made history!" Long's face beamed, and his voice was strong and triumphant. "Once again, California has led the nation. We have earned our way onto the ballot in record time, thanks to you!"

The crowd roared.

"I have asked a delegation made up of the top petition gatherers in the state—one of whom collected over five thousand signatures by herself"—another cheer from the crowd—"to walk into the capitol with me and present these petitions to the secretary of state." The delegation of volunteers gathered around Long, nervously smiling for the cameras. "The people have spoken—they want a real choice for president in November. And with your help, we're going to give it to them!"

Long handed the microphone back to an aide, and with the volunteers holding stacks of petitions in their arms, they marched up the stairs and into the cavernous dome of the state capitol. Preening for the media, Long strode confidently across the marble floor and opened the door to the secretary of state's office. The staff at the counter (the secretary of state was a Republican, and these were his appointees) wore grim expressions, not pleased at being reduced to props for Long's media show. They stacked the petitions on the counter as still photographers flashed away.

Standing to the side, Jay Noble looked on with unrestrained joy. Dan Dorman wandered over, wearing a thin frown. Jay took one look and knew he was going to try to rain on their parade.

"Very impressive, Jay," Dorman began. "But what about the states where filing deadlines have passed? You aren't on the ballot in Texas, Illinois, and Michigan, right?"

"We're going to sue them," shot back Jay. "And we're going to win."

"And what if you don't win?"

Jay just looked at him. The truth was, he didn't know.

———

MELINDA LIPPER WAS THE total package. Her striking good looks and traffic-stopping figure melted the hearts and excited the libidos of middle-aged men with money, and she had a rare talent for getting them to part with it in very large sums. Her beauty, however, could be deceiving, for Melinda had the killer instincts of an NFL linebacker. In fact, she had nearly married one, becoming engaged to a defensive starter for the New York Giants the year the team had won the Super Bowl. But he had turned out not to be man enough for her: just another crybaby trapped in an Arnold Schwarzenegger body. She liked men who were tough, ambitious, with a sense of humor, and preferably wealthy, with a nose for the jugular—men, in a word, like her. Her jet-black hair, doelike eyes, formfitting Versace suits, and a svelte body that swayed when she walked appeared at times to be a deliberately feminine façade masking an uncommon meanness.

That was why it was so unusual for Lipper to find her stomach churning and fingers shaking as she dialed the phone number of Michael Kaplan.

"Mike, it's Melinda. Did I catch you at a bad time?"

"No, this is fine. I'm seeing your daily reports. You're doing great."

In a business where money was king, Melinda was the queen of fundraising. She had raised an eye-popping $750 million for Democratic candidates during her career. But the price of success was high. She had developed the rough exterior of a street fighter. Her profanity-laced tirades were legendary. She had once humiliated a big donor in front of an entire click line by yelling at him that his last check had bounced and if he wanted to get his photo she needed a credit card number—right then and there. (He dutifully gave it to her, and she charged twenty-five thousand dollars on his American Express card.) Melinda had the best Rolodex in the party, and when Salmon

Stanley had hired her as a consultant to his presidential campaign, it had been a turning point in the "money primary."

"We're on track to do two hundred million dollars more by Election Day," she boasted. "We could do even more if you would put Betsy Hafer in the luggage compartment of a Greyhound bus and ship her to the Ozarks for the rest of the campaign." Melinda stuck the knife in and enjoyed twisting it. "Mike, she's killing us."

"We're working on it," replied Kaplan.

"We're doing our job in finance. Meanwhile, we're running third in the polls, behind Bob Long, who's a fruitcake. Throw me a bone, will you?"

"We're working on it, Melinda," repeated Kaplan.

"Anyway, that's not what I'm calling about," she said, her voice turning serious and worried. "I . . . have a problem."

"What?"

"I received a subpoena from the Department of Justice."

"I see," answered Kaplan.

"It's exhaustive," said Melinda, trying to keep the fear out of her voice. "They ask for every email, document, cell phone records, even my calendar and travel schedule." She began to read from the subpoena. " 'All correspondence, emails, notes of meetings, contracts, agreements, planning documents, lists of donors, copies of checks, bank deposits, records of wire transfers, credit card transactions, and any and all other related documents between Melinda Lipper and Associates, LLC, the Salmon Stanley for President campaign, the Committee for a Better America, Inc., the Democratic National Committee, and the Virginia Democratic Party.' "

Kaplan let out an expletive.

"What do you want me to do?"

"We need to narrow the scope of the subpoena," Kaplan said calmly, his mind racing. "We'll handle your legal representation. How much time did they give you?"

"Fourteen days."

"We can get an extension."

"Mike, they have asked for everything related to the Committee for a Better America," Melinda pointed out gravely.

Kaplan let out another expletive. "Didn't you get rid of that stuff?"

"I got rid of a lot, but not everything. We ran CBA out of my firm so that it wasn't sitting over at the campaign, remember?"

It was not something Kaplan wanted to be reminded of at the moment. "Just sit tight and I'll have someone from our counsel's office call you this morning. In the meantime, fax the subpoena to our legal department."

"How do they know about CBA?"

"Maybe one of the Virginia delegates. Who knows?"

"Well, *I* know," Melinda said with characteristic bluntness. "Someone is talking to the FBI. Mike, they knew exactly what they were looking for."

"We've got everything under control, Melinda," Kaplan said with barely disguised impatience. "Look, they want you to be afraid. Just take a deep breath, and I'll have our lawyers contact you today. It will be fine. Trust me."

But as he hung up the phone, Kaplan knew that everything was *not* fine. If DOJ was playing hardball, this was not a problem that could be resolved by hiring lawyers. They were targeting the best operatives in the party, lobbing subpoenas like grenades, forcing everyone to hire lawyers, and threatening to drag them in front of a grand jury. As Kaplan saw it, it was an abuse of power and a politically motivated prosecution. It was time to go to war. He swung around in his chair to his computer to pull up his contacts. There was only one person he knew in the Democratic Party with the gonads for this fight. He reached over to dial the number of G.G. Hoterman.

———

SENATOR TOM REYNOLDS GLIDED through the Senate Dining Room with his usual fare-thee-well flamboyance, greeting colleagues by grabbing them affectionately by the arm, waving to lobbyists at nearby tables, and yukking it up with the waitstaff. If life was a play and the world a stage, Tom Reynolds stood under an eternal spotlight. In the U.S. Senate, where egos were oversized and preening peacocks plentiful, Tom Reynolds was a man in full. As Reynolds surveyed the menu, his mind wandered back to his morning workout with his personal trainer and the urgent need to lose a few more pounds—especially if the rumors of David Petty's elevation as the GOP presidential nominee were true. Petty would need a conservative as his running mate, and who better than Tom Reynolds? He needed to look his best. His media consultant told him that the camera added ten pounds, which gave his struggle with his waistline a new urgency. He ordered a cup of minestrone and a lettuce wedge.

Joining him was Randolph Snow, who was in Washington for the RNC meeting. Rumors about the GOP presidential nomination shifted daily like trade winds. One webside, Presidentialhorserace.com, tracked the contest among the contenders, giving odds like a Vegas Internet gambling site. That morning the website ranked David Petty's chances of being nominated as 3 to 2; Reynolds was a long shot at 6 to 1.

"What are you hearing from RNC members?" asked Reynolds as he spooned a mouthful of soup.

"They are scared to death of the prospect of David Petty," answered Snow, scarfing down a french fry as he cut his cheeseburger in half with a knife.

"It might happen," said Reynolds, his lips curled into a smirk. "They may just have to put ketchup on it and eat it."

Snow stopped chewing in midbite. He put his knife down, swallowed the food in his mouth, and leaned forward, speaking in a half whisper. "Senator, I assure you that . . . is . . . not . . . going . . . to . . . happen."

"How do you propose to stop it?" replied Reynolds, surprised.

"By counting votes," continued Randolph, ignoring his food. He picked up his knife and used it as a pointer, punctuating his point. "There are forty-seven votes pledged to support a conservative candidate—and I've only been whipping for two days. I only need a third of the membership, as long as it comes from the right states. And I have two of the three RNC members from both California and Texas. That's 240 delegate votes right there. Our hard count right now with our forty-seven votes is 859 delegate votes, which is only two hundred short of what we need for a majority." Snow had rounded up his total by a hundred or so votes, but he was close enough.

"But who's your candidate?"

"You are," replied Snow, his eyes steady.

Reynolds laughed. "Seriously, who's the candidate?"

"I'm serious, Tom," said Snow, his facial expression growing sober and expansive. "If you were to walk out there right now"—he pointed toward the

Senate press gallery—"and announce you were a candidate, you could win. I've got nearly a third of the committee already, and that's *without* a candidate!"

"Well, I—"

"Petty's a moderate and an empty suit, and you know it."

"David's flawed, no question. But I'm concerned about opposing the president," replied Reynolds. "He's no shrinking violet. At some point, he will make his views known. In my experience, the RNC members talk a big game in the locker room, but when the White House steps in, they collapse like a chocolate soufflé. Your hard count will crumble if RNC members start getting calls from the West Wing."

"Less than you think," shot back Snow, growing visibly agitated. "The president is a lame duck. Besides, people are tired of taking orders." He paused. "I trust you're not reluctant to run because you have delusions of being picked as Petty's running mate."

"Of course not," Reynolds fibbed. Snow's shot had landed a little too close for comfort. "But why do you say that?"

"You mean other than the fact that the president can't stand you?" replied Snow.

The comment hit Reynolds like a sucker punch.

"Senator, my point is," Snow continued, "if the president can force Petty down the throat of the party, he'll do the same with the vice presidential nominee. Either way, he's going to want someone he can control, and that is not you."

"You're right about that," agreed the senator, regaining his composure. "They can't control me, and they know it. Randolph, you keep working your whip operation and keep me posted. I'll see if the Petty candidacy is real. And I'm going to make one other phone call to someone who could have a say in all this."

"Who's that?"

"Andy Stanton. If Andy said something on his radio show, it would help a lot."

"Try to get his endorsement," urged Randolph. "Stanton *despises* Petty. If Andy Stanton gives you a wet kiss on his radio or TV show, millions of people will follow him to the kissing booth."

As they left, Reynolds felt the cold stares of his colleagues. It wouldn't take long for them to see his lunch companion and connect the dots. He knew they were jealous of him, resentful of his high media profile, but he didn't care. He hoped to be what Randolph Snow and all good political jockeys needed: a horse to ride.

25

D AN DORMAN TOOK HIS seat in the front row of a hastily assembled news conference in the Oval Office. He flipped open his steno pad and turned on his digital tape recorder. Everyone was jumpy, which usually meant something big was about to go down. The door swung open and the president strode into the room. Behind him, David and Anne Petty and their two adult children walked in single file.

It was 8:59 A.M. A live national television audience watched as the president stepped to the small podium bearing the presidential seal. The cramped quarters of the Oval Office deepened the sense of drama. Dorman could reach out and touch Senate Majority Leader Sal Stanley, the Senate minority leader, Speaker of the House Gerald Jimmerson, and the House minority leader, who sat to his right. Dorman saw Stanley's jaw drop when Petty walked in.

"My fellow Americans, the loss of Vice President Harrison Flaherty at the hands of extremists whose only ideology is hatred and whose only weapon is terror has left our nation in mourning," the president said in a resolute voice. He read from a stack of cards on the podium, but he seemed to know the words by heart. His black eyes stared into the camera. "Let there be no doubt. We will defeat these terrorists and democracy will triumph. We are further resolved that the democratic process will go forward. Therefore, after consultation with members of Congress of both parties, this morning I am announcing that I will submit the name of David Petty to Congress for confirmation as vice president of the United States." The only sound in the room was the *click-click-click* of still-camera shutters recording the scene. The tension in the room was palpable. Only twice before in American history had a president submitted the name of a prospective vice president to Congress, both times during Watergate. No one currently a candidate for national office had ever been so elevated.

Dorman could hardly believe it. *The guy has no shame*, he thought. It was an audacious move by a man not known for timid thinking. The president was seizing control of the presidential campaign by executive fiat, running over Congress, the electorate, and even his own party.

"General Petty is one of the most accomplished public servants in recent national memory," the president continued, his regal manner masking the cutthroat politics at play. "He is eminently qualified to serve at a time when our nation faces challenges at home and abroad. I ask Congress to confirm him quickly."

The president yielded the podium, his arm extending to invite Petty to assume the stage. More camera shutters clicked as Petty stepped to the lectern.

"Mr. President, I am deeply humbled by your confidence." He turned to the president and bent slightly from the waist in an obligatory bow. The president nodded. Petty studiously ignored Stanley, who sat three feet from him. "The circumstances that have brought us here this morning underscore the gravity of our times. As the first person selected to serve as vice president because of the death of my predecessor, I want to assure the American people that I will have no higher priority than protecting the homeland. This is a job not only for our military, but for all Americans." He paused, cocking his head to emphasize his point. "Mr. President, on behalf of a grateful nation, let me say *thank you* for your leadership. It is a *great honor* to serve my country."

Petty glanced left and right, smoothly seeking stage directions, as he pulled his wife Anne toward him and grabbed her hand tightly. His children stood motionless like deer caught in the headlights. A White House staff member jumped up and opened the door and the presidential party turned to its left and exited. Just like that, it was over. The press conference had lasted a total of nine minutes.

Dan Dorman bolted for the door, knocking over a chair. Out of the corner of his eye, he caught a glimpse of a stunned Salmon Stanley turning to a fellow member of the Democratic leadership, shrugging his shoulders, arching his eyebrows and frowning as if to say, "Well, we're really in it now, aren't we?"

"SENATOR, I HAVE MARVIN Myers on line one."

Senator Tom Reynolds looked at the phone as if it were a ticking bomb. Marvin Myers! Should he say he was out of the office? That would only make things worse. He winced as he reached for the phone.

"Marvin?"

"Hello, Senator. Or should I call you Mr. President?" Myers had the story.

Reynolds let out a nervous laugh. "Marvin, I'm just a backbencher in the U.S. Senate trying to do my job."

"Don't give me that. I wasn't born yesterday," Marvin said.

"What do you mean?" responded Reynolds, playing dumb.

"I'm hearing that you have agreed to be nominated for president at the RNC meeting tomorrow," revealed Myers coolly. "Conservatives on the committee claim to have sixty-four committee members representing nine hundred and fifty delegate votes for your nomination. They claim they are close to having enough votes to defeat Petty."

Reynolds gulped, trying to wet his throat. Randolph Snow was singing like a canary to the media and his numbers kept growing. He had gained a hundred more votes in less than a day without even announcing. Funny how that happened.

"Off the record, I have *not* agreed to have my name placed in nomination."

"You haven't?"

"No. I was contacted by some RNC members and they asked me to consider it. I was polite but I told them I could not commit. That's all." Reynolds was like a cat burglar hurrying down a fire escape.

"That's funny," Myers drawled. "Because I heard you were having lunch with Randolph Snow yesterday in the Senate Dining Room."

Ouch! Was Snow running his mouth or one of his Senate colleagues? "We're old friends," said Reynolds curtly.

"So you didn't discuss your candidacy with him?"

"Marvin, I'm not going to divulge private conversations," Reynolds fired back. "Like I already said, some of the conservatives on the RNC came to me. I committed to nothing. End of story."

"Come on, Tom, quit playing games. Feed the beast!" Marvin bellowed. "Are you running or not? Are you going to let a liberal like Petty become the Republican nominee for president without winning a single vote in a primary?"

"I . . . I have not decided," stammered Reynolds. "Off the record," he said, lowering his voice, "the White House has asked me if I am interested in being Petty's running mate." It was a bald-faced lie, but Reynolds hoped it might work its way into print. "It's a tough call. I have a lot of options."

"Can I report that?"

"Let me tie up some loose ends first," Reynolds answered, praying that Myers was taking the bait. "When does your column run?"

"Tomorrow," drawled Myers. "So you need to get back to me by the end of the day. I'd like to include your side of the story."

Reynolds hung up the phone. He didn't have much time left. If Myers reported that he was running for president, any chance he had of being named as the vice presidential running mate would go up in flames.

———

"DR. STANTON ON LINE TWO," announced Ross Lombardy's assistant as she stuck her head through his office door. This wasn't just any phone call—the presidency hung in the balance. Ross felt his adrenal glands kick in as he adjusted his headset.

"Hello, Andy."

"I just hung up after talking to your old boss," Stanton replied.

"Let me guess," chuckled Ross. "He wants you to endorse him for president." It bothered Ross that Tom Reynolds had not called to ask for his advice. But this was presidential politics, and Reynolds was playing for the golden ring. He didn't want any training wheels.

"He asked me to say something nice about him on my radio show. I guess they want to generate support for him at the RNC meeting and he knows we control a bloc of votes. What do you think?" Stanton's voice projected doubt.

Ross glanced at the crystal desk clock. The time was 2:37 P.M. Stanton's radio show would go on the air in eighty-three minutes. Reynolds had not checked with Ross, so Ross owed him nothing. "I'd be careful, Andy," he warned. "You don't want to saddle up a three-legged horse. From what I hear, Petty has this thing wrapped up. If you give Reynolds a love hug and he loses, it makes us look weak."

"What does the vote count look like?"

"Randolph Snow is telling people he has forty-seven votes—"

"Randolph is all hat and no cattle," interrupted Andy dismissively.

"He's a blowhard," Ross agreed. "But even if he has forty-seven votes, then Reynolds gets twenty-eight percent of the vote, Petty seventy-two percent. And if Randolph's votes are concentrated in the larger states, the conservative candidate gets one-third of the vote to Petty's sixty-six percent."

"Wow!" exclaimed Stanton. "That's a whipping."

"Nobody wants to take on the White House," explained Ross.

"So I blew the horn with my statement criticizing Petty, and no one followed." Stanton sounded dejected, an emotion that rarely surfaced in his sunny disposition.

"Not necessarily," Ross corrected. "These RNC members are state Republican chairmen, lobbyists, and money types—they're party insiders. If they challenge the president, they're dead meat. The word is out that the White House is not taking a vote against Petty lying down. They're playing hardball."

"I thought we had a say in the party," moaned Stanton. "But the White House controls everything."

Ross knew that, for Andy, this was a jarring wake-up call. The empty flattery, pushing mints across the table in the Roosevelt Room, presidential cuff links, whispered confidences in the Oval Office, sitting next to the queen of Monaco at a state dinner—it all added up to: nothing. The president had all the power; they had none. "Go ahead and put some lipstick on Reynolds's collar if you want, but don't wear his class ring," advised Ross. "Stay out of camera range."

"Stay out of camera range? I may have to leave the country," joked Stanton.

Ross hung up the phone. He turned in his chair to look out his window at the grounds of New Life Ministries. He could see Georgia 400 cutting through the Atlanta suburb like a concrete ribbon. By the time Andy went on the air, the afternoon rush hour would turn 400 into a parking lot, and many of those people stuck in traffic would tune their radio dials to Andy as he opined on the day's news. Ross chuckled. This was why he got paid the big bucks. He had just saved Andy from going down in flames with Reynolds, and he had thrown his former boss under the bus in the process. He didn't feel guilty about it. His job was to watch Stanton's back, not carry water for his ex-boss. But it begged the larger question: what would Stanton and the Faith and Family Federation do when David Petty was the Republican nominee for president? They were staring into the abyss.

SAM SYMS SAT IN his West Wing office, doing his best to control his slow-building anger. Marvin Myers was calling all over town, turning over rocks, pushing the absurd story that Tom Reynolds had the votes to defeat David Petty for the Republican presidential nomination. Could these people not count?

The *New York Times* claimed Petty had only 38 percent of the delegate votes to 25 percent for Reynolds. Merryprankster.com had a link to the *Times* story under the lurid headline, "Delegate Survey: RNC Members May Reject Petty." But the *Times* survey had been conducted before the president chose Petty as vice president; since then the White House had rounded up all the votes. It was time to end the charade.

He dialed Reynolds's office and asked to speak to the senator. The voice of Tom Reynolds came on the line, dripping syrup.

"Sam, to what do I owe this honor?"

Syms ignored the suck-up. "Senator, I'd like to be calling under more pleasant circumstances," he said, a harsh edge in his voice. "But Marvin Myers is reporting tomorrow that you are opposing David Petty for the nomination. Since that would be counterproductive for the president and the party, not to mention you, I can only assume that Myers's report is false."

"It's nonsense. I told Marvin this morning categorically it was not true," said Reynolds. "I told him I was approached by conservatives on the RNC, but that I had committed to nothing."

"Senator, that sounds like a nondenying denial. Why didn't you give us a heads-up when Randolph Snow approached you?"

"Look, Sam, it was nothing," Reynolds backpedaled. "I didn't take it seriously. I would have called you or someone at the White House if I was considering it."

"I'm afraid we're past that point, Senator," Syms replied coldly. "This thing has gotten out of hand. We need to knock it down."

"What do you suggest?" asked Reynolds, bracing for the answer.

"You issue a statement saying you will not allow yourself to be nominated under any circumstances. It needs to be a Shermanesque statement."

"Isn't that overkill? That could make the story bigger. Why deny something I'm not even contemplating?"

"What is driving this story," shot back Syms, "is being coy about it. You're reluctant to issue a statement so you can get press for a nonexistent campaign." He was getting hotter by the minute. "Tom, let me be blunt: you're on the verge of being dropped from the list for veep. The choice is yours. So what's it going to be?"

Reynolds was shaken by the full-throated ferocity of Syms's blast. He was threatening to keep him off the ticket. "All right. You'll have a statement within the hour. Do you want to be the one to get it to Myers, or do you want me to do it?"

"You do it," replied Syms. "Email me the release so we can take a look at it."

"Sorry about the misunderstanding," apologized Reynolds obsequiously. "Myers is a snake."

Syms thought that Reynolds's self-abnegating exercise in Maoist self-criticism, followed by publicly shooting himself, was as pathetic as it was unconvincing.

"Believe it or not, Senator, this is not the biggest problem I'm dealing with today," replied Syms, pretending to put Reynolds at ease while making him feel even more uncomfortable and insignificant. "The big problem today is the Russian foreign minister saying that he doesn't see a problem if Iran has nukes." He paused. "Get the statement out. Petty will win the nomination tomorrow and all this will be forgotten."

———

THE CONSERVATIVES GATHERED IN Randolph Snow's suite at the Marriott Marquis, two blocks from the White House, were despondent. The previous day they'd had a legitimate shot at nominating a conservative for president. Then the White House blitzkrieg had begun. The president elevated Petty to the vice presidency and forced Reynolds out of the race. Now it was the night before the prom and the conservatives had no date. RNC Chairman Dick Pepper, the president's pull-toy, predicted that Petty would win with 75 percent or more of the vote. The fat lady had sung.

"Ladies and gentlemen, we find ourselves in quite a jam," said Randolph Snow, his face pale and drawn. "Our horse has been shot out from under us."

"What about Congressman Tony Peters? He told me he would be willing to be nominated," suggested Beverly Hunt, the committeewoman from Alabama. Awkward silence followed. Peters was a wild man. His main claim to fame was delivering stream-of-consciousness speeches to an empty House chamber while a national TV audience watched on C-SPAN. They had officially reached the bottom of the barrel.

"What about voting for 'none of the above'?" asked the committeeman from Wyoming.

"That would trivialize our effort," Snow objected.

"What worries me," said the committeewoman from Missouri, "is that the grass roots may not turn out at all. They might stay home. Or they may vote for Bob Long. That'll teach the Republicans a lesson they won't soon forget."

"The party establishment thinks conservatives have no place to go," interjected the Texas committeeman. "They're wrong. We can vote for Long. I received over two hundred emails today from grassroots conservatives who say that if Petty is the nominee, they will not vote for him under any circumstances."

Snow wrapped up the meeting and the dejected caucus filed out. It was nearly midnight. He flopped in a chair, put his head in his hands, and began to weep. The party he had given his life to had turned its back on its principles. A horrifying thought entered his mind. What if the terrorists had murdered Harris Flaherty to divide the Republican Party and put a liberal Democrat in the White House? There could be no doubt that once elected, Stanley would beat a rapid retreat in the war on terrorism. It all seemed too Machiavellian, too evil, but now it was coming true.

26

THE GRAND BALLROOM OF the Marriott Marquis crackled with electricity. The RNC members resembled department store mannequins, decked out in their best suits and colorful dresses, lapping up their Andy Warhol–like fifteen minutes of fame. A restless mob of hundreds of reporters, television cameras, and foreign press from every continent jammed the press riser in the back.

RNC Chairman Dick Pepper gaveled the meeting to order and dispensed with the usual formalities. In a roll call vote devoid of suspense, David Petty won the Republican nomination with 82 percent of the vote.

Speaker of the House Gerald Jimmerson of North Carolina, a strong conservative with street cred among the GOP base, had been pressed into service by the White House to introduce Petty, who would then accept the nomination. It was fervently hoped that Jimmerson's embrace would give conservatives the warm fuzzies they needed to swallow Petty whole. Jimmerson had been happy to oblige: it was one more chit he would call in later with the White House. Jimmerson was an ideological ally of the movement conservatives on the RNC, but he did not see them as serious players. In his estimation, the adults were taking charge, and the conservatives had to be rolled.

"We must remember Ronald Reagan's admonition that an eighty percent friend is not a twenty percent enemy," Jimmerson proclaimed. He tried to compensate for the skepticism hanging in the air with a burst of arm-waving and shouting. In a glaring faux pas, he urged that "conservatism comes in many shades and colors" (apparently oblivious to the fact that David Petty was black) and invoked Ronald Reagan's name repeatedly. He grandiloquently claimed that a nation at war with terrorism needed "a leader with the moral courage of a battlefield commander, the negotiating skill of a diplomat, and the vision of a Thatcher and a Reagan. David Petty is that leader."

Petty walked across the stage to an explosion of camera flashes and a standing ovation. It was downhill from there. He read his remarks, head down, reading glasses on the end of his nose, never once making eye contact with his audience. Describing the pacification of Baghdad, he ticked off a litany of statistics that sounded more like the recitation of a military briefer than the poetry of a presidential candidate. Turning to the war on terrorism, he split the baby. "We will not allow state sponsors of terrorism to gain the world's most destructive weapons and hold the Middle East hostage," he said. Yet he also asserted that "we cannot triumph with military force alone." The RNC members, especially the conservatives, looked stunned. Petty made no reference to social issues, refusing to pander. He seemed to say, sotto voce, that the party needed him, not the other way around. Petty's candidacy rested on a simple rationale: I can win.

After Petty left the stage to a muted reception, things got interesting. The chair recognized the chairman of the Iowa Republican Party, a known flack for the White House.

"Mr. Chairman," said the Iowa chair into a handheld mike, holding it a little too close and pulling it back when the speakers screeched with feedback. "I am proud to nominate for vice president a great Republican and a proven reformer, Senator Edward Bell of Colorado."

Ed Bell? There were audible gasps.

To grassroots conservatives, Ed Bell was Satan. He had been the only Republican in the Senate to vote against a GOP-sponsored tax cut ("welfare for coupon clippers"), opposed a new aircraft carrier for the U.S. Navy ("a boondoggle for armchair admirals"), and sponsored climate change legislation with Salmon Stanley (!). These sins paled in comparison to his smearing of Supreme Court nominee Henry Stonecipher—a devout evangelical and favorite of the Federalist Society—by raising a legal malpractice suit early in the judge's career. Bell's opposition doomed Stonecipher's nomination, and the judge withdrew his name rather than face certain defeat. Though five years had passed, conservatives had never forgiven Bell.

"Mr. Chairman! Mr. Chairman!" shouted Randolph Snow.

"The chair recognizes the national committeeman from Michigan."

"Mr. Chairman, I move for a recess."

Dick Pepper glared down at Snow, his eyes aflame. "The gentleman's motion is out of order."

Snow jumped up again. "Mr. Chairman, I nominate Senator Tom Reynolds of Oklahoma for vice president."

"Second!" shouted several delegates loudly.

Pepper gazed out at pandemonium. Delegates had gotten up from their chairs to hold caucuses in the back of the room. Finger-pointing and shouting began to break out between allies of the White House and the conservatives. "The meeting of this committee will come to order! Everyone return to your seats!"

"Mr. Chairman," said the Texas committeeman in one of the stand-up microphones. "We lick the envelopes, man the phone banks, and walk the precincts to elect Republicans. Your attempt to ramrod a vice presidential nomination without—"

"Does the gentleman from Texas have a motion?" asked Pepper, his face contorted with anger.

"I move we give the grass roots a say in choosing our candidates! That is my motion, Mr. Chairman!" Cheers rose from the crowd.

"If you have no motion, the chair requests that you relinquish the microphone."

"I will *not* give up this microphone until you . . . *give . . . us . . . back . . . our . . . party!*" Applause rippled through the delegates.

The roll call vote proceeded by state in alphabetical order. The result was far closer than anyone had anticipated. Edward Bell received 1,153 votes, or 57 percent, to Tom Reynolds's 923 votes, or 43 percent. Not since Reagan's insurgent presidential candidacy forced Nelson Rockefeller off the ticket in 1976 had the GOP felt such powerful tremors of ideological schism.

After the vote, Randolph Snow wandered toward the exit, surrounded by fellow conservative members of the RNC, who slapped his back in support. A clutch of print reporters charged over, eyes wild, perspiration beading on their foreheads, white-knuckling steno pads and tape recorders. At the head of the scrum was Dan Dorman, wearing scuffed shoes, a rumpled oxford shirt, a soiled paisley tie, and a blue blazer draped over wrinkled khakis.

"Will conservatives support Petty and Bell?" Dorman asked, his beady eyes peering over the top of his eyeglasses. "Or will they stay home?"

"The Republican Party that I grew up in no longer exists," Snow replied, his eyes dazed and teary. His lower lip trembled. "Conservatives have not just been given the back of the hand—they have been stabbed in the back," he seethed. "The Republican Party will pay a heavy price for ignoring its conservative base."

The reporters scribbled across their pads. The reporter from McClatchy Newspapers glanced over Dorman's shoulder to make sure she got the quote right.

"Will they abandon the party?" asked the *Los Angeles Times*.

"I wouldn't be surprised," answered Snow. "The Republican Party has given conservatives up for adoption, and Bob Long may find millions of orphaned conservative voters on his doorstep."

MARVIN MYERS WAS ALREADY in his chair on the set, having sat there throughout the bizarre session of the RNC. The director counted down, "We are live in three-two-one," then threw his index finger at the anchor.

The red light on camera two illuminated, cuing the anchor to turn to Myers. "Marvin, your column in today's *Washington Post* predicted this decision by the RNC, even David Petty's margin of victory. But the selection of Senator Edward Bell as vice presidential nominee was quite a surprise, was it not?"

Myers returned the question with an intense stare. Why had his sources not fed the beast? "It is a *huge* surprise," he answered with bravado. "According to senior aides in the campaign that I have talked to in the last hour, this decision was David Petty's alone."

"And what do you think is the strategy behind the selection?"

"It is an appeal to independents," answered Myers. "Bell has broad appeal among independents. Republican strategists hope he can prevent Bob Long from gaining traction with those independent voters."

"What about the downside? How will the Democrats criticize Bell?"

"Democrats will claim that in spite of his image as a maverick, Bell has a very conservative voting record," replied Myers. "He was also reprimanded by the Ethics Committee for failing to list the financial holdings of his wife on disclosure reports, violating Senate rules. The Democrats will raise the ethics issue."

"Tom Reynolds received over forty percent of the vote for vice president. Will there be further fallout from conservatives?"

"Count on it," answered Myers, the side of his mouth turning up in a half smile. "Conservatives never cared for Petty, and Andy Stanton has all but said he will not vote for him. Bell makes things worse. The big beneficiary may be Long."

The anchor smiled. "Marvin Myers, thank you as always."

Marvin nodded. As he unclipped the mike from his tie and pulled the
IFB from his ear, his only regret was that the White House had forced Tom
Reynolds out of the race, ruining his scoop before he could publish it. He
would have to be more careful in dealing with Bill Diamond and Sam Syms
in the future—they could not be trusted. He wondered what Andy Stanton
would do now that Petty was the presidential nominee. Myers decided to
find out. That might make for an interesting column.

ROSS LOMBARDY LEANED BACK in his leather chair and dialed Andy Stanton's private home number. He knew Andy would be at home surfing the
Internet, doing show prep for his radio program.

"What's up?" Andy asked.

"I'm sitting here looking at the *National Review* website."

"What does it say?" asked Stanton, his voice rising an octave.

Ross began to read from the editorial, then stopped. "Pull it up for yourself. It's Nationalreview.com."

Andy went to the website. The headline read "Why Conservatives Cannot Support David Petty." The editors of *National Review* thundered that the
nomination of Petty and Bell "removes any remaining doubt that the party
of Ronald Reagan has lost its way." They conceded that Petty was a war hero,
but "conservatism is not government by biography; it is a set of core beliefs,
not a cult of personality." The editorial blazed with indignation:

> *Petty's views on immigration, affirmative action, abortion,
> campaign finance, and gays in the military are identical to those of
> Salmon Stanley and the far left of the Democratic Party. Petty lacks
> the temerity to stand for Republican principles. His intellectual
> cowardice is more revealing of his political character than his mili
> tary valor. Petty's selection of Edward Bell indicates that he lacks
> political radar as well as philosophical ballast. Bell's character as
> sassination of Henry Stonecipher was a low point in confirmation*

politics, and that "borking" now bears Petty's imprimatur. We can-
not recommend the Republican ticket of David Petty and Ed Bell.
They may be Republicans, but they are assuredly not conservatives.
And as such, they are unworthy of conservative support.

"Unbelievable," said Stanton. "This is devastating. And dead on, by the way."

"I emailed it over to the studio for you. You may want to read it over the air."

"I'll do more than that. I'm going to post a link on my website," chuckled Stanton. "You may want to give *National Review* a heads-up. Their server may crash."

Ross laughed. This was fun. "I think they will be most appreciative."

"Listen, I have to head over to the studio," said Stanton. "But there's something else I've been thinking about."

"What's that?" asked Ross.

"Do you think you might be able to get hold of Bob Long?"

"Probably."

"I think it's time for me to sit down with him. I've heard through the grapevine that he's become a Christian. I don't know if it's true, but he may be someone we can do business with. We've got nothing to lose, with Petty choosing Bell."

"An inspired idea. I'll get on it." Ross hung up the phone.

In less than an hour, millions of radio listeners would hear Andy trumpeting the *NR* editorial. The White House would be livid, and Ross's working relationship with Bill Diamond would be over. The break between the GOP and conservatives was tragic, but Ross had reluctantly concluded that this marriage could not be saved. David Petty had thrown acid in the face of the religious base of the party, and the result was a political version of the *Phantom of the Opera.*

There was one possible lifeline left, and his name was Bob Long.

———

"GOD SAVE THIS HONORABLE COURT!"

The members of the Texas Supreme Court filed in to take their seats, their black robes rustling as they walked. The gallery before them was jammed with attorneys, political consultants on retainer to all three major presidential campaigns, and reporters. After claiming expedited appellate court jurisdiction, the justices had read the briefs and had prepared questions for oral arguments in the case of *Robert W. Long v. Hernandez,* which challenged the May qualifying deadline for independent presidential candidates in Texas. The tension in the court chambers was thick.

Phil Battaglia rose from his chair. He had argued four cases involving election law before the U.S. Supreme Court, and won them all. He was ready.

"Your Honors, the issue before you today," he began in a firm voice, "is whether the citizens of Texas will have their First Amendment right to free speech and their Fourteenth Amendment right to freedom of association protected, or whether those rights can be denied arbitrarily by legislators acting on behalf of a political party." He paused to glance down at his notes. "If voters are denied the right to cast a ballot for the candidate of their choice—"

"How are they denied that right?" interrupted the chief justice. "They can write in the candidate's name, correct?"

"That is an effective denial, Your Honor," Battaglia replied. "The history of write-in candidates is not one of viability. A right impinged is a right denied."

"Isn't the issue here not the voters, but Governor Long's desire to punish the Democratic Party?" fired another justice. "He's already been on the ballot in Texas—as a Democratic presidential candidate. The voters were not denied, he simply lost his party's nomination. Isn't Long's ambition the reason you are before this court?"

The question was a vicious rejoinder, and Battaglia leaned over his podium, absorbing the blow. "No, Your Honor. As the Supreme Court ruled in *Anderson v. Celebrezze,* voters have a right to vote for candidates in a *general* election, including those who lose primaries. That was the case with John Anderson in 1980 when Ohio required him to qualify for the general election ballot before the primary. Texas's law is similar, and if the law denies voters a choice in the general election, the law is unconstitutional under the *Celebrezze* standard."

"But what if Bob Long had lost the Democratic nomination at a convention in September? Wouldn't you then be claiming Texas should move its filing deadline to October? Where does the law draw the line?"

"Your Honor, that is an excellent question," Battaglia said with appropriate flattery. "As the *Celebrezze* court made clear, any filing deadline within the range of seventy-five to ninety days before the election protects the rights of citizens to petition their government for other choices, and also balances the right of the state to ensure the integrity of the electoral process."

"So if the filing deadline is ninety-one days before the election, it is unconstitutional—is that your claim?"

"I am simply citing existing case law from the Supreme Court, Your Honor."

"Counselor, you are going beyond the case law," said the chief justice, a scowl on his face. "Many states have filing deadlines more than ninety days before the general election. None have been struck down."

Battaglia was momentarily stunned. "That is true, Your Honor, but only because the Supreme Court has not revisited the issue. If it did, those deadlines would have to fall by the Court's own precedent."

"I'd be careful about trying to tell a Supreme Court what it had to do. That goes for this one as well," shot back the chief justice.

The justices glowered down at Battaglia; they were clearly unconvinced. They fired questions for another thirty minutes, most of them openly hostile. When he sat down, though his experience told him it was always hard to predict an outcome based on oral arguments, Battaglia knew it was unlikely the Texas Supreme Court would rule in Long's favor. Mentally, he made a note to check on next steps. They would have to prepare an appeal immediately to the Fifth Circuit Court of Appeals. If they lost that appeal and the U.S. Supreme Court declined to hear the case, they would be out of options.

IS THAT REALLY JOHNNY Whitehead?" asked someone in the press corps. "That's him all right, in the flesh," answered Hal Goodman. "What a coup."

Bob Long walked in a slow lope across a cleared field in the midst of towering redwood trees in a California state park, the picture-perfect setting arranged by the campaign for the much-anticipated announcement of his vice presidential running mate. Walking beside him with a determined gait was former Republican U.S. Senator Johnny Whitehead from the state of Kentucky.

The two men, wearing matching khaki slacks and blue blazers with open collars, came to a stop in front of the massive trunk of a redwood tree. They maneuvered up a temporary set of steps and stood together on the stump.

"Thank you all for coming," said Long as camera shutters whirred and clicked. "I gave a great deal of thought to the selection of my vice presidential nominee, and I am pleased to introduce him to you. He is one of the most distinguished public servants to be produced by either political party in the last quarter century. He has served at the state and the federal level, with extensive foreign policy experience. Please welcome my running mate, the next vice president of the United States, Johnny Whitehead."

Whitehead's salt-and-pepper hair had turned almost completely gray in his retirement years. His heavily lined face and slightly stooped shoulders showed every bit of his seventy-two years, while his prominent Roman nose and twinkling eyes revealed the dying embers of his youthful charisma. As the former chairman of the Senate Foreign Relations Committee, Whitehead had advised presidents and traveled the world dealing with issues from nuclear proliferation to counterterrorism. After the Republicans lost control of the U.S. Senate, he had grown weary of minority status and responded to the pleas of the GOP to return to Kentucky and run for governor. Frustrated by a recalcitrant legislature that blocked his education and tax reforms, he had abruptly retired, out of the game. Until Bob Long came calling.

"Governor, thank you so much. At my age, you don't always know if you will get another opportunity to serve your country," he said, his eyes bright and a smile creasing his face. "But when Governor Long contacted me, I knew this was a once-in-a-lifetime opportunity to fix Washington and address the public's disenchantment with the two-party system." He snapped his head in Long's direction, his blue eyes piercing. "Governor, I have the fire in the belly, and I look forward to campaigning enthusiastically for you."

Shouted questions echoed through the redwoods from the large pool of reporters, who spread around the two like so many insects, their microphones and cameras jittering with excitement.

"Senator, you endorsed Harrison Flaherty for president," shouted Hal Goodman. "How do you explain such a flip-flop to the voters of Kentucky and the country?"

"Harrison Flaherty was a dear friend," replied Whitehead. "I served with him in the Senate, and respected him greatly. But he is no longer with us, and I believe with all due respect to other candidates that Bob Long is the right man for the job given what the country needs at this time."

"Governor Long, you've had a much more moderate record in social issues than Senator Whitehead," asked the Associated Press. "Is this part of a strategy to appeal to social conservatives in the South?"

Long's face lit up like a Roman candle, clearly expecting the volley. "I didn't think in terms of left or right. Johnny and I think alike in that he is conservative on foreign policy and defense. But he also worked to reform Kentucky's tax and educational systems. He proposed making sure wealthy corporations paid their fair share, and he expanded health care to poor children." Long leaned forward and gestured with his right hand. "His foreign policy experience is extensive, and I will rely on his wisdom and counsel as we seek to defeat the terrorists and build support among freedom-loving allies." He paused and smiled. "I hope southerners appreciate the fact that I chose a son of the South, someone who knows their region and their values, to run with me. But I also think they'll like what I have to say during the course of the campaign."

Long and Whitehead embraced in a traditional running-mate pose as photographers recorded the moment. Then they quickly stepped off the massive redwood stump, ignoring shouted questions, and walked in the direction of a black Suburban, holding hands with their wives.

Jay Noble stood to the side, beaming. It was a home run.

Hal Goodman wandered over, already firing away, steno pad in hand. "Jay, what about Whitehead's age? Isn't that a liability?"

"He's fit as a fiddle, Hal," answered Jay. "He had a full physical at Mayo before the selection and passed with flying colors. He's got the body of a forty-year-old."

"But hasn't he had prostate cancer?"

"Six out of ten men over fifty get it," Jay replied. "He's been cancer-free for years."

Goodman frowned.

"We can get you on the phone with the doctors if you want a backgrounder."

"That's usually a snow job," said Goodman dismissively. "We're going to want his medical records."

"Up to the doctors, Hal. See you on the trail." He flashed Goodman a fake smile, refusing to let him ruin his chipper mood. He walked away, heading for the motorcade, then turned back. "It's a two-fer. He's a pro-life Catholic and a southerner. So you can dig through his medical records all you want, we just put millions of Catholic votes in one back pocket."

"You'll be hearing from us," Goodman promised.

G.G. HOTERMAN WORKED HIS way through an egg-white omelet filled with basil and spinach, tomatoes and cheddar cheese. As he chewed, he turned on his BlackBerry, which he hadn't checked since the night before. An email from Walt Shapiro read, "Tough piece in today's *Post* by Dan Dorman. Call when you get a chance." Hoterman felt his blood pressure spike. If the story was under Dorman's byline, it was bound to be a drive-by shooting, and his romantic weekend in the Adirondacks was ruined.

Deirdre was at the stove whipping up an omelet, looking sexy and mussed in her bare feet and tousled hair, her creamy white skin contrasting with her black kimono bathrobe, its silk hemline at her knees.

Hoterman grabbed his cup of coffee and hurried back to his study, turning on the computer and logging onto the *Washington Post* website. The screaming headline jumped off the screen: "Stanley Campaign Laundered Funds Through Nonprofit Group to Pay Delegates." Hoterman read the lede: "The Stanley for President campaign utilized a tangled and complex web of tax-exempt organizations to funnel money to delegates and elected officials pledged to support his candidacy in apparent violation of federal election and tax laws, according to documents obtained by federal investigators conducting a criminal probe into allegations of bribery and perjury by campaign officials."

Nice touch, Dan, thought Hoterman. Dorman had managed to squeeze innuendo, guilt by association, and unsubstantiated rumor into a single sentence.

The story featured a "cast of characters" diagram with photographs and bios (including Hoterman's) and a sinister "follow the money" diagram with arrows leading from donors to nonprofit groups to Virginia delegates.

What he read next almost made his heart stop: "Democratic lobbyist G.G. Hoterman led the effort to raise funds for the Committee for a Better America, which in turn made payments totaling $675,000 to Virginia delegates, family members, and elected officials, according to internal Stanley campaign documents." Who were they getting the documents from? Hoterman certainly hadn't kept anything—that was why he had a paper shredder. "According to election law experts," Dorman's article continued, "expenditures by nonprofit groups coordinated with the Stanley campaign may have constituted illegal corporate contributions, violating federal election law and Internal Revenue Service guidelines."

"What a joke!" exclaimed Hoterman, shaking his head. The Committee for a Better America was a qualified 501(c)(4) issue organization. The law allowed it to engage in political activity, and Dorman knew it. The article was a smear job!

He read on. "Payments to Virginia delegates, if made in exchange for supporting Stanley, may also run afoul of federal antibribery statutes. The payments have become a major focus of the investigation, and the Justice Department has issued subpoenas to, among others, Melinda Lipper, the Stanley campaign's fund-raising consultant."

Melinda Lipper! If the FBI had Melinda's records, then someone was going down, and the only question was who. The timing for G.G. could not have been worse. His FBI interview was the following week.

Hoterman went back to the kitchen. Deirdre reclined at the kitchen table, her legs curled beneath her, eating from a bowl of fresh berries as she lazily flipped through the Sunday *New York Times*.

"What's wrong, honey?" she asked. "You look like you've been hit by a bus."

"There's a hit piece on the front page of the *Washington Post*."

"About Virginia?"

"Yes. The focus is on the Committee for a Better America and the people it hired to do work in Virginia. It was all legal. But the *Post* smells blood."

"I thought Melinda Lipper raised most of that money."

"She may have gone over to the dark side," he said.

Deirdre shifted in her chair, her cheeks flushing red.

"They hit her with a subpoena and it looks like she cracked. She's leaking. Now the focus is on me," he said. And he knew why. He had hosted early planning meetings for the Committee for a Better America, which carpet-bombed Long with negative mail, phone banks, and radio ads. Later CBA joined in the mad scramble for delegates in Virginia. Its activities crossed into gray areas—every candidate had a 527 or 501(c)(4) to do his dirty work.

"Why you?" Deirdre said. "You did *nothing* illegal."

"That and a quarter will get you a cup of coffee in Washington," answered Hoterman matter-of-factly.

Deirdre pushed her plate away and got up to freshen her coffee. "Good people are going to be ruined." She looked at G.G. with desperate eyes.

G.G. smiled. "Washington scandals burn like funeral pyres, and they only go out after the angry mob has tossed someone to the flames to pacify the gods."

Deirdre put down her coffee and walked over to G.G., placing her hands on his broad shoulders and pushing him down into the kitchen chair. She sat on his lap, legs dangling, and he wrapped his arms around her waist. She put her head against his chest. "I'm scared, G.G.," she said quietly.

Hoterman stroked her hair gently. "Don't worry. Shapiro's a great lawyer. The press is going to be brutal, but we'll survive." The truth was, he was up to his armpits in the scandal, but he didn't want to ruin the weekend more than it had already been wrecked by Dan Dorman's story.

"I hope you're right," Deirdre whispered, burying her nose in his collarbone.

"THIS IS THE BEST fried-egg sandwich I've ever had in my life," exclaimed Bob Long, a gigantic bite bulging out of his right cheek like an acorn in the mouth of a squirrel. "Go back to that country store and get me another one of these fried-egg sandwiches!" he shouted to the bus driver. "I promise every American family fried-egg sandwiches for breakfast and a chicken in every pot!"

Everyone laughed uproariously. Wasn't Bob Long a stitch!

Long rumbled down the interstate in his customized touring bus on his way to the fifth stop of the "Your Choice, America!" tour. Along for the ride was his newly minted running mate, Johnny Whitehead, on his maiden campaign trip. The ostensible purpose of the tour was to fire up the volunteers circulating ballot access petitions. But Long's crowds had gotten so large that the campaign had hired two more buses just to accommodate press. Ten thousand people in Chicago, twelve thousand people in Saint Louis, and the crowds kept growing. Long was like a rock star on the rise, playing to packed arenas, and among the press on the bus were reporters from *GQ* and *Rolling Stone*. A hundred cars and trucks loaded with Long groupies joined the caravan. They honked horns, waving to people who lined the road by the thousands, campaign flags fluttering in the wind. Long's bus tour resembled Ken Kesey and his Merry Pranksters but without the hallucinogenic drugs.

The press was grateful for the show. The Stanley campaign plane had become a funeral hearse. David Petty crouched inside a hermetically sealed bubble of handlers, granting no interviews, holding no news avails, and blowing off the Sunday chat shows. Into this miasma of boredom had stepped Bob Long, the pied piper of American politics. He had sparked a modern grassroots rebellion, with an army that now numbered three million volunteers. His rolling, off-the-record news conferences had become legendary.

"What do you make of the uproar on the right over Petty choosing Edward Bell?" asked the Associated Press, the reporter's face lit with anticipation.

"This is off the record, right?" asked Long.

"But of course," giggled the AP to the knowing smiles of his colleagues.

"Ed Bell is a legend in his own mind," answered Long. Happy faces looked up from steno pads. Johnny Whitehead grinned awkwardly (Bell was a former Senate colleague and longtime nemesis), while Lisa Robinson shot

Long a disapproving glare. He was walking on a high wire, flirting with danger, toying with the press. "The Republican base hates him for the same reason you guys love him. He's good copy. But he's going to hurt Petty among conservative voters."

"Senator, do you agree?" asked *USA Today*.

Whitehead flashed a nervous smile. "Yes, but don't quote me."

"To whom do we attribute this nugget of wisdom?" asked the *Los Angeles Times*.

"How about a 'senior Long strategist'?" Long joked. "Come to think of it, that observation was so brilliant, you should attribute it to Jay." They guffawed.

Jay Noble stood in the aisle, swaying with the bus while he guzzled from a water bottle. His face cracked into an embarrassing grin.

"Five minutes!" shouted an advance man.

The bus pulled off the interstate and rolled in front of the state capitol in Jefferson City, Missouri. Long's handlers had estimated the rally would draw a crowd of five thousand people. Long peered out the window. Hundreds of supporters ran alongside, waving, slapping the side of the bus, calling out his name. A sea of humanity spread out across the capitol grounds. Everyone in the bus felt their pulse quicken.

Jay Noble barked orders into his cell phone. "I want the kid to come onstage and hand his petition to the governor!" A pause. "Really? Wow!"

"What?" asked Long excitedly.

"The police estimate the crowd at twenty thousand people. Apparently there's a traffic jam from all the people coming."

Long's eyes widened like saucers. The bus door flew open and Long bounded down the stairs to a deafening roar.

"There he is! There he is!" shouted the crowd.

John Mellencamp's "This Is Our Country" boomed from gigantic loudspeakers on both sides of the stage. Long hugged, grasped, kissed, and high-fived his way down the rope line to the stage. When he bounded onto the platform, he raised his arms, and a guttural, primordial roar filled the air.

"Are you tired of the partisan bickering in Washington?" Long shouted.

"Yes!" the crowd shouted back.

"Then get some skin in the game and help me change it!" Loud applause.

Long introduced the thirteen-year-old boy who had gone door-to-door collecting petition signatures. The boy came out onstage with his beaming, nervous mother and Long conducted an impromptu interview.

"What's your name, young man?" asked Long.

"Jason," the lad answered.

"How old are you, Jason?"

"Thirteen. I turn fourteen in December."

"Still not old enough to vote. Sorry about that," Long joked to appreciative laughter. "How many doors did you knock on to collect your signatures?"

"I don't know. I didn't count them."

More laughter. Long threw his head back and dropped the microphone to his chest, sharing the moment with the audience.

The boy leaned forward again and Long lowered the microphone to his mouth. "Not many people turned me down, sir."

"And how many petitions did you collect?"

"One thousand, two hundred and sixty-eight." Audible gasps and cheers. The crowd applauded enthusiastically.

A smiling Long turned to Jason's mother. "Your son is different, isn't he?" The crowd erupted with laughter.

"Yes, he is. He doesn't spend a lot of time watching MTV. I tell him he's an adult trapped in a teenager's body. Governor . . . you inspired him."

As the crowd applauded, Jason raised his stack of petitions and handed them to Long, who bent over from the waist, peering into his eyes. This was the money shot. Camera shutters whirred and clicked. Jay Noble stood to the side of the stage, smiling like a proud father. His arms were folded across his chest, and his eyes darted over the crowd. Bob Long was starting to look like a winner.

There was only one problem: Missouri's ballot petition deadline had already passed. If the campaign didn't win the lawsuits it had filed to force him on the ballot, the entire exercise was moot. This was what kept Jay awake at night. The worst part? It was all in the hands of the lawyers.

28

G.G. HOTERMAN GAZED OUT the window at the emerald-blue ocean below as the pilot made the final approach into Bermuda. It was a clear day, not a cloud in the sky. As the plane dipped over the causeway leading to the main island and landed on the runway, Hoterman gathered up his papers and shoved them into his brown leather satchel. Waiting for him at the FBO was Stephen Fox, Internet billionaire and Democratic donor extraordinaire.

"G.G., I hope you had a good flight," Stephen greeted him.

"Thanks for seeing me on short notice," replied Hoterman, his handshake firm.

Fox's company, Future Networks, was a client of Hoterman's firm. Fox had founded a travel website as a graduate student at UC–Berkeley, later taking it public. When the stock soared, he became an instant paper billionaire, and he used the inflated stock to fund acquisitions, methodically building an Internet business empire. His net worth stood at $3 billion.

Hoterman sank into the smooth, creamy leather seat of Fox's midnight blue Bentley. Fox skillfully guided the car out of the airport and onto a busy highway, its buttery ride navigated by his two fingers on the steering wheel. The car turned up a hill toward Tucker's Point, a high point on the island with a breathtaking view of the harbor. They drove down a long, winding driveway to the gigantic main house, painted a startling yellow, where a houseman stood at attention.

"Orlando, please show Mr. Hoterman to his room," said Fox. "G.G., make yourself at home. Felicity's down by the pool. Why don't you change and join us?"

Hoterman slipped off his street clothes and changed into a swimsuit and T-shirt. He headed across the marble floor to an open patio leading to the pool. Stephen relaxed shirtless in a lounge chair under an umbrella, in a pair of khaki shorts, leather sandals, and silver-framed, smoke-lensed Chrome Hearts sunglasses. His well-defined pectoral muscles looked like slabs of rock above his washboard abs. His wavy pompadour of silver hair had been combed to the back of his head, where it collected in a mass of little-boy curls. He was in midsentence on his cell phone.

"How much a share?" He waved Hoterman to a chair. "Thirty-eight? Okay. What's the exit strategy?" A long pause. "Keep me posted." He hung up. He let out a long sigh and looked Hoterman up and down. "Sell health-care stocks short, old boy," he said. "I'm shorting them for all they're worth . . . and I'm making a killing!"

"I'll keep that in mind," answered Hoterman.

"Felicity!" Stephen shouted. "Come and join us!"

Hoterman turned to see Felicity, Fox's second wife, gliding down the pink marble stairs. Her dark brown, wavy hair had been piled into a bun, and her platform sandals made her look even taller than her five-foot, nine-inch height. She wore a black string bikini with a wraparound skirt, her skin tanned to a deep bronze, Chanel sunglasses completing her stunning outfit. Her back, shoulder, and thigh muscles rippled as she walked.

"G.G., hello, my darling!" Felicity called as she slinked toward their table.

"Felicity, you look fantastic," G.G. said, he hoped not too enthusiastically.

"Thank you, honey," she answered in her distinctive Long Island accent. "The architect is coming on Friday," she informed Stephen, changing subjects.

The men just gazed at her.

"We're redoing our bedroom," she told G.G. "I *adore* this architect. Stephen and I met him at a charity benefit and I *loved* his work. The wall treatments are *to die for.* They were white and I ran my hand over them. They felt like patent leather!" Her face lit up at the recollection. "They looked almost silver, and bumpy like the hide of an elephant. His work is *beautiful.*"

Hoterman's eyes drank her in, paying no attention to anything she said.

"Anyway, we're tearing down the wall that leads to the kitchen and he's doing the entire hallway," she continued. "I can't wait."

"Felicity, why don't you join us for lunch?" asked Stephen.

"I'd love to, darling, but I'm meeting a girlfriend," she demurred, crossing her legs. "Besides, all you and G.G. will do is talk shop. *Boring!*"

Stephen's cell phone shrilled. He picked it up and looked at the display.

"This guy's a loser," he said with disgust. "The last time I took his call he conferenced-in his banker. Can you imagine?"

"I'm boiling," complained Felicity. "It is burning up. Aren't you boiling?"

"Boiling," agreed Stephen.

"Boiling," repeated Felicity. "I need to get in the water." She untied her skirt and draped it over her chair, dipping a toe into the water and then delicately stepping into the pool. A rainbow butterfly was tattooed on the small of her back.

Stephen's cell phone rang yet again. He listened attentively for a minute or two. "How much?" he asked the caller. "A hundred and forty-five million?" A pause. "I'm willing to make an offer, but I have no interest in driving up the price. If he's serious, then let's talk."

Orlando appeared with a tray of lemonade and iced tea. G.G. took an iced tea and Stephen grabbed a lemonade, slowly twirling the ice with the straw.

"So what brings you here?" asked Stephen. "Something tells me you want money."

"I need your help," said Hoterman, turning serious. "Bob Long is raising a lot of money on the Internet, and he's rising in the polls. Our lawyers are fighting him tooth and nail, but he's getting on a lot of state ballots. He can do to Stanley what Nader did to Gore in 2000. It could elect Petty."

"He has to be stopped," agreed Stephen. "What's your strategy?"

"I'm helping to set up a new 527 organization called Citizens for Truth," answered G.G. "We're going to hit Long high and hard."

"Good. You need to. Long supports the secret war against Iran. How can I help?"

"We need folks to step up to the plate with cornerstone contributions. We have three levels: one million, five million, and ten million. Our plan is to spend ninety million dollars on television in the targeted states. If we can raise the money, we will knee-cap Long. He'll drop like a rock in the polls and Stanley will win."

"I love it. Count me in," said Stephen.

"What level can I put you down for?"

"Ten million," snapped Stephen. "And I'll tell you what else I'll do. I'm going to call some friends and get them to match me. If I'm going to step up, I don't want to go alone. Put my partners down for another five million. If they don't give it, I will. How does that grab you?"

"Can I hug you?" asked G.G. He had his cornerstone investor! And not only that, Stephen was going to help raise more. G.G. was in tall cotton.

"No, you can't. By the way, are you going to be all right on this Virginia delegation investigation?" asked Stephen, looking concerned. "The press is really raking you over the coals."

"I'm fine," assured G.G., his facial features hard. "I've hired Walter Shapiro. He's never lost a case. But in the meantime, the media is going to get its pound of flesh." G.G. chose not to mention the fact that his FBI interview was any day now and that his deputy and mistress were likely to be called before the grand jury.

"Good," said Stephen cheerily. "I hope Michael Kaplan will be all right."

"Mike's got issues. He's getting ready to go through the dry cycle with a box of razor blades."

"I don't know if I told you, but the Justice Department sent me a subpoena."

"You're kidding!" exclaimed G.G.

"I wrote a $250,000 check to the Committee for a Better America, so they wanted a bunch of records from me, including emails with you and the Stanley campaign. I told my lawyer to tell them where they could shove their subpoena."

"Good for you," said G.G. His mind raced—if his name was turning up in subpoenas, it was not a good sign. He made a mental note to alert Walt Shapiro.

"I can't prove it," Stephen said, "but I think that's why the Federal Trade Commission is slow-walking one of our acquisitions. They claim it raises antitrust concerns. Pure baloney. They're messing with my stock price."

"People in the Nixon administration went to jail for less than that."

"We're going to have to fumigate the White House when this crew is gone," Stephen said.

Felicity waded over to the side of the pool and pulled herself out of the water. The water dripped off her brown skin and formed small pools at her feet. She threw her head back and arched her back as she patted herself with a towel, her arms and legs stretched. G.G. tried not to gawk. Her cell phone rang and she picked it up.

"I can't do Hard Rock Cafe," she said. "Stephen and I have an out-of-town guest for dinner." She winked at G.G. "Ooooh, not him! I can't take him. He's just icky. Ickily egoistic." Another pause. "Are you sure it's kosher? Because if it's New York strip, it can't be kosher, honey."

Stephen's cell phone rang again. He began to bark orders, rattling off financial figures and deal details. They sat a foot apart, ignoring each other, chattering away on their cell phones. G.G. wondered how much of their lives was spent this way.

Stephen hung up and glanced at his watch. "I lost track of the time! Let's go." He looked over at Felicity. "Which watch is that?" he asked.

"This is my Piaget," she said proudly, extending her wrist. "Do you like it?"

Stephen shook his head. "Women change watches like they change clothes," he said, wincing. "I can't do that. If I take off my Rolex, it stops, then I have to adjust the time. It's a pain."

G.G. and Stephen jumped in the Bentley and drove to the Mid Ocean Club, which boasted one of the finest golf courses in the world. Over a lunch of conch salad and beer, Stephen impulsively suggested they play golf. G.G. protested that he had neither proper clothes nor his clubs. Stephen was unmoved. At his insistence, they blew through the pro shop, buying a shirt, shorts, and golf shoes for G.G., and headed to the first tee.

Stephen stretched and loosened up on the tee box, chatting it up with the caddy, who instantly became his best friend. Without having hit a single practice ball, he proceeded to rip his drive 280 yards over the three fairway bunkers on the left, cutting the distance to the hole, and safely landed his approach shot on the green. He scored a par; Hoterman bogeyed. They agreed on a friendly wager, and needled each other mercilessly as they worked their way around the course. Hoterman was up by one hole when they reached the par-three seventh, but Stephen landed a six-iron within three feet of the cup and sank the birdie putt.

They slugged it out for eighteen holes, consuming massive quantities of beer and cigars, all the while talking about how best to stop Long from hurting Stanley and how to keep David Petty from winning enough moderates to make up for the exodus of social conservatives.

When they reached the eighteenth hole, 421 yards straight into the wind with the ocean on their right, Hoterman was down a skin and needed to win the final hole to halve the match. Hitting into a stiff breeze, they both needed three shots to reach the green. After Stephen lagged his first putt to within a foot of the hole, Hoterman needed to drain his putt from twenty feet to avoid defeat. He wanted to win. Taking his time, he walked back and forth, reading the grain of the green, and finally leaned over the ball, lining up his putt.

"Hey, wait! We never agreed on the stakes," Stephen said.

"Makes no difference to me," shrugged Hoterman, "because this putt is going in."

"All right, tell you what—if you make the putt, I will raise my contribution to eleven million dollars. If you don't, I drop it to nine million."

Hoterman stood paralyzed as the blood drained from his face. Fox burst out laughing, slapping his knee like a little boy. He turned to the caddy. "Have you ever seen a two-million-dollar putt?" he asked.

"No, sir, I can't say I have," answered the caddy.

G.G. didn't know if Stephen was kidding or not. As he stood over the putt, it looked to him as if the green broke toward the ocean, but he couldn't be sure. To make matters worse, he was using rental clubs. He firmly rapped the ball. It rolled rapidly along the bent grass. At the last second, just before it reached the cup, the putt slowed, dove toward the hole, and fell in the side of the cup. Stephen raised his arms and let out a yell. He gave G.G. a big hug.

"You made a two-million-dollar putt on the eighteenth green at Mid Ocean!" he shouted.

Stephen handed a pair of hundred-dollar bills to the caddy with a slap on the back, then walked up the steps to the clubhouse and into the bar, where he proceeded to tell everyone who would listen about the putt. He and G.G. drank celebratory pints of Guinness and watched the sun go down over the ocean.

"What a great night for a cruise," Stephen announced spontaneously. "We can eat on the boat. I'll call Felicity."

After a flurry of rapid-fire phone calls and a quick shower in the locker room, they jumped in the Bentley. G.G. guessed the kitchen staff had been thrown for a loop. But in Stephen Fox's economy, everyone else rode in steer-age when they bought a ticket to life, and they would just have to roll with the punches.

As they pulled up to the dock, G.G. was stunned by the yacht's size and beauty. Its fiberglass hull rose from the water like a floating palace, with blue siding and an observation deck complete with a crow's nest and radar and communications antennae. The crew scurried about untying lines and ready-ing the boat for the evening sail. They found Felicity below at the bar mak-ing drinks. She had changed into a yellow top and gold-embroidered white jeans with matching gold Jimmy Choo shoes.

"Felicity makes a mean martini," Stephen bragged.

"In that case, a martini it is," G.G. said.

"My shoulder's killing me," announced Stephen, looking for sympathy.

"Did you give yourself a charley horse with one of those 280-yard drives?"

"No, I fell off a horse playing polo." He let out a low groan. "I need to see my chiropractor."

As Felicity poured the drinks, Stephen excused himself to make a phone call.

"You're going to absolutely *love* this cook," Felicity said, spearing a rasp-berry in her razztini with a toothpick. "He is *brilliant*. We found him through a mutual friend in New York. He can design an entire menu around what-ever diet you're on."

"Really?"

"Yes! Atkins, the Zone, South Beach, Weight Watchers—doesn't matter. When Stephen and I were doing Atkins, he went heavy protein and low carb, lots of salmon and chicken. No pasta. I told Stephen I don't want cellu-lite—ever! Ugh!" She closed her eyes, grimacing as if drinking vinegar. "Any-way, he's *wonderful*."

G.G. was enraptured, but he was beginning to feel a little self-conscious. His idea of a diet was to cut back to only two bourbon-and-waters a day.

Stephen breezed in from the master bedroom. "G.G., I just found out I have to go to L.A. I have a business meeting with Jeffrey Gabel. Why don't you come with me?"

L.A. was on the other side of the continent. But Gabel was one of the biggest Democratic givers in Hollywood. He was A-list.

"But my plane is here."

"Send your plane back to D.C. and ride with me. My plane is nicer anyway," chuckled Stephen. "I'll drop you off in Washington on my way back to Bermuda."

"You men and your toys!" Felicity rolled her eyes. "I've told Stephen we need another plane," she said, sipping on her martini. "Sometimes when you need your plane, it's in the wrong place."

"Come on, G.G.," Stephen urged. "We'll have fun. We'll stay at the Four Seasons, hang out with Jeffrey, have a nice dinner, and then we'll fly back the next day."

"Sure," shrugged Hoterman, smiling. "Why not?"

His grin masked an unpleasant secret: he needed to get back to D.C. for his FBI interview. People had gone to prison for making false statements to the FBI. Hoterman still had thousands of pages of documents to review, and the L.A. trip was going to put even more pressure on him. But he couldn't say no to Stephen, not after he had just agreed to give or raise $16 million.

They sat down at the dining room table. A waiter brought a foie gras appetizer.

"I told you, darling," Felicity whispered, patting G.G. on the arm. "This chef is an *absolute master*." She gazed down at the foie gras, the meat sliced and fanned across a piece of crustless toast, a bed of sliced apples surrounded by a mango puree. "Oh, Stephen, I wish I could cook like this," she sighed.

"You don't have to, honey," Stephen replied, not missing a beat. "You have other talents that are far more desirable."

Felicity smiled.

As G.G. took a bite of his foie gras, he realized he had no clothes for the trip to L.A. The thought entered his head to send his plane back to D.C. to pick up one of his nice Italian suits and fly it back to him, but he figured that would be bad form.

———

"THE TEXAS SUPREME COURT'S decision is a devastating blow to the Long campaign," boomed Marvin Myers as the enraptured anchor looked on.

"His legal team *had* to win this case. He's doing well in the polls in Texas and he desperately needed its thirty-eight electoral votes. This puts his entire campaign strategy in jeopardy."

The Supreme Court in Texas had just announced its decision in the Long ballot access case, and the news rocked the political world: the court had rejected Long's claim that the state's early qualifying deadline was unconstitutional.

"Long is getting on the ballot in most states," the anchor noted. "For Texas and other states with early filing deadlines, does he have any legal recourse?"

"He can appeal today's decision to the federal courts," Myers replied. "But there is no guarantee they will hear it. If they don't, today's decision, for all practical purposes, marks the end of the Long campaign as a genuine national effort."

"A major setback for Bob Long," said the anchor. "Thank you, Marvin."

Myers unclipped his microphone and strode off the set, walking out of the studio and down the hall to the makeup room. As he stood in front of the mirror wiping the powder off his face with a wet towelette, his cell phone shrilled.

"Marvin, why are you trying to kill us!" screamed the voice on the other end of the phone. It was Jay Noble, and he was livid.

"I'm not," Myers protested. "I'm reporting what happened."

"Bull!" shouted Noble, his voice shaking. "We knew Texas would rule against us. We've already got the appeal ready and it will be filed with the Fifth Circuit Court of Appeals *today*. We're doing same thing Anderson did in 1980, and we will have the same outcome. We're going to be on all fifty state ballots."

"I know that's your plan, Jay, but it isn't going to be easy."

"It's going to be a lot harder if you keep distorting the facts, Marvin!"

"Hold your horses. I have reported when you won state ballot contests, but this is a setback. Don't shoot the messenger."

"Our lawyer, who has won four Supreme Court decisions, tells me a filing deadline outside ninety days will not withstand federal appellate court scrutiny. Now that's a *relevant* fact. Next time, you might want to mention it."

"It's not a fact," Myers said. "It's an opinion."

"Marvin, I took care of you in Chicago!" yelled Jay. "All I'm asking for is fairness."

"Yes, and then you lied to me about Long running as an independent."

"Good-bye, Marvin." The phone line went dead.

29

G UESS WHO BEAT ME to the punch?" Andy Stanton half whispered into
the phone.

"Who?" asked Ross.

Stanton liked to keep Ross off-balance, keeping him guessing, playing
twenty questions. Andy was always one chess move ahead. In the strange
Hegelian construct of their relationship, there was no question who was
master and who was slave.

"Bob Long. I just hung up with him."

"Sounds like great minds think alike," Ross said.

"Come over to my office. I want to discuss this face-to-face."

Ross hung up, grabbed his gray pin-striped suit coat, and jogged out the
door, calling out to his assistant that he would be available on his cell phone.
Driving across the sprawling campus of New Life Ministries in his Lexus
400 sedan, his mind raced, anticipating what the contact with Long would
mean, what Andy would want to know, what the wise response on their part
would be. He took the elevator to Stanton's office, where he found Andy in
front of M.J.'s desk, flipping through a ream of papers, eyes darting across
the pages from behind gold-framed reading glasses that rested at an impossible angle at the end of his nose.

"Ross!" he bellowed. "That was quick." He placed the papers on the desk,
sighing wearily. "M.J., give those to the lawyers."

"What is it?" asked Ross.

"Another lawsuit. This time it's a ten-million-dollar libel suit by an abortion doctor who claims I hurt his practice."

"Good grief," sighed Ross.

He ushered Ross into his private office and closed the door. They settled
into the two wing chairs in the formal sitting area off to the side. Andy's eyes
bored into Ross like lasers, his fingers making a chapel steeple across his
chest, his massive legs crossed. Ross leaned forward expectantly.

"Bob Long has come to Christ," announced Andy with dramatic flair.

"You're kidding. Really?"

"It happened six weeks ago at the hospital where his oldest daughter was having a baby in a breech delivery. The baby almost died. It was a very moving testimony." Andy paused, letting his hands fall to his laps. "I believe him."

"That would make it easier for us to help him," said Ross, wheels turning. Whatever he had expected, this wasn't it. "But he will have to move on the moral issues. He's pro-choice."

"He's coming our way. He said when he committed his life to Christ, for the first time it stopped being about him and became about the Lord." Stanton's eyes grew wide and he dropped his chin. "Brother, if this is true, this presidential race may blow wide open."

"The Whitehead pick sure indicates he's moving in the right direction."

"He's a changed man," Andy said.

"If this is true, God has a well-developed sense of humor," Ross chuckled.

"God's bigger than all of us, Ross. His plans are always better than our plans," Stanton answered in his firmest ministerial baritone. "Here's what I want to do. The Bible says there is wisdom in a multitude of counsel. I don't want to be a lone ranger. If we help Long, it has to be a team effort if it's going to be effective."

"What do you have in mind?"

"Let's put together a meeting with Long and some evangelical leaders. The usual types: Max Van Buskirk, as difficult as he can be sometimes; Jerry Patterson with the Southern Baptist Convention; and Paul Parks for starters. The meeting is invitation only, off the record, and no more than a dozen people in attendance. Real players. People with large audiences, big churches, and troops."

"Excellent idea."

"Let's invite Long to come to the top of the meeting and share his testimony and discuss the issues. No holds barred."

"I'll get on it today," Ross answered. "We can find a central location in the middle of the country and get a meeting room at an airport hotel so people from both coasts can get there conveniently."

"Call Long's campaign guru—you know, the smart guy—to arrange his attendance. What's his name again?"

"Jay Noble."

"Right, Noble," Andy recalled, snapping his fingers. "When you get to my age, you'll have a hard time with names." He rose from the chair, towering over Ross, his charcoal slacks and tailored blue blazer flowing perfectly over his athletic frame, a matching silk burgundy tie and handkerchief in the pocket. He smiled broadly, and his blue eyes blazed like headlights.

There was an angel in the whirlwind. Perhaps the good Lord had reached down and gotten hold of Bob Long's heart for a reason. They were about to find out.

———

BOB LONG HUNG UP the phone and narrowed his eyes, staring down the table at his Brain Trust. Everyone held their breath. The suspense cut like a knife.

"Stanton liked what I had to say," Long reported. "He offered to set up a meeting with evangelical leaders. That's good, don't you think?"

"Outstanding!" Jay exclaimed, clapping his hands. "Now we're talking."

"As long as it's private," said Lisa Robinson, looking concerned. Lisa was the eternal pessimist, her political radar permanently tuned to impending danger. "It is unsustainably incongruous if it looks like you're trying to become the candidate of the religious right."

"Whoa!" shouted Jay. "Give Lisa an apple. She wins the prize for using the biggest words at a strategy meeting."

"Where's the dictionary?" joked Hollywood.

David Thomas grabbed an apple from the wilting breakfast tray and placed it in front of Lisa. It rolled like an oblong soccer ball, to the cackles of her colleagues.

"What?" Lisa reacted with irritation. "You guys don't have vocabularies?"

"I have a vocabulary," shot back Hollywood. "It consists of three words: kill . . . the . . . opponent." He raised his three middle fingers from his clenched fist as he spit out the words.

"All right, enough of the stand-up routine," ordered Long, growing impatient. "Lisa raises a good point. What do we do when the evangelicals ask me to change my position on abortion and gay rights? I don't know that I can do a total flip-flop."

"Governor, here's what you should do," suggested David Thomas, his eyes intense. "Sit down with your minister, discuss what happened during the birth of your grandson, and talk about when life begins. Then meet with the evangelical leaders and tell them you've had an epiphany and a change of heart. Afterward, go to an evangelical college and deliver a major speech on values and explain your new position."

"You want me to manipulate my religion for political advantage?" Long asked, his face etched with disgust.

"Governor, I want you to win."

"So do I," Long replied, glaring at Thomas. "But if I do that, the Republicans and the Democrats will both attack me as a flip-flopper. They'll have videos of my old pro-choice statements on YouTube. They will say I exploited a personal tragedy—nearly losing my grandson—in a cynical play for votes."

"And you'd win."

Long looked around the table. No one said a word.

"I can't mention my grandson," he said at last.

"Governor, you have to mention him," Jay insisted in a firm voice. "Voters grapple with abortion on an emotional level. They need to see your heart, not your head."

Long looked deflated and defeated. He looked around the room for allies. There were none. "I've been pro-choice through twelve years of campaigning for and holding public office. How do I change now?"

"In a delicately calibrated way," Lisa said. "You can't come out for a ban on abortion. If you turn a hundred and eighty degrees, you'll lose your support among moderate and independent voters—they'll be turned off if they think you're beholden to Andy Stanton and a bunch of snake-handling, right-wing preachers."

"How about if I take the middle ground?" asked Long. "What if I favor restrictions like partial birth abortion and no federal funding, and say I will appoint strict constructionist judges? That's what they really want."

"Hogs in the middle of the road get run over," said Fred Edgewater, the pollster.

"The governor's right" interjected Hollywood. "If he totally flip-flops, he loses all credibility. It will kill us with independents. They like the governor because he is beholden to no special interest. He has to meet the evangelicals halfway."

Jay shot Hollywood a dirty look across the table. He wasn't used to being corrected in matters of strategy. Scottie just smiled back.

"Governor, if it makes you feel more comfortable," said Jay, "we can make the speech focus on faith and policy, and keep the part about your family brief. It could be a paragraph at most."

"This is not a spiritual striptease," added Lisa, trying to reassure him.

"All right, work up two versions of the speech," Long said. "One draft with the personal stuff in it, a second draft without it." He turned to Jay. "And set up the meeting with the evangelical leaders."

"Okay," replied Jay. "I'll get the speechwriters working. We also need a venue for the speech. I'll sound out Ross Lombardy—he's Andy Stanton's version of me."

"This is not an abortion speech," insisted Long, tapping the table. "It has to be broader, addressing poverty, the underclass, and human rights. It needs poetry and eloquence. Get me a Reinhold Niebuhr or C. S. Lewis quote."

"Now look who's showing off!" laughed Lisa. "Reinhold Niebuhr, wow!"

Jay raised his chin upward and stretched his neck as if he were singing in a choir. "We will bind the wounds of our nation with the healing balm of rhetoric," he said in a sarcastic falsetto. Everyone broke up—except for Long, who glared at him.

VIC GASKINS, CHIEF LOCAL political reporter for the *Quad-City Times,* was anything but a Bigfoot; he was about as low as one could be on the journalistic food chain. But that was about to change. Gaskins lurked in the shadows, leaning up against a concrete wall, waiting for David Petty's motorcade to pull up to the convention center.

Petty's limo screamed to a stop. He jumped out and bounded up the stairs of the loading dock, surrounded by Secret Service agents and advance staff. He strode to a line of "greeters"—the donors, elected officials, and grassroots leaders who had been selected by the campaign to shake Petty's hand and engage in a brief moment of false intimacy as a reward for their loyalty. As Petty stepped to the end of the greeting line, he turned to one of the party dignitaries (Gaskins thought he recognized him as a former state GOP chairman) and engaged in an animated conversation that Petty clearly intended to be private but that took place just within Gaskins's hearing. Instinctively, Gaskins whipped out his cell phone and recorded the scene with the phone's video camera. Was Petty saying what Gaskins thought he was? His eyes nervously darted from the screen to an advance man who watched him with a disapproving glare.

When Petty had finished, Gaskins slid his cell phone in his pocket and stepped forward. "General Petty?"

Petty turned.

"Vic Gaskins with the *Quad-City Times*. Can I ask you a question while you walk?"

"Sure," replied Petty hurriedly. His head was down, eyes studying the concrete floor, feet moving rapidly.

"Forgive me, but I could not help overhearing your conversation. Did I hear you say that your agreement not to change the Republican platform on abortion was only symbolic?"

"That was a private conversation," shot back Petty, clearly annoyed.

"But you said the party platform means nothing. Don't you think that will offend a lot of conservatives?"

"Right now, I have to do this rally," Petty said dismissively. He ducked into a holding area behind a blue drape.

An advance man who looked like a cross between an NFL linebacker and a bar bouncer guarded the entrance. "Sir, this is a secure area," he said. He peered down at the press badge dangling around Gaskins's neck. "This area is off-limits."

"No problem," responded Gaskins, his face flushed with excitement. He scurried back to the press filing room as fast as his legs could carry him. As he walked, he pulled up the video clip on his cell phone and played it back. The clip was only about ninety seconds long, but the sound and video quality were astonishingly good for a cell phone. Gaskins's hands were shaking as he held the phone. He dialed the number for his editor. He had hit the jackpot.

G.G. HOTERMAN AND STEPHEN Fox followed Jeffrey Gabel's African-American executive assistant as she walked down the hallway. Her hips swayed rhythmically in her designer dress, which was a tad short even by L.A. standards; her long legs were mesmerizing as they moved back and forth in four-inch heels. She led the way to Gabel's large, sun-splashed office on the sprawling campus of New Generation Studios.

Gabel sat behind his mammoth desk talking on the phone, deeply engrossed in conversation. His white-sneakered feet rested on the desktop, his athletic physique wrapped in a Dolce & Gabbana white T-shirt and snug designer jeans. The secretary directed Hoterman and Fox to the couch, where a late breakfast of freshly squeezed orange juice, coffee, fresh fruit, and bran muffins lay on the table.

"But you *will* get a production credit," said Gabel into the phone. "You're not being asked to just sing the songs for the sound track. Do you think I would treat you that way?" He paused. "Honey, I'm always looking out for you. Don't hurt me like this. You're hurting me." Another pause. "All right, that's my girl. Now get back to work. Love you too, honey." He hung up the phone and shot a quick glance at Fox.

"I spend half my life stroking egos," he said. "Welcome to Hollywood."

In a town filled with big fish, Gabel was a whale. He had made his first fortune in the record business, selling his label to Sony/BMG and using the money to launch his own film studio. He had three Best Picture Oscars on his mantel and hits on every network, including the number one show on HBO. He lived in a Malibu mansion with one of the finest wine cellars in California, collected Impressionist art (he had a weakness for Renoirs), and got his pilot's license so he could fly his G-5 to his vacation home in the Turks and Caicos. He also sat on the board of the Los Angeles symphony and had given millions to Democratic candidates and liberal causes.

Gabel shot up from his chair and walked over to G.G., extending his hand, his tanned face grinning widely. "So this is the famous G.G. Hoterman!"

"Infamous is more like it," joked Stephen.

"You're looking great, Jeffrey," said G.G., extending a beefy palm.

"Thanks. I've never felt better. I'm doing yoga," replied Gabel, flopping down on the white leather couch and putting his sneakers up on the oversized coffee table.

"Yoga?" exclaimed Stephen. "You seem more like the weight-lifter type."

"Yoga will kick your tail. Try it. It's the best workout you'll ever have." He turned his entire body to face G.G. "I understand you've got a plan to take down Bob Long." He flashed a wicked grin, the age lines on his forehead showing. "I'm all ears."

"We do indeed," replied G.G. "It's a group called Citizens for Truth. It's a 527. We're planning on doing ninety million in paid media, mostly in the battleground states but some national cable. Long is a bad guy. We're going to tell the truth about him."

"It's about time!" shouted Gabel, eyes afire. "I know Bob well, you know. Total chameleon. He's *evil*. And I don't say that about very many people." He stopped and smiled. "Well, maybe I do."

"No one's laying a glove on him. That's about to change." G.G. smiled.

"The guy sat right here in my office—as close as you are to me right now—when he ran for the U.S. Senate—this was about twelve years ago—and told me he opposed employment discrimination against gays and lesbians," said Jeffrey. "Now he's moving to the right on everything. Then he picks Whitehead—what a phony!"

It was feeding time, and G.G. decided to drop the hook. "We want to go on television immediately. We're going to hit him on a land deal in Southern California where the value of some land he bought skyrocketed because of plans for a major road by his own transportation department."

Jeffrey's eyes widened. He turned to Stephen. "I love this guy!" he blurted. "He thinks like me. I love a good pitchman!"

"After that, we're going to hit him on flip-flopping. But first we soften him up with ethics."

"Great!" exclaimed Gabel. He took his hands and placed them behind his head, leaning back. "So, how much do you want?"

Hoterman walked through the budget and the giving levels.

"I'm giving eleven million," said Stephen, his arms resting on his knees. "It was ten million, but then G.G. made a twenty-foot putt on the eighteenth hole at Mid Ocean, so now it's eleven million."

"I'm not playing golf with you guys," replied Jeffrey, rolling his eyes. "You don't need to sell me. I hate the little weasel. Put me down for five million."

"Thank you, Jeffrey," said G.G., trying not to sound too excited. "We'll put it to good use."

"I know you will."

Jeffrey called in his assistant, and in breezed the willowy African-American woman, smiling effervescently, the faint smell of her perfume in the air. "Stephen and I have some other business to conduct," Jeffrey informed her. "Can you take G.G. down to the animation studio? Have them give him a tour of the new production." He turned to G.G. "You'll love seeing how they do the computer animation. It's amazing."

"Just follow me, Mr. Hoterman," the assistant instructed.

G.G. walked down the hallway with a new spring in his step. He was $5 million richer and no worse for the jet lag. He was actually looking forward to the studio tour. Ever since he had gone to Disney films as a young boy, he had wondered how they made cartoons.

THE *QUAD-CITY TIMES* POSTED the video from Vic Gaskins's cell phone on its website just as David Petty finished working the rope line at the Davenport campaign rally. Word spread like wildfire on the press riser in the back of the auditorium. Reporters scrambled to pull it up on their laptops and BlackBerries.

Among them was Dan Dorman of the *Washington Post*, who happened to be along for the ride on Petty's maiden swing through the battleground states of the Midwest. Predictably, Petty's handlers would not let Dorman anywhere near the candidate. He was riding in steerage with the other journalistic cattle, and he didn't like it one bit. Now it was payback time. This was going to be a bonanza: David Petty, unplugged!

"I've never seen so much corn in my life," said Petty, the outlines of his image slightly blurry on the video. "I guess that's why I'm for ethanol." Petty chuckled, hiking up his pants, twisting his lips and making a funny face.

"Oh, you have to be, around here," replied the volunteer.

"So let me get this straight. In Iowa, you're *for* ethanol and *against* abortion," joked Petty as he made amusing hand gestures. He paused and laughed. "Right?"

"A lot of Catholics and corn farmers here in Iowa, sir," joked the volunteer.

"That's why I have to say to the right that I'm not going to change the

platform on abortion. But it doesn't mean a thing," continued Petty, enjoying the joke. "Nobody reads the platform." Petty sighed. "The things you
have to say in a campaign." Grabbing the volunteer by the shoulder, he
asked, "Are you planning to run for office someday?"

"I might. I've thought about it."

Petty leaned into the man, their faces inches apart. "Well, I've been
around Washington a long time. I've seen people succeed, and I've seen a lot
of people fall. Just remember: more people have dug their graves with their
peckers than with shovels."

The volunteer's eyes widened like saucers. He was speechless, obviously
taken aback.

Dorman was ecstatic. His encyclopedic political mind flashed back to a
choked-up Ed Muskie denouncing Willie Loeb in the falling snow of New
Hampshire, Gary Hart with a blonde in his lap sitting next to a boat named
Monkey Business, John Kerry jabbing his finger in the air as he asserted that
he "voted for the $87 billion before I voted against it," and his personal fa-
vorite, Michael Dukakis riding in the tank. The Petty video was going to go
down in history as one of the great gaffes of all time!

Dorman emailed the link of the video to his editor in Washington: "This
conversation between Petty and a campaign volunteer was captured on video
by a reporter for the *Quad-City Times.* I'll have a story for you within thirty
minutes. You may want to get this up on our website ASAP. If you don't, our
readers will go elsewhere to view it." He hit the send button.

"Have you seen the Petty video?" asked Gannett News, sauntering over
to Dorman and a group of reporters hunched over their laptops. "It's already
on YouTube."

"Beyond belief!" exclaimed McClatchy Newspapers.

"Someone just emailed it to me," replied CNN. "We're putting it on the
air in a few minutes. And get this: we're going to bleep Petty."

"You're going to bleep him?" said *USA Today.* "That's worse than broadcasting what he said!"

"What's the Petty campaign saying?" asked ABC News.

"Not a thing. They're curled up in a fetal position," replied CNN.

"How about something new and original like, 'He misspoke,' " came the
dry reply from *USA Today.*

The reporters cackled.

Someone walked over and turned up the volume on the television set. The anchor teased the story: "Caught on tape: Republican presidential candidate David Petty in a conversation picked up by a cell phone video camera in Iowa ridicules ethanol and the Republican Party platform and uses a vulgarity. A warning to parents: this video includes language that may offend some."

The video played, and everyone in the press room stared, as though watching a car crash in slow motion. After the video, the anchor introduced Marvin Myers. "Marvin, this video is already generating criticism from Democrats. The Democratic National Committee has issued a press release urging, and I quote, 'David Petty to apologize immediately for offending the sensibilities of and violating the innocence of American children and families with his profane language.' How damaging is this?"

"Very damaging," answered Myers. "Petty's selection of Ed Bell had already offended evangelical leaders like Dr. Andrew Stanton," Myers continued. "This comment—which includes the salty language many candidates use behind closed doors, but which is not generally broadcast to the world—will add fuel to that fire."

"Could it lead evangelicals to defect from the Republican Party, or just stay home?" asked the anchor. His expansive, intense face seemed to beg, *Please, say it's so!*

"It's possible," answered Myers, courteously following the suggestion of the anchor. "Petty has a lot of explaining to do to the socially conservative base of the Republican Party—or what's left of it."

"Bravo! Bravo!" shouted several members of the press corps slumped in chairs and leaning over a tray of stale sandwiches in the back of the filing room. Already, several reporters were speed-dialing Republican members of Congress to read them Petty's comments and dutifully transcribe their background comments confirming that the campaign was in a tailspin. Petty was imploding!

Dorman punched in Merryprankster.com on his laptop. Atop the home page was the headline: "Petty Ridicules Pro-lifers; Dirty Joke Caught on Video!" Underneath were the words: "Click here to view Petty's profane joke."

As Dorman dialed the number for a Republican strategist who was always good for a pithy quote, a reporter with the *Charlotte Observer* leaned over and asked in a half whisper: "How did we do our jobs before the Internet?"

———

AN AIDE STUCK HIS head into the front compartment of the campaign plane, where Bob Long was playing a game of hearts with Lisa, Jay, and another staff member. It was 8 P.M. on the East Coast, and Long was flying west to make up time before an early event the following morning. "Governor, it's Phil Battaglia and David Thomas on the phone. They says it's urgent."

Long looked up with a start. He took the phone from the aide.

"Governor, it's David. I have Phil on the line."

"What's up?" asked Long excitedly. "Is it the Texas case?" Battaglia's voice came on the line crystal clear, as though he were calling from the next room.

"Governor, the decision just came down from the Fifth Circuit Court of Appeals on our Texas ballot access case." He paused, and Long's heart skipped a beat. "They ruled unanimously that the early filing deadline in Texas is unconstitutional. They've ordered the state legislature to change the law. Sir, this is total victory."

"Wow!" exclaimed Long. "That is fantastic news, Phil. Well done!"

"The best part," Phil added, "is that they voided it on both First and Fourteenth Amendment grounds. That strengthens our case for the appeal."

"Governor, this probably causes other states to either stand down or drop their own appeals of our legal victories," Thomas said. "So it isn't just Texas. This victory changes the whole ball game."

"This is huge!" Long said effusively. He looked across the table at Lisa and Jay and gave them a thumbs-up. Jay smiled broadly.

"It's not over, though. The Texas attorney general has already issued a statement saying he plans to appeal," Battaglia reported.

"Do you think the Supreme Court will take it?" Long furrowed his brow.

"Hard to say," replied Battaglia. "I doubt it because it's such a hot potato. If the Supremes take the case, the process drags out, and we'll have uncertainty until they render their decision."

"When will we know?"

"The Supreme Court can technically take a case whenever they want. But they have to move quickly if they want to reverse the Fifth Circuit. The appellate court issued an injunction with its decision ordering you on the ballot pending any appeal."

"Fabulous! You're the best election law lawyer in the country, Phil." He and Jay and the rest of the crew in the front compartment of the airplane broke into loud applause for their legal eagle. Lisa put her middle fingers in her mouth and let out a shrill whistle.

"Oh, and it gets better," chuckled Thomas. "Some Iowa reporter caught David Petty with a cell phone camera telling a profane joke to a supporter and ridiculing pro-lifers in the GOP. The video's up on YouTube and already has gotten two million hits."

Long's eyes widened. "The guy's never been through the wringer. He's never run for office. He's a first-time candidate running for president of the United States."

"Well, I'd say we've had a banner day," Thomas said joyfully. "Petty's stepped in it and you just got on the ballot in Texas."

Jay leaned over and whispered in Long's ear: "Do you have any idea how many evangelical voters there are in Texas?"

Long nodded his head vigorously.

30

I F A GRENADE WENT off in this room, it would mark the end of the vast right-wing conspiracy!" laughed Andy Stanton, his eyes twinkling with mirth. He had just walked into the conference room of the Hyatt hotel at Dallas/Fort Worth International Airport to find the most important evangelical players in the country standing in front of a table of food, nibbling on muffins and drinking coffee.

"Andy, as a charter member of the conspiracy, I can tell you we're in trouble whether a grenade goes off or not," said Wayne Hawkins, pastor of the 25,000-member Church of Living Water in Houston, Texas. Hawkins was famous for his seeker-friendly sermons, but his Norman Vincent Peale–like exterior masked a nose for political combat. "I'm not sensing any excitement out there for David Petty at all."

"None!" exclaimed Andy, warming to the topic. "He kicked us in the teeth and now they have no troops."

"Andy, I sure hope you have a plan," offered Paul Parks, the silver-haired, ambitious president of Trinity University, the largest evangelical college in the nation. "As bad as Stanley is, it's not enough to be against someone—we need to be *for* someone." Trinity had 18,000 resident students and 27,000 more enrolled in online distance-learning classes, a law school, and a business school. The president had delivered the university's commencement address during the last presidential campaign.

"I think I have a strategy to recommend." Andy winked. He knew the men in the room could elect a president in a three-way race. It was a little heady to think about the influence they could have on the election, and a far cry from Jesus' admonition that the first shall be last and the last shall be first.

The door opened and into the room burst Bob Long as if fired from a cannon. He flashed a winning smile, his white teeth gleaming, not a hair out of place. He blazed with kinetic energy, his eagerness to please transparent. He worked the room like a city council candidate, shaking every hand, slapping every back, making eye contact, drinking in the faces of his new friends, and interspersing his conversation with disarming comments like "I am reading your book right now in my daily devotions" and "Claire and I watch your program every night before we go to bed." He seemed to know each individual and their ministries, possessing perfect recall of the titles of their books and newest CDs.

Ross Lombardy stood in the back of the room, admiring as only a strategist could the rare display of a candidate's mastery of the personal touch. He had prepared the briefing memo on the meeting for Long. For once, a candidate had actually read it. *This guy is really good*, he thought. He slid next to Jay and gave him a knowing smile.

Stanton called the meeting to order and turned the floor over to Long, who took a seat at the head of the table. "Thank you, Andy. And thank all of you for what you do for the Gospel and to strengthen the family in America. I mean that." The leaders exchanged approving glances. Long had cleared the suck-up bar.

He briefly shared the outlines of his Christian testimony. "For most of my fifty-five years," he said, "politics was my god. But six weeks ago I was hit by two things that shook my world to its foundation. First, I lost the Democratic nomination for president. I can't say this publicly, but the outcome involved criminal misconduct, which is now under investigation." He paused, letting out a long sigh. "Second, when my oldest daughter almost lost a baby in childbirth, I promised the Lord that if he spared my grandson's life, I would serve him with whatever days I have left."

"Praise the Lord," they murmured.

"God took me up on it," Long said. "It's a commitment that has demanded a higher price than I had anticipated." A wry smile crossed his face. The leaders nodded, chuckling knowingly.

Long leaned forward in his chair, his body language conveying that he was speaking strictly off the record. "You have the ability to elect the next president. Whether you choose to do so or not is up to you. I know in the past you have been supportive of Republican candidates. But if the Republicans are treating you this badly before the election, just think how they'll treat you if they win."

"We're like abused spouses," agreed Andy as if on cue. "We keep coming back for more punishment. I've seen it in marriages. It's a self-destructive codependence." It was an arresting metaphor, one that elicited grunts of agreement around the table. They were united in their frustration with Republicans, who in their view were too afraid of their own shadow to stand firmly for the moral issues.

"I want to have a relationship with you," said Long. "I'll promise you this: when I tell you something, you can take it to the bank. But I'm not here to ask for your endorsement. I'm here to ask for your prayers and your friendship."

The leaders were stunned. In a brief monologue Long had touched every evangelical erogenous zone—their reflexive reliance on personal testimony as a demonstration of God's grace, their resentment at being looked down upon by the larger culture, their hunger for legitimacy, their yearning for leaders who honored the moral values that gave meaning to their lives.

"Governor, I thank God for your salvation," said Wayne Hawkins in a silky baritone. "But you are a baby Christian. I wonder if you know *why* you believe *what* you believe. If you were standing before God today, and he asked you why he should let you into heaven, what would you say?"

The room fell silent. Every head turned to Long, who dropped his chin to his chest as if deep in thought. Only the hum of the air-conditioning could be heard. Someone cleared his throat. Tears began to fall in drops on Long's tie and suit coat. He was crying! He slowly raised his head.

"I wasted most of my life chasing my ambition and ignoring God," Long replied at last in a firm but emotional voice, wiping the tears from his eyes with his fingers. "The only reason I could give for letting me into heaven is that Christ died on the cross and paid the price for my sins. I would plead the blood of Jesus."

The leaders sat in silence. Long had answered with the simplicity of a sinner saved by grace. He was the real deal.

"That's beautiful," said Max Van Buskirk, his voice catching, wagging a finger for emphasis. "If more of our preachers said that from the pulpit, we'd be in much better shape as a nation." Van Buskirk was chairman of the Bethany Broadcasting Network, with eighty-five radio stations, thirty-six television stations, an inspirational cable channel, and a state-of-the-art television studio. The network had more daily viewers than ESPN, Lifetime, and HBO combined. BBN brought in $260 million a year in advertising and another $185 million in donations from viewers.

"Governor, I don't need to tell you this is a dirty business," observed Jerry

Patterson, president of the Southern Baptist Convention. "I'm convinced your profession of faith is genuine. But if you stand with us, you're going to be subjected to vicious attacks. We're not just lightning rods—we're targets on an artillery range." A rumble of laughter rolled up and down the table. "Are you sure you're up for this?"

Long knew Patterson well by reputation. He was the pastor of the Sonshine Church in Orlando, Florida, and had been heralded as one of the leading members of a new generation of Southern Baptist leaders. Patterson believed the church could attract more converts with honey than with vinegar and should say what it was for more than what it was against; he eschewed the hellfire-and-brimstone preaching that had once characterized many evangelical leaders.

"It's going to get ugly," Long replied. "But I can't serve the Lord if I walk in fear. Jesus said not to fear those who can kill the body. He said to fear the one who casts into hell or heaven. So I fear no man." He smiled. "And that includes you guys."

It was a startling rebuke to one of the nation's leading evangelical figures. The evangelists had spent their entire lives preaching the Gospel over the airwaves, and in packed auditoriums and jammed stadiums all over the world. As they sized him up like political bosses in a smoke-filled room, a career politician (and a Democrat until a few weeks ago) had corrected them by quoting Scripture.

Paul Parks pulled a large, leather-bound Bible with gold leafing out of his briefcase and set it on the table. He flipped through the pages. "Luke chapter twelve, verse five," he began in a sonorous voice. " 'My friends, do not be afraid of those who kill the body. But I will warn you who to fear; fear the one who after he has killed has the authority to cast into hell; yes, I tell you, fear him!' "

"Amen," seconded the leaders in a chorus. The political strategy meeting had turned into a Bible study. None of them had ever had such a meeting with a politician.

"What about the issues of marriage and abortion?" Patterson asked directly. "You've been a centrist Democrat, and you obviously paid a price for that in your party. But we can't sell your positions on abortion and gay rights."

"I understand that," replied Long, clearly expecting the question. "Let me be transparent with you. My views have changed for the reasons I've already indicated." He spoke deliberately, choosing his words carefully. "But I'm running to win, and I can't do that if I flip-flop on every issue." He glanced around the table. Heads nodded. The evangelical leaders were increasingly pragmatic about where they found themselves.

Sitting in a chair against the wall, Jay turned to Ross and winked.

"I'd like to do an interview in which I discuss my faith," Long continued. "It needs to be a friendly interview. After that, I'd like to give a speech at a college or similar venue and explain my views. I will need your guidance as to the necessary points I should make. If I say that the first bill I sign as president will be a federal ban on abortion, it will strain credulity. I can favor no taxpayer funding for abortion, no partial-birth abortion, and parental consent. But if you push me too far to the right, I can't win the independent votes I need to defeat Petty."

"We get that," said Andy, jumping in. "You can't do us any good if you don't win. Governor, the most important thing that you can do as president is appoint conservative judges who will not legislate from the bench."

"Hear, hear," echoed J. D. Welch. "The courts are the ones legalizing abortion on demand and redefining marriage." Welch had sold more books than any other living author. His twelve-title *Faith on Fire* series, which recounted spiritual warfare in a small Nebraska town, had sold 133 million copies in thirty-five languages. "You should say you believe those decisions should be left to the people, not nine people in black robes."

"I can say that," agreed Long. "The courts have overstepped their bounds."

"Governor, I'd like to invite you to give your speech at Trinity University," piped up Paul Parks enthusiastically. "We'll roll out the red carpet."

"What Paul really wants," Hawkins said with a playful laugh, "is for the media to write more stories about Trinity University."

"What's wrong with that?" protested Parks.

"Governor, I would like you to come on my radio and television shows and tell my audience your testimony and where you stand on the issues," said Andy. "I think the whole world needs to hear what we have heard here today."

"I'd be honored," answered Long, his eyes fixed on Stanton's.

Not to be outdone, Van Buskirk invited Long to appear on the BBN flagship program in prime time. Welch offered to write a column about why evangelicals should consider Long's candidacy. After a half hour of brain-storming, Long rose to leave, hugging and shaking hands. He gave out his cell phone number and told the leaders to call him personally any time of the day or night. Before he left, the leaders gathered in a circle and prayed for him. When they finished, Long's eyes were filled with tears.

Andy grabbed Long by the arm and pulled him into the corner of the room in a power clutch. Their bodies were so close together they almost touched.

"Andy, thank you so much," said Long.

"Listen, I was *glad* to do it. You were terrific."

"I hope I didn't say anything stupid," responded Long humbly.

"You were fantastic. These guys"—Andy gestured toward the room, his other hand touching Long's arm affectionately to drive home the point—"will go to the wall for you. And they have millions of people who listen to them."

"I won't let them down," replied Long.

"I want you to do me one other favor," said Andy. "I want you to call Bishop Frank Weeks in Philadelphia. Do you know him?"

"I know *of* him," answered Long.

"He has the largest African-American church in Philadelphia. He's a dear friend. And just as important, he's no fan of Salmon Stanley's. He wants to visit with you. Call him—it's important."

"I'll call him," Long promised. Jay came over and dutifully wrote down the bishop's phone number on a white card. "Now, Andy, I'd like you to do me a favor. I want you to read this draft of my speech on faith and values," Long replied. He turned to Jay, who pulled a draft copy of the speech out of his leather binder and handed it to Stanton. "I want your input and your edits."

"I'd be happy to," said Andy. "I'll look it over and then give you a call."

They turned and left the conference room. Ross escorted Long and Jay down the hall to the elevator.

"Well?" asked Long.

"Governor, I think you did extremely well," answered Ross. "Frankly, the Republicans could learn a thing or two from you."

"Let's keep it a secret for now," laughed Long, shooting a wink at Ross. "We'll tell them after the election."

The door opened, and Long and Jay stepped onto the elevator. Long held the door open with the palm of his hand and stuck his head out of the elevator until it was no more than six inches from Ross's face. "You know those postcards you guys send out to your members and to pastors comparing the candidates?" He formed the shape of a postcard with his left index finger and thumb.

"Yes."

"I want those postcards!"

"You'll get them."

"How many?"

"Fifty million."

"Good!" Long smiled widely, satisfied with the answer. The elevator doors closed and he was gone. Ross headed back to the boardroom. They had a lot of work to do—and only sixty-five days remained before Election Day.

"YOU *CAN'T* GIVE THAT speech!" shouted Claire, standing in the kitchen with her hands on her hips, the veins in her neck showing, madder than Bob had ever seen her. "It makes my skin crawl!"

Bob sat at the kitchen table, arms across his chest. "Why? What's the problem?"

"You sound like Cotton Mather. You're a centrist, for crying out loud, not a right-wing nut! This is going to turn off the moderates who support you. And using Kate and the baby as political props is beyond the pale." Claire took another drink from her glass of red wine. It was her second glass since they'd arrived home from yet another fund-raiser, this one in Phoenix.

"It's an early draft," Bob said, hoping to defuse the situation. "I haven't decided yet what I'm going to say."

"Bob, you and I agreed we would *never* use the children. That's why our children are well adjusted in spite of their father being governor and a public figure." She glared at him. "You're their *father*. Protect them—don't use them to get votes!"

"That's not fair, Claire," Bob protested. "I'm trying to explain my faith in God. The fact is I came to Christ as a result of what happened with Kate. I can't *lie* about it."

"You don't have to tell the whole world," Claire shot back. "That is, unless your purpose is not to share your faith but to win the support of the religious right."

"I can't believe you would say that!" shouted Bob, his anger rising. "You think my faith is political? Let's face it, Claire, you just don't like the fact that I've become a Christian. You don't want people to think I'm a religious nut."

"All right, your becoming a Christian has certainly thrown me for a loop, I admit that," Claire acknowledged. "But people change, and I still love you for who you are. If finding God makes you happier, then I'm for it." She paused, her eyes narrowed. "But it's not Bob Long the Christian who worries me. It's Bob Long the politician."

Bob winced; that blow landed a little too close to home. "Claire, I know how to give a speech," he replied, wagging his finger. "And the first rule of public speaking is to know your audience. I have to speak to my faith, and it is intensely personal and private. If you're uncomfortable with that, I'm sorry."

"You can't fool me, Bob. I know you too well," said Claire. She took another sip of wine. "I've known you for thirty-five years, remember?"

"All right, then, I'll ask Kate. If she has a problem with it, I'll drop it. Since it involves her and her baby, I think that's only fair."

"It's *wrong*, Bob," Claire replied, her eyes filling with tears. "You don't use your own flesh and blood to con the right wing into voting for you. It's *wrong*. And if that's what you plan on doing, don't ask me to go with you when you give the speech." She marched out of the kitchen and into the bedroom.

Bob sat in the kitchen alone. Yes, Claire had a point, but increasingly lately, Bob had found himself worried about her. So often she had seemed emotionally unstable. She was drinking again. It was bad enough that he had to fight the media and his political opponents. He had no desire to fight with his own wife.

MICHAEL KAPLAN CLOSED HIS office door and picked up the phone, dialing a number. The phone was answered on the second ring.

"G.G. Hoterman."

"G.G., it's Mike. I just wanted to check in with you and see how your extracurricular activities are coming, totally on the Q.T."

"It's going outstanding," G.G. replied smoothly. "We've raised forty-five million dollars in cash and pledges for Citizens for Truth. I think we can get on the air in a week, maybe sooner, and stay on the air through Election Day."

"I think it's high time," Kaplan said.

"It's past time," agreed G.G. "It has taken a while to raise the dough because I'm having to do most of the solicitation. We're raising it in such big chunks that I've had to flop around the country in a jet. No one's giving less than half a million."

"Glad to hear it. We need to start hitting this guy hard."

"The good news is I think the press is going to turn on Long. I'm hearing that the *New York Times* is lining up a series of pieces on his record as governor that are going to be devastating."

"What's the angle?"

"Apparently Long invested in a land deal with some campaign contributors and then his own highway planners put a limited-access highway right by the land parcel. He apparently made millions. The guy's as crooked as the day is long."

"Holy smoke!" exclaimed Kaplan. "That will *kill* him."

"Yeah, my guys are working up an ad on it now. It will be a head shot."

"You've got a good media team? You can't use anybody who's working for us or the DNC for legal reasons—you do understand that."

"Mike, I've got a whole back office of election-law lawyers, remember?" G.G. answered. "Don't worry, there will be no links to the campaign—none. CFT will have one of the best ad teams ever assembled. All you have to do is pop the popcorn and watch us work our magic."

"I love it," said Kaplan. "Keep me posted. But no email."

"I don't put anything in email," said G.G.

———

BOB LONG STOOD BEHIND the podium bearing the Trinity University logo after an embarrassingly effusive introduction by Paul Parks. In the front row sat a constellation of evangelical dignitaries, pastors, and broadcasters. In the back were no less than forty television cameras and probably another hundred print reporters. The press stared down on the roughly ten thousand students and faculty who had jammed into the university's basketball arena. Even before he had delivered it, Long's address was being billed as the official divorce ceremony of social conservatives from the Republican Party that they had considered home for almost a half century.

"America's greatness is not its streets of gold, skyscrapers of silver, or cities of alabaster," Long asserted after the obligatory acknowledgments and opening remarks. "America is great because America has good and decent people of character who work hard, help those less fortunate, and care for their families. That essential goodness, ladies and gentlemen, is impossible to separate from the upward call of faith.

"Too many in public life are caught between the demands of their party and the dictates of their conscience," he said. This line was not in the prepared text, and reporters scrambled to keep up with Long's extemporaneous aside. "The pursuit of public office for its own sake is an empty exercise. Indeed, the modern emphasis on worldly success is misplaced, and can even be destructive," he continued. "A focus on one's personal ambition absent one's calling by God can breed selfishness, a cold disregard for the needs of others, spiritual poverty, and despair. Believe me, I know, because I experienced it in my own life, before I went to my knees and found God in a hospital chapel."

Jay and Lisa stood together backstage, flipping frantically through the text. They looked up from the pages, staring at each other. It wasn't there. After Claire's blow-up, Long had ordered the personal references deleted from the speech. Now, inexplicably, it was all back—Long was extemporizing, he was on a roll, and he was baring his soul! Just as he had in announcing his independent candidacy on national television, he had fooled everyone, including his own campaign handlers.

"We see this in our culture's lack of concern for the poor, a failure to address human rights around the world, and in the treatment of the elderly and the disabled as a burden rather than a blessing." Having seized the thematic high ground, Long turned to the political red meat. "I confronted the coldness of my own heart recently when my daughter nearly lost her baby in a difficult delivery." Reporters in the back of the room searched in vain for the words in the text. "By God's grace, my grandson's life was spared. As I stood in the delivery room, holding him in my arms, I understood that life is a gift from God. In Jefferson's words, we are all endowed by our creator with the inalienable right to life." He paused, returning to the text. "Our goal as a nation should be to see a day when every member of the human family is welcomed in love and protected by law." The standing ovation that followed lasted a full minute.

Paul Parks turned to Andy Stanton, who sat to his right, and gave him a look of stunned approval. They were almost pinching themselves with joy. Stanton had edited the remarks, so he was not surprised by their content, but the personal force of Long's faith testimony was overwhelming.

"The founders intended for sovereignty to reside with the American people," Long continued. "That sovereignty is undermined when federal judges try to play the role of legislators." This set up the money line. "Judges should interpret the law, not legislate from the bench. And the Senate should confirm judges based on their qualifications"—he paused for dramatic effect— "not litmus tests or the demands of special interests that have turned the judicial confirmation process into search-and-destroy missions." The arena exploded with a standing ovation. The line was a clear reference to the lynching of Henry Stonecipher, in which both Ed Bell and Sal Stanley had participated.

"The call of our time," Long continued, "is to care for the sick and the elderly, remember the rights of the poor, protect the sanctity of life, and overcome the hate-filled dogma of terrorism. This is a high calling. But I believe it can happen in our time. As Jesus said, all things are possible to those who believe." On the front row, Stanton, Parks, and the evangelical leaders blossomed in their seats like sunflowers in the afternoon sun. A Democrat— even an independent Democrat—quoting Jesus and mentioning the rights of the poor and the unborn in the same sentence was nirvana to them.

"As we do so, let us act in humility, not haughtiness; in brokenness, not self-righteousness. No political party has a monopoly on righteousness. We all fall short of the glory of God," Long added. It was a deft maneuver —Long's words signaled his independence from social conservatives even as he embraced them. He was cautioning religious folk against the sin of pride. There was more. "As Ronald Reagan once correctly observed, 'God has truly blessed this country, but we never should fall into the trap that would detract from the universality of God's gift. It is for all mankind. God's love is the hope and the light of the world.' " This was Long's veiled critique of American exceptionalism, using the words of Reagan, no less. But it seemed to fly right over the heads of his listeners.

In the front row, the evangelical dignitaries nodded approvingly. They had completely missed the fact that Long had skillfully distanced himself from their clutches even as he sought their support. For the moment, such nuances went ignored. The evangelical leaders, desperate to find a presidential candidate whom they could work with and who could win, hurled themselves headlong into his arms. All they cared about was that Long had come to a citadel of evangelicalism and quoted Jesus Christ and Ronald Reagan. And unlike the spineless wonders who led the Republican Party—who treated them like lepers—he was not afraid to be seen with them in public.

Long finished the twenty-two-minute speech, almost one-quarter of which he had delivered extemporaneously. The audience gave him his fifth standing ovation, and he stood at the podium, head cocked in relief and appreciation. Paul Parks walked to the rostrum to present Long with a Trinity University sweatshirt and coffee mug as gifts. Long dutifully donned the sweatshirt to loud cheers.

Parks led the way across the campus to a VIP reception for major donors and local dignitaries. As Long entered the room, he was met by a wall of applause and cheering. Startled by the response, Long turned to Parks.

"They love you, Governor," Parks said soothingly. "You did yourself a world of good here today."

Long dove into the crowd, hugging, laughing, touching. He soaked in their affection and drank in their praise. He had come, spoken, and conquered. He was mobbed by the crowd as he posed for photographs and autographed programs. Finally, Parks went to a podium in the front of the room and hushed the crowd, which was buzzing with excitement. He called Long up to still more applause.

Jay and Lisa huddled in the back of the room with Ross Lombardy, who had flown in for the speech with Stanton.

"They sure love a convert, don't they?" asked Jay in a whisper, his hand cupping his mouth.

"The prodigal son has come home," replied Ross. "Parks has killed the fatted calf and laid out a banquet table."

At the podium, Long was on autopilot. He thanked Stanton and Parks profusely. He stared unseeing at the faces, lost in thought, the words pouring forth with ease. What a strange business politics was, Long thought. If Harris Flaherty had lived, and if his grandson had not nearly died, he would not be at Trinity University today, and the evangelicals crowding around him would have held their noses and pulled the lever for the GOP ticket. The murder of a vice president and near death of a baby had changed the course of his life and perhaps the life of the nation. But now that he had been embraced by religious conservatives, he knew he was about to get hit by a furnace blast of criticism. He felt a strange foreboding.

A campaign aide came into the room, looking worried. She pulled Lisa to the side. "Dan Dorman wants to talk to you," said the aide. "He says it's urgent."

"About what?"

"He wants to know why Claire is not here."

"Tell him she was scheduled to be somewhere else."

"I did," the aide said. "He's not buying it. He said he's hearing there's some kind of problem with Claire, and that she is opposed to the governor coming here."

"What?" Lisa blurted. She pulled Jay over in the corner and explained about Dorman. "Can we get Claire on the phone with Dorman on background and spin him? We don't want him to write a piece saying Claire and Bob had a falling-out over today's speech."

"No can do," said Jay. "Claire's no longer available for interviews. Those are the orders from the governor."

"How am I going to talk Dorman out of sliming us?"

"I don't know," said Jay impatiently, his eyes watching Long at the podium. "Shame him. Just make it go away."

Lisa followed the aide out of the room, her stomach churning, trying to figure out how she could spin Dorman off the story that Claire Long was no longer on board with her own husband's campaign for the presidency.

31

A T 8:20 A.M. ON the Tuesday after Labor Day, the red phone rang on Jay's credenza at Long campaign headquarters. The staff jokingly called it "the bat phone" because the only person with the number was Bob Long. "Jay Noble," he answered.

"How goes it?" asked Long. It was his normal conversation starter.

Long was, Jay knew, in Tampa for a fund-raising lunch. "Are you sitting down?" he asked. "The new Gallup poll is out." He paused. "You're leading."

"What?" Long shouted. "Really?"

"It's close. Among likely voters, 31 percent for you, 30 percent Petty, and 24 percent Stanley, with 15 percent undecided," Jay reported. "The crosstabs are scary. The likely voters are 37 percent Democrat, 30 percent Republican, and 33 percent independent. Republicans are not punching through the likely-voter screen, and the independent vote is soaring."

"Are the conservatives sitting on their hands?"

"Looks like it. If this turnout model holds, it's going to be the biggest turnout of independents since 1976. They'll decide the election, and you're leading among them."

Long let out a whistle.

"And get this—you're getting 38 percent of the evangelical vote. Petty is getting 39 percent, and Stanley is getting 14 percent."

"So the Trinity speech worked."

"Big-time," said Jay. "And even with our tack to the right, the independents think you're an outsider. We're even holding our own among women—Stanley is up by only four percent. We're also getting fourteen percent of the black vote. That will fall, I would think."

"We need to go see Bishop Weeks," interrupted Long.

"We're in the political equivalent of a physical world without gravity. Everything is upside down," said Jay, working up an analytical sweat. "You've got the first African-American nominee, an imploding Democratic ticket, and the strongest independent candidate ever. And on top of all that, the surge of independents is reshuffling the deck. We've not seen a turnout model this surreal in a half century."

"It's a long way until November," Long cautioned.

"A lot can happen and probably will," Jay agreed. "But this much is clear: we can win." He was alone in his office, the door closed. The walls began to spin.

"We need to run scared and like we're behind." It was a placeholder, conversational filler, and Long said it at least once a day.

"Roger that, sir," replied Jay. "The press is now going to fire at us with both barrels. They're going to try to bring us down to earth."

"Why do you say that?"

"We're wearing a bull's-eye. No one has ever lost the presidency if they were leading on Labor Day," answered Noble. "People have lost leads— Nixon in '68 and Carter in '76. But if you're ahead on Labor Day, you win in November."

"Let's make sure I'm not the first to lose," Long ordered, only half in jest.

"We will," answered Jay. "But get ready. The love affair with the press is over."

"What keeps you awake at night?" asked Long, turning philosophical.

"Ballot access," said Jay. "We've got court cases galore, and for the most part we're winning. But if the Supreme Court doesn't order us onto the ballot, we're in trouble." He paused. "What about you?"

"I'm afraid we may have peaked too soon," said Long.

"Me, too," Jay responded in a distant voice. "I can feel it. The sharks are circling."

BILL DIAMOND WAS AT his desk in the West Wing when he heard the ping of an incoming email. The subject line read "Gallup Poll Shows Long Leading Presidential Race."

"What in the heck?" Diamond said aloud. The campaign had been picking up bad vibes about the Gallup poll for days, and now he knew why. As he opened the email and read it, his heart pounded and a wave of nausea passed through him. He picked up the phone and dialed the direct number to Matt Folger, the Petty campaign pollster.

"Have you seen the Gallup poll?" he asked.

"Yes," replied Folger matter-of-factly. Folger was unflappable, and Diamond swore he had ice in his veins. Everyone else in the campaign could be jumping out of windows, and Folger would be calm enough to perform an autopsy on his own mother's body.

"This is pretty unsettling, isn't it?" Diamond pressed.

"Bad timing. We got hammered by the earned media on the Iowa video. My guess is that if this poll were taken before the Iowa video hit YouTube, we'd be up."

"That hurt us."

"Worst possible timing," Folger repeated. "I see two other things. They have a seven-point spread on party turnout, thirty-seven D to thirty R. That will not hold up. Even assuming a five-point spread, that would put us up two, rather than down one."

"Seven points is absurd. They're screening out Republicans," agreed Diamond.

"The second thing is the movement of evangelicals to Long. We're seeing it in all the published polls. We need to hit him on his pro-choice, pro-gay-rights record in California. That'll peel off some religious voters and we can gain another three to four points on the ballot."

"We waited too long to define Long. We thought as long as Stanley cratered, we couldn't lose. That was a mistake."

"We're suffering from the 'other guy' syndrome," said Folger.

"What's that?"

"Voters are mad at both parties—it's a pox on both your houses. Long is the other guy. He's an amorphous quantity. We have to tell voters who this guy really is. We need to define him as a flip-flopper and drive up his negatives, especially on the values stuff."

"Can you work me up a one-page memo? I'd like to get that out as talking points for the surrogates. Our people are going to panic when they see Long ahead."

"I'll shoot it to you in fifteen or twenty minutes. Hey, one other thing," added Folger.

"What's that?"

"Make sure Petty is ready for the debates. If he does well, this thing will come back our way. But if he falls off the stage, our job gets really hard."

"He knows that," answered Diamond. "He's focused on it." Diamond hung up the phone. Actually, Petty was not focused at all. Diamond had tried to get prep sessions on the calendar to no avail. He was worried. Stanley was a U.S. senator who had been debating in the Senate for years. Long was a natural performer. Petty was used to the fawning treatment of reporters who covered him at the Pentagon and Foggy Bottom. He wasn't used to walking into a ring with guys swinging bicycle chains. Diamond had to get his attention, and fast.

———

WALT SHAPIRO SAT BEHIND his desk looking like a department store mannequin in a pin-striped custom-tailored suit, starched blue shirt with white collar and French cuffs, and matching tie and suspenders. The computer on the credenza bonged every time he received an email.

G.G. Hoterman sat in a chair next to Shapiro's deputy, Erin Koslowski, gazing at the breathtaking view of Pennsylvania Avenue stretching toward the Capitol in one direction and the White House in the other. *So this is what my legal bills are paying for,* Hoterman pondered: *Shapiro's million-dollar view of D.C.*

"Okay, let's recap," said Shapiro in a gravelly baritone. "There are three rules for today. First, answer the question asked, not the question you think they meant to ask."

Hoterman nodded.

"If they ask when you met someone, give the date only," added Koslowski. "Don't tell them how you met, where you met, or who introduced you.

"Second rule: don't try to recall something you don't remember," said Shapiro. "When people try to reconstruct events from a foggy memory, they get into trouble. If you don't remember, just say, 'I don't recall.' "

"I got it," replied Hoterman.

"Third, stick to yes and no answers. Don't lead them. If they are blind, you are not their Seeing Eye dog. They might be six inches from a gold mine; don't open the door and show them the way."

"Understood," said G.G.

"Okay, let's go," said Shapiro. They walked across the hall to the conference room. Hoterman entered with Shapiro, Koslowski, and a partner from Hoterman & Schiff. Anyone who walked into an FBI interview with Walt Shapiro was making a statement that they had come to play. Three FBI agents rose to their feet, clearly relishing the opportunity to question a political celebrity. The agents slid their business cards across the table to the lawyers. Hoterman clutched a tall cup of Starbucks coffee in his left hand and shook each agent's hand with his right.

"Mr. Hoterman, we want to ask you some questions," began the lead agent, wearing a gray suit, white shirt, and striped tie. His coat was draped over his chair. "At this point you are not a target of the investigation."

Hoterman did not feel any particular relief at the news.

"I want to ask you about the Virginia Democratic delegation, and in particular your role in raising and dispensing funds through the Committee for a Better America."

"All right," replied G.G.

The interview started with a mind-numbing recitation of dates, names, places, and biographical detail. It took fifteen minutes to get to anything substantive. Hoterman was about to get bored when the first uppercut landed.

"Deirdre Rahall works in your law firm, is that correct?" asked the agent.

"She is my deputy at the firm." (Hoterman caught himself—he had not answered the question as a "yes" or "no," and had volunteered more information unsolicited.)

"Do you recall the date when she began her employment?"

"Approximately three years ago."

"And how did she come to work for you?"

"She worked for another partner in my firm. She assisted on a project that I was managing. It went on for about three months, and she stayed with me after that."

"Is your relationship with Ms. Hall professional, or would it be accurate to say that it is personal as well?" asked the agent, his eyes steady.

Hoterman's wheels turned as anger boiled up. What a pathetic excuse for a criminal investigation! They were trying to trick him into denying his affair with Deirdre. To do so would violate 18 U.S.C. Section 1001, lying to a government agent, which was a felony. Among its victims: former secretary of Housing and Urban Development Henry Cisneros (misleading FBI agents about a former mistress), Martha Stewart (lying to investigators about an otherwise legal stock sale), and Bill Clinton (lying about his sexual relationship with Monica Lewinsky). And who could blame them? Hoterman knew them all, and felt they had each made mistakes but paid far too high a price. He was not going to get indicted for lying about whom he slept with. If he went to jail, it wasn't going to be for having sex.

"It is personal and professional," he replied, a sharp edge in his voice.

"And would it also be accurate to say that you have a *physical* relationship?"

"Yes." Hoterman winced inside. His affair was now on the record.

Walt Shapiro had heard enough. "My client is far too nice," he hissed. "Could I ask what my client's personal life has to do with this investigation?"

"It is material, counselor," answered the FBI agent coldly, not backing down. "Ms. Rahall's brother received payments from the organization for which Mr. Hoterman raised funds." He cut his eyes toward G.G. "The nature of their relationship is germane. No one wants to embarrass Mr. Hoterman, but we have a job to do."

"You can do your job without prying into personal lives," shot back Shapiro, his face angry. "It is hardly necessary to rummage through people's bedrooms."

The agent visibly bristled. "Mr. Shapiro, if Mr. Hoterman does not want to answer these questions, you can terminate this interview at any time. Then we will decide whether we need to subpoena him to appear before the grand jury."

Shapiro knew that he held few cards. His goal was to avoid indictment. The interview continued. The score: FBI 1, Shapiro 0.

"How long has your physical relationship with Ms. Rahall gone on?"

"Approximately two years."

"Do you recall how it came about that her brother received a ten-thousand-dollar consulting fee from the Committee for a Better America?"

"As best I can recall . . . it was . . . he was . . . helping CBA in Virginia," replied Hoterman slowly, fumbling his words. "They were building a grassroots organization in the state."

"Was he suggested by Ms. Rahall?"

"I don't recall."

"Your firm incorporated CBA and did its legal work. Do you know who handled the books or who made decisions regarding consulting contracts?"

"I believe the CBA books were kept by someone at Melinda Lipper's firm."

"Just to confirm that we are all referring to the same individual: Melinda Lipper was the fund-raising consultant to the Stanley campaign?"

"Correct." The lead agent turned to one of his colleagues and nodded. They each made notes on their legal pads.

"To whom did Ms. Lipper report?"

"Michael Kaplan."

"Did you ever discuss payments by CBA to individuals in Virginia with Mr. Kaplan?"

This was the question that Hoterman dreaded even more than the probing into his affair with Deirdre. He wanted to protect Kaplan, but not at the cost of his own hide. "Yes," G.G. replied.

"When was that?"

"I could not put an exact date on it, but it would have been late March or early April. It was prior to the Virginia Democratic state convention in early May."

"And what do you remember about that conversation?"

"Mike told me there were a number of people in Virginia working for CBA as consultants. He asked me to make sure that Melinda Lipper had the funds to pay them."

"He asked you to help raise the money then?"

"Yes."

"Do you recall how much he said he needed to pay the so-called consultants?"

"My recollection is that it was $750,000."

The lead agent handed a copy of a document to Hoterman. It was the transcript of an email from Kaplan to Melinda Lipper dated April 5, and it included a list of individuals with dollar amounts next to their names. Hoterman felt the walls closing in and his heart rate accelerating—it was the smoking gun! It tied Kaplan directly to the CBA payments and, worst of all, G.G. was copied on the message.

"Mr. Hoterman, this document shows an email message from Mr.

Kaplan to Ms. Lipper directing payments to individuals from CBA. Have you ever seen this before?"

"Not that I recall."

"You are copied on this message. You don't recall receiving it?"

"I receive over three hundred emails a day, on average," G.G. explained. "I have over ninety attorneys who work in my firm, and they copy me on emails all the time. Usually when I'm copied on someone else's email traffic, I either delete it right away or review it in a cursory manner."

"Even from the campaign chairman of a presidential candidate who is the Senate majority leader?" inquired the agent, his body language conveying his disbelief.

"I'm not saying I didn't receive it. I just don't recall it."

The agent nodded. The score was even: FBI 1, Shapiro/Hoterman 1.

The questions continued for three and a half hours, at which point they took a brief lunch break. Hoterman, exhausted and drained, followed Shapiro back to his office, where deli sandwiches and soft drinks awaited them. Shapiro noticed the hunted look in G.G.'s eyes.

"You're doing great," he said, trying to buck him up. "Of all the witnesses I've represented who have done a deposition or an FBI interview, you're in the top five percent."

"Thanks," replied G.G., trying to maintain his macho composure. "Walt, is it just my imagination, or do they have Kaplan in their crosshairs?"

"He's the target," agreed Shapiro.

G.G. took a bite out of a roast beef sandwich. The gigantic scale of the scandal suddenly hit him. Kaplan was toast. He and Deirdre were skating on thin ice—Walt would have to warn Deirdre to tell the truth about their affair when she did her own interview. Then a sick feeling came over him. His admission of his affair would leak, and he needed to tell his wife before she read about it in the *Washington Post*.

———

"I'VE BEEN SAVING THIS bottle of champagne like a good luck charm for this occasion," announced David Thomas as he pulled a bottle of Dom Pérignon out of the refrigerator on the campaign bus. The Long campaign's "Change America" bus tour was rumbling through southeast Ohio, where the lush green and gold fields of the family farms they passed showed the first colors of early fall. The election was fifty-one days away, and Long had just gotten the biggest break of the entire campaign.

"What's the special occasion?" asked Long.

"I just got off the phone with Phil Battaglia. The Supreme Court has denied certiorari in the Texas ballot access litigation," Thomas replied. "The Fifth Circuit Court's decision stands. You're on the ballot in Texas." A guttural cheer erupted from the staff on the bus. Thomas waved them to be quiet so he could finish. "It gets better. Phil says the Supreme Court's decision not to take the case means that now you'll be on the ballot in all fifty states. Congratulations!"

Another cheer from the staff, and this time the clutch of reporters sitting around them allowed themselves a smile. They had a vested interest in seeing Long qualify for the ballot if only to preserve their own beat. Thomas popped the champagne cork, and the bubbly spilled forth as he poured it into paper cups. Long stuck with Diet Coke as he held an impromptu news conference.

"Governor, how important is the Supreme Court deciding to let the Texas decision stand?" asked *USA Today*.

"Extremely important," answered Long. "This was one of the biggest challenges we faced when I entered the race, qualifying for the ballot where deadlines had already passed. People can't vote for you if you're not on the ballot." The reporters hung on every word.

"How many total ballot petition signatures have you gathered?" asked the *Miami Herald*.

Long turned to Jay Noble. "Jay, what was the final number?"

"We needed approximately 750,000 signatures to qualify on all the state ballots. We submitted 1,262,425," Jay answered proudly. "We exceeded our goal by 512,000 signatures. We also have had over two million people sign up as volunteers."

"How much did you spend getting on the ballot?"

"Counting legal bills?" joked Long. "Not counting litigation costs, five million dollars."

"What about the lawsuits that have been filed by the Democratic National Committee claiming that some of your signatures are fraudulent?" asked AP.

"Fraudulent!?" Long exclaimed, a broad smile spreading across his face. "The DNC and the Stanley campaign accusing me of fraud? Isn't that like being lectured on ethics by Richard Nixon?"

"Whoa!" shouted the reporters.

"Are you comparing Salmon Stanley to Richard Nixon?" asked the Associated Press. Several tape recorders rose in the air to capture Long's answer. They were praying his skull would go through the windshield—another "gotcha" moment that would soon be all the rage on YouTube and send the bloggers into orbit.

"No, no, that's not what I said," corrected Long, backpedaling. His staff stared into their paper cups of champagne. The party was over. "I'm just saying it's odd being lectured on ethics by the Stanley campaign."

He smiled again. The reporters were not smiling.

"What about the upcoming debates?" asked the *New York Times*. "The Commission on Presidential Debates is going to announce their decision any day now. If they decline to include you, what will you do?"

"I'll show up in a bus caravan of supporters," fired back Long. "And if they still won't let me in, I'll stage a counterdebate in the same city. We'll set up two empty chairs for David Petty and Sal Stanley if they don't show!"

"Really?" asked the *Times* euphorically. "You'd do that?"

"Sure, why not? We're either leading or competitive in every national poll, we're raising a record amount of financial support, and I'm going to be on the ballot in all fifty states. If I'm not included in the debates, there will be a grassroots rebellion."

Lisa Robinson stood silently behind Long in a slow burn, arms crossed, her facial expression growing tighter. When the spontaneous news conference ended, she leaned into Long.

"Could I see you for a moment?"

He followed her to the back of the bus. Several staffers were sprawled on a couch, talking on cell phones or banging away on laptops. Lisa asked them to leave.

"These reporters are not your friends!" she shouted in a loud whisper as she closed the door. "Now that you are leading the polls and you're on all fifty state ballots, they are going to turn on you like a pack of wolves. You are nothing but a piece of meat to them!"

"I'm just showing them a little leg," replied Long. "It's harmless. The earned media we've gotten has been essential. I'm going to be on the cover of *Time* next week. Do you think that would happen if we were not sucking up to the Big Feet and yukking it up with the press?"

"They are the *enemy*, Governor!" Lisa shot back, the vena cava in her neck bulging through her fair skin. "And if you don't believe me now, you will soon enough. They are planning to *destroy* you. They did it to Petty. He was their darling and now they're tossing dirt on his grave. They're going to do the same thing to you."

"But why take me down? I'm selling newspapers."

"The only thing that sells more newspapers than building you up is when they take you down."

Long nodded grimly.

"Andy Stanton just gave you a bear hug in front of the entire press corps," continued Lisa, her voice shaking. "You don't think you'll pay for that? Let me tell you, for giving that speech at Trinity University, the press will bust a baseball bat right across your kneecaps. They're just waiting for the right moment."

"Okay, okay," said Long plaintively. "I'll be more careful."

"You'd better be," Lisa replied. "I now get to deal with the story of you comparing Sal Stanley to Richard Nixon. Thanks a lot for that one, by the way."

She opened the door and walked briskly back to the front of the bus, leaving Long standing alone. He had never seen her so mad! But he realized that he should be grateful for the reminder. They were now getting closer to the prize, which meant the real artillery was about to start exploding. He had to be more careful. No more winging it. He had to stay on message.

———

"I WANT YOU OUT of the house!" shouted G.G. Hoterman's wife, Edwina. Her voice was shaking, her facial expression hard and unyielding.

"What are you going to say to the children?" asked G.G. He was worried about his sixteen-year-old daughter and fourteen-year-old son. What would they think?

"Don't worry. I'm not going to tell them the truth, which is that their father is sleeping with his secretary."

"She's not my secretary."

"Don't nitpick the details, G.G.," shot back Edwina. "She's an employee. Anyway, I don't want you here. Pack your things and go."

"Edwina, I'm in the fight of my life against the Justice Department. I need you to stand by me now more than ever," G.G. begged.

Edwina's eyes were aflame. "Get out." She stomped out of the bedroom.

G.G. went into the closet and stared at his clothes, trying to figure out what he should take. But he was too stunned to collect his thoughts. His world was coming apart. With Walt Shapiro's help, he would probably avoid being indicted. But the DOJ and the media were going to destroy him anyway. His clients were getting nervous about the negative publicity. His wife had now kicked him out of the house. Was the marriage over?

If he could, he would end the relationship with Deirdre now. But it was dicey; she was a witness, and he couldn't afford for her to turn on him after a lovers' quarrel. He had to wait until he was in the clear legally before he could break it off.

He pulled out a suitcase and started folding his dress shirts. He sighed, stacking them on top of one another so they wouldn't wrinkle. He had no idea where he was going to stay.

———

"RASSEM, WAKE UP!"

Rassem el Zafarshan awoke with a start. It was pitch-black. He could make out the voice of one of his handlers. His mind was a fog.

"Wake up! We have to leave. Right now."

"What is it?" asked Zafarshan groggily.

"Someone in the village tipped off the police. They are on their way now. We need to move immediately."

"All right," replied Zafarshan. He was in a safe house in a remote village along the Pakistani border with Afghanistan. In the five weeks since the assassination of Flaherty, he had been constantly on the move, traveling first to Mexico, then to Cuba, then on to Damascus, whence he was spirited into an area of Pakistan along the Afghan border considered a safe haven. But the

CIA and the Pakistani secret police were in hot pursuit. He was moving his location every few days. It was getting old.

"Grab your things. We have no time," whispered the handler.

Zafarshan took a flashlight from his handler and began to throw his few personal effects into a canvas bag: 9 mm pistol, bullets, a diary, some books, a copy of the Koran. If he was going to hide, he needed to get to Iran. But word had come back that he was not welcome—he was considered too hot to handle. His presence in the country, his sponsors had explained, would only give the United States the pretext to take military action. Zafarshan was a man without a country, and he could feel the Americans closing in.

32

"Could I speak to Stan Anderson please?" Long paused. "Tell him it's Governor Bob Long." He glanced at Jay, raising his eyebrows and shrugging his shoulders.

Long sat on the edge of the bed in his room at the Marriott in Charleston, West Virginia. Jay Noble leaned forward in a wing chair wearing blue jeans and a Polo shirt, legs crossed, drinking a large cup of Starbucks. At Jay's suggestion, Long had called Stan Anderson, president of the United Mine Workers. The UMW was the only union in the AFL-CIO that had refused to endorse Salmon Stanley, primarily because of its strong opposition to his plan to cap carbon dioxide emissions. Jay thought Anderson might just be in the market for a dance partner.

"Stan? How are you? It's Bob Long." He listened attentively as the voice on the other end chattered away. He looked at Jay, bobbing his head back and forth to indicate that Anderson was on a roll. "I understand, Stan. No question . . . I would be pleased to work with you." Another pause. "Absolutely . . . consider it done . . . not a problem . . . you bet . . . Let me put you on with my associate Jay Noble. He will work out the details. He's your new best friend." He handed the phone to Jay.

"Mr. Anderson?" said Jay.

"Hello, Jay, Stan Anderson. First of all, let me repeat what I said to Governor Long: *I despise the ground Salmon Stanley walks on.*"

Jay felt his heart skip a beat. He was in love.

"I went to Washington to meet with Stanley in the Senate majority leader's office about the energy bill. He glad-handed me, talked a big game, took me around the room and showed me all the paintings. Then you know what he did? *Nothing!* And his radical environmental agenda does not sell with my members. To coal folks, he's the devil incarnate. He's worse than Al Gore."

"We agree," said Jay, beginning to feel warm and fuzzy. "It sounds like we have the basis of a mutually beneficial relationship."

"I hope so, but I need your help. Over 160,000 miners are on strike fighting for better health care and black lung benefits. We need Governor

Long to make a statement supporting the miners. If he does that, I can help him."

"Sure, Mr. Anderson. The—"

"Call me Stan."

"The governor will be happy to do it, Stan," replied Jay. "The question is, when, where, and what does he say?"

"How long are you in West Virginia?"

"We're leaving after lunch."

"Have one of your speechwriters call me and we'll work out the language."

"Forget the speechwriters," Jay said. "Dictate to me."

"I want some of my miners standing around him when he makes the statement."

"Done. Obviously, we're doing this on sound public policy grounds—there is no quid pro quo," he lied. "But how do you think you can help the governor?"

"I'll get the word out," answered Anderson. "I can say something very complimentary after his statement. Later on, I'll take a swing at Stanley for his wacko position on global warming. That will do the trick."

"We need to win in West Virginia, Kentucky, and Ohio. They could decide the outcome of the election. Your membership is critical," said Jay, lathering him up.

"We need more federal assistance for black lung. We need something done about the atrocious record of this administration in mine safety—we have already lost nine miners this year. And we need more investment in clean coal technology," said Anderson. "Salmon Stanley's climate change proposal will destroy the coal industry and throw my guys out of work. I've told the AFL-CIO leadership. They're busting my chops, but that's just the way it is in coal country. You follow me?"

"One hundred percent," said Jay as he began to rock slightly on the edge of his chair. "Get me a backgrounder on clean coal and black lung and I'll get it staffed by our policy shop. I don't see an issue. The governor supports clean coal." Actually, Long had signed a carbon cap-and-trade bill in California, but at this moment of heated political passion, with the election on the line, that seemed a minor inconsistency. Jay figured if Long was going to evolve on abortion, why not climate change?

"I've got a quarter of a million members," boasted Anderson. "With family members, we can deliver six hundred thousand votes. I'm going to put them in your back pocket."

"Music to my ears," said Jay. He uncapped his pen and began to take notes as Anderson dictated the wording for Long's statement. Given Long's green environmental record as governor, it would require a deft touch. That was why he made the big bucks, Jay thought.

"I CAN'T FIGURE OUT these polls," whined Salmon Stanley, kicking the seat in front of him as they drove from the Saint Louis airport to a fund-raiser. With forty-four days to go, the campaign had become a mind-numbing blur of airports, motorcades, hotel ballrooms, and press avails. Stanley was running on empty. He turned to Michael Kaplan, who sat next to him in the back of the car, stoically absorbing the blows. "How can Bob Long possibly be *leading*? We beat him like a drum in the primaries!"

"We picked up serious negatives when we won the nomination ugly. The same thing happened to Bush in 2000 and to Clinton in 1992. People were sticking a fork in Clinton after the primaries. That's when Ross Perot was the 1992 version of Long."

"Yeah, but Perot was a grenade with a crew cut," Stanley shot back. "Ultimately, he blew up. When does Long blow up?"

"I don't know. But if he doesn't, we'll blow him up," said Kaplan, his lips curled in a sardonic smile.

"We need to change the dynamic," said Stanley.

"It's been a perfect storm," agreed Kaplan. "First we had Long's walkout in Chicago. Terry Tinford turned out to be amateur night at the opera. Betsy Hafer was not ready for prime time."

Stanley rolled his eyes knowingly.

Kaplan continued: "And now eight weeks of earned media on the FBI investigation—"

"Vicious!" seethed Stanley. "The most biased press coverage I have ever seen!" His face turned red, the capillaries beginning to bulge. "They're crucifying me!"

"And it isn't going to let up, not with Dan Dorman chasing a Pulitzer."

"What do we do?"

"We take the skin off Long," replied Kaplan smoothly. "Hit him on ethics—he lined his pockets in land deals from road projects approved by his own office."

"He's a crook."

"He's *worse* than a crook," Kaplan corrected him. "He got rich because of his official actions as governor. He *profited* from public service."

"Oh, that's good," said Stanley, calming down. "I like that a lot."

"Then we slam him on hypocrisy. Show his canine obedience to Andy Stanton and the religious right and contrast it with his record in California."

"Don't attack the evangelicals," cautioned Stanley. "That could backfire."

"Don't worry," agreed Kaplan. "We won't. The issue is Long's hypocrisy. He's a chameleon who changes whichever way the wind is blowing."

"Will it work?" asked Stanley skeptically.

"It's a body blow," assured Kaplan. "According to our polls, after we hit him with the land deals and flip-flopping, his fav-unfav goes from four-to-one favorable to two-to-one unfavorable. He goes from leading by two points to trailing by thirteen points." He put his palms together and then flipped them. "He'll be upside down."

Stanley nodded, clearly impressed.

"It'll kill him," breathed Kaplan in a whispered baritone. "I'm telling you, by the time the 527s, the union PACs, the 501(c)(4)s and the DNC get done, they'll have to identify him with dental records."

"When do we start?"

"You don't know . . . and you don't want to know."

"Good answer." Stanley smiled. "I want total deniability."

The car pulled up to the back entrance of the hotel where a line of "greeters" who had raised the bulk of the money for the event waited. An advance staffer stood ready to open the door. Stanley motioned to him to leave the door closed.

"Can we keep Long out of the debates?"

"I don't think so," said Kaplan. "My talks with the debate commission have not been friendly. He's viable by their criteria: ballot access, financial resources, and standing in the polls." Kaplan shot him a wicked grin. "You're just going to have to kick his tail."

"I relish the prospect," Stanley replied. "By the way, I don't know anything about this other stuff."

"Senator, this conversation never happened." Kaplan opened the car door, jumped enthusiastically to the pavement, stood at attention, and gave everyone a theatrical Gomer Pyle salute. "Is this the A team?" he fairly shouted. "Is this the group that broke every fund-raising record in the history of Saint Louis?"

Everyone grinned from ear to ear.

———

BOB LONG STOOD COATLESS, his striped necktie loosened at the collar and sleeves rolled to his elbows. Small beads of sweat broke out on his forehead, which glistened under a hot afternoon sun. Two dozen coal miners stood behind him as camera crews jostled for position. The United Mine Workers' strike was in its sixth week, the price of coal had jumped 30 percent, and electric bills had spiked across the country. Long had stepped right into the middle of one of the biggest stories in the nation.

Camera shutters clattered as Long began to read his statement. "It is critical that we reduce our dependence on foreign oil, especially from those regimes that aid and abet terrorism," he said in a firm voice into outstretched microphones. "It has never been more critical for us to increase domestic sources of energy that are affordable and environmentally sound. That is why I have come to West Virginia to express my solidarity with these mineworkers who are the backbone of our economy."

The workers erupted into a full-throated cheer and raised their fists in the air. Cameras snapped the dramatic image of their leathery faces framed by mine helmets with lanterns on the brim.

"I call on the president to invoke his statutory authority to bring the parties to arbitration." Long paused, knowing the line would grab headlines. "I have spoken today to the UMW leadership and to executives of the coal companies and urged them to do all they can to reach an agreement. I have not taken sides in the negotiations. But I do believe better safety and adequate health-care coverage for brown and black lung disease should be a high priority. Thank you all very much."

The reporters shouted questions, which Long ignored. He wasn't about to step on his own headline. A *New York Times* reporter grabbed Lisa Robinson by the arm and stuck a sweaty nose and quivering lip in her face. He appeared to be about to have a coronary. "Why isn't he taking any questions?!" he sputtered.

"Take it from the statement," Lisa shot back as she hustled to the motorcade.

"I can't!" he yelled frantically. "It's about something else."

"What are you working on?"

"The Pomona land deal."

"Email me your questions," replied Lisa. Her heart skipped a beat. It was the story the Brain Trust had feared would break, and now their fears had come true. "I'll call the press shop in L.A. from the plane and they'll get you the answers before your deadline."

As they clambered into staff vans for the ride to the airport, Lisa felt her stomach go queasy. It wasn't just the lack of sleep and the greasy breakfast she had scarfed down that morning. It was a sense of foreboding. Money was pouring in over the Internet, a new ABC News poll showed Long ahead, and they had just tied a red ribbon around the UMW vote. Now the counterassault of their lives was about to begin. The first artillery shell would be fired by the nation's paper of record.

THE CAMPAIGN PLANE LANDED at John Wayne Airport in Orange County a little past 10 P.M. Jay had spent half the flight talking with Lisa and Nicole, who was back at campaign headquarters, answering the detailed financial questions submitted by the *Times*. It was going to be an ugly hit piece. At one point, Lisa got into a screaming match with the reporter.

They still had the UMW endorsement headline, so everyone remained relatively upbeat. When they walked into the FBO, Nicole was waiting for Jay in the lobby looking like a brunette lollipop in white jeans and red lipstick, a fire-engine-red Chanel purse on her shoulder and matching red Ferragamo heels. As Jay slipped his arm around her tapered waist and crooked his finger into the belt loop of her jeans, Bob Long called out, "Don't keep him up too late! He's got to work tomorrow."

Nicole let out a throaty laugh. "Actually, I plan to keep you up all night," she said under her breath to Jay as they walked to her car.

Jay decided to celebrate the UMW endorsement by going to Spago, one of his favorite high-end haunts in L.A. where the celebrities and glitterati mingled. When they were seated at their table around 11 P.M., Nicole ordered a gin and tonic and gave Jay a briefing.

"The *Times* is in heat over the Pomona land deal," she reported. "They've retained an outside accounting firm to review the land transactions by the governor. I think it's going to be a front-pager."

"In Sunday's paper," Jay predicted. "Circulation is higher then and they want to drive the Sunday talks. I always knew the press would turn on us."

"Lisa emailed me talking points, but I still don't completely understand the issue," said Nicole, squeezing a lime into her drink. "I don't have any institutional memory."

Jay leaned forward and lowered his voice. "Bob had a couple of good friends and major donors, former Larson Company executives, who approached him about a land deal. They were buying a parcel of land they hoped to develop and then sell," answered Jay. "When Bob sold his house in L.A. after being elected governor, he took the money and put it in the Pomona land development. The real reason he did it was to avoid paying capital gains taxes on the proceeds from the sale of his house. That's it—there was nothing nefarious about it at all."

"Then why is the *Times* going ape?"

"The problem came later. The state Department of Transportation was planning a major highway by the land parcel. Bob's enemies and the *Los Angeles Times* have always claimed that he knew about the state highway in advance and influenced where it was located to turn a profit. We've battled it in every campaign since."

"What's the truth?"

"Ah, the truth—that elusive, Aristotelian concept!" joked Jay, spinning the wine in his glass. Nicole stared back, unsmiling. "Bob did nothing wrong, but he was not well served by his friends. That's the truth." He shrugged his shoulders. "So what else is new? As long as his partners keep their mouths shut, we can ride it out."

"Sometimes your friends hurt you more than your enemies," Nicole said. "How did the governor's partners find out where the highway was going?"

Jay stared back, his face expressionless.

"Well?"

"The governor appointed one of their wives to the DOT board." He smiled. "It was pillow talk."

"I get it now. How much did they make?"

"About eighty million dollars. Not bad for two years of turning dirt. The governor made four million on a one-million-dollar investment. What is this—sixty-four questions? Lighten up!"

Nicole shrugged. "I was just curious, that's all."

Out of the corner of his eye, Jay saw a striking blonde approaching their table. Immaculately coiffed, she wore the L.A. glamour girl uniform of tight jeans tucked into spike-heeled suede Gucci boots, a black leather jacket, and a lace blouse with a plunging neckline from which Jay could barely avert his stare. As she approached, Jay figured she had to be an actress or model. But who in L.A. wasn't?

"Excuse me," she asked. "Aren't you Jay Noble?"

"Who wants to know?" Jay asked with a smile.

"Kate Curtis, pleased to meet you," she said, smiling right back. She extended a delicate, pale hand with polished red nails. "I'm a big fan."

A wave of egomania and sexual tension rolled through Jay's body. "No, I'm a big fan of *yours*! I *knew* I recognized you—I watch your show all the time." Actually, he couldn't remember the name of the show. "I love your work!" Jay was stunned by her beauty, but also by how impossibly thin she was. Was she living on sesame seeds?

"That's me," she said, bobbing her head, giggling, shooting a glance at Nicole.

"You look fabulous . . . you look . . . just great," Jay blubbered.

"Oh, thank you. I don't usually interrupt people—I hate it when people do that." She laughed. "I feel like a . . . teenybopper! But my husband and I are big supporters of Bob Long. We're behind him all the way." She turned and pointed to her husband, an A-list movie star, who smiled and wiggled his fingers in a wave. "We're also fans of yours. We saw you on Marvin My-ers's show—you did a great job."

"Well, thank you. It's not hard when you're defending Governor Long," replied Jay, basking in the compliment. He introduced Kate to Nicole and gave her his business card, making a major production of writing down his cell phone number. "You guys call me anytime. I'm on that number 24/7."

"We will!" She beamed, flashing a million-watt smile. "Good luck! Let us know if we can do anything to help."

"Send money!" exclaimed Jay, laughing.

"We did—we contributed on the website. We both gave the max."

"I love your show even more now, sweetheart."

She smiled. What perfect teeth! "Maybe we could host a fund-raiser?" she said.

"I'd love it!" He made the shape of a phone with his hand and pointed flirtatiously at her. "Call me."

"I will. I definitely will," she insisted. She waved his business card for emphasis. Since it was Hollywood, Jay could safely assume he would never hear from her again.

She walked back to her table clutching Jay's business card as if it were a talisman. Jay had spent decades toiling away in anonymity as a political hack, and now he was being recognized at Spago by movie stars.

"You're such a sucker," said Nicole, shaking her head and rolling her eyes. "You acted like a groupie. It was *embarrassing*!"

"Hey, I'm just trying to raise money for the campaign," Jay protested.

The waiter came to the table and flipped open two dessert menus. Jay was feeling on top of the world. Crème brûlée with a cup of espresso sounded good.

"What are you going to have for dessert?" he asked.

"I thought I was dessert," Nicole replied, batting her eyes.

Jay closed the dessert menu. "You know what?" he said to the waiter. "On second thought, we'll take the check."

33

B OB LONG STOOD IN the center of his office, hands on his waist, a stoic look on his face. Jay Noble perched behind his desk, his poker face on as he tore into a breakfast of Starbucks and a Butterfinger. Lisa slumped in a wing chair, her legs crossed, looking pensive, legal pad on her lap. David Thomas leaned against the wall, his shirt sleeves rolled, chewing the nubby fingernails of his right hand. Hollywood sprawled on the couch, his countenance pale, sweat beading on his upper lip. The television set in Jay's office was tuned to one of the cable news networks, where a camera was trained on a cluster of microphones outside a downtown office building in D.C.

The stress of the campaign team had spiked with the distribution of that morning's press clips. In the top of the stack was the *New York Times* front-pager on the Pomona land deal, with its gaudy headline: "State Officials Helped Long and Donors Reap Millions in California Land Deal." Lisa and Jay had both predicted the media worm would turn; it had done so with a vengeance. Now they awaited the verdict of the Commission on Presidential Debates.

First to the microphone strode Dirk Bulloch, former chairman of the Republican National Committee. "The Commission on Presidential Debates has reached a final decision regarding the manner, location, and formats of this fall's debates." Paper rustled among the press corps. "The first presidential debate will take place on the campus of Emory University in Atlanta next Sunday evening, September 30, and will be devoted to foreign policy and national security. The second will be one week later on the campus of the University of California at Los Angeles on October 5 and will focus on domestic issues. A vice presidential debate will be held in Orlando on the campus of the University of Central Florida on October 7. The third presidential debate will be October 12 at Washington University in Saint Louis. The commission will extend invitations to Republican nominee and Vice President David Petty, Democratic nominee and Senate Majority Leader Salmon Stanley . . . and independent candidate Governor Robert Long."

Long's face folded into a wide smile as the senior staff erupted into loud cheers. The commission's decision was a political thunderclap. Long was the first independent candidate included in the presidential debates since Ross Perot and was guaranteed an audience of 120 million people on three nights just a few weeks before the election—and equal stature with the major party nominees.

Lisa bolted from her chair. "They couldn't keep you out!" she exclaimed.

"We needed a boost after that *Times* hit piece," growled Long. The story on the Pomona land deal had sparked a brushfire in the liberal blogosphere and unleashed a flurry of critical editorials, some of which compared it to the first Whitewater story by the *Times,* which had ultimately led to the appointment of a special prosecutor, a scandal, and Clinton's impeachment.

"The press giveth, and the press taketh away," said Jay in a flat monotone, staring at the chocolate-smeared wrapper. "From here on out, it's fastballs at the head."

"How did the *Times* find out that I appointed that Larson Company executive's wife to the DOT board?" asked Long.

"It's public record." Jay shrugged. "Are your former partners talking?"

"Talking?" replied Long. "They're hiding under their desks. Their lips are sealed." He shook his head. "I hope we don't have a leaker."

"It could be someone in state government leaking," observed Jay. He made a mental note to check with Nicole and make sure she hadn't inadvertently told someone else in the campaign.

"Whatever the source, it's going to get worse before it gets better," said Lisa. "The *L.A. Times* is working on a piece claiming you flip-flopped on gun control."

"I didn't flip-flop," Long said with a smile. "I evolved." Everyone chuckled.

"Keep that between us," joked Thomas. "Remember: Andy Stanton doesn't believe in evolution."

Long turned serious. "What do I do when I walk out on the stage at the first debate and both Petty and Stanley start blasting away at me?" he asked.

"Look into the camera and smile," said Scottie, looking exhausted. He had stayed up half the night producing ads to respond to the negative attacks on the land deal that were rumored to hit the airwaves any day now. "You need a line like Reagan's in 1980: 'There you go again.' "

"Yes," agreed Long, bobbing his head in affirmation. "Get me some one-liners."

"Forget witty lines. Focus on projecting confidence," Jay corrected him. "When 120 million people turn on their television sets and see you looking presidential, it won't matter what Petty and Stanley say. Their attacks will bounce off you."

Nicole Dearborn stuck her head in the door, making eye contact with Lisa. She walked in and slipped her a piece of paper. Lisa silently read, eyes widening. "Listen to this!" she said. " 'Coal Companies and United Mine Workers Reach Labor Accord.' The AP is reporting the coal strike is over. The UMW got the health benefits they wanted."

Long looked over at Jay. "Get Stan Anderson on the phone," he instructed. "I came through for him. Now it's time for him to deliver for me."

THE CARTOON POPPED UP on YouTube and quickly jumped to Merryprank ster.com, Drudge, Huffingtonpost, and the major news sites. By that first evening, it led news broadcasts on Fox, CNN, and ABC.

The spot, which rivaled the finest animation of Pixar or Disney, opened with Bob Long drawn as a Gordon Gekko caricature, a Master of the Universe pacing in his Wall Street office, smoking a cigar and snatching up land parcels through straw buyers while ogling a shapely female assistant. "I want to be *rich, rich, rich!*" he shouted into his speakerphone. When an earnest protégé asked how he could be certain the land deals would be profitable, he replied, "Because I decide where all the roads go, pal." Then, blowing cigar smoke in the kid's face, the Long character added, "It's the American way."

"How do I get in on that action?" asked the naive protégé.

"Easy—get elected governor!" joked Long.

In the final scene, Long was shown in the Oval Office, a large map of Panama on the wall, holding court with his staff. "I want to buy these parcels here . . . here . . . and here," he barked, pointing at the map.

"But why buy land in Panama, Mr. President?" asked one of his naive staffers.

"Because I'm widening the Panama Canal!" Long guffawed. "This dirt will be priceless. And it's *mine—mine, I tell you—all mine!*"

By its second day in circulation, the cartoon had 3.9 million viewings on YouTube and Merryprankster. The Internet, which had fueled Bob Long's meteoric rise and built his two-million-strong grassroots army, was now the vehicle for the first major blow struck against his candidacy. But who had produced it? It was the best-kept secret in the country.

———

LISA CLOSED THE DOOR to Jay's office and collapsed on the couch, her face drained. She looked like she had seen a ghost. Jay quickly wrapped up his phone call.

"I just got a call from Hal Goodman," she said, then paused. "He has a copy of your memo outlining the strategy for the entire campaign."

"*What?*" Jay slumped low in his chair. "You mean the one I wrote in Mexico?"

Lisa nodded.

Jay sat in shock. It was an unspeakable breach of security. His mind raced a thousand miles an hour, trying to figure out how the memo could have fallen into the wrong hands.

"Who do you think leaked it?" asked Lisa helplessly.

"I have no clue. We numbered the copies and took them up after the meeting."

"No hard copies floating around?"

"None. We only had nine copies and we shredded them."

"Does anyone have access to your laptop? Have you left it lying around?"

"My laptop never leaves my side," Jay replied defensively.

"Well, somebody gave the memo to Goodman. He's doing an exclusive tomorrow, and it's going to be the hook for a cover story on the governor. Word is the cover photo is you and Long walking together in conversation."

"Great," muttered Jay. "This is a disaster. We have to find out who leaked it. We need to notify law enforcement. If this is campaign espionage, it's against the law."

"We're going to investigate our own campaign staff?" asked Lisa in disbelief.

"We have to plug the leak," Jay replied, visibly agitated. "Battaglia may have to contact the FBI. I don't think the California state police can do it because they ultimately report to the governor."

"Two FBI investigations going on at once—that's got to be a first for a presidential campaign," sighed Lisa. "What do I say to Goodman?"

"We can't accuse a rival campaign of stealing it without evidence," Jay said, thinking aloud. "Just say this was an internal brainstorming document that does not constitute policy or reflect the thinking of Governor Long. We find this leak highly suspicious, and whoever is behind it is trying to harm the governor."

"And when he asks: such as whom?"

"That's for law enforcement to determine."

Lisa scribbled on her legal pad. She stood up to leave, then caught herself at the door. "You need to tell the governor."

"He's going to love this," said Jay sarcastically. He tried to retrace his steps, desperately searching his memory to figure out who might be the leaker. It had all the markings of an inside job. He didn't know who it was yet. But he would find out, and when he did, they would never work in politics again.

———

STEPHEN FOX SAT BY the pool at his Bermuda estate, his laptop online via a wireless broadband connection, giggling as he watched the parody of Bob Long. Orlando the houseman poured him lemonade and laid a fresh towel on his lounge chair. Still laughing, Fox picked up his cell phone and dialed the Washington office of Hoterman & Schiff.

"G.G., it's simply brilliant," he bubbled. "It's hilarious! And the animation is beautiful. It really cuts through the clutter."

"We didn't want a typical drive-by shooting," G.G. boasted. "So you like it?"

"I don't like it; I *love* it. So does Felicity—she emailed it to her entire contact list! It's the best spot of the entire campaign." He chuckled. "Who did it?"

"I could tell you but then I'd have to kill you," said G.G. playfully.

"Whoever did it deserves a medal when this is over."

"I told you we'd get it done, didn't I?" bragged G.G. "We're going to cut

Long's face with a rusty blade every day between now and Election Day. By then, he'll be the elephant man."

Stephen fell silent, recoiling at G.G.'s savagery. G.G. realized that he had spoken too candidly. He had pulled the curtain back on the slaughterhouse, allowing a civilian to see the blood and guts that had to be spilled to win. "We wouldn't have to do this if the media would just do its job," he backpedaled. "We've done this reluctantly."

"Look, I know you're in a tough business," replied Stephen, trying to assert his own machismo. "It is what it is."

"I've been accused of a lot of things, but pulling punches ain't one of them," Hoterman growled.

"You've got less than six weeks. Is that enough time?" asked Stephen, his voice conveying concern. "Don't you need longer to soften Long up?"

"We've got plenty of time, trust me," G.G. assured him. "Wait until you see what we hit him with next."

"That's why I stroked you the big check, old buddy. You're doing exactly what you need to do. Just keep hitting him. And stay out of trouble with this Virginia delegation investigation. Whatever you do, don't let up."

———

BILL DIAMOND SAT IN the front cabin of Air Force Two, working his way through a bowl of chicken noodle soup and a plate of tuna salad. His free hand guided the cursor on his laptop. Vice President Petty was on his way to Pittsburgh and Air Force Two was high in the clouds somewhere over the Alleghenies.

Diamond was feeling better about the campaign. The deadly toxins of the Internet were eating away at Bob Long. After heated debate, the Petty campaign chose not to add a link to the Long cartoon parody to its website, letting the RNC do it instead. Some of the campaign's testosterone-addled advisors were livid, but Diamond saw no need to get cute. Internet vigilantes had taken justice into their own hands. Their venom spewed forth from the Web like lava from a volcano. It was almost too good to be true. As Long took the incoming, all Diamond had to do was pull up a chair and enjoy the show.

Diamond logged on to the *Newsweek* website and scrolled down the home page. Goodman had not disappointed—the story was a head shot. "Long's Secret Plan to Destroy America's Political System," heralded the headline. The subhead was just as juicy: "In Confidential Memo, Jay Noble Called for Destruction of Two-Party System, Lashed Out at Democrats." His eyes darted to the lede:

> *Bob Long portrays himself not as a wild-eyed bomb-thrower but as a reformist governor who will transcend partisanship and unite the country. But an internal memo obtained by* Newsweek *reveals the harsher underside to Long's candidacy. Penned by Jay Noble, Long's strategic guru, it vows to destroy both political parties, compares the two-party system to communism, and promises to replace it with a new political order made in Long's image. "The existing two-party system is hopelessly corrupt and must be destroyed. But as with Soviet communism, history needs a push. The Long candidacy will signal the death knell of the current party system," Noble wrote in the confidential strategy memo.*

Vice President Petty came into the cabin and sat down across the worktable from Diamond. As he spooned his chicken noodle soup, Diamond swung the laptop around so the vice president could read the screen.

"Looks like someone left their luggage on the tarmac." Petty grinned. His eyes narrowed as he stared at Diamond. "I assume we had nothing to do with it."

"Nope," answered Diamond, holding up the palms of his hands. "We're clean."

"This will slow Long's momentum," Petty predicted. "Big-time."

"You bet. This and the Internet cartoon—which we also had nothing to do with, by the way."

"Who did the cartoon?" Petty asked, chuckling. "Funniest thing I've ever seen." He signaled to an attendant for some soup of his own.

"I don't know, but if I had to guess, Kaplan's fingerprints are on it."

"Well, at least it knocked my Iowa video off YouTube's greatest hits."

"I wasn't going to say that, but it does have that added salutary effect." Diamond smiled. "The two people behind it are clearly Kaplan and Hoter-

man. They're the meanest, toughest, most vicious political team I've encountered in my career."

"Is that right?" replied Petty. "I've met Hoterman a few times. He's always Mr. Big Shot, obsequious, laying on the schmaltz. He's self-important,
an inveterate name-dropper, and insufferable. He's a parody of a Washington
lobbyist."

"Don't let appearances fool you. He's a killer. He and Kaplan are really
hanging ten on a high wire," observed Diamond. "Can you imagine doing
this kind of stuff when you're being investigated by the criminal division at
DOJ?"

Petty shook his head, slurping a spoonful of soup. "It's beyond reckless. I
can't tell you how many O-6's in the army I saw flush their careers over a
needless firefight. I guess campaigns have the same effect. People lose perspective."

"It's all good for us. We benefit more than Stanley from Long taking on
water. You never know, we might even see some of the evangelical vote come
home."

"They can come home, but they're in the doghouse," spat Petty, putting
down his spoon and wiping his mouth with a white, monogrammed cloth
napkin. "Especially after the way they've played it. Andy Stanton has intimi-
dated this party for years. He balloons up like a porcupine and everyone runs
for cover. When we win, those days are *over*."

"Noble's memo makes it clear Long planned all along to play the socos
for fools. And they fell for it," Diamond marveled. "They must feel like
idiots."

"How is it different from the way we've played them?" asked Petty.
"They're just being used by someone else now."

Diamond was startled by Petty's honesty. For his part, Diamond wished
he could rewind the tape and prevent the breakup of the Reagan coalition,
which had provided the durable framework for the GOP since 1980. Though
frayed and threadbare, it was still comfortable, like an old winter coat. But it
was too late. Harris Flaherty was gone now and David Petty was the head of
the party. The divorce papers had been served.

34

J AY TOOK ONE LAST bite from the crab appetizer as the waiter laid a siz-
zling, medium-rare filet mignon in front of him. The wine steward appeared with a second bottle of Brunello from Tuscany. He uncorked the
bottle and poured a small amount into a fresh wineglass. Jay spun it in the
bottom of his glass, breathed in its aroma, and took a sip, letting it flow
across his tongue. He nodded approvingly.

It was thirty-eight days until the election and the night before the first
presidential debate in Atlanta, and Jay and the Brain Trust were blowing off
steam in a private room at Bone's, the popular Buckhead steakhouse. The
table overflowed with sautéed mushrooms, garlic spinach, hash browns, and
asparagus. Lisa dispensed with her usual Southern California salad fixation
and dug into a New York strip. David Thomas had downshifted from his
usual flamethrower intensity by a gear, laughing loudly and seemingly enjoying himself. Everyone was feeling good.

They had made it to the bigs, improbably pushing Bob Long to the top
of the mountain, and they would never again wallow in that lonely purga-
tory populated by mediocre and defeat-checkered political consultants. Assuming Long did well the following night, they had a shot at an historic
victory. In the world of politics, a presidential win was like an Academy
Award—it was a career maker. For Long's team, victory would be even
sweeter because they would be electing the first independent president in
history. If they won, the members of the Brain Trust were going to be rich
and famous, and loyal friends forever. A soothing combination of professional comradeship, white-hot ambition, friendship, and alcohol bound
them as they gorged on their red meat and Italian wine. Nor was that all.
Nicole's hand slowly stroked Jay's thigh under the table. He was having a
hard time concentrating on the debate, but he didn't want to tell her to
stop.

Hollywood polished off his vodka martini (Status with ginseng, straight
up with three olives, please) and was sufficiently lubricated that he was sending the entire table into explosions of laughter with his comic, smashmouth

vows to destroy David Petty. Jay noticed that Hollywood's eyes were blood-shot, his skin pale and pasty, and he had barely touched his lettuce wedge. He hoped he wasn't overdoing the chemicals.

"Let me tell you what we're going to do to pretty-boy Petty," vowed Hollywood, a sneer spreading across his face. "We're going to take off both layers of his skin. I've got ads documenting that Petty gave billions of dollars in no-bid contracts to cronies for bogus Iraq reconstruction projects. Our troops went without body armor while Petty's friends got rich!" He lowered his voice to a whisper. "I've got a combat vet—an Army Ranger—who looks into the camera and asks Petty why he didn't do more for the soldiers. When voters learn about Petty's sleaze, he'll have to wear a mask in public. Little children will see him and run."

"Hollywood, a person doesn't have two layers of skin—they have three," corrected Lisa.

Hollywood didn't miss a beat. "Then I'll cut another ad and take care of the last layer."

Everyone laughed at Scottie's over-the-top stand-up routine. He was simply fun to be around. He was the kind of crazy genius who stayed up until 2 A.M. making an ad he knew would never air for the sheer amusement of it. Scottie was brilliant, creative, and increasingly strung out on cocaine. Jay's job was to keep him on a short leash, make sure that the only ads that aired were the ones that worked, and get him to rehab as soon as the campaign was over.

The Big Feet gathered down the street at the bar at Posh, knocking down drinks, trading gossip, and stargazing as political celebrities floated in. When they heard the Brain Trust was at Bones, they headed over in search of more gossip. They hung out at the bar, hoping for an invitation to join them, but Jay ignored them. He was in the bunker now, and he was no longer kibitzing with his old pals in the press.

Dan Dorman wandered over, a scotch-and-water in his hand, his hair a tangled mat of gray, a red stain on his white shirt, looking more disheveled than usual.

"Thirty-eight days to go," he announced. "How's the team that put Bob Long within reach of the presidency?" he asked, warming them up with flattery.

Jay said nothing. That was Lisa's cue to swat away Dorman's compliment. "Tomorrow night is a big night," she said with a total absence of candor. The fun began to drain from the table. "We're under no illusions. We're determined and sober. It's still a long way to November."

"Sober politically or sober period?" joked Dorman.

"Both," answered Lisa.

"Speak for yourself!" bellowed Scottie. "I'm not sober politically or chemically. It's my strategy to lull the opposition into underestimating me."

"I don't think anyone is doing that anymore, Scottie," deadpanned Dorman.

Dorman pulled up a chair and began to regale them with war stories from campaigns before most of them were born. He was a throwback to the "boys on the bus" era, before reporters were assassins and presidential candidates were hunted prey. To his young sources, only two of whom were over the age of forty-five, it was ancient history. Jay glanced at his watch. He had one more debate prep session with Long in the morning and some research to do. Plus Nicole had his engine running. He waved for the check.

Nicole's cell phone went off. Jay assumed it was a press call. She left the table to take it.

Breezing through the bar area and out the front door, she walked past the parking valet and into an empty parking lot, far from earshot.

"Michael, is that you?" she asked nervously.

"Got your voice mail. I'm sorry things are getting a little dicey."

"What were you *thinking* leaking Jay's memo to *Newsweek*?" She spat the word.

"I don't know what you're talking about," Kaplan lied.

"Don't give me that. I *know* you leaked it. The only person with that memo besides me and Jay is you! Do you want me to get smoked out?"

"Of course not. You've been a terrific asset."

"Well, I may not be for much longer." It was a threat, and Nicole enjoyed hurling it at him. "Long is suspicious. When the *Times* found out about the developer whose wife was appointed to the DOT board, they started clamming up. They know there's a leaker, and it's only a matter of time before they figure out who it is."

"You knew the rules. You asked to do this, remember?"

Nicole didn't like being reminded of that inconvenient fact. "I didn't want my own team telegraphing my position with a smoke grenade!" she angrily shot back, her voice rising. "Phil Bettaglia is conducting an investigation. He's interviewing every member of the staff, pulling cell phone records, reviewing emails and text messages. They're going to bring in the FBI, Mike. I never agreed to become party to a crime, and I'm not going to go to prison, do you understand me?" Her voice trembled.

"Take it easy, Nicole," said Kaplan. "No one is going to jail. I'll get you the best attorney money can buy. You're going to be *fine*. Don't talk to Bettaglia, the FBI, or anyone else about this without a lawyer present."

"Don't you think that will raise suspicions?"

"Just explain to Phil that your attorney is a family friend and you would feel more comfortable with him present. He'll understand."

"I hope so," Nicole replied, a hint of resignation in her voice. "Because if you're wrong, we'll end up with a story that will make Jay's memo look like a yawner."

"Hang in there, Nicole. You're doing *great*. It will be duly noted when this is over."

"Have the attorney call me ASAP," said Nicole. "I think from now on we should talk only on a hard line."

"You'll hear from the attorney tomorrow. Keep your chin up. We're hurting them, which is why they're circling the wagons. And remember: we don't forget our friends."

Nicole hung up and walked back into the restaurant, her hips swaying in a Bebe cocktail dress with a wide belt that accentuated her waist; heads turned among the male patrons as she moved. Jay shot her a sly smile. The waiter brought the check and David Thomas shoved a campaign credit card across the table, but Jay would have none of it. He tossed a personal credit card at the waiter. The campaign had bumped up the fall media buy by another $25 million—and Jay's commission had just increased by a whopping $750,000. With money like that, what did it matter if he dropped a thousand on dinner? He reached over and began to rub Nicole between her shoulder blades, his hand slipping underneath her hair while everyone thanked him for dinner.

———

BOB LONG SAT IN his suite at the Grand Hyatt in Buckhead at 7:30 A.M., gazing out over the Atlanta skyline. He had a breathtaking view, with Stone Mountain to the east and the smoky outline of the Blue Ridge Mountains to the north. His BlackBerry vibrated on the dining room table. He answered it.

"Bob, it's Andy Stanton. Welcome to my state, my friend," he said with affection. "I hope I'm not calling too early. I was going to leave a voice mail."

"I'm glad you called," replied Long, walking back to the window. The morning sun reflected off the skyscrapers, lighting them up like pillars of fire. "Andy, why don't you come to the debate tonight as my guest? You can sit with my family."

"I'd be honored, but I think I better lay low," Andy demurred. "If I'm sitting with your family, I'll be criticized when I have you on my television and radio shows to share your testimony." He let out a burst of laughter. "I generally steer clear of Emory—I graduated from the divinity school, and they've been kicking themselves ever since!"

"I hope you're not declining because of that story in the *Washington Post* claiming that Claire objected to my values speech," Long said.

"Of course not. I don't believe a word I read in the *Post*. You should see what they say about me."

"Good," said Long. "Because Claire thinks the world of you." It was a white lie, but Long didn't have the stomach to tell Andy that his wife thought he was a snake oil salesman, a charlatan.

"Bob, I'd like to offer you something more powerful than my coming to the debate. Would you mind if I prayed for you?"

"Not at all. I'd be grateful, Andy."

Stanton began to pray in an intimate, conversational style with which Long was unfamiliar. Andy seemed to be talking to God as if he were his best friend. Not the distant, fearsome God of Long's Methodist upbringing, but a God who was in his corner, cheering for him, fighting his enemies for him, and celebrating his triumphs. He felt warm and relaxed.

"God, I thank you for Bob and Claire, for their willingness to stand up and be counted for the Gospel in the political arena," Andy prayed. "When Bob walks out onstage tonight, give him a peace that surpasses all understanding. Even as Jesus told His disciples not to worry about the words they would speak when dragged before courts, assuring them that words would be given to them, even so I pray, Father, give Bob the words tonight that you would have him speak to the American people."

Long felt his nose tickle and his eyes begin to fill with tears.

"Protect him, Lord, bless him, prosper all that his hand touches, and give him *victory* tonight," Andy fervently asked. "Give him wisdom, eloquence, and favor with the voters beyond his own ability. We praise you in advance and thank you. Amen . . . and *amen.*" Andy fairly shouted the final "amen," signaling the prayer was over.

"Thank you," Long managed, choking back the tears.

"All right, you're covered with prayer," exclaimed Andy in his booming, infectiously optimistic voice. "The Holy Spirit is going to fall on the Emory campus tonight like it has not done in a century. Now go out there and get 'em!"

"Don't worry. We're going to have fun tonight," replied Long.

"And Bob—"

"Yes?" Long interrupted.

"Remember when you walk out onstage, you belong to God. Don't worry about what you will say. You're going to be like Daniel in the lion's den. The Lord will go before you and not a hair on your head will be harmed."

"I believe that," Long said.

"Stay on your knees, Bob. God is on the throne."

Bob thanked Andy and hung up. He was beginning to believe that Andy was right: God really was in charge. He let out a relaxed sigh. Had the Lord heard Andy's prayer, and if so, what would be his answer? Bob would know in twelve hours.

35

A KNOCK ON THE DOOR: three insistent raps. "Governor, it's time."
Out of the dressing room stepped Bob Long in a tailored blue suit
and a blue patterned Ferragamo tie, a crisp white shirt, and black slip-on
shoes polished to a deep shine. That afternoon Long had dispensed with his
final debate prep session and had instead sat on the balcony of his suite at
the Grand Hyatt, letting the sun toast his face to a healthy glow. His makeup
and hairstylist had told him a good tan was the best makeup for television.
And she was right. He looked great—tanned, relaxed, and ready.

"Showtime," said Long, walking down the hallway to the set in long
strides. He glanced at Jay and Lisa, who walked beside him, their faces
stricken with fear that bordered on sheer terror. It wasn't what Long needed
just before he stepped onstage. They stopped at the edge of the stage as an
assistant director prepared to cue Long to walk to his podium. Long suddenly wheeled and said, "Calm down!" in a stage whisper, his hand cupping
his mouth. "I'm going to do fine!"

Lisa and Jay exchanged smiles. Long was loose—it was a good sign.

Long made his entrance under the lights with Salmon Stanley and David
Petty to loud applause. The candidates went through the formality of shaking hands, awkwardly and nervously rounding one another like partners at a
square dance, and then went to their corners, standing behind their respective podiums.

Marvin Myers sat solemnly before the cameras like a high priest on holy
day, clearly relishing his role as debate moderator. The toughest interrogator
in broadcast journalism, he had been selected by the debate commission
after a tug-of-war with the campaigns, and he had come loaded for bear.
Myers briefly explained the rules, then the candidates delivered opening
statements, basically *Reader's Digest* versions of their stump speeches. For the
first few rounds of questions, the candidates spoke haltingly, relying on tapes
of talking points playing in their heads. Their answers droned on with no
spontaneity as they avoided one another like bulls in a ring. It would be

twenty minutes before the fireworks began—and it came in a sharp exchange between Long and Stanley, who hated each other.

"Senator Stanley," asked Myers pointedly, "you oppose the administration's efforts to aid prodemocracy forces in Iran, claiming it is a 'secret war' that violates international law. But how do you plan to stop Iran from obtaining nuclear weapons?"

Stanley leaned into the question with ferocity too hot for TV. "This is a clear difference between me and the other two candidates, who are ideological twins when it comes to America acting unilaterally. If Iran obtains a nuclear weapon, it will destabilize the Middle East and undermine the nuclear Non-Proliferation Treaty. But two wrongs don't make a right. This administration violated international law and misled Congress, and it has cost us dearly. We have lost our moral authority in the world. One of their most vocal supporters in my party—that is, before he *left* the Democratic Party"— he shot Long a nasty look—"was Bob Long."

"Governor Long, would you care to respond?"

Long smiled and cocked his head, glancing at Stanley with a twinkle in his eye. "Well, first of all, I didn't leave my party; my party left me. And apparently I was not alone in my decision." It was a kidney punch, a reference to Stanley's listless poll numbers and the Virginia delegation scandal. Stanley's face was frozen with disdain. "Second, I think the vice president must be surprised to learn that he is my twin." The audience broke into spontaneous laughter. Long had deftly turned Stanley's attack into a joke about their different skin colors. Petty smiled at the remark and looked back down at his notes. Stanley did a slow burn.

Myers scowled and leaned into his microphone. "The audience will please refrain from reacting to the comments of the candidates." The laughter slowed to muffled giggles and died.

"Chief among the reasons for the disaffection with the Democratic Party by me and millions of others," Long continued, "is the majority leader's lack of a plan to deal with Iran. He proposes a regional conference. I'm all for talking, but Iran has defied the international community. We need action." He paused and dipped his chin. "Yes, I supported the president's policy to aid democracy groups in Iran. But I disagreed with the administration's failure to inform Congress. That was a terrible mistake that undermined our credibility. It wasn't the policy—it was our government's secrecy that was wrong."

As the debate's pace quickened, Long was light on his feet and Stanley circled, looking for an opening for a killing blow. Petty, by contrast, appeared slow and listless, almost as if he were medicated. His canned answers lacked fire. He seemed to be playing four corners, hoping to get through the ninety minutes without making a mistake. His caution backfired when Myers stunned him with a sudden, crippling blow.

"Vice President Petty, imagine you are in the Oval Office and your national security advisor walks in and tells you that Iran has just tested a nuclear missile and is threatening to fire additional missiles. What would a President Petty do?"

Petty's eyes blinked nervously. He stood gripping the podium. He said nothing for ten seconds. "Well," he began slowly. There were, in fact, specific—and highly classified—battle plans for such a scenario, but Petty could not reveal them on national television. His mind reeling, he punted the answer. "I would first consult with our allies, both in the Middle East and outside the region," he said. "My objective would be to isolate Iran . . . That is the goal. After that, I would see how Iran and others responded."

"And if Iran did not back down?"

"I can't address a hypothetical. There is no way to know the answer." He stood deflated. He would have loved to give a complete answer, but he'd been handcuffed by his knowledge of the president's plans. And in a glaring error, he had failed to take Iran to task for its involvement in the assassination of Harris Flaherty.

"Governor Long, you have one minute."

"I wish this was a hypothetical situation," answered Long, leaning into the question. "It is not. Iran is close to weaponizing a nuclear device, and it has happened on this administration's watch. There is also evidence that Iran was involved, directly or indirectly, in the assassination of Vice President Flaherty." He paused for dramatic effect. "We cannot appease Iran. They are outside the community of civilized, law-abiding nations. If they successfully test a nuclear device, I would seek action by the U.N. Security Council and moderate Arab states in the region to do whatever is necessary to end the threat. If Iran failed to respond appropriately, it would face grave consequences, including a military response by the United States."

Myers's face lit with surprise. "Just to be clear, you are promising a military attack on Iran if it were to test a nuclear weapon?"

"If the U.N. Security Council and moderate Arab states are not able to end the threat, then we will act," Long replied. "We cannot allow Iran to have a nuclear weapon."

IN A HOLDING ROOM in an adjacent building on the Emory campus, the Brain Trust watched the debate, legal pads open as they took notes, nerves on edge. Runners from the rapid-response team dashed in and out, carrying notes from Jay or Lisa for instant press releases popping Stanley and Petty. Lisa Robinson shot up from her chair. "He won that exchange! Score that one for us. He looks like a strong leader."

Jay nodded, never looking up as he furiously scribbled on his pad.

"How does the general who won the battle of Baghdad screw up that question?" asked David Thomas aloud, shaking his head.

"He's got the same problem Nixon had in 1960," pointed out Hollywood, his sneakered feet resting on the coffee table. "Nixon knew about the CIA's plans to invade Cuba. He had to keep his mouth shut, so he looked weak."

THE TEMPERATURE IN THE studio rose as the debate grew more heated. A bead of sweat appeared on Petty's upper lip. He wiped it with a handkerchief.

That was when Myers went for the jugular. "Vice President Petty, Governor Long began airing a television ad today that accuses you of wasting billions in reconstruction funds in Iraq," Myers observed. "A study by the Government Accountability Office concluded that the awarding of no-bid contracts in Iraq lacked adequate financial controls and violated government contracting guidelines. Sir, what went wrong?"

Petty rose up in righteous indignation, his lips forming a thin line and his eyes flashing with contempt. "What happened?" he asked, acid dripping from his voice. "Marvin, what happened is we liberated twenty-five million people and turned a nation that had been a sanctuary for terrorists into an ally in the war on terrorism. For that, I make no apology *whatsoever*. Unlike

Governor Long"—he glanced in Long's direction, his eyes aflame—"I didn't have the luxury of being an armchair general. We moved quickly to get financial resources flowing to revive the Iraqi economy. Our brave war fighters saved the capital of Iraq and won a major victory in the war on terror."

Myers was not pacified. "What about the GAO report showing financial mismanagement? Does it not raise questions about your competency?"

Petty sighed in frustration before jumping down Myers's throat. "That's a Washington game played by the media to second-guess people who are risking their lives to defeat the terrorists. We were dealing with billions of dollars needed to get Baghdad functioning. Sometimes in war you have to move faster than you would like." He turned to Long and shot him a look of disgust. "As for Governor Long's negative ad questioning my integrity, it is beneath contempt, especially coming from someone who never served his country in uniform."

"Governor Long?" Myers asked, arching his eyebrows expectantly. Like a referee in a heavyweight fight, he stepped back to let the punches fly.

"First of all, no one is second-guessing our soldiers," Long corrected. "The best way to support our troops is to give them the tools they need to win the war. That's what made the fraud that took place on Vice President Petty's watch so indefensible." He turned to Petty, his stare steady. Petty glared back, hatred oozing from every pore in his body. "Mr. Vice President, the billions that lined the pockets of those who ripped off the taxpayers could have been used for body armor, armor plating for Humvees, and ammunition." He turned back to Myers. "I'm not questioning anyone's integrity. But Vice President Petty supervised the reconstruction. Instead of trying to pass the buck, he should accept responsibility."

"I can't let that go unanswered!" blurted Petty, shaking with rage, a small vein bulging at his temple.

"Mr. Vice President, I need to allow Senator Stanley—"

"He is impugning my character! He's lying!"

"Vice President Petty, the rules state—"

"I'm not going to stand here and allow someone who never served in a war to question my integrity!"

Myers gave up. "All right, since Governor Long's answer dealt directly with your role, I will give you thirty seconds to rebut his rebuttal, which is permitted under the rules."

Petty pointed to Long, his face filled with fury. "I guess it's easy for blow-dried, flip-flopping politicians like you to question those of us who have served in battle," he spat. "But my men were under attack by a vicious enemy. I had a job to do, which was to liberate Baghdad. And today Baghdad is the free capital of a free Iraq. For some slick career politician hiding behind a bunch of negative attack ads to now—"

"Mr. Vice President, your time is up."

"—when he never served a day in the military—"

"Time."

"—is an insult to those who have served our country!"

"*Time!*" Myers said firmly, cutting him off.

———

AFTER THE DEBATE, HUNDREDS of reporters and campaign staff jammed into the "spin room," a cavernous basketball arena in the Emory physical education complex set apart for one of the most bizarre rituals in American politics. It was a political meat market. Volunteers carried signs above the designated spinners, whose rank on the totem pole could be discerned by the number of journalists crowding around them. Mobs of reporters pressed against Jay Noble, Michael Kaplan, and Bill Diamond, peppering them with questions. Diamond tried to step away, if only to get some air, but was blocked by the scrum of reporters that resembled a human blob.

"Long obviously got under Petty's skin. Did he blow his top?" a reporter shouted.

"Not at all," insisted Diamond. "It was a desperate move by Long, who is dropping in the polls like a rock, and that's why he's hiding behind attack ads. We're going to set the record straight so that voters know the facts."

"Are you worried that Petty's outburst might make him appear unstable?"

Diamond's face hardened. "The vice president was appropriately indignant about Governor Long's false attacks on his distinguished military record. He responded forcefully, as he should have. Does Bob Long really believe that the way to win this election is to smear a man who liberated Baghdad from the terrorists?"

"Did anything surprise you?"

"I was surprised Long promised to attack Iran if he is elected. Does he want a nuclear exchange in the Middle East?" (Like Petty, Diamond knew that the administration was planning an attack on Iran, but he kept it to himself.)

"Does it worry you that Long came off more forceful on Iran than Petty?"

"Bob Long has given us nothing but rhetoric and hot air; David Petty has actually defeated the terrorists. There is no one more forceful than the vice president in dealing with state sponsors of terrorism seeking nuclear weapons." He stared out at a sea of skeptical faces. They circled him like sharks, and they smelled blood in the water.

Suddenly a "reporter" with a Comedy Central late-night show shoved his way toward Diamond. He had a sock puppet pulled over his right hand and a cameraman in tow. The program had created a franchise out of ambushing politicians and getting them to say idiotic things to the puppet. It was Ali G. meets *Sesame Street*. Diamond braced for the encounter.

"Don't talk to the puppet," whispered a press aide in Diamond's ear.

"Are David Petty and Bob Long twins?" asked the ventriloquist as his hand mouthed the words for the puppet. The reporters paused from their steno pads and chuckled.

"Don't talk to the puppet!" said the aide more firmly, his voice growing louder.

"Were they Siamese twins separated at birth?" asked the puppet, craning his neck.

"Bill, say something to the puppet," joked *Time*.

Diamond turned and walked away. As he moved across the basketball arena's polished wooden planks, a dozen reporters following, he could hear the puppet machine-gunning questions to the laughter of the crowd.

"Bill, why couldn't David Petty find Rassem Zafarshan?" shouted the puppet.

———

BACK IN THE PRESIDENTIAL suite of the Hotel Intercontinental, the phone rang. It was just past 11 P.M., and David Petty was changing in the closet.

"David, it's the president!" shouted Anne from the bedroom.

Petty rushed in in his underwear, dark socks on his feet, shirttail flapping. He took the phone from Anne.

"David, I just wanted to call to tell you I thought you were terrific tonight," said the president in a hollow voice.

"Thank you, Mr. President. I think we landed a few punches," Petty said, his posture wilting from the empty compliment.

"Long is slippery, no question, but I thought you stunned him during the exchange over his saber rattling on Iran. The guy's a demagogue, calling for war in the Middle East. You're doing *fine*. Don't let the media tell you otherwise."

"Thank you, Mr. President. This is going to be a tough campaign for all the reasons we've talked about, but we're going to get the job done."

"I hope you're not letting all this Baghdad reconstruction nonsense bother you."

"No, it's Monday-morning quarterbacking by the usual chickenhawks."

"Good." The president sighed. "It's a nasty business. I did what I had to do eight years ago. So will you. I've got total confidence in you."

It was the pained, stilted exchange of a father with the son who never quite measured up, but was loved in spite of himself. Petty hung up and turned to Anne.

"What did he say?" she asked, her face betraying concern.

"He said I did great," Petty said.

"Well, that's good, isn't it?" she asked hopefully, her eyebrows arched.

"I don't know," he replied skeptically. "You don't call up someone who just knocked out his opponent and say, 'Hang in there, kid.' "

Petty's relationship with the president was a tangle of ambiguity, a combustible mixture of appreciation and resentment, loyalty and ambition, indebtedness and jealousy that bordered on the Oedipal. They had been thrown together by the murder of Harrison Flaherty, and Petty remained haunted by Flaherty's ghost. Now he was in the fight of his life. It was not a fight he had sought, any more than he had sought the presidency itself, but he had to find a way to win. No one—not Harrison Flaherty, God rest his soul—not the Republican Party, not even the president, could win it for him. The thought hit him: he was going to have to destroy Bob Long.

BILL DIAMOND BREEZED THROUGH the lobby of the Hotel Intercontinental on his way to the elevators when he saw a group of Petty campaign operatives in the bar. It was 1:30 A.M. and they were imbibing heavily. He sauntered over.

Taylor Sullivan, Republican rapid-response guru, held court with his unique brand of politics-as-performance-art. Sullivan had spread the sleaze that splattered Stanley and Hafer, sending the Democratic ticket into a tailspin, and he was now a legend. The grizzled political hit man's bald head glowed in the semidarkness like an evil Mr. Potato Head, his chin incongruously covered with two days of beard growth, his eyes hollow with the distant stare of a long-distance truck driver. A half-smoked cigar rested between the fingers of his right hand. Before him sat an empty margarita glass the size of a small bathtub.

"Taylor, maybe you should order a bigger margarita," joked Diamond.

"This isn't a margarita," replied Taylor with a cold stare. "It's a strategy—a strategy for bouncing back from this debate. And I may have another one to advance the strategy further."

"You really think it's that bad?"

"Let me put it to you as simply as I can," muttered Taylor, his speech slightly slurred, punching each word for emphasis. "We had a chance to deck Long tonight—fight over. I'm talking the kind of beating where you punch him through the ropes and he falls into his wife's lap and she cradles his busted face while his blood gets all over her pretty dress." Everyone gazed down at their drinks as Sullivan drew a picture of the carnage. "That's what we *should* have done. Instead, our guy had his arms dangling at his sides." He paused, dropping his hands toward the floor and making a silly face. "We never landed a punch!"

"How much will it hurt us?" asked Diamond. He had learned to trust Sullivan's violent instincts and twisted insights—perhaps too much.

"We'll lose three to four points on the ballot within forty-eight hours. The media is going to pound us."

Taylor's dark prophecy sank in around the table. It had taken weeks of negative ads blasting away at Long to open up a slim lead for Petty. Now, in a single night in Atlanta, weeks of hard work and progress had gone down the tubes. If Taylor was right—and he usually was—they would wake up in four hours and be trailing again. A morbid silence filled the air.

"We'll bounce back," said Diamond, trying to buck them up. "The veep just needs to get back on his game. He'll get there." He pulled up a chair. "He always does."

"Well, that settles it," Taylor said to no one in particular. "We have to go negative." The table erupted in cathartic laughter.

"The media was dying to write this story. They're sick of us after eight years. They loath the president," observed Dick Pepper with clinical detachment. "When Petty became vice president, he became the president's guy." The gel in Pepper's black hair had mixed with sweat, his beard dark against his pale skin.

"From a process standpoint, they don't want the campaign to be over," added Matt Folger, the campaign pollster. "They want a horse race. So they're going to cut our hamstrings."

"They had this story written before the debate even began," said Pepper.

"Darn right," agreed Sullivan. "I saw Dan Dorman with the *Post* an hour before the debate. He was already writing his story."

"What?! He wrote his story before the vice president even walked out on the stage?" shouted Diamond, straightening in his chair. "Pathetic."

"Dorman's an assassin," said Taylor as he sucked his margarita through a straw. "The only difference between him and the terrorists in Miami is they used guns and he uses a Macintosh." Folger glanced at Diamond, shocked at the macabre analogy. "We're going to get pounded in the papers tomorrow, pummeled by the talking heads, and we're going to get eviscerated on the Sunday shows. By the time the weekend is over, the conventional wisdom will harden that our guy fell off the stage and Long won the debate."

"Why does Long get such a free ride?" asked Pepper.

"He's the white albino monkey. The circus has come to town, and he's the bearded lady. To some extent, he's entertainment value and people are gobbling it up."

"I agree," said Pepper. "Now what?"

"Simple," responded Taylor. "It's a two-man race now between Petty and Long. Stanley's done, stick a fork in him. So now we're going to have to send our flying monkeys over to attack Long. We take the gloves off."

"Forget about gloves," said Folger. "We need brass knuckles."

"Taylor, when you send those flying monkeys, make sure they're packing heat," laughed Pepper. "We need the NRA vote!" He took a long swig from a bottle of Bud.

Everyone cackled—they were punch-drunk from exhaustion. Taylor ordered a second margarita and pecked furiously on his BlackBerry.

The postdebate polls were rolling in. "ABC has us down two points," Sullivan announced, his eyes scanning the screen. "That's a three-point drop in the overnights. When asked who won the debate: 48 percent Long, 27 percent Petty, 16 percent Stanley, rest undecided."

The bartender wiped the bar with a towel. It was approaching 2 A.M. Diamond walked to the elevator, his legs rubbery, feeling lightheaded. The muscles in his neck and shoulders had twisted into knots. As the elevator doors closed, the last thing he saw was Sullivan, hunched over his BlackBerry, his thumbs flying across the keyboard, perspiration streaking down his bald head, a determined look on his face. Tomorrow, Diamond thought, the Petty campaign would come out blasting.

36

Yᴇʜᴜᴅᴀ sᴇʀᴡɪᴛᴢ, ɪsʀᴀᴇʟɪ ᴀᴍʙᴀssᴀᴅᴏʀ to the United States, was no stranger to the White House. As he waited to see the president, he made small talk with friends in the West Wing lobby as they filed out of a senior staff meeting in the Roosevelt Room. He contemplated that with the election only thirty days away, there must be an important reason for his being summoned to the Oval Office on such short notice.

The president's assistant appeared at his side and walked him into the Oval. He was startled to find the president standing at attention in front of a cream-colored armchair, surrounded by his entire national security team.

"Yehuda, my dear friend! Have a seat," said the president, motioning him toward the chair next to him. As he sat down, Serwitz felt the stares of the others. National security advisor Geoffrey Davis and White House chief of staff Sam Syms sat on the couch to the president's right. Doug Parks, secretary of defense and the leading hawk in the administration, sat on the couch to his left, joined by acting Secretary of State Nicholas Butler. Clearly something was up.

"The prime minister sends his greetings," offered Serwitz with diplomatic aplomb. "He knows we are meeting today. He asked me to tell you that he looks forward to seeing you next month." The president had invited the PM to be his weekend guest at Camp David after the election.

"Give the prime minister my very best," replied the president. He crossed his legs and leaned back in his chair, resting his right arm on the armrest and pulling his body toward the ambassador. The president was giving Yehuda the full treatment. "I know he's having a tough time keeping his coalition together in the Knesset. I can relate, given what I have to deal with in Congress." The president shifted gears, his face turning deadly serious. "I know you and Geoff have been talking about Iran."

"We have, sir," answered Serwitz.

Normally an ambassador would not have merited such a powerful audience in the Oval Office, but Yehuda was no ordinary diplomat. He was a rising star in Israeli politics, a protégé of the prime minister, and the new and friendly face of a resurgent Likud party. Serwitz was married to an American woman, spoke flawless English, was a regular fixture on television chat shows, and a sought-after table guest at Georgetown dinner parties. Everyone expected him to be the prime minister of Israel someday.

"We have confirmed that the Iranians were behind the assassination of Vice President Flaherty," said the president, his eyes steady. "Eight of the terrorists who attacked Marine Two came from Iran. We have also confirmed the flow of funds from Iran to a bank in Venezuela."

"Rassem el Zafarshan was the leader of the cell, no question," Geoff Davis said, jumping in. "He fought with an Iranian-backed militia during the battle for Baghdad. The CIA recently tracked him to a safe house near the Afghan-Pakistani border and came within an hour of killing or capturing him. He got away. But we'll get him."

"I am hardly surprised it is Iran, Mr. President," said Serwitz. He wondered why the president was going through the motions of sharing U.S. intel. The Israelis had been tracking Zafarshan for years as he moved through the shadows of Iranian-backed terrorist networks. As usual, they knew more than the U.S. intelligence community.

"Nor are we. If we could, we would have already retaliated." The president glanced at the wary faces of his advisors. "But we have to stroke the Saudis and cover our bases with the Iraqis. If we attack without laying the groundwork, we will weaken our friends in the region and embolden our enemies."

"Iran is a tough customer," said Serwitz, his face grave. "If the United States takes military action, they could do anything—including attacking Israel."

"That's right, Yehuda. Saddam did it when he fired Scud missiles into Israel during the first Gulf War. Your government showed remarkable restraint, allowing us to take care of Saddam. We believe Iran may try the same thing. I wanted to make you aware of our plans and request that Israel show similar restraint."

Serwitz paused before answering. "Of course, Mr. President. You have our full support." He paused. "However, if Iran strikes Israel, we would have no choice but to act to protect ourselves."

"We hope it doesn't come to that," replied the president. "If Israel launches a preemptive military strike against Iran, the Saudis will be off the reservation and all bets are off. If we do our job correctly, we won't have to worry about it. We'll disable the Iranian military before they know what hit them." He nodded toward Parks, who nodded back slowly, not saying a word.

"Mr. President, I realize you may not be able to share this, but when do you plan to set the plan in motion?"

"My problem is the election is just around the corner," the president said with a sigh. "If we act now, it will look like we are trying to influence the outcome. Our plan is to act after the election but before the new president is inaugurated in January."

"The sooner the better," gingerly suggested Serwitz. "The longer you wait after the assassination of Vice President Flaherty, the more the memory slips from the public's consciousness. The American people are angry now, as they were after September 11, but that anger will fade with time."

"We won't delay," said the president. He rose from his chair and grabbed Serwitz's right hand with a vise grip, their eyes locked. "Before I leave this office, the people who murdered Harris Flaherty will pay. And we will be rid of one of the most evil regimes in modern times."

Serwitz stood nodding silently, transfixed by the president's intense stare.

"Iran should have been taken care of years ago," said the president, his face inches from Serwitz's. Their bodies were so close they were almost touching. "It was not dealt with—and look what happened. They killed my vice president. I promise you, I'm going to take care of the Iranians—*once and for all*. I'm not leaving this to my successor."

Serwitz left the Oval Office, Geoff Davis flanking him, their bodies brushing as they glided down the narrow hallway. Yehuda's mind reeled as he contemplated the implications of what the president had said: a military strike on Iran, almost certain pan-Arab opposition, a possible attack against Israel, and the danger of a nuclear exchange in the Middle East.

He had been struck by the president's obsession with avenging the murder of Harrison Flaherty, but something else about his conversation with the president sent chills down his spine. If the president felt such an urgency to act before he left office, it could mean only one thing: he was no longer sure his successor would be David Petty.

G.G. HOTERMAN'S SHOT FLEW the green on the twelfth hole at Robert Trent
Jones Golf Club, landing in the bushes. RTJ was one of the most exclusive
golf clubs in Washington, and had once been a favorite haunt of Bill Clinton's. G.G. liked bringing his clients there, especially the Japanese golf nuts.
It had been a week since Stanley's disastrous performance in the first debate,
and Hoterman was playing golf with a potential major donor to the Citizens
for Truth. The election was just twenty-eight days away, the ads were on the
air in every key battleground state, and he was only $17 million short on
CFT's media budget. Disgusted with his poor shot, he reached into his golf
cart and grabbed his BlackBerry. As he scrolled through his emails, he saw
one from a *Time* magazine reporter he knew, and the subject line stopped
him cold: "Stanley Campaign Official Resigns Amid Growing Scandal."

His stomach turned somersaults as he read the Associated Press dispatch:

> *A top official at the Salmon Stanley campaign resigned today*
> *after an internal investigation found she had raised funds for a*
> *tax-exempt group that made secret payments to Virginia delegates*
> *to the Democratic convention. The payments are the central focus*
> *of a criminal probe by the Justice Department. A grand jury in*
> *Washington is reviewing evidence for possible indictments. Me-*
> *linda Lipper, the Senate Majority Leader's chief fund-raiser, be-*
> *came the first Stanley campaign official to step down in the*
> *growing scandal.*

Hoterman could not believe it—they were tossing Melinda to the wolves!
It was beyond disloyal; it was stupid. She was one of the best operatives in
the party, and she knew where all the bodies were buried at the Committee
for a Better America. She could turn state's evidence in a New York minute.

> *The campaign declined to elaborate on Lipper's resignation,*
> *saying it was a personnel matter. A senior campaign official who*
> *asked not to be identified said Lipper raised funds for both the*

tax-exempt group and the campaign, and "the lines became blurred beyond a point we were comfortable with."

You can say that again, thought Hoterman.

Lipper's resignation brings the scandal closer to Stanley campaign chairman Michael Kaplan. Sources say Kaplan and Lipper arranged for payments to delegates who gave favorable testimony in the credentials dispute with Long. Lipper is to appear before the grand jury next week. Repeated calls to her office were not immediately returned, and her attorney declined comment.

Hoterman put down his BlackBerry, sick to his stomach. He could no longer focus on his golf game. He skulled his next shot through the green, picked up the ball after he reached double bogey, and fell apart on the closing holes. Following the round, after a glass of wine with his donor prospect and golf partner (which netted another half million dollars for Citizens for Truth), G.G. stepped into a phone booth off the men's locker room to ensure privacy and whipped out his cell phone.

"Hello, G.G.," said Melinda. "I haven't been answering my phone, but I saw your number. It's nice of you to call."

"Melinda, I'm sick over this," he said. "Please tell me you were not forced to resign."

"I was," she replied coldly. "Duke Barrett was gunning for me. He said I violated FEC rules by soliciting funds for CBA, which is baloney. The real reason is I'm going before the grand jury next week and the leaks from DOJ continue to mention me, so they want me off payroll. I said I was willing to defend myself, and Duke said, 'It's not your job to defend yourself. Your job is to do what's best for Senator Stanley.'"

"That's it?" hissed G.G. "Just like that—after you've raised two hundred million dollars for him!"

"I said, 'What if I don't resign?' And Barrett said, 'Then we will fire you, and we'll do it tonight.' That pretty much ended it. So I sat down last night with a bottle of red wine and wrote my resignation letter. It was hard. I gave this campaign two years of my life."

"Why didn't Mike protect you?"

"That's the disappointing part," she answered. "Why force me out? All we had to do was ride it out for four weeks, and then I could go quietly. The grand jury is secret—I'm not talking. By forcing me out, they've made it an even bigger story."

"Much bigger, and this doesn't help Mike," observed Hoterman. "It paints a bull's-eye on his forehead."

"That's what I told them."

"I can't discuss the particulars," he said, dropping his voice to a low rumble. "But I saw some documents during my FBI interview that involve you. You and I can't discuss them, but have your attorney talk to my lawyer, Walt Shapiro."

"I think I've seen everything, but I'll mention it to my lawyer," Melinda answered. Her voice grew quiet and worried. "G.G., they're trying to make me the scapegoat."

"This is not how you treat your friends," G.G. said indignantly. "Sal Stanley would not have won the nomination without you—and this is how they repay you." Hoterman's righteous anger at Melinda's mistreatment contained a large measure of calculation. She was going to be a witness before the grand jury; he wanted her to view him as a friend. If she turned state's evidence, she could bring down a lot of people, and he didn't want to be one of them.

"I guess they figure I'll take the fall to save Mike and the senator."

"They're kidding themselves," said G.G., spitting out the words. "The Justice Department isn't going to be satisfied until Mike is doing a perp walk."

"Well, they just shafted the wrong person," Melinda said bitterly. "And after what they've done, I don't know why I should protect them any longer."

———

TWELVE MILES FROM ROBERT Trent Jones Golf Club, Fairfax County police squad cars surrounded a red-brick McMansion in one of the most exclusive gated communities in McLean. Residents of the community included prominent lobbyists, politicians, corporate executives, and professional athletes. Police tape circled the house. Soccer moms with children loaded in the back of their SUVs slowed down as they drove past the crime scene, trying to figure out what evil had invaded their pleasant neighborhood.

Plainclothes detectives walked out the front door carrying boxes, computers, and stacks of videotapes, placing the evidence in the backs of vans. News helicopters, alerted by the district attorney's office, buzzed overhead.

A blond woman in her early forties emerged from the house escorted by two deputies, her hands cuffed behind her back. Her hair was pulled back and she wore no makeup. She was strikingly attractive but disheveled, her face distraught. She wore faded blue jeans, Nike tennis shoes, and a University of Virginia sweatshirt. The deputies opened the door of one of the squad cars and she slid into the backseat.

Within an hour the news rocketed across the Internet that Jessica Cruz, a lobbyist for a prominent defense contractor, had been arrested for operating a prostitution ring out of her McLean mansion. The Fairfax County DA charged her with prostitution, operating a house of prostitution, cocaine possession, cocaine distribution, and mail and wire fraud. The story posted on Merryprankster.com reported that prominent Washingtonians were rumored to be on Cruz's client list, and that police had seized as evidence computer hard drives, phone records, and credit card vouchers. Merryprankster christened her the "McLean Madam," and everyone in D.C. waited for the next shoe to drop.

———

"WHILE WASHINGTON GRIDLOCKED, PLAYING politics instead of solving our nation's health-care challenges, we led in California," said Bob Long with a confident flourish, his facial expression earnest and expansive. "Republicans and Democrats came together and enacted a plan that covers every uninsured person in our state, starting with children, with quality, affordable health care. Not everyone gets a Cadillac, but everyone receives basic and preventative care. That's what we did in California, and that's what I'll do as president."

Twelve days after the first debate, the candidates were locking horns in the third and final one, on the campus of Washington University in Saint Louis. It was a cold and blustery night, but the temperature in the studio rose to a boil. With only twenty-five days left before the voters went to the polls and with absentee and early voting already under way in some states, it was the last opportunity for the candidates to make their case before a national television audience, and the debate turned into a spirited, three-way slugfest.

"Vice President Petty, your response?" cued Marvin Myers.

"He covered everyone, all right," Petty said, shooting a withering look in Long's direction. "He did it with a huge tax increase that has driven small business from California. It was a Soviet-style system. He created a gigantic new bureaucracy. His prescription for every issue can be summed up in two words: raise taxes."

"Mr. Vice President, are you comparing Governor Long's health-care plan to the Soviet Union?" asked Myers provocatively.

Alarm bells should have gone off in Petty's head, but he was unfazed. He plowed ahead, oblivious to Myers's challenge. "It's a government-run health-care system—"

"—but you called it Soviet-style—"

"Who am I debating, Marvin, Governor Long, or you?" asked Petty, his eyes flashing with anger.

Republicans in the audience began to applaud. Myers ignored them.

"You're debating your opponents, but as the moderator, I ask the questions," Myers said firmly. "Do you want to give an answer?"

"Can I answer without being interrupted, please?"

"By all means. The floor is yours, Mr. Vice President." Myers extended his hand in a mock gesture of courtesy.

"Thank you," said Petty with a bob of his head. "The point is that you either rely on big government, as Governor Long and Senator Stanley do," he said pointing at Long with an accusing finger, "or you rely on individuals and the marketplace." He pivoted back toward Myers. "Government-run health care has not worked anywhere it has been tried—not in Canada, nor in Great Britain, and not in the former Soviet Union. That was my point, Marvin."

As Petty delivered his answer, Sal Stanley looked as though he was about to bust. He wiggled his index finger to grab Myers's attention.

"Senator Stanley, you wanted in on this topic?"

"I certainly do," Stanley said forcefully. "In my first term in the Senate, I worked to add a prescription drug benefit to Medicare. As majority leader, I took the lead in allowing the government to negotiate with the big drug companies. I also expanded the S-CHIP program to cover ten million uninsured children." He shot a venomous look at Long. "Bob's plan in California does not cover every person. My plan would. And unlike my opponents, I've been a champion for affordable health care for two decades, and I've delivered."

"Governor Long?"

"Well, first of all, I think the Republicans in the California Assembly who voted for my health-care plan would be amused to find themselves compared to communists in the old Soviet Union," joked Long. "Vice President Petty," he said, turning to Petty with a wry smile. "I have a news flash for you. The Cold War is over, and we won." The audience tittered in appreciation. Petty glowered at his podium, his hands gripping the sides. Long ignored Stanley's salvo, primarily because he was fading in the polls. He had another target: the millions of viewers watching at home. He glided out from behind the podium, stepping toward the audience, and looked solemnly into the camera. "This is typical Washington politics. In Washington, if they don't like your ideas, they call you names and try to tear you down. Meanwhile, a single mother working two jobs can't get a mammogram. Her children can't get basic checkups. That's wrong. And when I'm president, we're going to stop talking about it and do something to fix it."

———

BOB LONG, STILL RIDING high from his performance in the debates, which had won accolades from the chattering class and had given him a lift in the polls, gazed around the cavernous room like a child at Disneyland. He shot a quick glance at Jay Noble, his eyes saying, *Do you believe this place?* They were in the conference room at the New Harvest Church in south Philadelphia, with its two-story atrium, balcony, wet bar, oak-paneled walls, overhead projector, African-themed murals, and hand-carved white maple conference table about twenty feet long.

"You could shoot hoops in here," chuckled Long admiringly. Over soft drinks, they chatted with an aide to Bishop Frank Weeks, killing time. After about fifteen minutes, the aide excused himself, apparently to go in search of the good bishop.

"Where is he?" asked Long, by this time clearly irritated.

"On a mountaintop praying, perhaps?" replied Jay with a smirk.

After a long delay, the aide reappeared, clearly distraught. He suggested they watch a ministry video. As they watched the slickly produced video, Long began to rap his knuckles impatiently on the table and shot Jay a dirty look.

"Ahem," said Jay to the aide, clearing his throat. "I don't want to be rude, but the governor has another appointment, and we really need to—"

At that moment, as if on cue, Bishop Weeks burst through the door grinning, his face lit like a Christmas tree. A bundle of energy, his bodybuilder frame compact and musclebound, he wore orange-beige pin-striped dress slacks, a silk shirt that resembled a second skin, matching leather vest, and designer lizard-skin shoes. His hair was slicked back in a gel-sculptured pompadour, and he gave off the sweet aroma of cologne.

"The next president of the United States!" Weeks boomed. "Governor, thank you for coming," he said as he grasped Long's hand and shook it vigorously. "Please forgive me for being a bit tardy." He shook his head. "My staff runs me too hard." He flashed a grin. "What's the word I'm looking for? I am *overscheduled*. But you know all about that!"

"No problem," replied Long, his anger dissipating in Weeks's effervescent presence.

Weeks sat at the head of the table and got down to business. Long noticed that Weeks's biceps bulged like canned hams beneath his shirt. The guy was ripped! "Governor, I have twenty-eight thousand members. Our ministries touch over four hundred thousand people in greater Philadelphia, from cradle to grave, from the jailhouse to the courthouse to the schoolhouse."

"Incredible!" said Long, glancing at Jay, eyes dancing.

"I'm not beholden to either political party," Weeks said firmly. "Our church is above politics. Our mission is to preach Jesus Christ, free people from sin, turn their lives around, make them earthly good and get them on the road to heaven."

"Beautiful," nodded Long, his face breaking into a Cheshire-cat grin.

"Jesus said, 'If I be lifted up, I will draw *all* men unto me,' " bellowed the bishop. "That was a *prophetic* statement. All means *all*—rich, poor, powerful, dispossessed, hurting, brokenhearted, young, old. As we have lifted up

Jesus, they have come—by the tens of *thousands*." He smiled. "That includes a lot of politicians."

Long pondered the biting comment—was it a veiled shot? He didn't really care where Weeks was going as long as it led to those tens of thousands of voters.

"I'm not in the 'hood carrying water for massah like Joe Johnson in New York." His face wrinkled into a look of contempt. "Johnson is an ambulance chaser, a shameless self-promoter and a publicity hound. He gives our community a bad name."

"You're right," Long said. "He's the worst kind of demagogue." So there it was: the explanation for Weeks's sudden interest in his candidacy. The Reverend Joe Johnson had delivered the black vote in New York to Stanley, helping him win the Democratic nomination. Weeks and Johnson were bitter rivals for leadership of the African-American community, and Long would, if he played it right, be the accidental beneficiary of their mutual disdain.

"I support faith-based initiatives and school choice," Weeks plowed on. "I believe black folk should be able to send their children to good schools just like white folk. That offends some elements of the Democratic Party." He paused, his eyes gazing into Long's. "You know what I'm talking about."

"Do I ever!" Long exclaimed. "When I abolished teacher tenure in California, the teachers' union blistered me. They *despise* me."

Weeks barreled ahead with his monologue. "But I'm not a conservative, either. I'm for social justice. I've fought predatory lending by banks that redline and prey on our people with junk subprime mortgages. I oppose discrimination in the criminal justice system. Take crack and cocaine. Crack is the drug of the poor black man, powder cocaine is the drug of the rich white man. Why is the sentence for the black man twice as long as for the white man? That's wrong. So I don't fit into either party very well."

"That makes two of us," quipped Long.

Weeks smiled. "And you've paid a high price," he said. He lifted his elbows and straightened his back. "The African-American community has been the property of one party for too long. I'm tired of eating crumbs from the Democrats' table."

"Frank, you and I have the chance to bring about a new era of racial healing," Long said, working up a froth. "White evangelicals have also been taken for granted by the Republican Party. African-American and white believers can make common cause."

Weeks nodded emphatically. "Governor, God allowed you to be defeated for the Democratic nomination. He did it so he could use you for a greater purpose."

"I believe that," Long said. His mind raced back to the book his pastor had given him. It struck him: God really did allow bad things to happen in order to do something greater. He decided to close the sale. "Frank, I'd like to visit your church and worship with you. If you can recognize me from the pulpit, I'd be honored. If not, I still want to come. I want to show my solidarity with you and your leadership."

"Oh, goodness, a silver-tongued wonder!" Weeks roared. He winked at Jay, the first time he had acknowledged his presence. "I'll have you at a televised service—we are on the Spirit Channel, BET, and the number one TV station in Philly. We have over three million households who tune in between cable, broadcast, and radio."

"I get the feeling you've done this before," chuckled Long.

"There are only three Sundays left before the election," said Jay. "We can't do it this Sunday, but next Sunday will work, assuming that works for you, Bishop." He looked apprehensively at Long, who turned to Weeks, his eyes anxious. Long knew he needed Weeks's national TV audience in time to make a difference.

"The last Sunday in October will work just *fine,*" Weeks replied. He turned to his aide and caught his eye, as if to say, Make that work. His cheeks rose in an impish smile, his cleft chin deepening and his Adam's apple bobbing. He stood up and wrapped Long in a bear hug. Long's face pressed up against the man's massive chest, the musky smell of cologne filling his nostrils. "You would have made a great preacher, Governor," Weeks boomed. "But you're doing what God has called you to do. And I am going to help you."

Long felt the warmth of Weeks's affection pass through him. He was going to steal black votes from under the nose of David Petty, the first African-American presidential nominee in history, and Salmon Stanley, to whom they rightfully belonged. He was going to steal them both blind—and it was perfectly legal.

MARVIN MYERS PULLED DOWN his suit coat to straighten the wrinkles as a makeup woman applied Vaseline to his lips. He rubbed his lips together.

The red light on the camera lit up; they were on the air.

"Joining us now is Marvin Myers, who has some breaking news regarding a new poll in the presidential race that has everyone talking," said the anchor.

"That's right," Myers replied. "With eighteen days remaining before the election, a new series of state polls in the battleground states conducted by our polling division shows the race closer than ever. In the aftermath of a lackluster performance in the first debate by Vice President Petty, who had pulled ahead, Bob Long now leads by just two points, 29 percent to Petty's 27 percent, and Sal Stanley is at 24 percent."

"What about the situation in the states?" asked the anchor.

"That's where it really gets interesting," Myers teased, leaning forward in his chair. "Bob Long leads in most of the South and his home state of California, Stanley in the Northeast, and Petty in the rock-ribbed-Republican Rocky Mountain states. But many states are still too close to call, and no candidate is anywhere near having a majority of the Electoral College."

"The president is actually elected by the electoral votes, not the popular vote," the anchor interjected helpfully, providing a quick civics lesson for viewers. "Where does it stand as of today?"

"The picture in the Electoral College is muddled, to say the least."

A graphic appeared on the screen:

Long	148
Petty	121
Stanley	89

"Long leads by more than four points only in California and some southern states which, added together, give him 148 electoral votes. Petty and Stanley trail behind. But no candidate is even within a hundred electoral votes of having the 270 needed to win on Election Day."

"Do you think this pattern will hold?"

"In a highly competitive race with each candidate having a strong geographic base of support, the arithmetic of reaching 270 electoral votes is almost impossible. Unless something changes, this election is heading to the House of Representatives."

"What happens then?" asked the anchor, eyebrows arched, plastic face animated.

"Each state will have one vote," replied Myers. "And twenty-six votes are needed to win. Having the election in the House hurts Long the most because his base is California, which is the most populous state in the country, but it will have only one vote, the same as less populous states like Wyoming or Delaware."

"Who does it help?"

"No question: Vice President Petty. Primarily because the Republicans control the House and, more importantly, they control a majority of state delegations in Congress. If the Republicans hold the House, and Speaker Jimmerson decides to play aggressively, it is theoretically possible that Petty could win, *regardless* of how he does in the general election."

"So Republicans in the House could reject the presidential candidate who wins the popular vote and leads in the Electoral College?"

"Yes. That's exactly what happened the last time the House elected a president, in 1824. It rejected Andrew Jackson, the winner of the popular vote, in favor of John Quincy Adams. It happened then and it could happen again." Myers's lips curled into a smile, his eyes dancing.

BILL DIAMOND LEANED FORWARD in his chair in his West Wing office as the thirty-second ad played on his laptop. When it was done, he hit the replay button and watched it again. He didn't say a word. His eyes narrowed as he rubbed his chin. There were two weeks to go and Diamond needed a silver bullet. Taylor Sullivan and Dick Pepper leaned forward expectantly like parents giving birth to a child. They nervously awaited his verdict.

"I like it," Bill said at last.

Sullivan's face lit up. "You don't mind the mug shot?"

"No. The guy's white," replied Diamond. "You couldn't use the mug shot if he was black—the media would compare it to Willie Horton. But he's white. Don't you guys agree?"

"Absolutely," seconded Dick Pepper. "It's not a racial thing."

"Heck no," said Diamond, warming to the topic. "Bob Long's parole board released a child rapist from prison, who then molested and killed a seven-year-old girl. Her death was caused by Long's failed policy."

"Now you're talking," smiled Sullivan, strumming his fingers on his knees excitedly.

"How soon can you get this on the air?"

"Tomorrow or the next day."

"I'll have to run this by the veep. But plan to email it out to the entire RNC press list and activist file tonight at around midnight," ordered Diamond. "That should put some blood in the water."

"I can advance this to Marvin Myers," suggested Sullivan. "He'll eat it up."

Diamond nodded his assent. "Good idea. Okay, what else have you got?"

Sullivan opened a file folder and scanned his notes. "We've got Claire Long's booze problem. It popped up four years ago and did some damage. It's kind of faded since, but from what I hear she's hitting the bottle again."

Diamond listened impassively.

"Sometimes drunk by noon," said Pepper. "It's pretty bad. They're barely letting her appear in public." Diamond raised his eyebrows.

"We've got a good whisper campaign going on it," reported Sullivan, his obsidian eyes bright. "Reporters on the Long campaign plane know about it. It's an open secret. But no one will report it."

"I saw Dan Dorman worked a veiled reference to it into his story about Claire refusing to go to Long's speech at Trinity University," Diamond said.

"Right. It's bubbling just beneath the surface. We could try to goose something on Merryprankster.com and see if that caused it to blow," suggested Sullivan.

"How about starting a rumor that her *Ladies' Home Journal* pie recipe has bourbon in it?" joked Petty. "I don't think Andy Stanton wants a shot of Jack Daniels with his pecan pie."

"Have we done public record searches?" asked Diamond, in no mood for levity. He uncrossed and crossed his legs, appearing uncomfortable with the topic. "If there was a DUI or a recent visit to rehab, that would be news."

"We looked," reported Sullivan. "We turned up nothing. Zip. If it exists, we can't find it."

"Then it will be hard to turn this into more than a one-day story. We need more. We need a mushroom cloud."

"I've got something else," said Sullivan. He paused, folding his arms across his chest and arching one eyebrow. "Scottie Morris, Long's media guy, is a cokehead."

Diamond rubbed his chin.

"He's high constantly. He's cratering. I hear his girlfriend is a dealer."

Diamond sat up in his chair. "She's a dealer? Can you get it into the water?"

"We have our ways," replied Sullivan with a sly lilt in his voice. "We've got good contacts in law enforcement in California." He shot Diamond an evil grin. "Scottie might just get pulled over on his way home from dinner one night."

"Be very careful," ordered Diamond. "I don't want any fingerprints of people at the campaign, the RNC, or the White House. Use a bank shot. Can you do it with an anonymous tip?"

"I think we've talked about this enough already," said Sullivan, his eyes unblinking.

Diamond rose from his chair and shook Pepper's and Sullivan's hands, signaling the meeting was over. He walked them to the door, placing his hand on the doorknob. Pepper held the door closed with the open palm of his hand.

"Wait until the religious right finds out that Long's media consultant is a drug dealer," Pepper said in a half whisper. "So much for family values."

Diamond opened the door and Sullivan and Pepper walked through the outer office, greeting the secretaries and other staff aides, a new bounce in their step. Sullivan clutched a leather case containing his laptop and oppo files. He waved back at Diamond as they headed out the door and down the hallway.

"Great job, guys!" yelled Diamond. "Love the ad. Brilliant!"

———

"THIS IS A GOOD man!" shouted Bishop Weeks.

"Amen!" responded the congregation.

He twirled to his right. "He is a man of moral courage who lives by faith, not by sight!" He spun to his left. "He is a man of Gaaawd!"

"Amen!" Their voices echoed off the rafters of the sanctuary, which seemed as large as Madison Square Garden.

The service was in its second hour, and Bob Long sat onstage like a lily-white buoy bobbing in a sea of pulsing, dancing, singing, and shouting black humanity. Eighteen thousand members of New Harvest Church packed the pews, waiting for Weeks to introduce Long. But Weeks was in no hurry; he had been preaching for forty-five minutes and was just warming up.

"He serves no party!" Weeks blasted, wiping dripping sweat from his face with a white handkerchief. "He has only one master—the humble servant who walked in Judaea and Samaria two thousand years ago!"

"Preach it!" someone in the front pew shouted.

The crowd began to shout, clap, and stomp its feet. Organ music blared as the choir swayed. Carried along by the energy of the crowd, Weeks began to bounce on his toes, moving from behind the pulpit, his head swinging, arms dangling at his sides. Several couples rushed the altar and began to do a jig. They jumped rhythmically to the roll of the drum and the clang of a cymbal.

Long shot a nervous look at Jay Noble, who sat in the front row next to Weeks's stunningly attractive wife. Jay stared back, eyes darting, utterly helpless.

Weeks stopped and pulled the microphone to his lips, his heavy breathing filling the air. Then he bounced over to Long, pulled him up from his chair, and waved him to the pulpit. *So that was my introduction*, thought Long: *a dance.*

Long flipped open his Bible and prowled around the pulpit like a lion, confidently resting his left hand on the edge. He began to read from the Gospel of Luke about Zaccheus, the tax collector who climbed a tree in order to catch sight of Jesus.

"Zaccheus was a sinner," whispered Long in a slightly hoarse voice. "He was a tax collector. Tax collectors were the dregs of society." He paused, his gaze looking over the congregation. "Do you ever feel unworthy, ashamed, looked down on?"

"Yes! Yes!" the congregation shouted.

"Zaccheus was small in stature," bellowed Long. "Do you ever feel small, powerless, ignored, stepped on?"

"Amen!"

"Zaccheus could not see for the crowd. Do you ever get tired of the crowd pushing you, forcing you this way and that"—he bobbed his head back and forth as he spoke—"not letting you see over their heads?"

"Hallelujah!"

Bishop Weeks, smiling broadly, rested his hands on his chest in a modified prayer pose. In the back of the room on the press riser, jaws dropped. Long was preaching!

"Zaccheus climbed up a tree that the Bible says may have been forty feet high." Long raised his left hand high above his head to dramatize the tree's height. "I don't know if he was afraid of heights or not, but I know I am." The crowd laughed appreciatively. "The point is, he overcame fear . . . his small stature . . . peer pressure . . . the shame of his sin . . . because he wanted to see . . . what the whole world yearns to see . . . Jeee-sus!"

"Perr-fect. Just perrr-fect," Weeks cooed behind him.

"I don't know about you," said Long in a controlled shout, "but I don't want to be down here in the mud." He stooped down to the carpet, placing his hand in imaginary soil. Then he popped up to his full six-feet, one-inch height. "I want to be up in that tree where I can see!"

"Amen! Preach it, brother!"

"I want to see Jesus!"

"Hallelujah!"

Long's voice fell to a whisper. "Verse ten says, 'For the Son of Man has come to seek and save that which was lost.' "

"Mmmmmmm," the crowd assented.

"In ten days, the American people will go to the polls and choose a new president. So some of my friends in the media have shown up to hear me ask you for your vote." Knowing laughter rumbled through the pews. "They're going to be disappointed. Because I didn't come here to ask for your vote." He wagged his finger to scattered applause. "I came here to ask you to climb that tree. And whatever is lost in your life—a dream, a relationship, your health, your marriage, your finances—Jesus will seek it and save it. Let's climb that tree together and build a better world! God bless!"

Long abruptly spun on his heel and went back to the thronelike chair next to Weeks and took his seat. The auditorium exploded in cheering and applause, many members of the congregation cheering and waving handkerchiefs.

Weeks returned to the pulpit, his countenance assuming a serious expression. He waited patiently for the applause to die. Church bulletins folded into fans fluttered across the congregation like the wings of a thousand paper butterflies.

"I'm not going to tell you who to vote for," Weeks began. "I never do. But I am going to ask you to pray for this *good* man. We *need* leaders like this who love God and fear *no man*. So pray that God will use Governor Long to do mighty things. Amen?"

"Amen!" shouted the congregation thunderously.

In the back of the room, Dan Dorman leaned over to Hal Goodman of *Newsweek*. "How in the world did Long get Stanton and Weeks on the same team?" he whispered. "It's like Jesse Jackson and Jerry Falwell endorsing the same candidate."

"Two words," replied Goodman, his lips raised in a sardonic smile. "Joe Johnson."

"Amazing," Dorman chuckled and shook his head in wonder. "Even in the kingdom of God, the enemy of my enemy is my friend."

37

THE PHONE JANGLED ON the nightstand, waking Jay with a start. He looked at the clock, which read 3:06 A.M.

"Jay, it's Scottie."

"How's it coming? Do you have something yet?" Jay asked. He assumed Hollywood was calling from the studio, where he was pulling yet another all-nighter to cut a response ad to Petty's new attack ad about Long releasing a child rapist.

"I'm afraid not, Jay," Scottie replied. "I'm calling from the L.A. County Jail."

Jay sat up on the edge of the bed. "What?"

"A few hours ago, while I was working on the spot, the police showed up at my house with a search warrant. They tore the place apart. They found a small amount of cocaine. They arrested me and my girlfriend and charged us with cocaine possession and distribution."

"*What?*" Jay exclaimed, the blood rushing to his head. "How much did you have?"

"A little over an ounce," Scottie replied, his voice shaking. "Anything over an ounce and they can charge you with distribution." He paused. "I have to resign from the campaign."

Jay's head was spinning. Strangely enough, the first thought in his head was how to get the response ad off Scottie's laptop—they needed to get it on the air the next day. "Do you have a lawyer? We need to get you out of jail."

"My bail hearing is tomorrow. I should be able to make bail, but if Phil can find me a good criminal lawyer who's wired in L.A. County, I need it."

A horrifying picture flashed through Jay's mind of Hollywood, disheveled and in handcuffs, shuffling into an L.A. courtroom in an orange jumpsuit. The cable news networks were going to have a field day. "I'll call Phil right now and have him come to the jail tonight. He'll get you a good attorney."

"Thanks," said Scottie. He choked back sobs. "I'm so sorry. I really screwed up. Please tell the governor how sorry I am. I hate that I let him down . . ." He broke down.

"Scottie, just sit tight—and don't talk to anyone," instructed Jay. He hung up the phone and turned on the lamp. He could not believe he had lost his media wizard just as Petty pounded them with attack ads. Every newscast in the country the next day would lead with the story about a senior Long campaign official arrested for distributing cocaine. The timing was suspicious—Jay suspected that Scottie had been set up. Nothing in politics happened by accident. Was Hollywood the victim of the same mole who was leaking Jay's strategy memos to the press?

Nicole stirred in the sheets next to him. "What is it?" she asked, rubbing her eyes.

"Scottie's been arrested for cocaine possession. He's in jail. I have to get a response ad up tomorrow in eighteen states and I've just lost my media consultant."

Jay picked up the phone. He had to get Phil Battaglia down to the L.A. County lockup right away and bail Scottie out of jail.

———

A BLACK LINCOLN NAVIGATOR pulled up in front of the Federal District Courthouse building in Washington. As the doors opened, a mob of a hundred reporters surged toward the vehicle shouting questions, throwing elbows, and stepping over one another. Melinda Lipper emerged from the car, her jet-black hair waving in the wind, her glamorous looks muted by the determined, stoic expression on her face. She wore a smart red Versace dress, sheer hose, Bruno Magli stiletto-heeled boots, and Chanel sunglasses. She walked arm in arm with her attorney, an alligator Prada bag over her shoulder, clutching a cup of Starbucks with her free hand. Together they walked with great difficulty through the press scrum.

"Melinda, are you going to take the Fifth Amendment?" shouted AP.

"No comment, folks," fired back her attorney, Cliff Knox, one of the most respected criminal lawyers in Washington. "Melinda will have a statement after she's finished testifying."

"Are you going to implicate Michael Kaplan? Did Kaplan tell you to pay bribes to Virginia delegates in exchange for their votes and testimony?" asked *Roll Call*.

"Please, everyone, give her room. She can't move!" shouted Knox, jostling with the press. A security guard extended his arm like a cowcatcher, shoving them back. A photographer tripped and went sprawling, his camera clattering across the concrete. "Please! Make room!" begged Knox. The scene was pandemonium.

"What are you wearing, Melinda?" asked *People*.

Melinda stopped and wheeled toward the reporter, the fear on her face melting away. Suddenly and inexplicably, her face brightened. "Versace," she said. She disappeared into the courthouse.

"What about the boots?" someone shouted. "What are they? Gucci?"

SIX HOURS LATER, MELINDA emerged from the courthouse, looking drained but relieved. Her hair and makeup glowed under the afternoon sun, having been freshened in the ladies' room for the cameras. She leaned into a cluster of microphones and began to read tentatively from a piece of paper.

"I am innocent of wrongdoing, and I have fully cooperated with this investigation," she said, her voice growing firm. "Today I testified completely and truthfully. I am confident the evidence will show I did nothing wrong." Knox stood stoically at her side. "I ask the media and the American people not to rush to judgment or needlessly destroy people's lives. We must not criminalize political activity that is protected by the First Amendment. So please wait until the facts come out. Thank you all very much."

"Melinda, are you angry about being fired by the Stanley campaign?"

"What about the boots?"

"Melinda has nothing further to say. Thank you!" shouted Knox over the scrum.

"Who were the donors you solicited? Did they know the money was for bribes to delegates?"

"The boots! What are they?"

Melinda and Knox walked swiftly to the Navigator, eyes straight ahead, ignoring the shouted questions. The Lincoln was ten feet away, passenger doors open, engine warming up.

"Melinda, how do you feel about being called the 'D.C. Diva'?"

Melinda turned. "I've been called worse," she fired back. The door closed and the Navigator pulled away. The driver turned onto Pennsylvania Avenue.

Knox turned around in the front seat. "Well, how did it go?"

"I think it went well. The prosecutor was very thorough," she replied clinically. "They've clearly done their homework. They had copies of checks, consulting contracts, the works." She was still a little jumpy. "I can tell you this: Kaplan's in trouble."

"I'm not surprised. What did they ask you about him?"

Melinda looked out the window with a distant stare, then her eyes shot back toward Knox. "They asked me if he knew the purpose of the payments. I told them he approved everything." Her face suddenly hardened. "I gave him up. And you know what's strange? I don't feel bad at all."

"Do you think they believed you?"

"The prosecutor did. He could hardly wipe the smile off his face," she answered. Kaplan and Stanley had tried to make her take the fall. It was payback time. "They kept asking over and over again: Who controlled the flow of funds, you or Kaplan? It seemed to be the central issue in the case they're building. I said he did, which is the truth."

Knox nodded. "Do you want to grab some dinner or are you too tired?" he asked.

"You know what sounds *great* about now?" she said, perking up. "Crab-cakes and a bottle of chardonnay at Oceanaire." She winked at Knox. He was very capable and had done a great job getting her ready for her testimony—and kind of cute, too.

"Take us to Oceanaire," Knox instructed the driver. "Twelfth and F."

The driver nodded. He turned the car to the right, accelerating as they headed up Fourteenth Street and into downtown. The paparazzi trailed them in rental cars, weaving in and out of traffic, flashbulbs exploding.

She sighed with relief. Her grand jury testimony was behind her, and she was home free. She glanced down at her lizard-skin boots and laughed. She began to hum the words to the old Nancy Sinatra song: *One of these days these boots are gonna walk all over you.* The paparazzi had missed the point. Her Bruno Maglis were not a fashion statement—they were a political statement. She was tired of women getting walked all over by the likes of Kaplan, doing the dirty work and then being run over like roadkill.

The photos of Melinda and her attorney emerging from the federal courthouse would be splashed across the front pages of the *Post* and the *Times,* and *People* magazine would run a special two-page spread on her wardrobe that day. Soon no woman in Washington or New York would be able to find the Versace dress she wore for her testimony—they had all flown off the racks. Melinda was not just at the center of a scandal. She was a bona fide celebrity.

———

JAY SAT AT THE coffee table in his office staring down at the documents in front of him, stunned. He heard the voices of the others in the meeting, but he couldn't quite make out the words. The room had suddenly gone foggy, and the floor was spinning.

"Jay, look at these old clips from *Newsweek,*" Battaglia insisted. "Two articles from the primary campaign under Hal Goodman's byline mentioning Governor Scott Ballard, and both quote Nicole, who was his communications director. She was one of Goodman's sources. You know Goodman— he'd have kept in touch, kept the pressure on. She could have given him your memo."

"And look what we found in her cell phone records," said Lisa, handing him a phone bill. "She called Goodman two days after the meeting at which we discussed your memo."

"Hal Goodman talks to everybody," Jay protested. "*I'm* one of his sources, for crying out loud. So are you, Lisa. We can't fire her based on this."

"There's more," Phil said. "We have text messages. Here's one to Michael Kaplan on August 12." He slid it across the table.

Jay picked it up. The message was cryptic but damning: "Call me ASAP."

"I bet she set up Scottie," said Lisa.

"Me, too," Phil agreed. "No one gets raided by narcotics detectives with a detailed search warrant unless someone tipped them off. Nicole knew enough about Scottie to give him up."

Jay slumped lower, devastated. It was widely known in the campaign and among the press that Jay and Nicole were an item. When the news broke that Nicole was a mole, it would be a major embarrassment.

"You know," he said at last with a sigh, "I got suspicious when the story about the DOT appointment leaked to the *New York Times*. I asked her about it and her answer was convincing. She said I hadn't told her until after the story went to press."

"Guess who her roommate was while she worked at the DNC?" asked Phil.

"Who?"

"Deirdre Rahall's sister."

"The Deirdre Rahall who works for G.G. Hoterman? The one caught up in the Dele-gate scandal?"

"Bingo."

Jay nodded slowly, morosely. "How did you find all this out?"

"We hired a private investigator. One of the best," answered Phil. "Jay, we need to terminate her today . . . before she does any further damage."

Jay nodded again. "What about the FBI?"

"The investigation will be over now that we know who the mole is," replied Phil. "But they might still charge her."

"Okay, how should we proceed today?"

"It needs to be a public execution," advised Phil. "Our press statement should say she gave proprietary information to Stanley's campaign. We don't want to open ourselves up to a defamation lawsuit, but we have to shoot her."

"We have to get in front of this story," echoed Lisa. "We're already dealing with Scottie's arrest. When we whack her, it's going to be big news—the second campaign official fired in two days. We need to blame the Stanley campaign. We have to lay this at Kaplan's feet."

"I'll fire her. I assume you'll want to stay away, Jay," suggested Phil.

"If I do, people will say I was too ashamed to face her," Jay shot back. "I have to be in that meeting. I need to confront her with witnesses present."

"Okay, let's go," said Phil, rising from his chair. They walked down to Phil's office and closed the door behind them. Phil sat behind his desk, while Jay and Lisa plopped down on the couch. Phil buzzed Nicole's extension. "Nicole, could I see you in my office for a minute?" He hung up the phone and let the silence hang in the air, the suspense building.

The door opened and Nicole walked in. As soon as she saw the looks on their faces, her posture wilted and her face fell. She slunk to the empty chair by Phil's desk. She looked at Jay, her eyes desperate.

"Nicole," Jay began slowly, "we have incontrovertible evidence that you have been providing information to the media and the Stanley campaign."

Nicole stared back, her facial expression blank.

"You have been a valued member of our team and contributed greatly to the campaign," Jay continued. His emotions roiled inside him, but he held them in check. "My disappointment in you is profound. There will be serious consequences." He paused. "First, you are being terminated, effective immediately. Second, because the FBI is involved we cannot rule out a criminal prosecution. To some extent, our decision depends on how much you cooperate with Phil."

Nicole's eyes began to tear up. "I know I deserve to be fired," she said, her voice faltering. "But I just want you to know it was nothing personal against you, Jay."

Jay ignored her expression of affection. He stood up to leave. "Phil will take it from here. I recommend you tell him everything. Even then, I can't guarantee we won't prosecute. Lisa will work out how we are going to handle the press." He walked out.

PHIL AND NICOLE HOLED up in his office for the next five hours. Phil's strategy was to keep her under his watchful eye so she couldn't contact Kaplan or her attorney. The strategy worked, and Nicole spilled her guts. She told Phil how she had arranged the romantic encounter with Jay in Mexico, maneuvered her way into the press operation, and provided Kaplan with documents and internal polling data. But she adamantly denied tipping off the LAPD about Scottie Morris.

At a few minutes before 3 P.M.—pushing up against print deadlines on the East Coast—Phil emerged from his office with a signed confession and a draft press release. He handed it to Lisa, who emailed it out to the campaign's press list. The explosive headline said it all: "Deputy Press Secretary Nicole Dearborn Dismissed, Admits Giving Internal Documents to Stanley Campaign."

Nicole hung back in Battaglia's office as news of her treachery spread, hoping to wait until most of the staff left before exiting the headquarters. But no one would leave—they wanted to watch her go, tail between her legs, and jeer at her as she departed.

Jay returned to Phil's office, closing the door behind him. Nicole sat alone, face turned to the wall, slumped in a chair. She spun in the chair and their eyes met, his filled with disdain, hers weary and drained.

"How could you do it?" he asked.

"At first I was mad at Long for hurting the party," she replied haltingly. "But after a while . . ." She sighed. "I got in over my head . . . in more ways than one."

"That makes two of us," Jay replied, his voice growing softer.

"Jay . . . I just want you to know . . . how sorry I am. I know you've got enough to deal with today with Scottie's arrest without having to deal with me."

"It's certainly been an interesting twenty-four hours," Jay said, shaking his head. "By the way, there's one thing that's been eating away at me. How in the world did you track me down in Manzanillo?"

"Kaplan had someone follow you to the airport. When he found out where you were going, they flew me down ahead of you in a private jet. I got there before you did because you changed planes in Mexico City. I waited around for three hours for you to arrive and then followed you to El Tamarindo."

Jay shook his head. "And all along I thought I had met the girl of my dreams in paradise."

"When I fell for you, it was real." She paused. "I loved you, Jay."

Jay's face hardened. "No one who loves me could do this." He paused. "I remember you telling me that first night that you didn't like to live a lie. Obviously, that was itself a lie."

He turned and left, closing the door behind him. Between the damage Nicole had done—she had single-handedly turned the Pomona land deal story into a major story—and Scottie blowing up, the Long campaign was running in the political equivalent of the Daytona 500 on two blown tires. The only way to win now was for someone else to hit the wall. Jay thought he knew how to help make it happen.

IT WAS APPROACHING MIDNIGHT, and Jay ordered another round of beers. The Brain Trust—or what was left of it—gathered round a table at a Mexican bar and restaurant around the corner from the campaign headquarters. He was drowning his sorrows, an all-too-familiar tale in his decades of political combat. He had lost his media consultant in a drug bust, lost his girlfriend, and was responsible for bringing a mole into the campaign. It was humiliating.

Lisa, David Thomas, and Battaglia tried to buck him up—they needed his head in the game. As the night wore on, the others peeled off, leaving Lisa and Jay alone at the table to bond in mutual sorrow and conversation.

"Eight days to go," said Jay into space, his facial expression sullen, his eyes hollow. "What do you think? Do we win?"

"We'll win," Lisa predicted. "We have time to recover. We just have to get that response ad on the air. Scottie's assistant told me he just about finished it."

"We *have* to win." Jay stared disconsolately into his beer mug.

"Don't be so hard on yourself," Lisa urged. "How could you have known?"

"There were signs. She read all my memos, with a disturbing level of interest. She asked a lot of questions—too many, in hindsight. I missed it." He paused, cutting Nicole a rare glance of self-reflection. "I was thinking with my hormones instead of my brain."

"She fooled all of us. I didn't know, and she reported to me! You know what's odd? There was no one better at spinning a reporter."

"Oh, yes, there is," Jay said. "You're the best in the business." He raised his glass in a toast. "You proved it today. You turned my screw-up into another example of Kaplan's corrupt perfidy. Well done!"

Lisa looked at him with playful eyes. "You've got a thing for identifying talent, don't you?" She patted his arm. Jay felt a jolt of sexual energy shoot through him. He felt another bad romance on the rebound coming on. He reminded himself to be careful. Lisa was attractive, but they had a job to do.

After they polished off their drinks, Jay and Lisa strolled back to the headquarters. He walked her to her car, gave her a professional hug, and she drove off. He turned to go back to the office. He still had work to do.

He scanned his passkey and entered the building, taking the elevator to the third floor. He stepped off the elevator and walked down the dimly lit hallway. A few rapid-response worker bees toiled away at cubicles, monitoring cable news shows, but otherwise the office was deserted. Jay turned the key in his office door, pulled down the blind to cover the window, and locked the door. He sat down behind his desk and slowly put on a pair of rubber surgical gloves, then opened the bottom drawer of his credenza, pulling out a plain manila envelope. He reached inside and pulled out a DVD. He popped it into the DVD player on the nearby TV stand and watched it with the sound turned down. It was even better than he remembered it. He reached over and picked up the phone.

"I've got the package," he said discreetly. "It's everything I promised you and more. But I'm not giving this to you or anyone else without assurance that it will receive the full-blown attention it deserves."

"I'm *very* interested," replied Jay's contact. "We're the perfect outlet. But I can't promise how we'll use it until I see it."

"It's too late for that," shot back Jay. "If you take it, I want Hiroshima headlines. I've got several other major news organizations barking like seals." It was a lie, but he needed to play hardball. "Are you going to play . . . or do I give this to someone else?"

"Okay, we will give it prominent play," said the voice on the other end of the phone. "You won't be disappointed. Now, what's the best way to get it to me? Can you overnight it?"

"No," replied Jay firmly. He wanted no express delivery records—that was how people got caught. He arranged to meet his contact at a restaurant off Sepulveda Boulevard later that night. At this late hour, there would be few witnesses. He hung up the phone and ejected the disk from the DVD player, placing it back in the envelope. It was the last bullet he had left, and he was about to fire it right at David Petty's head.

———

BILL DIAMOND SPRAWLED ACROSS the couch in a temporary staff office at the Detroit Renaissance Hotel. Vice President Petty was in a holding room waiting to deliver a speech to the Detroit Economic Club. Diamond cradled his cell phone with one hand, scrolling through emails on his BlackBerry with the other. On the television set, video of Scottie Morris appearing at a bail hearing in an L.A. courtroom ran, accompanied by copy proclaiming, "Long Campaign Aide Arrested on Cocaine Charges."

"Long still doesn't have a response ad up?" Diamond asked. "Incredible."

"That's right," Taylor Sullivan reported gleefully. "Our buyer tells me the stations are just now getting calls about some new traffic from Long for tomorrow."

"How late could they send it tonight and still get it into rotation tomorrow?"

"Technically, up until around nine or ten P.M., but it won't clear the morning shows. It'll be noon tomorrow, in some places the evening news, before the stations get their new ad on the air. We got a two-day jump on them."

"I guess Jay Noble was too busy bailing staffers out of jail and firing moles to stay on top of his ad buy."

"Without Scottie Morris, Jay's a three-legged horse. Long is going to stagger to the finish line."

"I heard that Dearborn chick was Jay's girlfriend," Diamond said. "Is that true?"

"The guy's got great taste in women, eh?" Sullivan let out a staccato burst of laughter. "Almost as good as his taste in candidates."

"Got to go," said Diamond, hanging up. Matt Folger sauntered over, a crooked grin on his face, his blue blazer and khakis wrinkled from days on the road. He clutched the remnant of a gigantic chocolate chip cookie in his right hand. In his left hand was a stack of papers, his latest tracking poll.

"Long lost another point in the overnights," Folger reported. "His unfav is now forty percent. The ads are working. So is the earned media beating he's taking over Morris's arrest. He's in a free fall."

"What's the ballot?" asked Diamond.

"Thirty-five Petty, 31 Long—but that's only last night," Folger answered. "The three-day roll has us up two, 34 to 32 percent. Stanley is stuck at 28. He's not moving."

"Those numbers reflect only one night of polling after Morris's arrest. What will a few more nights of that do?"

"It should accelerate Long's descent. As voters get closer to the election, they have a gut check, almost like buyer's remorse," Folger explained. "Long's support was always a mile wide and an inch deep. Now it's evaporating."

"What worries you?" Diamond asked, probing.

"That the election is not tomorrow," Folger sighed. "Six days is an eternity in politics. Any late development will have an exaggerated effect. Look at Morris's arrest and Dearborn's firing. The former hurts Long, but the latter might help him, reminding voters he was the victim of dirty pool by Stanley."

Diamond nodded. He felt good about the state of the campaign. His strategy was working—insulate Petty from the media, put him in front of friendly audiences in controlled settings, and hammer away unmercifully at Long. Taylor Sullivan had come through in the clutch—Scottie Morris was a jailbird. Better yet, Kaplan had been caught putting a spy in the Long campaign. Sal Stanley's political machine—favor-seeking lobbyists, shadowy tax-exempt organizations, wealthy donors, favored reporters who transcribed leaks, and an army of take-no-prisoners political operatives—was collapsing. Diamond could feel the touch coming back to his fingertips. The murder of Harrison Flaherty had rattled his confidence and temporarily shattered his dreams of being White House chief of staff. But as the campaign entered the homestretch, he felt the tide turning. The attack ads bombarding Long (lobbed in a lethal crossfire by both parties) were having the desired effect: Long was slipping, his negatives rising. Petty was getting better on the stump, peaking at the finish. Diamond had his mojo back.

As he flipped through Folger's overnight polling, Diamond raised a warm Diet Coke to his lips. His cell phone rang.

"Bill, it's Kate Higgins, how are you?"

"Pretty amazing, huh?" he asked. "Long has now fired two senior aides in two days. Maybe they should install a revolving door at the campaign headquarters in L.A."

"You think you're having fun now, wait until Kaplan gets indicted," cracked Kate. "I hear it's imminent. Listen, I'm picking up some rumblings that may interest you." Higgins blogged for the Heritage Foundation, appeared regularly on Fox and freelanced for Merryprankster.com. She was smart and well sourced, the right's savvy and saucy foil to the MoveOn.org crowd in the blogosphere.

"What?" asked Diamond.

"A sex scandal is breaking. There are a couple of liberal websites digging around and Dan Dorman at the *Post* is on the case. Heard anything?"

"No. Who does it involve?"

"That tart who lobbied for a defense contractor and was arrested for running a high-end prostitution ring out of her house a few weeks ago. Remember that?"

"Vaguely," Diamond responded. "What did they call her . . . ?"

"The McLean Madam," said Kate. "Anyway, here's the story. Her real name is Jessica Cruz. She ran a call-girl operation out of a mansion in a gated community in McLean. Her network of prostitutes spanned the globe—L.A., Vegas, London, Tokyo. Her clients paid five thousand dollars a night, some up to ten grand for a threesome. Not sure how one gets into that line of work, but apparently Ms. Cruz was quite the entrepreneur."

"Okay, what about it?" asked Diamond impatiently. Where was this going?

"Bill, someone in the DA's office is leaking that David Petty's phone number has turned up in her computer."

Diamond nearly dropped his phone. He felt the air knocked out of him, as though someone had just fired a cannonball into his gut. His mouth turned to cotton. "I have not heard anything about that," he heard himself say. He got up from the couch and walked down the hallway. He did not want anyone to hear the conversation.

"Cruz's day job was as a lobbyist for General Support Solutions," added Kate. "GSS did business with the Pentagon—Baghdad security and reconstruction work. So his number was on her computer and in her cell phone."

"I'll look into it," replied Diamond curtly. "But I'm highly skeptical. This is the silly season. There are dirty tricks, phony rumors, whisper campaigns. Most of it is garbage. So I'd be real careful if I were you." Diamond didn't want Kate to break the story, as that would only give it more credibility on the right.

"I agree," she replied. "But Bill, I'm warning you, this is going to blow. The liberal bloggers are going nuts. And Dan Dorman's no slouch. You . . . uh . . . might want to check out Cruz's website. It's called Silky smooth.com. Pretty catchy, huh?"

"Thanks, Kate," said Diamond, hanging up the phone, his mind racing.

What exactly was on Cruz's laptop and cell phone? Was it incriminating and, if so, was it already in the hands of Dorman or a far-left website? He needed to find a Republican lawyer who could back down the DA and the media. And as uncomfortable as it might be, he needed to tell the vice president right away.

38

OVER GRAY SLACKS AND blue oxford shirt, David Petty slipped on the blue flight jacket with the vice presidential seal on the right pocket. A steward brought a cup of hot herbal tea loaded with lemon and honey to soothe his raw throat. He sipped it slowly. It calmed his nerves as he prepared to take a power nap on Air Force Two, which was hurtling toward the West Coast. He hoped his voice would hold up for another six days.

A rap came at the door. "Come in," he instructed.

Bill Diamond walked in, closing the door behind him, his paleness telegraphing a problem. "Mr. Vice President, you have a personal attorney, right?" asked Diamond cryptically.

"Yes. He's my business lawyer. He negotiated my book contract when I came back from Iraq. Why?"

"We have a . . . situation," replied Diamond, his gaze piercing. "We may want to consider hiring some high-powered legal gun, a Bob Bennett or Clark Clifford type who can play hardball."

"Okay, spit it out. What's going on?"

Diamond took a seat across from Petty. "I talked to a conservative blogger today who is really plugged in," related Diamond. "She freelances for Merryprankster.com."

Petty nodded.

"She says a sex scandal involving the McLean Madam—the lobbyist who ran a high-end call girl ring—is about to blow. Liberal bloggers and the *Washington Post* are digging around looking into whether you are somehow connected to her. Her name is Jessica Cruz."

Petty did not flinch. "Connected how?" he said.

"The rumor is your phone number is in her laptop and cell phone."

Petty's face betrayed nothing. He leaned forward in his chair, gazing out the window, lost in thought for several seconds. "I knew her," he said quietly. "She was a lobbyist for GSS." He turned, his eyes locking on Diamond's. "GSS did a lot of contract work in Baghdad—reconstruction, security, and so forth."

"Any idea how your cell phone number might have turned up in her laptop?" Diamond was not backing down. He lived by the rule that there were three people in life that you told everything: your attorney, your priest, and your political strategist. He had to know the truth.

Petty visibly bristled, his spine stiffening ramrod straight. "I don't know," he said with resignation. "I dealt with her because our office did business with GSS. We might have had a drink or two, or gone to dinner." He shot a look at Diamond as if to say, You've asked enough questions, thank you very much. "That's all there was to it."

"If your number is in her records, that will be small consolation," warned Diamond. "The DA is a big Dem and he's leaking."

"Just deny it," said Petty. "My phone number turning up somewhere is proof of nothing. We need to hang tough. There's so little time left until the election we can't possibly litigate this in the media and win."

"We can do that and survive—but not if she says something different."

"We need to find out what she's going to say. If we deny it and she denies it, we're fine." Petty put his hand on his chin. "We need Walt Shapiro—"

"He's representing Hoterman, remember?" said Diamond. "It's a conflict."

"That's right—there are so many FBI investigations going on I lost track." Petty chuckled morbidly. "Call Walt on the Q.T. and ask him to suggest someone who can represent me. We need a street fighter."

"Will do." Diamond turned and headed for the door. He had just conducted a gastrointestinal exam on the vice president. He felt queasy. He needed a stiff drink.

"Walt is an old friend. Call him right away," Petty said.

Diamond turned and left the room. He hoped Shapiro could refer them to a legal eagle who could reach out to Cruz's lawyer and get her to keep her mouth shut, read the riot act to the DA, and get the media back in its cage. They also needed Cruz to fly away like Peter Pan until after the election. Otherwise, Petty's slim lead in the polls would evaporate overnight.

———

DEIRDRE'S STOMACH CHURNED. The grand jury had been much tougher than she had anticipated—and not just the prosecutor, but the jurors themselves, who had peppered her with probing and, in some cases, borderline accusatory questions. Burned into her memory was a middle-aged, African-American juror sitting in the back of the room, his arms crossed over his chest, a scowl plastered on his face. It was always hard to read the body language of jurors, but his was not a good sign.

For the media, it was déjà vu all over again: the second of the "D.C. Divas" appearing before the grand jury in the Dele-gate scandal. Rumors of impending indictments rifled through the salons of the nation's capital like a bullet ricocheting through a corporate boardroom, everyone laying bets on who went down. For that reason, the press contingent covering Deirdre's grand jury appearance dwarfed even that of Melinda Lipper's. The election was only five days away, and Deirdre was G.G. Hoterman's mistress, which gave the scandal an irresistible sexual angle.

"Lipper and Rahall—two damsels in distress. Who says politics is show business for ugly people?" joked *Time*.

"I may never cover an apropos committee markup again!" laughed *Politico*.

"It sure beats Linda Tripp and Monica Lewinsky," laughed CBS. "Lipper and Rahall are major eye candy. All we need now is a Ken doll and we have a regular sitcom."

"Can we get G.G. on NutriSystem?" suggested the *Washington Examiner*.

"Not likely," deadpanned *Politico*. "He'll never give up the Maker's Mark."

———

A SECURITY GUARD LED Deirdre and her attorney to the elevator.

"We're taking you out the back way," he said. They moved quickly down a long hallway in the bowels of the courthouse. They rounded the corner and came to two glass doors. A horde of reporters twitched to attention, their bodies pressed against the glass.

"I thought they were out front!" shouted Deirdre's attorney.

"I guess they figured it out," said the guard. "Want to try another exit?"

"There's no other way except the front of the building!" He turned to Deirdre. "They've covered every exit," he said. "Let's just get it over with."

Deirdre gamely straightened her clothes and put on Dior sunglasses. The ssshhk-sssshhk of camera shutters exploded when she stepped into the blazing sunlight. Led by her attorney, Deirdre walked to a waiting sedan, her Christian Louboutin heels clicking on the pavement, her long legs highlighted by billowing Escada charcoal pants. She wore a matching satin-ribboned spectator jacket tapered at the waist and a Dolce & Gabbana black leather belt with a gold buckle. Her blond hair waved in the wind, revealing a long neck, high cheekbones, and lipstick that matched her cherry-red jacket. She looked more like a runway model than a woman caught in a Washington scandal.

"Was your brother paid to lie for the Stanley campaign?" asked Fox News.

"Did you and G.G. Hoterman know that the affidavits you filed with the credentials committee were false? Isn't that suborning perjury?" shouted Gannett.

"Deirdre, what do you think of being called a 'D.C. Diva'?" asked *Newsweek*. "Is it flattering, or do you find it sexist?"

"What are you wearing?" asked the *Hill*. "Is it Brooks Brothers?"

Deirdre had ignored their shouted questions until now, but she stopped dead in her tracks. She wheeled to face the offending reporter and pulled her sunglasses down on her nose, her eyes over the frames. "Brooks Brothers? You can't be serious." Her voice dripped with sarcasm. "Honey, this is Escada." She stepped into the sedan and the driver sped off, leaving the reporters standing on the sidewalk.

"For an Alabama fat boy, G.G. Hoterman is quite a chick magnet," chuckled AP, dropping his voice an octave. "You know that's his squeeze."

"I can see why," replied *U.S. News*. "I hope she was worth it."

A few feet away, a Fox News reporter did a live stand-up:

"Five days before voters go to the polls, the second of the 'D.C. Divas' appeared today before a grand jury in Washington in the ongoing federal investigation into the cash-for-delegates scandal that has hobbled the Stanley campaign," he said. "Did Deirdre Rahall drop a bombshell today? Or was the only bombshell in the federal courthouse the stunning deputy to G.G. Hoterman, one of Washington's most powerful lobbyists?"

———

THE STORY APPEARED ON Merryprankster.com at 11:30 P.M. on the Thursday night before the election beneath a banner red-letter headline: "David Petty Linked to 'McLean Madam' Call Girl Ring." Billed as a "Merryprankster Exclusive," the story reported that Petty had hired Jessica Cruz's client, General Support Services, to do private contracting work in Baghdad. It quoted anonymous "senior Defense Department sources" who claimed that Petty and Cruz were an item on the Washington cocktail party circuit. Merryprankster claimed the *Washington Post* had investigated the story but its editors were sitting on it out of deference to Petty.

Bill Diamond's cell phone went off as he sat in Air Force Two on a tarmac in Toledo, Ohio.

"Bill, it's Dan Dorman."

A call from Dorman was invariably bad news. "What can I do for you, Dan?" Diamond asked, trying to stay calm.

"Have you seen the story on Merryprankster?"

"No, I'm on the plane and we're getting ready to take off."

"It says Petty had a relationship with Jessica Cruz. I'd like to get a comment from you on it."

"Off the record, I don't know anything about it," Diamond lied.

"Petty gave no-bid contracts to GSS, which Cruz represented as a lobbyist," Dorman said in a dull monotone. "You're . . . uh . . . not going to . . . uh . . . say anything?"

"You're not actually writing a story on this, are you? This is tabloid trash!" seethed Diamond, spitting out the words.

"We . . . uh . . . I don't have a lot of choice," Dorman stammered. "My editors are all over me. The *Times* is also doing something. It's on the wires. ABC News has it on its website. We have to report that it's on the Internet."

"I can't believe you're hiding behind Merryprankster's skirts, Dan!" shouted Diamond. "Don't tell me you're doing this as a media process story—that's the oldest trick in the book for getting tabloid sleaze in a family newspaper."

"Look," Dorman fired back. "If you don't comment, it's only going to get worse. Don't take it out on me—I'm just doing my job."

"Sure, Dan," Diamond replied sarcastically. "Look, Cruz represented a contractor and the vice president dealt with her at DOD. End of story. *He had no personal relationship with her.*" He had made up the last part. He hoped it worked.

"Can I use that?" Dorman asked.

"No. We land in an hour, and I'll have a statement then," Diamond said. "But, Dan, this is a far cry from Woodward and Bernstein."

He hung up without waiting for Dorman's reply and walked to the front of the plane. He had to tell Petty. What had the vice president said? Hang tough. He was right. They had to plow through the muck and find a way to win.

————

JAY NOBLE STOOD IN the midst of a large room filled with work cubicles at the campaign headquarters in Los Angeles, pacing up and down, occasionally sticking his head into one to ask a question or fire off another order to his field staff. His encyclopedic memory carried vote goals for every battleground state in the country. He had a two-page memo from David Thomas detailing the massive get-out-the-vote effort, which he had dubbed "Operation Breakout." A large tote board on the wall tracked the ground game in the key states— which had ballooned based on tracking polls to twenty-two states. It was the Friday night before Election Day, and a third of all registered voters had already cast their ballots by mail or in person via early voting.

The Long campaign had fused traditional grassroots technology with Madison Avenue marketing and the instant tracking capability of the Internet. In campaign parlance, it was called "microtargeting." Pollsters "oversampled" Long supporters, creating a representative database of Long voters from every key demographic. From this sample, they created forty-seven distinct demographic "subgroup profiles" of likely Long voters. By using consumer databases (magazine subscription lists, personal property records, DMV records) the Long operatives had created targeted voter lists for their get-out-the-vote efforts. In Louisiana alone, the database totaled over nine hundred thousand voters. It was the largest grassroots army in the history of presidential politics.

Noble gazed at the tote board. He walked over and picked up a blue Magic Marker, writing "4 Days to Go" on the whiteboard. Underneath, he wrote: "Goal: 50 Percent of Long Vote in Before Tuesday." It was an audacious objective, like everything else in Jay's master plan for the Long campaign. The GOTV program had been under way for four weeks, beginning when early voting opened in Oregon and Florida. Jay's strategy to get half of all Long voters to vote before Election Day was partially predicted on his fear that an October Surprise would trip up Long in the closing days. He had been more right than he ever imagined: the Pomona land deal, the child rapist ad, his leaked strategy memo, the firing of Nicole, and Scottie's arrest had all hit the campaign like torpedoes. The more votes the Long campaign drove to the polls early, the less likely they would be tripped up by another last-minute attack.

"How are we doing in Louisiana?" asked Jay.

"Off to a slow start," reported Thomas. "The RNC had us on our back heels the first three days. But we've recovered, and I think we'll exceed our vote goal."

"How does it look in Lake Charles?" Jay was infatuated with Louisiana. He believed that its open primaries and runoffs made it the ideal laboratory for an independent candidate. It was also a bellwether of how the South would go.

"Why don't we get our parish coordinator on the phone?" suggested Thomas. He pressed a speed-dial button. "Billy, it's David Thomas," he announced with dramatic flair. "I'm standing here with Jay Noble. How is it going?" He paused and listened, his brow furrowed, his eyes intense. "That's terrific. Keep the pedal to the metal."

"Well?" inquired Jay.

"Billy says by COB today we'll have forty-five percent of our vote goal in Lake Charles already cast."

"Wow!" Jay allowed himself a smile. Similarly encouraging reports were flowing in from Florida, Ohio, and Missouri. Just as he had hoped, the McLean Madam story had dropped on Petty's skull with exquisite timing. They still had a chance.

BILL DIAMOND STEPPED OFF Air Force Two at midnight and stood on the tarmac at Phoenix International Airport, desperately trying to calm an unruly mob of reporters.

"Bill, will you categorically deny that David Petty was a client of Jessica Cruz's prostitution ring?" shouted McClatchy Newspapers.

"Were the no-bid contracts to GSS made in exchange for sexual favors?" asked the *Wall Street Journal*.

"I have a brief statement," Diamond announced. Boom mikes bobbed over his head and TV lights cut through the darkness. "Vice President Petty dealt with Jessica Cruz in his capacity as the senior military official overseeing the reconstruction of Baghdad. She represented a defense contractor that performed essential reconstruction and security functions. Vice President Petty's relationship with Ms. Cruz was limited to their professional interaction and was entirely appropriate." He paused, moving his head on a swivel to catch every camera angle. "The suggestion that the vice president had any involvement with Ms. Cruz's alleged criminal activity is completely false. It is a disgraceful example of tabloid journalism and attack-and-smear politics at its worst." He folded up the paper, his face flushed, his eyes flashing.

"Bill, do you regret not making the relationship between Cruz and the vice president known earlier?" asked CNN. "Why didn't you level with the American people sooner? You knew that she was arrested weeks ago."

"Your question presupposes there was something to say. The vice president deals with many people in Washington. He had no special relationship with Ms. Cruz."

"What about the no-bid contracts?" shouted the *New York Times*. "Doesn't that raise questions about the nature of their relationship?"

"GSS did work in Baghdad that required unique expertise and the highest possible security clearance," Diamond replied. He leaned into the cluster of steno pads, jabbing his index finger. "The contracts to GSS were awarded based on the merits alone, not based on who represented them."

"When is the vice president going to speak to this issue?" asked the *Washington Post*.

"The vice president will have something to say very soon," Diamond assured them, trying to lower the temperature. "But it's after two A.M. on the East Coast now."

"Is he hiding? Does he have something to hide?" asked *Time*.

"No," Diamond fired back. "Absolutely not."

"What are you waiting for?" asked AP. "The election is in three days."

"That's it for tonight. See you in the morning." Diamond ended the impromptu news conference. He began to walk to a staff van when Hal Goodman of *Newsweek* slid to his side.

"Have you heard about the McLean Madam video?" he whispered in Diamond's ear. "It's on a website called Caughtintheact.com. Merryprankster is linking to it."

"No," Diamond answered, his face etched with terror. Could it get any worse?

"The traffic crashed Merryprankster."

"What?"

"Well . . . she's . . . in the buff. Four million hits in a half hour and it crashed their server," Goodman reported. "This is spreading like wildfire, pal."

Diamond stepped into the van, sick to his stomach. He immediately dialed the RNC. He knew Taylor Sullivan would be in the war room.

"Taylor, it's Bill. We just landed in Phoenix and I gave the press a statement."

"Yeah, I just watched you on TV. It ran live on all the cable nets," Taylor said. "You did well." He sounded downcast, as if all the energy had been drained from him.

"Hal Goodman said something about a video on the Internet. You know anything about it?"

"I'm afraid so. It's Jessica Cruz in a hot tub." He skipped a beat. "She's in her birthday suit. You get the picture. The others in the tub have their faces obscured."

Diamond's mind reeled. "Did the DA leak it?"

"I doubt it," Taylor answered. He let out a sigh. "If I had to guess, it's Noble paying us back for Scottie Morris."

It was not a topic Diamond wanted to discuss on a cell phone. "Was this woman nuts?" he sputtered. "She lobbied for a defense contractor while running a prostitution ring out of her mansion and making amateur porn flicks?"

"The chick is bad news. Worst part is, people are gobbling it up," said Sullivan. "Three websites have crashed." He paused. "It's a code red, Bill. The press is hysterical. Word is there are members of Congress on her client list."

"Let's do a conference call at six A.M.," Diamond ordered. "The veep will make a statement in the morning, then we go into full attack mode. Cash for trash, tabloid journalism, Internet filth, fear-and-smear politics, et cetera."

"Talk to you then," Taylor replied. He let the dead air hang. "Bill, is anything else going to come out?"

"No," Diamond said, when the truth was that he had no idea. He hung up. As the van pulled up to the hotel, he dialed the home number of Walt Shapiro.

39

I T WAS AFTER 4 A.M. on Election Day; Bob Long ladled scrambled eggs onto trays in the cafeteria line at The Villages, a major seniors development outside Lake Wales in central Florida. Dark circles enveloped his eyes. Running on no sleep and pure adrenaline, he had the giddy glow of an astronaut reentering the earth's atmosphere. He played to the cameras as they dutifully recorded his every move—grinning, throwing his head back and fake-laughing, pumping hands and patting shoulders as the residents came through the line.

Jay stood in the back of the auditorium, catatonic with exhaustion, scrolling through his BlackBerry by sheer force of habit. His body ran on fumes. As Jay's watch ticked past 4:16 A.M., Long served the last breakfast. He took off the apron and did a quick stand-up with reporters.

"Are you tired?" said the *Palm Beach Post*.

Long looked at him and laughed. "A little," he said with a plastic smile. "But it's a good kind of tired. I feel great. I really think we're going to win."

"How much of a blow was Scottie Morris's arrest?" asked the *Miami Herald*. "How did you work so closely with him and not know he had a cocaine problem?"

"Scott did a great job. I did not know he had a chemical dependency issue," said Long, turning serious, refusing to utter the word *cocaine*. "He's in our prayers. He has been charged with a serious crime, and because the matter is pending before a court of law, it is not appropriate for me to comment further."

"Isn't it a bit of a contradiction for a candidate who advocates family values to have a cocaine dealer as a senior campaign official?" asked the *New York Times*.

Ouch! Long cut him a withering look. "As soon as we became aware of the matter, Scott resigned. There is no contradiction whatsoever."

"Will you require members of your White House staff to take drug tests if you are elected?" shot back the *Times*.

"My administration will follow the guidelines on background checks for

White House staff," Long answered, the energy draining from his face. "Scott Morris was never on my gubernatorial staff. He was an outside consultant, so that is really irrelevant." By now, Long had grown to despise the *Times* correspondent covering his campaign, and the feeling was more than mutual.

"The mother of the girl who was raped and murdered by the convict released by your parole board says you're unfit to be president," said *USA Today*. "Your response?"

"I can't imagine the pain and sorrow she is going through," said Long, his answer rehearsed. "My heart goes out to her. When someone is in that kind of pain, I think it's best to let her speak without my responding. She has a right to her opinion. The American people will render their own opinion today."

"Do you feel responsible for her daughter's death?"

Long's face hardened. "The only person responsible for that girl's death is the man who murdered her. He is now on death row in a California prison awaiting execution."

"The mother says you're responsible."

Long ignored the comment.

"Do you believe Vice President Petty's denial that he had a personal relationship with Jessica Cruz, the so-called McLean Madam?" asked the *Chicago Tribune*.

"I take the vice president at his word," answered Long, his jaw thrust out, refusing to take the bait. "This election should be decided on the issues."

More scribbles on steno pads.

"The Stanley campaign claims that you are calling minority voters with Bishop Frank Weeks's endorsement and identifying yourself as a Democrat. Is your campaign deliberately misleading African-American voters?"

"I'd refer you to Jay and the staff on that question," Long shot back. He glanced over at Noble, who held copies of GOTV scripts aloft. "I am an independent Democrat. I've said that throughout the campaign. Jay can provide you with copies of the scripts."

The press nodded, scribbling some more.

"Governor, Nicole Dearborn, whom you fired for allegedly spying for the Stanley campaign, was reportedly involved in a romantic relationship with Jay Noble," said the *Orlando Sentinel*. "Along with Scottie Morris's arrest, doesn't this show a lack of judgment on your part in choosing the people around you?"

Jay glared at the *Sentinel* reporter with a look of hatred. *What a cheap shot*, he thought. He stood no more than ten feet from the reporter. Tension rippled through the press scrum. Everyone raised their heads from their pads to watch the punches fly.

"I don't have anything to add beyond the statement my campaign issued at the time Ms. Dearborn resigned," said Long, growing weary of the give-and-take. "But Jay has done a fine job and he has my full confidence."

———

JAY HAD HEARD ENOUGH. He had allowed these ingrates one last press avail—and this was how they paid him back! He was looking forward to the election being over when he wouldn't have to deal with them anymore. "All right, that's all. The governor has to say a few words and then we head back to California and cast his vote."

The press contingent parted. Long bounded onto a stage and stood next to the owner of The Villages, a white-haired, white-whiskered, cherub-faced man who looked to be in his mid-sixties. His wife, dyed red hair piled up in a beehive, skin tanned to a deep bronze, stood at his side, huge diamonds sparkling from her fingers, wrists, earlobes, and neck. Jay wondered how she could stay standing while wearing fifty carats of rocks. After the introduction, the owner handed the microphone to Long.

"How were the pancakes and eggs?" joked Long.

"Fantastic!"

"Glad you liked them," he riffed. "I cooked them myself!"

The crowd clapped and laughed appreciatively. Everyone was feeling a little punch-drunk at this early hour.

Jay stood against the wall, waiting for Long to wrap up. It was the final stop of the campaign, and he was feeling a little nostalgic.

A petite woman with gunmetal-gray hair and intense black eyes hurried up to him. She rummaged through her gigantic purse, which looked like it could hold a small animal, and pulled out a postcard. It was neon yellow with bold type in contrasting colors. "I got this scorecard from the Faith and

Family Federation," she said. "Bob Long is the only pro-life candidate. You've got my vote!"

"Can I see it?" asked Jay.

He was impressed by the catchy graphics and the skillful contrasting of the positions of the candidates. The postcard showed side-by-side comparisons of Long, Petty, and Stanley on all the key issues of taxes, health care, abortion, gay rights, gun control, climate change, and immigration. Ross Lombardy had told them the federation would mail tens of millions of them. Jay handed it back to the woman.

"Put this back in your purse. Don't show it to any reporters," he said, his voice lowered. The last thing he needed was Dorman writing a hit piece on the Faith and Family Federation's GOTV effort.

"Don't worry," the woman replied proudly. "I don't trust the liberal media." She reached up and hugged Jay around the neck. "Bless you for helping a godly man run for president!" She put the postcard back into her purse and rushed off.

"God bless you, Andy Stanton," Jay said to no one in particular.

———

ELECTION DAY DAWNED COLD and raw in the Northeast, sunny and warm in the South, with rain showers in the midsection of the country. Barring a hurricane or earthquake, no one expected the weather to affect turnout. With all three campaigns, the RNC and DNC, and dozens of 527s pouring an estimated $250 million into early voting, absentee programs, and GOTV, voter turnout was expected to hit an all-time high. It was the closest and most fiercely fought presidential election since Bush and Gore had gone to the Supreme Court in 2000. Everyone awaited the early returns with a mixture of anticipation and dread.

The first exit polls reported at 1:30 P.M. EST. By that time Bob Long had voted at his precinct in Sacramento and had gone home to get some sleep. Jay was busy checking on turnout in key counties and states across the country. Reports were scattered and anecdotal; it was all a subjective fog.

David Thomas came into Jay's office, face tense, a pencil stuck behind his right ear. He held a sheaf of papers. "Have you seen the exits?" he asked.

"No. I don't want to know." Jay paused. "Okay, what do they say?"

"They look okay," Thomas answered. "Got a pen?"

"Yes. Go."

"Florida, we're up 2; Ohio, up 3; Virginia, Petty up 2; Pennsylvania, Petty up 1; Stanley up 5 in New York; we're up 3 in Kentucky; Stanley up 2 in Michigan."

"Florida and Ohio are terrific," Jay replied, picking up the piece of paper on which he had scrawled the numbers. "Kentucky is a good sign. Maybe Johnny Whitehead and Stan Anderson came through. Pennsylvania is not good. New York is no surprise." He put the paper in his shirt pocket. "I never believe this stuff anyway," he said, as if trying to convince himself. "When were they ever right?"

"Not since 1992," said Thomas.

"That's a long time ago," Jay replied. "Merryprankster blew the lid on the flawed turnout model of the exits four years ago. Now, with so much of the vote cast early, they don't mean a thing. Forty-five percent of the vote in Florida was already cast. So the exit polls are missing half the voters."

"They survey early voters by telephone."

"Too imprecise. They're guessing."

Thomas nodded. They were not going to get their hopes up based on data compiled by the media. They had put all their hopes for victory in the success of Operation Breakout, their state-of-the-art targeted GOTV program.

"Is there a way to measure how the McLean Madam affected things?"

"Not really, it's conjecture," Thomas said. "But based on how the votes are falling, I'd say it hurt Petty badly. The Zogby poll shows undecided churchgoing voters breaking our way three to one."

"So a prostitute beats a cokehead and a spy," joked Jay.

"Yes, and not just among religious voters. Petty's losing the late-breaking undecideds, who were sixteen percent in Zogby's poll, two to one. That's death."

"Putting Jessica Cruz in the witness protection program didn't help, did it?"

"Made it worse," Thomas argued. "It looked like Petty had something to hide. The rumor is they flew her out of the country on a private jet. She's supposedly holed up in some castle in the British countryside."

"An English castle? You're kidding."

"No. The judge who set her bail allowed her to travel to England. Her lawyer said she had a client in London."

"What kind of client—a lobbying client or the other kind of client?" joked Jay.

"I think both," laughed Thomas. "The *Wall Street Journal* sent reporters across the pond looking for her. The *Washington Post* has organized a search party as well."

"It's a Monty Python movie. Reporters scouring the English countryside in search of a call girl." He burst out laughing. "You can't make this stuff up!"

"Who could have leaked the McLean Madam story?" asked Thomas, his eyes piercing. His gaze said what his words could not: he suspected Jay.

Jay was momentarily stunned by the question, but quickly put on his best poker face. "Probably the DA," he answered. "He's a big D and a headline hound."

Thomas shrugged.

"What's amazing is Petty is hanging in there," observed Jay, shaking his head in wonderment. "The exit polls show the GOP is solid, even hobbled and walking with a limp. Do you realize that if Flaherty had not been killed or Petty had not kicked the evangelicals in the teeth, we'd be dead? The Republicans would have won again."

"Our opponents were dumber than we were smart," Thomas said.

"It's always better to be lucky than good, pal," said Jay.

———

BILL DIAMOND WAS AT the White House, fielding calls, walking in and out of meetings, and checking on the ground game when Matt Folger walked into his office and closed the door.

"What have you got?" asked Diamond. "The exit polls are a mixed bag."

"I've looked at them," answered Folger. "I'm also looking at our last track." His face screwed into a grimace.

"Yeah?"

"Long is going to be ahead. But I don't think he'll get 270 electoral votes."

"So the CW was right. The election goes to the House."

"Yes."

"I've thought that since they killed the vice president," Diamond said. "I just never said anything. I didn't want to jinx it." He leaned back in his chair, deep in thought.

"If Long comes out of the South with 160 electoral votes and wins California, he'll have 220 electoral votes," Folger said, glancing down at a list of totals on his legal pad. "Stanley will win about a hundred electoral votes in the Northeast and pick up at least one industrial state." He frowned. "That leaves 218 electoral votes for us."

Folger's analysis hit Diamond hard. He picked up the phone and dialed the number of Gerald Jimmerson, the Speaker of the House.

"Mr. Speaker, it's Bill Diamond. I wanted to make you aware of the latest developments. According to Matt Folger, who is our pollster—and a darn good one at that, I might add—no one is going to win a majority in the Electoral College today, so the election is going into the House. It looks like you're about to become the most important man in America." He smiled, rocking in his wing chair, then burst out laughing. Putting his hand over the receiver, he gave Folger a wink. "He says he's already the most important man in America."

Folger nodded and smiled.

———

SALMON STANLEY SAT IN an overstuffed chaise in the presidential suite at the Four Seasons Hotel in midtown Manhattan. There was nowhere left to go—no more rallies, no more fund-raisers, no more rubber chicken dinners. A campaign that in a sense had begun a quarter century earlier was over.

The door opened after two knocks. In walked Michael Kaplan, looking beleaguered and grim despite his crisp blue suit, starched shirt, and immaculately combed black hair.

"The first round of exit polls are in," said Kaplan. "You want it with the bark off?"

"That depends," Stanley answered gamely.

"We're going to come in third." He paused, allowing the blow to sink in. "We're doing okay in the popular vote, twenty-nine percent." He steeled himself for delivering the bad news. "We're carrying most of the Northeast. I think we'll carry Pennsylvania. I think we'll win Michigan, Wisconsin, and maybe even Illinois." Another pause.

"That's not bad."

"No, it's not," replied Kaplan. He paused. "But that's it."

"That's it!" bellowed Stanley. "I thought we would do better."

"The soft Ds and casual independents broke for Long. The earned media on the Virginia delegation scandal scared them off."

"We beat him in Chicago and then he beat us," said Stanley, shaking his head. "He's the luckiest guy that ever lived. I can't believe it."

"It's not over," said Kaplan. "Maybe we can still return the favor."

"How?" asked Stanley, brightening.

"Long isn't going to make it to 270. The election goes to the House. Then all bets are off." He smiled. "Senator, Congress is right in your wheelhouse."

Stanley nodded silently. No matter what happened, it seemed his fate was intertwined with Long's. It had been true four years earlier when they were rivals for the vice presidential pick, again when they battled for the Democratic nomination, and now for the presidency. Each time, they were each the other's nemesis. Now it might happen again.

If the election went to the House, perhaps they could cut a deal with David Petty and beat Long. Stanley's mind turned over the possibility with anticipation.

BY 2 A.M. EST the morning after the election, the networks had still not called Florida. Jay Noble huddled over the returns in the conference room, growing more agitated with each passing moment. Long was winning Florida by 125,000 votes, but Jay could not get anyone to report it. He stood in front of the television set, glaring at the anchors and occasionally shouting in frustration as they predicted a gridlocked election. Two blocks away at the Century City Hilton, two thousand people gathered at the Long victory party, waiting in vain for their candidate to appear.

"Lisa!" Jay shouted. "Get in here!"

"Yes?" Lisa replied, jogging in from her office.

"Why won't they call Florida? You better read them the riot act!"

"They're claiming there are too many absentees," she said. "CNN claims there were close to three million early votes. Most are counted, but any absentees that came in Monday or today have not been."

"When will we know?"

"Tomorrow at the earliest. Maybe not until Thursday."

Jay shook his head. He reached over and dialed Long's home phone number for the twentieth time that day.

"What's the latest?" asked Long abruptly.

"We're up 125,000 votes in Florida," reported Jay. "We're going to win. If they would call Florida, that would put us at 255 electoral votes."

"Why won't they call it?"

"They're giving us lame excuses, but the bottom line is no one wants a repeat of 2000," seethed Jay. "I just got a report on the absentee ballots from our attorney prepositioned in Hillsborough County. We're winning the absentees there by six thousand votes. If Hillsborough is breaking that strongly, there's no way we can lose."

"Spending those last few hours along the I-4 corridor paid off."

"It didn't hurt to have the morning shows showing you serving eggs to seniors at four A.M.," Jay agreed. "Petty was in bed by then."

"Well, that's where I'm headed." Long sighed, his voice tired. "I'll talk to you in the morning."

"You don't want to make a statement to the victory party? Lisa says if you did, it will run on TV all day."

"Not tonight. It's past two A.M. on the East Coast. Petty and Stanley have both stayed off the tube. Besides, it's pretty clear we're going to the House."

"No question," said Jay. The House of Representatives had not elected a president in two centuries. The last time had been in 1824, when John Quincy Adams narrowly defeated Andrew Jackson after an alleged "corrupt bargain" with Speaker of the House Henry Clay. The Constitution stipulated that if no candidate received a majority in the Electoral College, the House would vote by state, with each state delegation casting one vote, until one candidate won a majority of twenty-six votes. No one knew how the process would actually play out. Jay shuddered.

"Jay, go to the Hilton and announce we're going to win Florida," ordered Long. "Stick it to the networks. Say we're winning the popular vote, and we have a plurality of the Electoral College. We need to claim victory but not be overly triumphant. Say that we look forward to taking our case to the House."

"How about this?" asked Jay. " 'The American people have spoken, and their choice is clear. We trust that the people's House will do the people's will.' "

"Great line," said Long. "I'll use it in my statement tomorrow."

They both laughed.

"By the way," Long said, changing the subject. "Nobody on our team had anything to do with that McLean Madam story, did they?"

"No, sir," Jay lied.

"Good."

"Sleep well." Jay hung up the phone. He grabbed a rep tie hanging behind his office door and began to knot it.

"Lisa!" She appeared instantly at his door. "Alert the media. I'm going over to the victory party to make a statement. Come with me."

Lisa nodded. They bolted down the hallway, low-fiving staffers who emerged from their work cubicles. As they rode down the elevator, Lisa speed-dialed reporters on her cell.

PART III

THE HOUSE OF REPRESENTATIVES

40

Marvin Myers waved his pen with dramatic flair, stabbing at a map of the United States that appeared on the display screen rising from the middle of the anchor desk. It was 7:20 A.M. the morning after the election, and Myers had been on the set all night.

"The election comes down to three words," he said. "Florida! Florida! Florida!"

The anchor turned to Myers, his right eye cast mischievously back at the camera. "It does indeed. And Marvin, I understand you now have a prediction to make."

"I do," Myers replied, his voice suddenly grave. "I've been on the phone in the last hour with officials at all three campaigns, as well as election supervisors in the three biggest counties with remaining absentee ballots—Dade, Broward, and Duval counties."

The anchor jumped in to quickly educate voters. "Those are the counties around the cities of Miami, Fort Lauderdale, and Jacksonville."

"Correct," Myers nodded. He paused, allowing the suspense to build. "Based on what we have learned, Bob Long will win the state of Florida and its 32 electoral votes. That will bring his total to 255 electoral votes, with 164 electoral votes for David Petty and 119 votes for Salmon Stanley. Bob Long is now just 15 votes short of the magic number of 270 electoral votes."

"You are confident that nothing in the absentees will change that outcome?"

"Totally confident," Myers said firmly. "There are eight hundred thousand absentee ballots remaining, half of them in these three counties. Long leads in both Dade and Duval counties. Bob Long will carry Florida." Canned music with trumpets and banging cymbals played as a graphic of Florida with a photo of Bob Long appeared on the screen.

"As we have been discussing all night," the anchor reminded his viewers, "the Constitution stipulates that in the event no one wins a majority of the Electoral College, the election will be decided by the House of Representatives."

"The last time that happened was in the early nineteenth century," Myers said. "That was a long time ago—even before I started covering presidential elections." He chuckled, satisfied that he had inserted a self-reference into the dialogue. "The election will be presided over by Speaker Gerald Jimmerson, a staunch Republican and strong supporter of David Petty."

"Do you have a prediction on the outcome in the House?" asked the anchor. "Will Bob Long, who is winning the popular vote with thirty-six percent and a lead now numbering 1.2 million votes, be denied the presidency by a Republican House of Representatives? Or will the House ratify his victory in the popular vote?"

"Hard to predict," Myers said, deflecting the question. "But the House does not view itself as a ratifying instrument. I have talked to senior Republicans in the House this morning, and they say that Long's election is by no means a foregone conclusion. To quote one senior House Republican, 'Gerry Jimmerson is no shrinking violet.'" The anchor smiled. High drama! Big ratings for another two months!

"Thank you, Marvin. Ladies and gentlemen, stay tuned," the anchor intoned, trying not to smile. "The polls are closed and almost all the votes have been counted. But this election is far from over."

———

THE PRESIDENT SAT BEHIND his desk in the Oval Office, doing a slow burn as he angrily flipped through the news clips. He had no doubt that Petty had botched the election—it had begun when he selected Ed Bell as his running mate, a ham-handed move with disastrous results. Then Bill Diamond—who the president thought was overrated—had pushed him to the sidelines, consigning him to the Rose Garden. Then there was the matter of Jessica Cruz. How could they not have anticipated that Petty's name would surface? Petty should have gone public with his business relationship with Cruz the minute she was arrested. At least that way the campaign could have gotten in front of the story. In the president's thinking, it was one of the biggest blunders in the history of American politics.

Sam Syms walked into the Oval Office, his face a picture of grim determination, the worry creases on his forehead deepened by lack of sleep. The sun-splashed cheeriness of the Oval belied the gloom that hung over the White House.

"Mr. President, Fox News just called Florida for Long."

The president shook his head. "Well, that does it." He leaned forward, putting his elbows on the corner of the desk. "They wouldn't listen to me, Sam," he said. "I *told* Diamond to keep hitting Long. They let up at the end. They closed with a positive spot about Petty's military record." The veins in his neck bulged. "*It was stupid!* Who in the country didn't already know that Petty was a war hero? They needed to take out Long!"

Syms sat stoically in the chair next to the desk, letting the president blow like a volcano. A legal pad rested on his lap. When the president was angry, a torrent of directives—many of them later retracted—would soon be forthcoming.

"I blame Bill Diamond," the president continued. "He's a smart guy in a cerebral way, but all thumbs when it comes to political strategy. And the Jessica Cruz thing—why didn't they just acknowledge that he knew her after her arrest?"

"Who knows? Even worse, they left their best political asset on the bench—namely you, Mr. President," said Syms, his suck-up juices flowing.

The president straightened in his chair. "I won two national elections and they *refused* to use me. I could have helped increase Republican turnout, which was abysmal. It was the Kentucky Derby and they left Secretariat in the stable."

Syms changed the subject before the president blew a fuse. "Sir, we have the Joint Chiefs at two P.M.," he said in a flat voice. "They will be presenting you with military options on Iran."

"*This afternoon?*" exploded the president. "Reschedule it. I can't meet with the Joint Chiefs. Who in the world put that on the schedule?"

"We've had it on the schedule for some time," Syms reminded him.

"Well, Iran is going to have to wait. It's more than the system can bear at the moment. We can't send a military authorization resolution on Iran to the Hill when the House and Senate are electing the president and vice president." His eyes flashed in disbelief. "Can you imagine the political flap?"

"Yes, Mr. President," agreed Syms. "I'll call the chairman of the Joint Chiefs and explain the situation. They may want to sit down with Parks and keep the ball rolling."

"Good idea. Tell Doug I recommend it."

"I hear the vice president is asking Republicans in the House to vote for him regardless of how their states or districts voted," Syms said.

"Well, he's going to have to do that one solo," the president shot back. He shifted in his chair in barely controlled agitation. "I did all I could. I made him vice president. I handed him the Republican nomination on a silver platter. I thought that would be appreciated." His disappointment welled up inside. "He's on his own now."

"Don't you think it will be bad form if you don't support him? He is your former secretary of state and your vice president."

"Sam, I know that. I will say something supportive. But I won't tell members of Congress how to vote. That's between them and their constituents."

"Mr. President," Syms said, clearing his throat. "You should call him."

The president sighed. "Where is he?"

"At the Naval Observatory."

"All right." He tapped the desk. "Sam, I don't want the White House involved in any lobbying effort. It will look like a palace coup. Tell Bill Diamond—no freelancing."

"Yes, sir, Mr. President." Syms walked out, closing the door behind him.

The president stared at the phone on his desk. He dreaded calling Petty. What could he say—sorry you blew the election, good luck on the speaking circuit? It was too painful to contemplate. Petty would want him to intervene in the House, the answer would be no, and that would mark the end of their strained friendship. But the president had bigger fish to fry. The Joint Chiefs had prepared action plans for a massive military strike against Iran, a strike that was supposed to take place in a matter of days. Now they were on the back burner. His plan to avenge the murder of Harrison Flaherty would have to wait.

CONGRESSMAN CHARLIE HECTOR HAD left the Long victory party at 1:30 A.M. and gone home to bed, but he had tossed and turned all night. The impending election in the House filled him with foreboding. For him, it wasn't a tough call: Long had carried California and he could hide behind voting with his state. But for most Democrats, it would be different. The liberal base hated Long for splintering the party, supporting regime change in Iran, and for his politically expedient embrace of Andy Stanton and the religious right. Their hatred bordered on the irrational.

At 6:40 A.M., the phone on Hector's bedstand rang.

"Hector! Jay Noble here." He didn't even pause to apologize for calling at the crack of dawn. "Listen, the guv asked me to call," Jay said. "We want to pick your brain as to how we should proceed in the House. Can you share some of your infinite wisdom?"

"Sure," Hector heard himself saying. "With Gerry Jimmerson in charge, it's going to be a Barnum and Bailey circus with all the wild animals on the loose. You'd better get loaded for bear."

Hector had known that he would be caught in the crossfire with the left wing of the Democratic Party. He had supported Long in the primaries and the general election. Now Long wanted him to deliver votes in the House. The liberals in the party would never forgive him.

"You're the expert," Jay flattered him. "But here's what we're thinking. We need to carry a majority of the congressional delegations in twenty-six states. We won nineteen states yesterday. So we focus on carrying those nineteen and adding seven more. We carried 266 congressional districts. Incidentally, 109 of those districts are represented by Democrats."

"Got it," replied Hector. "That's a good place to start."

"We gin up our supporters in those 266 districts by email and phone and urge them to contact their member of Congress. The message: vote as your district voted. Maybe we do patch-through calls and light up the Capitol switchboard. Then we set up a whip system by state and region to start counting heads and get a hard count. What do you think?"

"For someone who's never served a day in the House, that's good. You'd make a great deputy whip." Hector was surprised by Jay's elaborate strategy—how had he crunched the numbers and worked it up in only a few hours?

Hector began to pace the floor in his underwear and T-shirt. "Members need to hear from their constituents. If they hear from the people, they'll tune out the leadership, who will be pushing for Stanley."

"That's what the boss thinks," Jay said. "We've got an army of volunteers. Let's put them to work. Charlie, the governor wants you to head up the whip operation."

"Can I make a couple of suggestions?"

"Of course."

"You need ideological whips. You've got groups like the No War in Iran caucus, which is a lost cause, the Hispanic caucus, the Congressional Black Caucus, the Blue Dogs, the Conservative Action Team, all of which need someone acting as whip and head counter."

"Great idea. Can you get me some names?"

"Sure," Hector said. "The governor should start calling members. He needs to love-bomb these guys. They need their egos stroked."

"I'll get him on the phone," Jay replied. "Can you put together a list of the top thirty or forty members he should call? We need to start this morning."

"Sure, just email me the list of all the CDs that Bob carried, and I'll rank them accordingly and shoot you a call list," said Hector. "Also, have Stan Anderson with the UMW call congressmen with whom he has a relationship. Elected officials and major donors calling members would also be good. But keep it low-key and highly targeted."

"I like it—a grasstops program to go along with the grassroots effort."

"One last request," Hector said firmly, his voice suddenly deep and sonorous.

"What's that?"

"Can I get a Cabinet appointment? Because when this is over, I'm going to be persona non grata in the Democratic caucus."

"You betcha," Jay joked. "How about Homeland Security? That way you can be in charge of dealing with illegal immigration!"

"Very funny!" Hector laughed even louder.

Hector hung up the phone, brain spinning. He grabbed his BlackBerry and padded into the kitchen to make some coffee. He needed to get on the phone right away and start recruiting regional and ideological whips. Turning on his BlackBerry, he saw that Jay had already emailed him the grid of congressional districts carried by Long. This guy was on the ball, he thought. They just might win after all.

THE REPUBLICAN LEADERSHIP HAD called the emergency closed-door meeting of the House GOP caucus ten days after the elections to discuss strategy for the election of the next president. The proceedings were strictly off the record. The members packed into the cavernous Cannon Room in the Capitol, buzzing with kinetic energy. This was history! It was the stuff of Clay, Webster, Calhoun, and Cannon. Best of all, unlike Supreme Court confirmation battles or the ratification of treaties, the Senate would take a backseat to the people's House.

Gerald Jimmerson, the speaker of the house, strode into the room like the father of the bride. He moved down the center aisle shaking hands, winking, cackling at jokes, whispering intimate asides, and slapping backs. Jimmerson was a bantam rooster of a man, slight of stature but with a booming laugh twice his size. His boyish demeanor and helmet hair suggested a made-for-television dandy. But it was a mistake to underestimate him. His hunger for recognition, preternatural ambition, mastery of parliamentary procedure, and sense of destiny that derived from his evangelical Christian faith all made him a formidable adversary.

After the conference chair called the meeting to order, Jimmerson took the floor. A ripple of anticipation rustled through the audience.

"Seven weeks from now, you will cast the most important vote you will ever cast in Congress," he began slowly, his voice so quiet that people strained to hear. "It may be the single most important decision of your political career." He paused, eyes darting across their faces. "After you leave office, whenever and however you leave, you will look back on this vote and see it as the defining moment of your time in Congress."

A hush fell over the caucus. Every eye was on him. Not a single person moved.

"Some *in the media* have argued"—laughter rumbled through the members—"that we are somehow obligated to vote our districts. They claim our judgment is irrelevant. If your district voted for Stanley, you should vote for Stanley, regardless of your own beliefs." The smirk on his face mocked the idea. His eyes narrowed to slits. "This argument is not only an affront to this House, it is an insult to the Constitution and the founders. It is a *sick* notion advanced by liberal opinion elites."

His voice rose as he began a winding historical discourse. Relying on James Madison's notes of the debates at the Constitutional Convention, Jimmerson argued that the founding fathers had expected the House to exercise independent judgment in choosing a president. The entire process was inherently undemocratic, he argued, as was the Electoral College. He denounced those who disagreed as having no understanding of the Constitution.

"My mother used to tell me that two wrongs don't make a right," he said, his voice shaking with righteous indignation. "It was *wrong* when radical Islamic terrorists murdered Harrison Flaherty." Heads nodded in agreement. "It was *wrong* when a partisan Democratic prosecutor leaked lies about David Petty the weekend before the election." It was an explosive charge for which Jimmerson had no proof, but it fed the belief among conservatives that victory had been snatched from them by Flaherty's assassination and the McLean Madam scandal. "My friends, it would be *wrong* for me to violate my conscience by voting for someone for president whom I do not support."

Murmurs echoed through the caucus.

"More than a presidential election hangs in the balance. Something greater is at stake: the integrity of the House. We were sent here to do the right thing. Not the *popular* thing . . . not the *political* thing . . . not the *expedient* thing . . . but the *right* thing." His voice fell to a hushed whisper. Emotion choked his voice. "Why are you here? To do what is right—or to do what some poll or the press tells you?" Another shot at the media—Jimmerson knew his audience. "Follow your conscience. Guard your heart. Wait until the electors meet in the various state capitols and cast their votes, and then transmit them to the House. Then—and only then—will we vote." He lowered his chin to his chest, assuming a prayerful pose. "May God grant us the courage to do the right thing."

The members jumped to their feet in a standing ovation. Jimmerson staggered to his chair, drained and light-headed from his oratorical exertions. Loud cheers filled the air. The House majority leader, whom Jimmerson despised and who hated him right back in turn, walked over and shook his hand. It was a powerful sign of Republican unity.

Jimmerson watched as the House GOP leadership clapped. He trusted none of them. They loathed him and lusted after his office. But he had their number. That was why he had not shared with any of them his plan to line up enough Republican votes to elect David Petty as the president when the new House reconvened on January 5. Not since Henry Clay had a speaker been poised to be the kingmaker. It was the chance of a lifetime, and Jimmerson had no intention of wasting it.

41

B ILL DIAMOND WALKED DOWN the narrow stairwell leading from his office on the second floor of the West Wing, turning sideways on occasion to avoid bumping into other staffers as they came up from the other direction. Reaching the first floor, he hung a right and walked down the hallway to Sam Syms's office.

"He's ready," said Syms's assistant, smiling and waving him in.

Diamond walked into the spacious office, the afternoon sun breaking through the windows from the courtyard in the back. It was the office Diamond yearned for and hoped to gain in a little more than sixty days. Syms stood behind his desk, studying papers, lost in thought. Diamond realized that Syms hadn't heard him enter. He cleared his throat. Syms snapped up his head, surprised to see Diamond standing in front of him.

"Goodness!" he exclaimed. "I didn't hear you come in. Grab a seat."

Syms glided from behind his desk to the sitting area and slid into a wingback chair. Diamond plopped on the couch. Even though it was his meeting, Syms sat in silence.

"Jimmerson gave quite a speech to the House caucus," Diamond began.

"I've never seen an off-the-record meeting reported in such detail," chuckled Syms. "He might as well have released a transcript." The corners of his mouth turned down. "I hope the House guys don't go off a cliff."

"What do you mean?"

The relaxed look on Syms's face drained away, replaced by somberness. "Bill, the president has some thoughts on the election in the House."

"Sure. I'd love his thoughts—we're putting together a whip operation now."

Syms let out a long sigh. "The president believes that Long winning a plurality in the popular vote and the Electoral College makes it very problematic for the White House to engage," Syms said smoothly, his hands resting in his lap. "The president selected Petty as vice president and strongly supported him." He paused, reloading. "But the optics of the White House trying to influence the House vote are not good. The House has its own dynamic, its own players, and we need to let it play out."

Diamond could scarcely believe what he was hearing. The first election of a president by the House of Representatives in two hundred years, and the president seriously believed the White House should sit on its hands? "Sam, with all due respect, this is delusional," he fired back. "David Petty is the vice president, for crying out loud. Everyone in this building worked their tails off for him. He's the president's guy. Now we're in extra innings, and we're supposed to lay down our bats?"

"The president will say *very* supportive things about Petty," Syms said, his hands folded. "But he does not want a lobbying effort by the White House. Period."

Diamond could not disguise his disgust. "David Petty has served this president faithfully and loyally, and at no small personal cost. He deserves better than this."

"The president wants him to win. We all do. But if the White House intervenes, it will backfire. Jimmerson is in charge, and he's very capable." Syms shifted in his seat, a pained expression on his face. "Look at how we got hammered for ramming Petty down the RNC's throat. That gave the president pause."

"Let's see if this gives the president pause," replied Diamond: "riding down Pennsylvania Avenue in a limousine with Bob and Claire Long to the Capitol to watch Long inaugurated. Because that's what's going to happen. Is that what you want?"

Syms did not flinch. Diamond sensed the oxygen being pumped out of the room—the decision had been made, and it was the president's. "Bill, at today's press briefing we're releasing a statement from the president saying that if he were a member of the House he would vote for Petty, but he will leave the matter to the House. The White House will not treat this as a party discipline vote."

Diamond stood, shaking with anger. "Incredible. Sam, can I ask you a question? At what point have I ever done anything to give you the impression that I am an idiot?"

Syms stared back silently.

"I know what this is really about—the president is upset we didn't use him more and he thinks we didn't defend his record enough. To tell me that this is a sacred constitutional prerogative of Congress is an insult to my intelligence." His face flushed red. "This is a *knife fight*, and we better start swinging a blade! This is unilateral disarmament! We're getting ready to turn the White House over to a Democrat."

"I think you're overreacting, Bill."

"Overreacting?" Diamond shouted. "Wait until we announce the president is neutral on whether his own vice president should be elected as his successor. Oh, I can't *wait* to see that headline!"

"Bill, you're not being reasonable here."

Diamond's eyes shot darts. "You know, it's strange," he replied coldly. "I've had a hard time being reasonable since they murdered my boss."

Diamond opened the door and marched down the hall, bumping into others as he rounded the corner. He stomped up the stairs into his office and closed the door. He picked up the phone and dialed Gerald Jimmerson's cell phone. A staffer answered the phone and handed it to the speaker.

"Mr. Speaker, Bill Diamond. Your speech to the House Republican caucus was terrific. Too bad it leaked."

"Are you kidding? *I leaked it!*" laughed Jimmerson. "I figured I better do it before someone else did. They can't help themselves—they're members of Congress." He paused, shifting gears. "What's the update from the West Wing?"

"There are some very interesting things going down over here," Diamond related cryptically. "Mr. Speaker, can I be blunt? I think it's time to play hardball."

"It's about time," Jimmerson drawled. "Now you're speaking my language."

———

MARVIN MYERS INTRODUCED HIS guest as "perhaps the most powerful person in Washington at the moment, a man who is expected to greatly influence the election of the next president by the House of Representatives." Gerald Jimmerson sat on the set, his folded hands resting on the anchor desk, a mug of water before him, a Cheshire-cat grin spread across his face, slowly nodding.

"Mr. Speaker, let's get right to it," Myers began. "According to news accounts, you have urged House Republicans to disregard the popular vote cast on Election Day." He threw onto the screen a clip from the *Washington*

Post that reported on Jimmerson's fiery speech to the House GOP caucus. "Did you encourage your colleagues to vote for David Petty regardless of how the people of their district or state voted?"

"Marvin, the press rarely gets it right, and this was no exception," Jimmerson said, the chip on his shoulder quickly evident. "Our caucus meetings are off the record, so I can't comment directly. But those reports are not accurate."

Myers was not about to let Jimmerson get away with that canned answer. "Mr. Speaker, should members of Congress vote as their state or district voted on Election Day? It's a yes-or-no question."

"Each member of the House needs to decide that, and people of goodwill come to differing conclusions," replied Jimmerson, keeping his iron fist gloved. "Some House members will defer to the judgment of the voters, others will not. But the idea that the House is ipso facto bound by the popular vote or the Electoral College is ahistorical."

"Ahistorical?" asked Myers, arching his eyebrows.

"Contrary to the clear intent of the founders," the Speaker lectured. "The framers never intended Congress to act as a rubber stamp. They expected the House to consider the matter seriously and render its own judgment. Marvin, if the framers had intended this situation to be resolved by popular vote, why didn't they just institute a runoff among the top two vote-getters? The reason is because they wanted Congress to be the final arbiter. We did not ask for this responsibility, but now that it has fallen to us, we must fulfill it." He stared back at Myers, eyes steady.

Myers lapped it up. "A recent Gallup poll showed seventy-two percent of the American people believe the person who won the popular vote should be elected by the House; only eighteen percent said the House should choose a different candidate, with ten percent undecided. That's pretty overwhelming opposition to your viewpoint, isn't it?"

"I don't take a poll on the Constitution," Jimmerson shot back with cool self-assurance. "I don't do it for the Bill of Rights, and I don't do it for Article Two, Section One, which lays out the process for the election of the president."

"So you have no problem with the House electing Petty or Stanley?"

"None whatsoever," answered Jimmerson. "Now, I'm not saying it will happen. I think it's certainly difficult for Senator Stanley because he only carried eleven states. But does the Constitution allow for that possibility? It does."

"Who will get your vote for president when the House votes on January 5?"

"David Petty is the Republican nominee. I proudly voted for him in the general election, and I will vote for him again when the House convenes," said Jimmerson.

"The president has said this is not a party discipline vote. Do you agree?"

"The president was right not to interject himself into this process. I think it showed appropriate respect for the separation of powers. But for House members, it is different. I would certainly expect Republican members to support their party's nominee for president, yes."

"So will you pressure Republican House members to vote for Petty?"

"That's your word, not mine," said Jimmerson, a twinkle in his eye. "I will *persuade*. Should House members ask my opinion, and I expect they will, I won't hesitate to share it." He smiled. "And I can be a pretty persuasive guy."

Myers smiled back. "I have no doubt, Mr. Speaker."

Within minutes, the news rocketed across the AP wire: "Jimmerson Will Lobby GOP House Members to Elect David Petty in House Vote."

ROSS LOMBARDY HAD JUST loaded his four children into the car and was pulling out of the church parking lot when he noticed his BlackBerry was vibrating. He answered it. It was the communications director for the Faith and Family Federation.

"Ross, sorry to bother you on a Sunday, but you didn't happen to catch Jimmerson on Myers this morning, did you?"

"No, we just got out of church," Ross answered. "I TiVo'd it. What did he say?"

"He said he was going to whip House Republicans to vote for Petty. He also said—and this is a quote—'I can be a pretty persuasive guy.' He's throwing down the gauntlet. AP wants a comment from us."

"Is Jimmerson out of his mind?" blurted Ross. "I can't believe this guy!"

"He's crazy all right—crazy like a fox. What do you want to say to the AP?"

"Take a pass," Ross ordered. "I don't want whatever we plan to say to Jimmerson credited to AP. But email me the story ASAP. I need to get it to Andy."

Diamond hung up and turned to his wife. "Gerry Jimmerson just stabbed us in the back on national television."

"What did he do this time?" she asked.

"He just endorsed David Petty in the election in the House on Myers's show. He said he's going to lobby for Petty and, believe me, he will be cracking heads. This is *total* betrayal—he knows full well that Andy is supporting Long."

"Gerry is so full of himself," she sighed. "He's a loose cannon."

"That guy wouldn't even *be* speaker if it weren't for us," said Ross. "It's time to remind him of that." He turned to the backseat. "Listen, kids, Daddy has to take care of something. Mommy will take you guys to brunch and I'll catch up later."

Eight eyes stared back at him, transfixed. Ross realized that his children enjoyed a front-row seat to history, watching political bones snap and noses bloodied at close range. They wouldn't realize it until years later, but like Andy Stanton in his youth, they were soaking up politics at the feet of a father they loved, and they were hooked and repulsed at the same time. What a brutal business their father was in—and how exciting!

Ross pulled up behind the New Life Ministries sanctuary and hopped out, slipping in through the service entrance and heading to the executive offices where Stanton cooled his heels between services. A security guard stood outside the door. He smiled knowingly at Ross, who winked at him, knocked on the door, and walked in.

"Ross!" boomed Stanton, enveloping him in a bear hug. "I saw your face out there in the congregation with your beautiful family in the first service."

"It was a terrific worship service," responded Ross. He held up his Black-Berry. "Check this out. Gerry Jimmerson just stepped in it on Myers's show."

Stanton squinted as he tried to read the BlackBerry screen, then pulled out his reading glasses and placed them on the end of his nose. His eyes widened as he read. "Unbelievable!" He read on. He let out a long whistle. Then he shook his head, scrolling down the body of the story with his thumb. "*Who does he think he is?*" Finishing the story, he rolled his eyes and handed the device back to Ross. "We delivered the votes that elected him speaker, and this is how he thanks us? This guy has a bad case of Potomac fever. Looks like I'll be doing my radio show from Washington tomorrow."

"Will that be before or after your meeting with the speaker?" Ross chuckled.

"After. That way I can share on the air what we discussed in the meeting."

"I'll call his chief of staff. It's short notice to arrange a meeting with the speaker, but I'll tell them it's important."

"You do that," said Andy. "I think it's time Gerry and I had a come-to-Jesus meeting."

"He may come to Jesus in more ways than one," joked Ross.

"He'll either see the light or feel the heat." Andy smiled.

Ross left the office and walked to the front of the sanctuary. In his excitement, he had completely neglected the logistics—he had no way to get to brunch. He fumbled for his BlackBerry and dialed his wife's cell phone. She didn't answer. He flagged down a security guard, who offered to drive him to the restaurant to meet his family. Meanwhile he scrolled through his contact file, looking for the home phone number for Jimmerson's chief of staff. Either the speaker was going to meet with Andy the next morning or Stanton might just give out the speaker's phone number to fifteen million radio listeners.

———

DAN DORMAN WAS TWO hours outside London and hopelessly lost. His rental car didn't have a GPS system and he couldn't figure out the map. The road signs were so confusing they might as well have been in Greek. He pulled off the road and dialed his editor in Washington on his cell. The phone rang as crisply and clearly as if he were across the street.

"So, have you found the madam?" asked the editor.

"Not yet, but I'm close. Other than getting lost in the English country-side, it's going well," Dorman reported. "I'm supposed to meet with Cruz in an hour."

"Where is she hiding?"

"She's holed up at some weekend home of the vice president for public affairs of some London-based company that was a client of hers."

"Did she agree to an interview?"

"Sort of," Dorman confessed. "She agreed to talk off the record. But I'm going to tell her she's misunderstood, she's being made to take the fall, and she needs to get her side of the story out. That usually works like a charm."

"You need to get her to speak to her relationship with Petty."

"If it's gettable, I'll get it," Dorman promised, impatient at being lectured by his editor. "She's protecting Petty, but it's only a matter of time before she cracks. We just better hope she does it to us. The tabloids are like dogs in heat. The *Sun* has supposedly offered her a million dollars to tell her story."

"If she goes with the tabloids, she's Gennifer Flowers. We're her salvation."

"No question. We'll treat her with dignity." Dorman paused. "Well, maybe not dignity, but at least some close approximation of it."

The editor chuckled. "Thank goodness Petty couldn't keep his pants on! And to think that I was beginning to miss the Clintons."

Dorman hung up. The prospect of a front-page exclusive reporting the details of Jessica Cruz's relationship with the vice president was irresistibly tantalizing. It would be another coup for the *Post,* and probably win him another award. Dorman hung up and walked into the pub to ask for directions.

AS AN AIDE LED Andy Stanton and Ross Lombardy through the outer offices and reception area to the speaker's personal office, Andy gazed out the windows at the panoramic view of the Mall. From the Speaker's chambers, he could see the Washington Monument, Ellipse, the White House complex, and Lincoln Memorial in the distance. Their white granite façades gleamed in the midmorning sunlight.

Ross had arranged to slip Andy in a side entrance, so that the sight of him trundling through the halls of the Capitol wouldn't send tongues wagging.

"Andy, thank you so much for coming," Jimmerson purred as he came across the large Oriental rug to grasp Stanton's hand. "It's great to see you, my friend." He pulled Andy close, a fake smile frozen on his face.

"Mr. Speaker, thanks for seeing me on such short notice," Andy said. They stood there awkwardly, each trying to outsmile the other before the shooting started.

Jimmerson guided him around the room, proudly pointing out a photograph of his father as a young army infantry officer in Korea, photos of himself with heads of state, and two of his prized possessions: a section of an American flag that had flown from the Capitol during Abraham Lincoln's funeral, and a slab of concrete from the Berlin Wall. He waved Andy to take a seat at the conference room table, where Jimmerson, his chief of staff, Andy, and Ross took their seats.

"We live in interesting times, Gerry," Andy observed as a conversation starter.

"Historic times," agreed Jimmerson. "The war on terrorism, Iran, and the first election of a president by the House in two centuries. Andy, when I was elected Speaker, I never thought I would see anything like it."

"With that opportunity comes great responsibility," added Andy, turning serious.

"We cannot shirk it even if we wanted to," Gerry assented, perking up. "That's the difference between us and the Democrats, Andy. We want power to *do* something; they want to be a majority to *be* something."

Andy figured he'd better get to the point. He decided to kick the elephant in the room. "So what do you think will happen with the election in the House? I saw your comments yesterday on Marvin Myers's program."

"I don't know," Jimmerson replied. "I don't think Stanley can make it—he did so badly in the popular vote and only won a hundred electoral votes. The Democrats don't even like him, and they think he ran a horrible campaign."

"He imploded!" exclaimed Andy gleefully. "Dele-gate killed him."

"Long won the popular vote, but he doesn't have much support on the Hill. Being an independent served him well at the ballot box, but this is a new ball game." He crossed his legs and rubbed his chin as he engaged in a little armchair punditry. "Petty is strong in the Republican conference, but he came in second. That hurts him. Some of our guys are nervous about voting differently than their district or state." He looked at Andy intently, having ticked through an analysis of the process while saying absolutely nothing. It was a common practice in the nation's capital, Andy was discovering. People went to meetings and droned on, saying absolutely nothing, and then left.

"Andy, I know you're for Long. I respect that, especially given your history with Petty. But Petty is the Republican nominee and I have to support him." The speaker stated it as a fact, not an opinion.

"You're the Republican leader in the House. You *should* vote for him," replied Andy, agreeing with the speaker before he took his best shot. "But I think if you make it an all-out, orchestrated campaign, it will hurt the party badly. And it will hurt you."

"How do you mean?" asked Jimmerson, leaning away. Andy knew that Jimmerson viewed him as a Dennis Hopper character, plastic explosives strapped to his chest, always threatening to blow up the train. The Republicans wanted the votes of his millions of supporters on Election Day, and then they wanted to shove him (and them) in the basement and forget about him.

"Petty is pro-choice, he opposes the ban on gays in the military, he supports amnesty for illegal aliens, and he is openly dismissive of religious conservatives. On top of that, now you have this McLean Madam thing. Our community doesn't take kindly to that." Andy leaned forward, fixing his stare on Jimmerson. "My differences with Petty aren't personal. They're based on a disagreement on the issues."

"I don't agree with him on those things," Jimmerson said with a wave of his hand. "But I think we can move him." He cracked a nervous smile. "He's certainly better than Long or Stanley. He has fought the terrorists, beat them in Baghdad, and he understands the threat of radical Islam. What is more important when the nation is at war?"

"Marriage, family, the unborn, and the moral fiber of our nation, to name a few," Andy shot back. "I have never voted for someone who is pro-choice, and I never will."

"I respect that, but we have an honest disagreement," said Jimmerson, his face turning to stone. "I hope it can remain a disagreement among friends."

"Mr. Speaker, I have no problem with you voting for Petty." Andy's deference masked a steely resolve. He moved in for the kill. "But I must tell you, if you try to lead the Republican caucus in Petty's direction, there will be a full-blown revolt."

Jimmerson stared back, his ramrod posture telegraphing extreme displeasure. His chief of staff sat silently taking notes on a legal pad, a sour look on his face.

"On Election Day evangelicals were twenty-six percent of all voters," Andy continued, starting to get on a roll. "They voted—Ross, what was the percentage?"

"Sixty-one percent for Long, 27 percent for Petty, 12 percent for Stanley," Ross rattled like a machine gun.

"Better than two to one for Long," Stanton pointed out. "They are the grassroots of the Republican Party. Those same voters voted for Congress—"

"Seventy-eight percent Republican, 22 percent Democrat," Ross interjected.

"That's *twenty-one million voters* who voted for Long for president and then voted Republican for Congress." Andy paused. "Do you want to offend twenty-one million voters? If you do, they're *not* going to go to the polls and vote Republican in two years."

The veiled threat stunned Jimmerson, and he visibly bristled. His chief of staff looked like he was going to have a coronary. People didn't usually talk to the speaker of the house like this.

"Andy, I hear you," Jimmerson said. "But Republican House members not supporting Petty has its own consequences. It's a vote of no confidence. We'd be rejecting our party's presidential nominee, a war hero, and the incumbent vice president. No one has ever done that."

Andy shrugged, unimpressed. "They can vote as their district did."

"That's your recommendation?"

"Yes. The polls show that's where the American people are."

"Do you take a poll before you take a position on an issue, or before you preach on Sunday morning?" asked Jimmerson sharply.

The corners of his chief of staff's mouth turned up in a restrained smile.

"No, I don't," smiled Andy. "But I'm not a politician."

"I see," Jimmerson replied with disgust. "Well, Andy, some of us believe that elected officials should do the right thing—even when we don't have a divinity degree or 'reverend' in front of our name."

"I'm glad you feel that way," Andy said, hunching forward, shaking off the insult. "But our people are not going to understand how voting for someone who is pro-choice and pro–gay rights just because he has an *R* after his name is the right thing to do."

A female aide walked in gingerly carrying a piece of paper. She leaned over and silently handed Jimmerson the note. He read the contents, nodded, and handed it back wordlessly. Stanton guessed that was their choreographed way of ending the meeting. Even the way they end meetings in Washington was phony, he thought.

"Well, anyway, I appreciate the advice," Jimmerson said, his voice hollow. "In my position, I get no shortage of unsolicited advice, and I find most of it beneficial." He laughed, enjoying his own joke. "I appreciate you coming to tell me in person. That means a lot. Keep up the great work over the airwaves. My wife and I watch you every night on the Spirit Channel."

He shook Andy's hand vigorously. Andy, Ross, and the chief of staff filed out together, exchanging pleasantries in the lobby and telling each other to stay in touch as the House prepared to vote. Andy snapped a few pictures with the speaker's staff, who gathered around excitedly, pleased to be in the presence of a celebrity.

Walking briskly to the elevator, Ross asked, "Well, what do you think?"

"He listened," Andy answered with an edge in his voice. "But he didn't hear me. Let's see if he hears it if I say it on five hundred radio stations and national television." He put his hands behind his back. The elevator doors closed. Alone, he turned to Ross. "Let the fireworks begin."

42

Some of the columnists and talking heads, motivated more by visceral hatred for Jimmerson than affection for Long, had suggested that when the presidential electors met in the state capitols on December 19, enough Stanley and Petty electors might vote for Bob Long to give him 270 electoral votes, thus rendering an election in the House moot. The chattering class shuddered at the thought of Gerry Jimmerson anointing the next president.

Technically, their suggestion was legal and plausible, as many state laws allowed electors to vote as they pleased. In practice, however, the notion was a pipe dream. The electors were party loyalists, donors, and elected officials. The Democratic National Committee took the extraordinary step of threatening legal action against any Stanley elector who voted for Long, and December 19 came and went with no fireworks. As cable news broadcasts degenerated into a murderer's row of ranting partisans, the nation braced for a House vote in which no candidate had a clear majority of twenty-six states. Republican and Democratic strategists and Long surrogates traded insults, pointed fingers, and spewed venom. By the time Christmas rolled around, the entire nation was exhausted. People needed a break.

It was against this backdrop that David Petty laced his shoes in his upstairs bedroom at the vice president's residence, getting ready for the holiday party. It would be Petty's first and last Christmas at the Naval Observatory, and he knew he was on his way either to the White House or the private sector, never to see the residence again. Anne Petty emerged from her closet, looking stunning in a red beaded Donna Karan couture gown.

"Wow!" David Petty exclaimed. He stood there, admiring his wife of thirty-two years, and let out a long whistle. He pulled her close and pecked her on the cheek with affection. "You are one beautiful black woman," he said, eyes filled with admiration. "You're going to be the best-looking woman at the party tonight."

"You're just saying that because you want some action later," she said playfully.

"I am not!" Petty protested. He smiled. "So what?"

"I hope you're not attracted to me just because you think I'm going to be first lady."

"I do believe you will be the first lady," Petty predicted confidently. "But I was attracted to you long before that, wasn't I?" He paused. "Honey, I'm sorry you've had to put up with so much garbage." Anne had held up stoically as the tabloid press foraged through his connection to Jessica Cruz. "I want us to enjoy Christmas as a family. Let's shut it out, even if it's only for a few days."

Anne put her arms around him. "I'm glad you ran," she said quietly, her voice vulnerable. "I knew it would be bad—but I didn't know it would be *this* bad. Still, I'm glad you did it, and I've never been prouder of you." She lifted her head, looking into his eyes. "And you're going to win."

He smiled down at her. "And when we do, to heck with them all," he said.

"Yes, to heck with all of them."

He stepped away, then held his arm out, inviting her to slip her arm through it, and cut her a proud glance. "Are you ready to make your entrance, my dear?"

She smiled, striking a regal pose, and put her arm through his. They walked down the staircase to the foyer where guests were already arriving. Several gasped when they saw Anne Petty in her stunning red dress gliding down the stairs like the queen of the night.

"Isn't she beautiful?" someone exclaimed.

"She's going to be the most glamorous first lady since Jackie Kennedy!" gasped another. "She's positively regal."

The Pettys passed out hugs and air kisses, then took their place in front of the Christmas tree, where they endured a long click line of photographs with guests as an official White House photographer flashed away. A holiday cake the size of a small automobile—baked as a gingerbread house by the White House pastry chef—dominated the parlor. A lavish spread of appetizers lay on the dining room table. Everyone tried to enjoy the magical evening in the midst of the turmoil roiling Washington. Republican bigwigs, U.S. senators, governors, Supreme Court justices, ambassadors, and members of Congress all waited their turn to pay their respects and wish the second couple a Merry Christmas.

Petty noticed Gerry Jimmerson and his wife. "Mr. Speaker!" he boomed.

"Mr. Vice President!" Jimmerson bellowed back, his husky baritone incongruously loud for his slight frame. "Anne, you look beautiful as always," he grandly complimented, opening his arms in a hug. "You make us all so proud."

"Thank you, Gerry. You're the *best,* sweetheart." She leaned forward and brushed her cheek against Jimmerson's face, lightly touching her lips against his cheek. She then held his hands in hers and looked deeply into his eyes. "We're so grateful for your support of David."

Jimmerson grabbed her arms and gazed back. "Happy to do it, ma'am," he said with festive flourish. "You've handled everything with such grace and dignity. You're going to be a fabulous first lady."

Anne raised an eyebrow, a smile turning up her lips. "Never let them see you sweat, honey."

"Mr. Vice President, may I borrow you for a moment?" asked the Speaker.

Mrs. Jimmerson rolled her eyes. "Always plotting!"

"Don't hog him, Gerry. He has a house full of guests," Anne ordered. Jimmerson smiled and bowed from the waist in deference to her wishes.

Petty grabbed the Speaker by the arm and led him out onto the porch. The night was clear and cold, and their breath turned to fog as they spoke.

"I assume you saw the story in the *Post* about the calls coming into the Capitol," Jimmerson said. "The switchboard is jammed. Seven hundred thousand calls in a single day. That's a record."

"I did," Petty replied, visibly worried. "Who is it—the wing nuts? I'd guess Stanton and the right-wing talk radio hosts are behind it. I'm telling you, they are doing more harm than good. They're nothing but a bunch of demagogues and blowhards."

"It's the Stanton brigade—the Faith and Family Federation. Andy went on the air and gave out the switchboard number. And the Long campaign is using the Internet and email to generate calls." Jimmerson shook his head. "Mr. Vice President, a member from Michigan that I put on the Appropriations Committee came up to me in the cloakroom today and told me the calls in his office are running eight to one for Long. Normally he's a reliable vote, but now he's gone wobbly on me."

"I talked to the RNC, and they say they're countering it."

"I don't see it," Jimmerson sighed. "The House switchboard has received 1.3 million phone calls in forty-eight hours. It's heavily pro-Long."

"What can we do?" asked Petty.

"Well, that's what I wanted to talk to you about. Our whip count doesn't look good." Jimmerson looked away. "I'm afraid it's going sideways. Even if the president intervenes, it's going to be tough." He paused, his voice catching. "I've done all I can, but I feel like I've let you down."

Petty sucked in the cold air and slowly exhaled. The blood rushed to his head. When Jimmerson looked up, Petty saw his eyes were moist with tears. The speaker's look said what he did not have the heart to verbalize: it was over. Petty put his arm around Jimmerson and pulled him tight.

"It's all right, Gerry," Petty said. "You've given it your best shot. You're a patriot and a hero. I'll never forget what you've done."

They walked together back into the residence and Petty plastered a stage smile on his face as he dove into the crowd, projecting a false sense of confidence to his party guests. He saw Anne across the room greeting a VIP, her head nodding vigorously as she smiled and made small talk. Their eyes met. She read the look on his face. As Petty looked on helplessly, she quickly excused herself from her guests and walked briskly up the staircase, closing the door to the master bedroom, where she could cry in private.

———

AT 4:30 P.M. ON January 2, the Justice Department issued a single-paragraph news release announcing the indictment of Michael Kaplan. The seven-count indictment included five felony counts of perjury and two counts of obstruction of justice. Each perjury count carried a minimum sentence of one year in prison, while the two obstruction counts each carried a prison sentence of up to five years. Kaplan had lied repeatedly to the grand jury, the indictment alleged, and had also destroyed documents material to the investigation.

G.G. Hoterman was sitting in his office on K Street when Walt Shapiro called him with the bad news. Hoterman was floored. He'd known Kaplan was in trouble, but given his slippery history—the guy had nine lives—Hoterman had always expected him to slip the noose.

"What does it mean for me?" Hoterman asked.

"Good and bad," Shapiro observed clinically. "The bad news is that there will be a trial, and you'll probably be called as a witness. The good news is you're not going to be indicted. The prosecutors have all but assured me of that."

"And Deirdre?"

"She's fine," Shapiro said. "Home free. Her brother and she both told the truth, even the part that hurt, and that's ninety percent of this battle."

Hoterman sighed, relieved. His affair with Deirdre was on ice as he tried to save his marriage. His wife was already mad at him—he didn't need a two-front war with Deirdre. "Is it all right if I call Mike?"

Shapiro thought for a second. "I don't have a problem with that. But be careful, and don't discuss any facts or testimony you might give in the trial."

Hoterman hung up and dialed Kaplan's direct number. Kaplan answered on the first ring. "Michael, it's G.G. I just wanted to tell you how sorry I am. I don't walk away from my friends, and I'm not starting now. I want to raise money for your legal defense fund."

"Thanks, G.G.," replied Kaplan, his voice calm and steady. "I knew when this whole mess got kicked to DOJ that it would be hard to dodge an indictment. But this is still America. I'm going to get a jury trial, and I like my chances. And after the witnesses from the administration we plan to call, they will rue the day they did this."

"Good for you. They need to be made to pay for this."

"If the crime was trying to elect Sal Stanley, I plead guilty. But how can they indict someone for hiring consultants in a presidential campaign? It's crazy."

"And doing this right before the House vote shows it was political from day one."

"Well, I'm not going to roll over. I'm going to fight . . . and I'm going to win."

"You *must* win. Mike, I say this as your friend—you need to beef up your legal team. You need a junkyard-dog criminal attorney." Hoterman couldn't believe that Kaplan had allowed the campaign's lawyers to handle the case. It was like walking into a gunfight with a knife.

"Don't worry," Kaplan promised. "I thought it would send the wrong signal if I retained a criminal lawyer during the campaign. In hindsight, that was stupid. Now I'm going to get the best legal talent money can buy."

G.G. muttered a few more lines of awkward encouragement and hung up. He wanted to keep Kaplan close. After all, if Hoterman were called as a witness, he didn't want Kaplan to view him as hostile.

Within minutes, Kaplan resigned as chairman of the Stanley campaign and abruptly left the campaign headquarters. Camera crews recorded him walking across the parking lot to his car, head down, carrying a box filled with personal effects, looking like a broken man. The media loved it: oh, how the mighty had fallen. For Salmon Stanley, the timing could not have been worse. The House election of the president was only three days away.

THE EDITORS AT THE *Wall Street Journal* put the final touches on their page-one exclusive. In addition to the news of Michael Kaplan's indictment—which rumbled across Washington like an earthquake—the *Journal* had its own three-bell ringer. The editors posted the story on the WSJ.com website at 11:30 P.M.: "Petty Recommended 'McLean Madam' as Lobbyist for Defense Contractor." The subhead was no less explosive: "Company Paid Cruz $80,000, Received $6.5 Million No-Bid Contract." The lead paragraph asserted that "Vice President David Petty recommended Jessica Cruz, the Washington lobbyist arrested for operating a prostitution ring out of her tony McLean, Virginia, mansion, to a defense contractor at a time when the company had contracts pending at the Pentagon." According to the story, "the company later received what government watchdog groups describe as a highly unusual no-bid contract from the Department of Defense for $6.5 million."

Bill Diamond was at his home in Alexandria when he received the phone call from the campaign communications director. It was nearly midnight and his family had gone to bed.

"Bill, the *Journal* posted the story on its website."

"How bad is it?" Diamond asked.

"As bad as anything we've seen so far," she mumbled in a monotone. "They have an anonymous source claiming Petty referred Cruz to the company, then awarded them a no-bid contract."

"Cruz is not quoted, I hope."

"No, her attorney is. He says—let me find it here—'there was no connection whatsoever between Petty's recommendation and the contract.' "

"Well, at least she hasn't turned. Who was her client?"

"Advanced Logistics, a defense contractor in northern Virginia. They make a big deal out of the fact that the CEO contributed to Petty's campaign. Ever heard of them?"

"No." Diamond mentally reviewed their options. They had to fashion a tough response and get talking points to Jimmerson and the whip team ASAP. Otherwise, their supporters in the House were going to panic. "I'm calling Al Kirkpatrick right now."

Kirkpatrick was the editor of the *Wall Street Journal*. He was smart, tough, and normally a straight arrow. Diamond dialed Kirkpatrick's cell phone number.

"Al, it's Bill Diamond. Listen, sorry to call so late, but we have a problem."

"I assume you're calling about the Advanced Logistics story," Kirkpatrick said somewhat defensively. "Before you get started, we don't reference the call girl ring beyond mentioning Jessica Cruz's arrest. But the fact that Petty recommended Cruz as a lobbyist for defense contractors he did business with was new information."

"Give me a break, Al. Your reporters are roaming the English countryside like body snatchers looking for Cruz," Diamond shot back. "This is a sex-scandal story masquerading as a D.C. lobbyist story. You've gone tabloid, and frankly I'm surprised, given the fact that it's the *Wall Street Journal*."

"We're following the story," Kirkpatrick replied. "I think your beef is with Merryprankster.com and the cable shows. We never even reported on the Jessica Cruz hot tub video."

"Your story claims it was a no-bid contract. That's not true. This was a transport and logistics contract. The price is set by the Pentagon in advance, almost like a mileage rate for travel or a per diem for lodging." Diamond's voice was shaking.

"Have someone call with the specifics, and we'll take a look at it."

"You need to take 'no-bid contract' out of the headline," Diamond insisted.

"I don't write the headlines."

"Don't hide behind the headline writers!" screamed Diamond. "You're the editor of the newspaper, for crying out loud."

"I'll pass it on," Kirkpatrick replied coldly. "Your point is duly noted."

"Thanks for doing nothing to fix an erroneous story, Al," Bill sputtered, and slammed the phone down.

He would have someone on the national security staff call the *Journal* and explain how Pentagon transport contracts worked, but he knew it was probably too late to do any good. Even if they won a correction on the headline, the damage was done.

43

M R. SPEAKER, I PRESENT the vice president of the United States, accompanied by the members of the United States Senate!"

Vice President David Petty led the way as all one hundred members of the Senate entered the House chamber for the official counting of the electoral vote, to be followed immediately by the election of the new president by the House. The House rose as one, applauding. Petty acknowledged the applause, moving his head like a bobblehead doll and cracking a nervous smile and winking at friendly House members. As required by law, the senators walked to the front of the chamber and sat to the right of the rostrum. Petty took his seat as the presiding officer; Gerry Jimmerson sat to his left.

The certification of the electoral vote by Congress usually packed all the suspense of watching grass grow, with "tellers" (or counters) designated by the presidential campaigns carrying out honorific duties before an empty House chamber. This time was different. Every member of the House and Senate was in attendance, including one congressman from Nevada recovering from heart surgery, who was wheeled in on a hospital bed. Every seat in the gallery was packed to overflowing, and the Capitol teemed with political activists, lobbyists, and gawkers. A national television audience estimated at over one hundred million people watched as Petty brought the gavel down and called the session to order at 1 P.M. sharp.

"Mr. Speaker and members of Congress," Petty said in a firm voice, "I declare this joint session of the members of the House of Representatives and the Senate, called for the purpose of opening the certificates and counting the votes of the electors of the various states for president and vice president, to be convened."

The House clerk handed him a mahogany box, a replica of the wooden boxes once carried on horseback to the Capitol in the nineteenth century. The counting of the votes of the electors continued in alphabetical order by state without incident for a little more than an hour. When Petty reached the state of Texas, his back stiffened. Necks craned and a murmur rippled through the chamber in the direction of a group of rebel GOP House members from Texas who had threatened to object to Long's victory, arguing that their state's filing deadline had been violated. But parliamentary rules prohibited debate on the election, so the moment came and went without protest.

After the state of Wyoming, Petty announced the final tally. "The vote for president of the United States, as delivered to the president of the Senate, is as follows." He paused. "Robert W. Long of California has received 255 votes. David Petty of Virginia has received 164 votes. Salmon Stanley of New Jersey has received 119 votes." He gazed out over the chamber. "No candidate for president or vice president of the United States has received a majority of 270 of the 538 votes cast by the electors. As required by Article Two, Section One of the Constitution, the Senate and House will now proceed to the election of the president and vice president in their respective chambers. Until the two chambers have completed the election process, I declare this joint session adjourned."

Petty shook Speaker Jimmerson's hand and left the rostrum, leading the members of the Senate back across the Capitol Rotunda in a solemn procession to the Senate chamber. When the last senator had exited, the sergeant at arms closed the House doors and Speaker Jimmerson banged the gavel. The tension in the chamber grew thick. No one knew how long they would be there, or for how many ballots the vote would drag on. Conventional wisdom was that Long would lead on the first ballot but be unable to secure the twenty-six votes needed.

"Gentlemen and gentleladies of the House," Jimmerson declared. "The House will proceed immediately to the election of the president of the United States. State delegations will caucus in their assigned locations in the chamber." Each state voted as a delegation, with both Democrats and Republicans voting by secret ballot. Because so many members lied or had promised their vote to more than one candidate, it was impossible for anyone to confidently predict the outcome.

Congressman Charlie Hector walked to the front of the chamber for the California delegation caucus. Members stood around chatting informally. Long had won the popular vote in the Golden State and had locked up the delegation early; there was no suspense here. After the delegation voted, Hector's cell phone rang. He left the floor and stepped into the cloakroom.

"Congressman? Jay Noble."

"Jay, bad news," Hector said. "We've lost North Carolina, and Florida is now a jump ball." Long had carried North Carolina and Florida—if he lost them both, his hard count would fall to seventeen states.

"What?" shouted Jay. "How did that happen?"

"Jimmerson is pulling out all the stops," Hector said. "He's threatening to kick people off committees, kill their earmarks, and make sure their bills never see the light of day. He told one appropriations subcommittee chairman that if he voted for Long, he could kiss his chairmanship good-bye."

"He's taking on the cardinals!" groaned Jay, using Hill slang for the powerful appropriations subcommittee chairmen.

"He's doing more than that. We lost one of our members from Florida after Jimmerson strong-armed the chairman of Armed Services to threaten to pull F-22s from an air base in his district."

"That's a violation of House rules! He can't do that."

"He can do whatever he wants. He's the speaker."

"What do we do?"

"Have the governor call Mark Hudson right now."

Congressman Mark Hudson, Republican from Lancaster, Pennsylvania, was the chairman of the Values Caucus, a committed pro-life Roman Catholic, and frequent guest on cable news shows. He was a rising star in the House and a man in a hurry who wore his ambition on his sleeve. He had placed a call to Long the day before, a call that Long had so far declined to return.

"The governor doesn't want to be seen as cutting deals," replied Jay. "That's why he hasn't called Hudson back yet."

"Jay, this is Congress. Cutting deals is what we do." He paused. "Do you want to win or not?"

"What can you tell us about Hudson? If the governor is going to return his call, he doesn't want to be surprised."

"I know him almost too well," Hector chuckled. "He's an expensive date."

"He claims he can deliver forty to fifty social-conservative votes."

"He's a player and he can definitely deliver some votes," Hector said. "But watch your back. He's probably negotiating with Petty at the same time."

BOB LONG PLACED THE call from the governor's office in Sacramento, where he had decamped to await the House vote. "Congressman, how are you? It's Bob Long."

"I'm good, Governor." Congressman Mark Hudson stood in a small anteroom off the House floor, his hand cupped over his cell phone. The vote was already under way. He spoke in a hurried whisper.

"I understand you have an interest in joining our team."

"That's correct," Hudson said in a hushed voice, his eyes glancing to the left and right to make sure no one was within earshot. He stepped behind a column to shield himself from view of some reporters milling around. "The leadership is turning the screws for Petty. That's the path of least resistance, but the high-pressure tactics are turning off a lot of people. I can't get comfortable with Petty—he's pro-choice, bad on guns, too liberal for me. Then there's the McLean Madam—a lot of us are worried that if we elect Petty, we don't know where it leads." He shifted gears quickly. "I can deliver a number of votes from conservative members . . . assuming you and I can come to an understanding."

"What kind of understanding?" Long asked, his voice flat and noncommittal.

"I'd like to be your leader in the House." Hudson had gotten right to the point—he was not known for beating around the bush. "You don't have a party caucus, so I could be your majority leader and whip, if you will, lining up votes. You can't use Jimmerson—he's your sworn enemy. Any Democrat with influence will be too liberal." He paused, catching his breath. "I could really help you."

Long was stunned. He knew Hudson was ambitious, but this was unseemly. He had to be careful not to promise too much while ensuring that Hudson didn't wriggle off the hook. "I think we can find a very prominent role for you to play in advancing my legislative agenda," Long said smoothly, dangling the offer. "I have not fully thought through exact titles and how we will organize our supporters in the House, but I would welcome your input. I could see you acting as my floor leader or something along those lines." Long let the dead air hang on the line.

"I want to remain a member of the Republican caucus," Hudson said, raising the ante. "I really can't leave the party and be effective."

"Oh, I agree," Long said, his tone solicitous. "Have you given any thought to how you're going to handle Jimmerson and the Republican leadership? They are not going to take kindly to your voting for me. Gerry's been known to hold a grudge."

"Tell me about it." Hudson laughed. "Governor, we have eighty-six members in the Values Caucus. If the speaker goes after me, he's going after them. He won't be able to hold the conference together if he tries to punish us."

"Can you bring other folks along?" asked Long.

"Governor, I guarantee you I'll bring people with me," said Hudson confidently.

"Mark, I look forward to working with you," said Long. "Welcome aboard."

Long hung up the phone. He glanced at the television set, where the vote proceeded on the screen. He hoped Hudson could deliver. It was his last chance to win the presidency.

———

GERALD JIMMERSON CALLED THE House to order, ordering the members to clear the aisles and take their seats. The sergeant at arms stood at attention at the door. "The clerk will begin the roll call of the states," the Speaker ordered.

The entire House chamber buzzed with energy. Word of Hudson switching to Long at the last minute had rifled through the chamber, shocking the GOP leadership and creating turmoil on the floor. The Petty whips bounced from one state delegation to another, cajoling, urging, and pleading Republicans to hang tough. Jimmerson had kept the vote open long past the time when most state delegations had voted, in a frantic search for additional votes for Petty.

"Alabama!" the House clerk called.

"Mr. Speaker, the state of Alabama casts its vote for Robert W. Long of California."

"Alaska!"

"Mr. Speaker, the great state of Alaska votes for David Petty of Virginia."

The roll call continued. Everyone knew that Long was ahead but few expected him to reach twenty-six votes. Long narrowly held on to Florida, giving him a virtually solid South, as on Election Day. But when Petty carried Jimmerson's home state of North Carolina, a murmur rippled through the chamber. Rumors flew that Stanley might be cutting a deal to throw his support to Petty on the second ballot.

"Pennsylvania!" A hush fell over the gallery. All heads turned to a senior member of the delegation, who stepped to the microphone. He had a sick expression on his face.

"Mr. Speaker, Pennsylvania casts its vote for Governor Robert Long."

Hudson had carried enough Republican members of the Pennsylvania congressional delegation to give the state to Long, a shocking turnaround. It was simple arithmetic: Pennsylvania was a blue state at the presidential level but a red state at the congressional level because of redistricting by a Republican legislature. As a result, a key state—the home state of Elizabeth Hafer—won by Stanley on Election Day had gone to Long. As Mark Hudson felt the hate-filled stares of his Republican colleagues, he looked across the chamber to see Charlie Hector with an irrepressible grin on his face and his thumb up.

Texas and Tennessee stuck with Long, bringing him to twenty-four votes. Then came the bombshell.

"Utah!"

"Mr. Speaker, Utah votes for Governor Robert Long of California!"

"No! No!" shouted a chorus of angry Republicans. Petty had carried that state on Election Day, but now the explanation flew across the vast chamber in hurried whispers: another member of Hudson's Values Caucus had bolted from the Republican fold, taking Utah with him. No one had seen it coming.

With only two states remaining to vote, Long stood at twenty-five votes to Petty's fourteen votes and Stanley's nine when the clerk called West Virginia. Long had carried it on Election Day, but it had only two members of Congress, one Republican and one Democrat, neither of whom had announced their vote. If they canceled each other out, West Virginia would lose its vote. Because the only other state remaining was Wyoming, whose lone Republican member of Congress was pledged to Petty, the deadlock would force a second ballot. The House chamber fell silent, the suspense almost unbearable, as they awaited the announcement from West Virginia.

"Mr. Speaker, West Virginia votes for the next president of the United States, Robert W. Long."

The gallery, packed with Long supporters who had traveled from every corner of the country, erupted in a standing ovation. Jimmerson, visibly annoyed, banged his gavel. "Order! Order in the House!" he shouted. "Spectators in the gallery will maintain silence or they will be removed by the sergeant at arms."

The gallery gradually quieted, taking their seats.

"The chair recognizes the state of Wyoming."

As expected, the Wyoming congressman voted for Petty.

The roll call complete, the clerk approached the rostrum with the tally, handing it to Jimmerson. The Speaker glanced down at it and laid it on the podium. "Gentlemen and gentleladies of the House, in the vote for president of the United States, the totals are as follows. Robert W. Long of California, twenty-six votes. David Petty of Virginia, fifteen votes. Salmon Stanley of New Jersey, nine votes. As provided for by the Constitution, Robert W. Long is hereby declared to have been elected president of the United States."

The members rose from their chairs to applaud the new president. Jimmerson, a scowl frozen on his face, declared the session adjourned and quickly left the speaker's chair. The vote had been a stunning repudiation of his leadership by his own party.

Ashen-faced, he moved swiftly through the Capitol, surrounded by a phalanx of aides and security guards. Reporters trailed behind, shouting questions, which the speaker ignored. He flew down the stairs of the Capitol toward a waiting car.

"Mr. Speaker!" shouted one of the reporters. "Why did David Petty lose? Why couldn't you deliver your own caucus in the House?"

Jimmerson wheeled on the reporter, his face etched with pain, his eyes black and steady. "Two words: Jessica Cruz." He stepped into the car and the door closed behind him.

ACROSS THE CAPITOL IN the Senate chamber, word arrived by official messenger of Long's election. The Senate president pro tempore interrupted the proceedings to make the announcement.

Standing at his desk, Sal Stanley maintained a stoic expression. He knew everyone would be studying his reaction. He had just yielded the floor to the Republican minority leader when Senator John Diller of North Dakota ambled over.

"What happened?" said Stanley, bewildered. "How did Long make it to twenty-six votes on the first ballot?"

"You didn't hear? A group of right-wing Republicans from Pennsylvania and Utah went over to him," Diller said. "They swung the vote in Long's favor. It was identity politics. They voted for the Christian instead of the Republican."

"Incredible," said Stanley, shaking his head.

"Sal, there's only one thing left to do. We have to run you for vice president. We've got the votes to do it."

Stanley felt numb. "I can't do that. Can you imagine me serving under Bob Long?" He paused. "Besides, you can't elect someone as vice president who wasn't on the ballot as a running mate in the general election."

"We can elect anyone we want," chimed in assistant majority leader Lyman Lyall, who had joined them. "We're the Senate, remember?"

"No," said Stanley firmly. "You're wrong." The Twelfth Amendment limited the balloting for vice president in the Senate to the top two vote-getters in the electoral college. Not only could Stanley not run, he couldn't even vote for his own running mate, Betsy Hafer, who had come in third. He glanced in the direction of Senator Ed Bell, who looked pale and devastated after learning of Petty's loss. "Let's elect Bell. What torture for both of them!" He chuckled. "Talk about killing two birds with one stone—he and Bob will claw each other's eyes out." They laughed among themselves, but it was a hollow, defeated laughter.

"It makes me sick that we can't elect you at least as VP," said Diller. "We would have total control of the Senate."

"The best thing for the country is for me to be majority leader," replied Stanley. "If we're going to put a fox in Long's henhouse, it has to be Bell. That's why I'm voting for Bell, and so should you."

LACKING A POWERFUL PERSONALITY like Jimmerson to herd the cats, the Senate roll call for vice president took on a haphazard and anticlimactic feel.

Everyone got their dramatic moment before the cameras, but the drama was beginning to drain from the chamber. Long had won the presidency, and all that was left was for the fat lady to sing. Still, more senators voted their conscience than had been the case in the House, making it hard to figure out who would ultimately prevail.

With Hafer out of the running, the bizarre contest pitted Ed Bell against Johnny Whitehead. The mercurial and maverick Bell had as many enemies as allies in the chamber, and with Petty now officially out of the running, his more conservative Republican colleagues began to abandon him like a sinking ship. As senators rose to speak, an ironic dynamic unfolded. The Republicans were breaking for Whitehead, while the Democrats were trying to elect the Republican vice-presidential nominee.

Senator J. T. Koch, the chairman of the Senate Republican caucus and a dyed-in-the-wool conservative, took the floor to announce his vote for Whitehead. There were audible gasps.

"I have enormous regard for my friend and colleague, Senator Bell," Koch protested a bit too much. "But the American people and the House of Representatives have rendered their decision, and Bob Long will be the next president. It is not a decision I take lightly."

From across the room, Bell glared at Koch, his eyes like lasers.

"Had David Petty prevailed in the House, I would now be casting my vote for Senator Bell for vice president," Koch continued. "But that die has been cast by the lower chamber. I believe it is absolutely essential for the good of the country that the president and vice president come from the same party, or in this case an independent or third-party ticket." Koch cited the famously strained relationship of Vice President Thomas Jefferson with President John Adams, creating an administration so dysfunctional that Congress amended the Constitution to prevent it from happening again. Koch's real reasoning was less gallant: he despised Bell's moderate-to-liberal brand of Republicanism and viewed his possible elevation as a disaster for the GOP and the Senate.

He was not alone. Bell lost his Republican colleagues to Whitehead, an astonishing rebuke from his own caucus. Democrats voted heavily for him, but it was not enough. The final tally was fifty-two votes for Whitehead to forty-eight votes for Bell.

THE PRIVATE PHONE LINE on the credenza rang. Bob Long picked it up.

"Bob, it's Sal Stanley. I am calling to congratulate you on your victory," Stanley said. "It was a tough campaign and you were a worthy opponent. I want to do everything I can to work with you for the good of the country."

"Thanks, Sal. I appreciate that very much. I'm coming to Washington before the inaugural. I would like to get together and discuss how we can work together."

"I look forward to it," Stanley said—no doubt through gritted teeth. It was a brief call, no more than a minute in length.

When Long hung up, he spun around in his chair to face Claire, who sat on the couch in his office, watching the television. "That was Sal Stanley."

"Good," Claire replied. "So he finally conceded. Was he generous?"

"He was a class act," Long said. "But I still don't trust him."

"You shouldn't."

Stanley's call unleashed a flood of emotion for both Claire and Bob. It hit them: they were on their way to the White House. Claire stood from the couch and walked toward Bob, her eyes filling with tears. Bob walked from behind the desk as she nearly fell into his arms, their embrace emotional and intimate. As he held her, Long began to weep, as did Claire. The tension and stress of a two-year presidential campaign poured out of them both.

After a few moments, they collected themselves, pulling apart, each wiping tears.

"You're going to be a great president," Claire said, her voice shaking.

"And you're going to make a terrific first lady," he said. They stood looking at each other, both faces damp with tears, both feeling like emotional train wrecks. They laughed. It helped.

Long's assistant rapped on the door and walked in. Claire was still wiping tears and smeared mascara with a tissue. "Governor, sorry to bother you, but Vice President Petty is on the phone."

"Put him through." Long walked back behind his desk, picking up the phone as soon as it rang. "Mr. Vice President?"

"Bob, it's David Petty. I'm calling to offer my personal congratulations and tell you that you will have my full support." Petty sounded like a robot, his voice hollow and defeated.

"Thank you, Mr. Vice President. It's been difficult for us all. I just want to tell you that you should be proud of the way you've carried yourself. You can hold your head high." It was a veiled reference to the McLean Madam story that consumed the Petty campaign in the final days. Long might not have won without it, and both of them knew it.

"Thanks, Bob," Petty replied. "Let me know if I can be of help."

"I would value your advice. I want to stay in touch," Long said diplomatically. "No one knows more about the threat of terrorism than you. I hope I can call on you in the future."

"Of course. Can I be so bold as to give you some unsolicited advice? Have someone on your team reach out to Geoff Davis at NSC as soon as possible."

"Can you be more specific?" asked Long.

"Not really," Petty said. "But it concerns Iran."

Long hung up and turned to Claire, his face drained of color. He'd had no doubt that Iran had been complicit in the assassination of Vice President Flaherty. Was the administration planning to attack Iran as its final act before leaving office? Petty would not have warned him to contact the NSC unless something—something really big—was in the works. He wondered if America was ready to go to war again. Bob Long had been president-elect for only fifteen minutes, and he already felt like the dog that caught the car.

44

OKAY, SMART GUY," LONG said, his gaze piercing. "What do you want to do?"

Jay Noble sat across from him at the dining room table in the Governor's Mansion in Sacramento as they enjoyed a celebratory lunch the day after the House election. Long paused for a beat. "Why don't you come to the White House? I had originally planned to make you DNC chairman, but I can't do that now—I left the party!"

Jay laughed, putting his pen down on the legal pad on which he had been taking copious notes. He had barely touched his lunch. The levity of the moment masked the seriousness of the president-elect's offer. Jay had lain awake half the night thinking about how he would answer this inevitable question. "Governor, the only thing I know how to run is my mouth," he said with false modesty. "I've never had a real job in my life and I don't know if I can start now."

Long stared back at Jay, his blank expression revealing no emotion. The true purpose of their meeting on Long's final day as governor of California (he was resigning the following day) was out in the open, and Long had clearly not contemplated Jay declining his offer to join the White House staff. "You won't be in the bureaucracy or slaving away at some agency. You'll be working for me," Long said firmly. "I know that in a lot of administrations people leak and stab each other in the back. The White House can be a snake pit. But this will be different. We'll be a team. We'll change the government the way we changed politics."

"Sir, I think I'll be more effective on the outside," Jay demurred, sounding as respectful as possible even as he rejected Long's entreaty. The truth was less noble and mercenary. Between media commissions and his cut of the mail and phones, Jay had made over $6 million during the campaign. He wasn't about to walk away from that kind of money to make $120,000 a year at the White House.

"All right." Long shrugged. "But if that's what you want to do, you have to be a one-client man. You work for me—no one else." He pointed at Jay with his fork. "And no lobbying or outside consulting."

"Agreed," Jay said, wincing inside. Ouch! There went all the money he could have made on K Street helping clients figure out how to keep their ox from getting gored by the new independent political force he had built. "We need to institutionalize the movement, take the netroots and grass roots of the campaign and make it permanent. We need a third force that is a cross between a labor union and a political party."

"I like it. Well, there it is," Long said. He brightened. "You're a one-man firm with one client—and a lucrative one, I might add." He smiled broadly. "Write a political plan and get it to me."

They rose from the table and Long escorted him down the hallway to the front door. When they got to the door, Long stopped suddenly. He looked at Jay, his gaze intense. "We ran a great campaign. But in the end, God did this," he said.

"I'm normally skeptical of invoking the Deity in election outcomes," Jay replied with a wry smile. "But in this case, I don't think there is any other explanation."

Long smiled in reply.

Jay struggled to control his emotions as he walked out of the mansion for the final time. The reality hit him: Bob Long was going to the White House, and Jay wasn't going with him. He fought back tears, surprised at the volcano of emotion that felt like it was about to explode. With one eye on the clutch of reporters waiting by his car, Jay struggled to pull himself together, keeping his feelings bottled in for just a little while longer.

"Jay, what did president-elect Long offer you?" the *Los Angeles Times* asked solicitously. Jay knew that, like the other reporters, he'd been staking out the mansion to see who came and went, hoping to pick up tips on Long's choices for White House staff and the Cabinet.

"I came away empty-handed," Jay said with a wicked grin. "I wanted to be ambassador to the Court of Saint James, but I don't know if I could be confirmed."

The reporters chuckled at the sly, backhanded reference to the fact that Sal Stanley remained Senate majority leader. They glanced knowingly at one another, aware that they were in the presence of the most brilliant political operative of all time—at least, that is, until the next guy came along.

"You're not going to the White House?" asked the *Chicago Tribune*.

"Sure," Jay deadpanned. "I'm taking my family on the tour next week." The reporters laughed some more.

"What did the governor say to you? Did he thank you?" asked Dan Dorman.

"I don't discuss my private conversations with the president-elect," Jay said. "We had a great lunch. He and Claire are very special and rare people." He broke off, momentarily choking up. "It has been the privilege and joy of my life to serve them."

The reporters were taken aback. Most of them didn't think Jay even had a heart.

"Thanks for a great ride, Jay," said Hal Goodman, breaking the awkward silence. "Don't be a stranger."

"Don't worry, I'll be around." He had regained his composure. "And I'll still be a good source." More laughter. "I'd like to say I enjoyed every minute of it, but that would be a lie!" Back in character, he raised his arms like a circus barker. "Now get some rest! Dan—you're pale, dude! The campaign is over. Get a life!"

He walked to his car, slid into the front seat, closed the door, and put the key in the ignition. He sat for a moment frozen, staring at the dashboard, unable to turn the key. The greatest experience of his life was over. There was a crushing, even depressing finality to it.

Why hadn't Long thrown a fit, insisting that Jay come with him to the White House? Deep down, Jay suspected, Long viewed him the same way everyone else did: as nothing more than a hired gun, which was in a sense what he was.

Still, Jay knew he was not just a political hack, but a great strategist. He had led a near-perfect campaign that had achieved the impossible. How odd, then, that at this moment of the ultimate triumph, with the excitement and challenge of the campaign behind him, it just didn't seem like enough. Long would go on to do great things at the White House—where Jay would have felt like a fish out of water. Some of this feeling of despondency was just the adrenaline draining away at the end of the campaign. But was that all of it? Jay wasn't so sure. He suspected that the emptiness of the rest of his life, or the lack of any life outside of politics, was coming to the surface, and Jay didn't like what he saw.

And that reminded Jay of what, for him, had been the most puzzling—perhaps the *only* really puzzling—part of the just-ended fight: Long's new-found Christian faith, and the way it had enabled him to find peace in a business where war was a way of life. Long's faith allowed him to make common bond with people who would otherwise have been not enemies but simply aliens, people who lived in what Jay called "fly-over country" and spoke a different language. They were the people who loved their country even as they distrusted Washington, and they had found their voice in Bob Long. What was it that Long had found in his faith that had so far eluded Jay? He'd certainly spent enough years searching everywhere else: money, women, and professional success. But none of it satisfied past the moment, and even then only while it was happening.

He'd won a presidential election now—the pinnacle of American politics. He could see forever, and had more money than he had ever dreamed of. Even so, he still felt that old familiar emptiness. Maybe it was the bodies that had piled up on the way to the top, the blood he had shed in the name of winning, the carnage left in the wake of victory.

At least he had beaten Kaplan at his own game. Kaplan was the meanest, dirtiest political operative Jay had ever encountered. With Stanley's authorization, he had stolen the Democratic presidential nomination through fraud, bribery, and assorted crimes. He had burrowed a mole into the Long campaign—and into Jay's bedroom. And someone—probably Kaplan or Bill Diamond—had set up Scottie Morris. Jay had leaked the Jessica Cruz DVD not because he wanted to, but because he had to. He had no regrets. He just wished he knew how to fill the void now that the campaign was over.

Jay turned the ignition key and slowly backed down the driveway. As he drove to the Sacramento airport, he impulsively decided to finish the vacation he had begun almost four months earlier, before Lisa Robinson had tracked him down on the beach at El Tamarindo. It gave him a sudden inspiration.

ANDY STANTON SAT IN the book-lined study of his suburban Atlanta home, swigging from a mug of coffee as he pecked away on his computer, working on the blockbuster follow-up to *Lighting a Candle in a Culture of Darkness*. It was sure to be a bestseller. It would include his personal reflections on the presidential campaign, a theology of civic engagement, and a full-throated warning to Christians to keep the Gospel paramount. God was neither a Republican nor a Democrat, Andy would caution its readers. Andy's publisher wanted him to spill the beans on his private conversations with Bob Long and describe his bitter falling-out with David Petty. But Andy was not a kiss-and-tell kind of guy.

The phone rang.

"Andy, I just left the mansion," Jay Noble said. "The president-elect wanted me to convey his deepest thanks. You're a great friend."

"Thanks, Jay, but you're the hero," Andy replied. "You ran a superb campaign. Not a lot of people thought Bob could win, probably me included, but you did it."

"We couldn't have done it without you. The last week people were coming up to Long clutching your scorecards, asking him to autograph them. You guys delivered. And in a business full of blowhards, that's worth its weight in gold. We saw it out there. People were grabbing him on the rope line, telling him they were praying for him. It really moved him."

"The Trinity University speech was the turning point," said Andy, in a reflective mood. "When he welcomed our people, talked about his faith, his grandson, and pledged to appoint strict constructionists to the courts—well, he had them at hello. The exit polls show twenty-one million votes went from the Republicans to Long. He owes his election to them. If you guys are smart, you won't forget it."

"Don't worry, Andy, we won't," replied Jay. "We're not like the Republicans."

The comment cut through Andy like a knife. The break with the GOP had been a nasty divorce, filled with heartbreak and recrimination, and Andy was confident that the Republicans would discover that the grass was not greener on the other side.

"You're going to get a Supreme Court pick sooner than you think," Andy said, as though confiding inside information. "When that happens, it's going to be the battle of the century. Get ready."

"Long is not going to shrink from that battle. If Sal Stanley wants another fight, this time over judges, we'll beat him again."

"I hope so, for both of our sakes," said Andy. "If our folks feel betrayed, they get their backs up. Just ask David Petty—or Gerry Jimmerson."

As Jay hung up, his mind wandered back to when he'd handed Long the card with Andy's phone number on it. Not all of Jay's hat tricks had worked, but the bond that had developed between Long and Stanton had been a marriage made in heaven. As he hurtled down the freeway to the airport, Jay smiled.

SALMON STANLEY THREW A pair of Bermuda shorts and swimming trunks into the suitcase. His flight to Maui left in two hours, and he had rented a house for his wife and their children for their first real vacation in years. They were not scheduled to return to Washington until the inaugural in two weeks. The phone in the bedroom rang. It was Mike Kaplan.

"Senator, I just wanted to call and tell you to hang tough. We lost this one, but I for one don't think you're done. Far from it," Kaplan assured him.

"Thanks, Mike." Even under indictment, Kaplan was as smooth as molasses—the guy just wouldn't go down. Stanley was impressed.

"Did you see that Noble's not going to the White House? Just came over the wires."

"No," Stanley replied. "That's too bad. I would have liked to have gone after him."

"Can you say 'subpoena power'?" joked Kaplan.

Stanley paused, absorbing the news. "Well, maybe it's better. Long has no clue what to do without Noble whispering in his ear. Bob has lost his right arm."

"Senator, take some time to recharge your batteries, and then battle Long with everything you've got. The bipartisan lovefest will last thirty days, and then the shooting will start. The base of the party hates his guts, and they want someone to take him on, and you can be the leader. After that, who knows what happens? Nixon got a second bite at the apple. You might get another shot."

"Stranger things have happened," Stanley said. He checked his watch. Time to leave for the airport. "Thanks for the call, Mike. We're behind you one hundred percent." He hung up.

Stanley continued stacking Bermuda shorts and Tommy Bahama shirts in his suitcase. His wheels turned, already plotting his comeback. With Noble off making money, Long was sure to blow it. He might invade Iran and get trapped in a bloody quagmire. Stanley might just be president yet. He shook his head and laughed. Wouldn't that be ironic?

———

JAY WAS SLUMPED IN a chair at the Sacramento airport, firing off replies to congratulatory emails on his BlackBerry while he waited for his flight to L.A. He was planning to get out of town for a long weekend. As he scrolled through his BlackBerry, his eye caught an email from Lisa. She'd known he was having lunch with Long, and curiosity had gotten the best of her—her email read: "Okay, big guy, what job did you get?" Rather than email her, Jay dialed her direct line at the headquarters.

"Hey there, cover boy of the *New York Times*," she teased. "Tell me all about it." Jay had been the subject of a front-page, postelection profile in the *Times* that was so glowing that it bordered on the embarrassing. He had endured a lot of good-natured ribbing as a result.

"It went great," he said opaquely.

"So . . . which is it?" she asked, prying. "Chief of staff or senior advisor?"

"Neither," Jay replied drolly.

"You're kidding," she said, sounding deflated. "He must have offered you something big."

"He did," Jay said, determined to impress her. "I turned it down. I told him I could be more effective on the outside. It took some persuading, but he agreed."

Lisa was floored. "Wow, I guess I always thought the whole team would go together to the White House if we won," she said, a tinge of regret in her voice. She paused, searching for the right words. "We're all going to miss you."

"Don't worry, I'll be around. I hope you'll have lunch with me at the White House mess every now and again."

"Of course I will!" Lisa exclaimed. "You *better* be around. I *love* working with you. You're smart, you're funny, and . . . well, you're the brilliant Jay Noble. What can I say?"

Jay felt his heart skip a beat. Did she say "love"?

"Hey, listen, the president-elect and Claire are going up to Big Bear for a long weekend, so I'm heading to Mexico to chill out," Jay said, diving through the opening with reckless abandon. "I rented a house with a great view of the Pacific, and lots of extra bedrooms. Why don't you come down?"

"Oh, Jay . . ." she said, and paused.

She's going to turn me down, he thought, and was surprised at how disappointed he was.

"Lovely!" she chattered excitedly. "It'll probably be the last break I get until the August recess—that is, assuming I get offered a job in the White House. Where in Mexico?"

"That's a surprise. Get to LAX in four hours. Bring your passport."

"I love surprises!" Lisa said.

Just as Jay had hoped, she was game. Things were off to a good start.

———

THE AMERICAN EAGLE FLIGHT from LAX touched down in Manzanillo just after 10 P.M. It had been a long day, and a full yellow moon hung in the sky, illuminating the night. Lisa giggled as they went through customs; she was giving Jay a hard time about keeping their destination a secret. Jay liked her a lot—she was attractive, smart, and tough as nails, with a great sense of humor and a voluptuous figure. He liked strong women, and Lisa had grown into a battle-hardened press operative as they went through the grind of the campaign. For him, it was virtually an aphrodisiac.

They grabbed their bags and climbed into the back of a taxi. Lisa gazed out the window as the taxi flew down the highway, the ocean sparkling beneath the moonlight. After a long silence, she turned back toward Jay, her face serious. "Are you sure you're okay coming back to Manzanillo?" she asked. "I know this is where you met Nicole."

"That's why I came back," Jay answered. "I guess I'm exorcising demons. I'm finally finishing this vacation, four months and a presidential victory later." He paused, looking into her eyes. "I'm doing it with a nice girl this time. Are you all right with that?"

"All right?" She smiled. "Of course. The best part is, you don't have to worry about me being a mole!" They both laughed. Then, suddenly, Lisa's face grew serious again. "Jay, you can't let Nicole and Kaplan win—in your soul. *We* won and they lost. I don't mean the election—I mean our *lives*. You have no reason to apologize for what happened. You cared about her."

Jay smiled and touched her hand, looking into her eyes. "That's over now. Thanks for helping me bury it."

The taxi arrived at the security entrance at a gated community overlooking Manzanillo. The guard waved them through, and the cabbie drove slowly up the hill on the narrow, winding cobblestone road. They gazed out at the moon rising over the Pacific Ocean.

"Oh, Jay, it's beautiful," Lisa whispered.

The driver pulled up in front of the house and unloaded their luggage. Jay and Lisa opened the front door, walking through the foyer and down the pink marble staircase to the living area. The table was set for dinner. The house was eight thousand square feet of luxury: four bedrooms, a palatial master bedroom suite, Nautilus-equipped fitness center, a large infinity pool with a terrace, a game room, and a garden in the back. Jay had paid fifteen thousand dollars to rent it for the week, even though he would probably have to head back after four days. It was worth every penny.

They walked out on the veranda on the second level, gazing silently as the yellow moon reflected off the ocean. The houseman brought them margaritas on the rocks.

"I propose a toast . . . to the election of Bob Long as president of the United States," Jay said. He straightened his back, raising his glass. "May he serve two complete terms and go down in history as one of the greatest presidents of all time."

"Hear, hear," Lisa seconded. She took a sip from her glass. "And here's to the rest of our lives," she said gently. She looked deeply into Jay's eyes.

Her face glowed in the moonlight, and he was momentarily intrigued by her innocence and vulnerability. She had developed a tough exterior and still, somehow, retained an inner tenderness. He envied her. His innocence had died years earlier, killed off by decades of take-no-prisoners political combat. He wanted it back, and he hoped he could find it again.

As the moon rose over his personal paradise, Jay hoped he could escape the death grip of politics. But first he had a job to do, one he had to begin to prepare for now: to reelect Bob Long. It would be a long, hard slog, and it was only four years away. Just one more campaign, he promised himself. Then he was done.

Dark Horse

For Discussion

1. In the Democratic National Convention detailed in chapters 1 through 5, a lot of underhanded, if not illegal, maneuvers take place in order to win the nomination. Is that just good, intriguing fiction, or do you think similar things take place in our electoral process? If so, how regularly do you think things like this happen? Do they happen in both political parties?

2. Jay Noble thinks that he's found true love when he meets Nicole in Mexico, but it isn't until months later that he discovers he's been set up. Are there really campaign "moles" like Nicole?

3. *Dark Horse* has a rich and expansive cast of characters, many of whom undergo significant personal change in the course of the novel. Whose story would you say *Dark Horse* is, more than anyone else's?

4. Michael Kaplan goes so far in his attempts to get Salmon Stanley nominated and elected that he ends up facing criminal charges. Was his illegal behavior motivated by a legitimate political viewpoint, or did he simply want to win?

5. What figures can you think of in recent American history who went so far in support of what they believed in politically that they broke the law and faced arrest? Is such behavior ever morally justified? If so, under what circumstances?

6. Robert Long, during the campaign, experienced a spiritual conversion—but when that became known, his political detractors accused him of simply playing the God card in order to win the votes of Christians. Even his own associates wondered about that. Do you

think his conversion, in the story, was legitimate and true? Was there perhaps even an element in it of political expediency? Have you ever wondered about the veracity of the spiritual statements of real-life politicians?

7. Dr. Andrew Stanton seems to be a composite of a number of religious figures in real life who exert significant power over politics because they influence the votes of so many people. Do you think such power on the part of religious figures is legitimate in a republic founded on the principle of separation of church and state? Do you find that their recommendations and the resources they provide via broadcast or the Internet or print are helpful to you in establishing your own political positions?

8. Which characters in the book reminded you of which figures in real-life American politics?

9. *Dark Horse* was written well before the 2008 election and initially published in hardcover several months before the election, at a time when Barack Obama and Hilary Clinton were still battling for the Democratic nomination. What aspects of that 2008 election do you find foreseen in this novel?

10. The deciding of a presidential election by the House because no candidate can establish a constitutional majority in the Electoral College, as happens in *Dark Horse,* seems freakish, perhaps even nightmarish. But legally, it could happen. Is that a good solution to an awkward problem? Should the Constitution be changed to provide a different solution?

ABOUT THE AUTHOR

Ralph Reed is a Republican political strategist, the former executive director of the Christian Coalition, a bestselling author, TV commentator, public affairs advisor, and columnist. He has worked on seven presidential campaigns and has advised eighty-eight campaigns for U.S. Senate, governor, and Congress in twenty-four states. Most recently, he was chair of the Southeast region for the Bush-Cheney '04 campaign and was campaign manager that year in Georgia.

As executive director of the Christian Coalition in the 1990s, Reed built one of the most effective grassroots organizations in modern American politics. During his tenure, the organization's budget grew from $200,000 to $27 million, and its support base grew from two thousand to two million members and supporters in two thousand local chapters.

More recently, he founded the strategic marketing and public relations firm Century Strategies, of which he is now chairman and CEO.

Recognizing him as one of the most important political strategists in America, the *Wall Street Journal* called Reed "perhaps the finest political operative of his generation." *Newsweek* named Reed one of the top ten political newsmakers in the nation; *Life* named him as one of the twenty most influential leaders of the baby boom generation, and *Time* included him in 1994 as one of the fifty future leaders in America under the age of forty.

Reed grew up in Toccoa, Georgia. He earned his B.A. from the University of Georgia and his Ph.D. in history from Emory University. Reed and his wife, Jo Anne, live with their four children in Duluth, Georgia.